(UN)EXPECTED

A DISLIKE TO LOVERS, SMALL TOWN ROMANCE

SAINT STEPHEN'S LAKE
BOOK 1

K.C. BROOKS

For my younger self, the eight year old girl who spent her days creating worlds and dreaming of characters.
This one is for you.
(Except the smutty stuff. That's for the grown up version of me who discovered spice makes everything better)

AUTHOR NOTE

This book contains on page, sexually explicit situations. It also contains elements of verbal and physical abuse (past), alcohol abuse (past), and brief mentions of military based violence. While it is the author's intention to broach these topics with sensitivity, it could still be triggering for some readers. If that is the case, please skip this book.

Protect your peace, lovelies.

PLAYLIST

1. Faded- Conor Maynard
2. Over My Head- Judah & The Lion
3. In A Perfect World- Dean Lewis & Julia Michaels
4. Adore- Amy Shark
5. Say Don't Go- Taylor Swift
6. Lost- Dermot Kennedy
7. Don't Let Me Down- Joy Williams
8. Light Me Up- Ingrid Michelson
9. Perfectly Broken- BANNERS
10. Here We Go- WILD

Alex

PROLOGUE

"Where the hell am I?"

I craned my neck as I looked out through the windshield. The darkened highway was the only thing visible, a vastly different view from how I started my morning. I was barely five hours out of Manhattan, and already, the rush and pulse of the city had disappeared. The towering skyscrapers had faded into lines of tall, lush trees. Gone were the dim glow of traffic lights and the symphony of car horns. Now, all I could hear were my tires on the asphalt as my antique Jeep led me down an otherwise empty road.

If you'd told me a week ago that I'd be here, I would have laughed.

Then again, a week ago, I had a job I loved, a boyfriend I thought I adored, and the next ten years of my life carefully planned out.

Funny how a couple of hours could change your entire future.

"It's fine," I muttered through gritted teeth. "Not like anyone's ever been murdered on the side of a highway before."

Staring back out at the dark highway the unsettling feeling

of the unknown washed over me. It made my skin crawl. I wasn't used to having spare time to think. My life had been a constant blur of busy for as long as I could remember.

First, it was high school, fighting tooth and nail to get a scholarship so I could escape my hometown. Then, it was four years of college, pulling all-nighters to stay at the top of my class, determined to land the best job possible after graduation.

All that work had destroyed my ability to be aimless.

I'd been viciously fighting upstream, desperate to keep my head above water.

Safe to say, I didn't make it after all.

Looking over at the passenger seat, I reached for my worn, brown leather purse, cursing as the contents spilled out into the open. I needed something, *anything*, to get out of my head.

Reaching across the console, I dug for my ever-present pack of Wrigley's, but instead, my fingers hit my buzzing phone. I'd meant to turn it off before I left, but I had forgotten in my haste to get out of the city. *Ignore it*, my inner voice screamed, but it was too late for that. I hit the turn signal, pulling off the highway at the next exit.

Saint Stephen's Lake.

Dumb name.

I tried to find a place to stop, but there was only a narrow, two-lane highway and a couple of buildings that looked ripped straight from a horror movie. Instead of testing my luck, I continued down the road—there had to be somewhere to stop safely.

Hopefully.

After a couple of minutes, I passed a welcome sign for the town of Saint Stephen's Lake. Thank God the name fit the picture in front of me. It turned out to be a small, picturesque village, even at this late hour. Tall, antique street lamps illumi-nated the main road, aptly named Main Street—billowing window boxes stuffed with pink and yellow blooms laid in front of each store. The smell of the bouquets wafted through the cracked window of my Jeep, bringing a small smile to my face.

Continuing down the road, I took stock of the different shops. A neat little row of stores lined the street, all with aged brick façades. Family names adorned their matching awnings, along with the year they were established. There wasn't a single one less than fifty years old. Although the storefronts were closed, they were still quaint, the kind you appreciate more after living in the city for a while.

Typically, the quiet freaked me out—made my thoughts too loud to drown out. Tonight, however, the lull soothed me. My mind could finally catch up after running all day.

Finding a parking lot next to a strip of beach, I pulled my Jeep into one of the empty spaces, shut off the engine, and climbed out of the driver's seat, immediately heading down to the shore. There was no one else around—the only other living things were a couple of gulls in the air.

Rocks bit into the thin soles of my sandals as I moved closer to the water's edge, but I ignored it, too focused on the lake in front of me. The waters were deep and peaceful, almost as sleepy as the world around us. Mountains surrounded me, but I could barely make them out, only able to see their powerful outlines in the darkness.

Breathe, Alex.

The cool wind whipped through my long hair, and I filled my lungs with it. My body shook with exhausted, too tired to do anything other than sink into the sand and pull my knees up to my chest. Just as the serenity started to soak into my aching bones, my phone chimed in my pocket with an incoming text.

I slammed my eyes shut, hoping that if I ignored it, the sound, as well as the message, would disappear. That maybe if I wished hard enough, I could erase the past couple of years from my history. But it just kept chiming, message after message pouring in until my willpower broke down and forced me to pull out my phone. As I moved, the sleeve of my sweater pulled up but I quickly tugged it back to cover the black and blue mottled skin. The move was ingrained into me—covering up even when no one else was watching. It hurt, seeing those marks on my skin, ones left by a man who claimed to care about me. And the knife only cut deeper as my phone lit up, showing the picture I'd saved as my wallpaper months ago.

A couple so happy in love.

What a fucking joke.

My pulse hastened as I stared at the image, guilt and fear swirling through my veins when my phone buzzed again. Before I could think better of it, I glanced down and read the notification.

"You know I love you, Princess. Come home."

My eyes slammed shut, trying to keep the nightmares at bay, to forget the sound of those words whispered in my ear after hours of agony and terror. My heart hammered an increasing beat as the rest of my body froze and my vision blurred.

"He's not here," I told myself. "You're safe, *you're safe.*"

But no matter how many times I repeated them, the words failed to soothe me. Tugged back and forth between this moment and the past, I clung to the present like a lifeline.

The phone screen lit up again, and anger coursed through my veins, fighting through the anxiety until all I saw was red. Fingers that didn't feel like mine curled around the phone, willing it to snap into a million little pieces, to watch as each one faded into the sand, never to be seen again. The stupid plastic was an anchor, tethering me to the world I was desperately trying to escape.

And that tether finally broke.

All day, I'd kept myself together, only feeling numbness as I packed my two suitcases into the back of my Jeep. I'd only bothered to take what I could carry, which meant having to leave behind so many of my belongings. Tokens of my past that were probably lying in a garbage can by now. Or worse, destroyed when Nate figured out what I'd done.

Still, I didn't break. Didn't shed a tear as I closed the door to my home, knowing that I would never set foot in it again. I didn't shed a tear as I crossed the GW bridge out of Manhattan, didn't cry as I headed north with no other destination in mind.

But now, sitting here on some strange beach in a strange town hours away from home, this was the moment when the tears started running. They were like a riptide, and I was helpless to resist their pull. With the silent night surrounding me, I finally let myself mourn—for all that I lost, all that I would never gain, and all that was left behind.

It felt like a funeral, like I was bidding goodbye to the person I once was—the one I'd fought to become over years of hard work. Instead, now, all that was left was a shell of who I'd once been. Maybe I didn't know what was next—who I'd become on the other side of this change.

But it had to be better than before.

With that tiny tendril of hope, the world stopped spinning, and I started to feel my senses return to normal. It took a while, but my eyes eventually opened again.

Peaceful waves were the only things in front of me, slow, cascading white caps dancing along the shoreline. Tiny stones tumbled in the water, spinning a couple of times before settling on a new piece of land. I timed my breaths with the quiet crash of the tide, letting it wash an extra layer of comfort over me.

Better.

Not great, not even close to okay, but...*better.*

After a long time sitting alone on the beach, my tears finally dried, and I forced myself to get up. I brushed the dirt off my leggings and trekked back to my car. My entire body ached with exhaustion, and I would have given anything for a warm meal and a comfortable bed.

Luckily, as I walked past a bulletin board at the edge of the beach, a bunch of colorful brochures stared back at me. My fingers danced along each one, checking the hours until I found one that was open late. *The Lost Tavern.* They were the only place open past nine, which I took as a good omen, considering how loudly my stomach was growling.

As I walked back to the side of my car, my phone chirped again. My hand stilled on the door handle, looking around the parking lot. I smiled as I noticed the metal garbage on the side, most likely there to ensure tourists didn't leave trash on the beach. But I had a better idea.

I walked over, my steps hurried and determined. Reaching into my pocket, I pulled out my phone, staring at it one last time, before switching it off. Using my key as a tool, I jammed it into the side of the phone, repeating the action over and over again until the SIM card finally popped out. With a quick, silent goodbye, I broke the damn thing in half, dropping it and my lifeless phone into the bottom of the can.

I stared at the closed bin for a second, trying to see if I made a mistake. Maybe some pang of regret would hit me after throwing away that piece of my old life.

Instead, for the first time in days, I smiled.

ONE

Alex

"Fuck!"

The sharp word escaped my lips as I slammed on my brakes. I pushed the hair from my eyes as a neon blue Audi whizzed past me, the driver flashing their middle finger as they sped off. *Asshole.* Sure, it was *my* fault he was going 40 miles over the speed limit.

"Alex, you okay?" a voice called out from my phone propped on the dashboard.

"Yeah..." I trailed off, rolling down my window to flip off the other driver. "Debating all my life choices that have led to this moment."

"So dramatic." Javier snorted on the other end of the line. "Maybe if you didn't hit the snooze button fifteen times, you wouldn't need to rush around every morning."

"It's not *every* morning."

My best friend let out a loud laugh. "I'm not even going to dignify that with a response. Get here already. The Baroness is already on the warpath, and I haven't had enough coffee to deal with her bullshit."

The call cut off without another word.

"Breathe, just breathe...." I mumbled as I pulled down my mirror and tried to fix my face. My pulse still hammered in my chest, but one glance at the clock told me I didn't have time to wait it out. At least this time, when I inched my car into the street, I remembered to keep an eye out for any speeding tourists.

When I first found this house, it seemed like a drive. The small, lakeside cottage had practically been plucked out of my dreams. It was quiet, with only one neighbor close enough to see, and surrounded by nature.

For nine months out of the year, it was perfect.

Until the summer months, at least. Because the one negative about the location of my house?

The damn driveway.

It backed out into the main road of Saint Stephen's Lake. The same one that was littered with tourists during the summer months, making it almost impossible to get away from my house in one piece.

"Why the hell are you all still here?" I grumbled under my breath. The tourist season started on Memorial Day and was *supposed* to end on Labor Day, which was last week. The influx of strangers that invaded our town every summer should be gone by now, but the ridiculous number of drivers on the road said otherwise.

Finally, there was a break in the traffic, so I pressed my foot on the gas as quickly as possible. *Fifteen minutes.* I could make it.

Shit, I better make it.

"Double fuck," I hissed as I approached the beach, and saw the line of red brake lights. Traffic filled both sides of the single lane road, leaving no room to go around them. There was nothing I could do but stare out the window while I waited for them to clear.

I cursed under my breath as I dropped my head onto the headrest. *Why the hell did I hit snooze again?* When it came to self-preservation and sleep—*sleep* always seemed to win out. Minutes ticked by as I waited for people to turn into the parking lot. With nothing else to fill my time, I rolled my head to the side, taking in the new sign everyone was in an uproar about.

I could see why. Most of our town stuck to a more rustic, aesthetic, but this sign was bright, a shiny green that was like a beacon for drivers. Probably why the town council designed it. The original wooden was a victim of last summer's visitors, destroyed by a drunk college kid. And while most of the town wanted to repair it, the damage was too much, and it needed to be torn down.

I frowned as I read the pristine golden letters naming Guardian's Beach. A pang of nostalgia hit me at its perfection, missing the old, weathered welcome sign—the same one that directed me to this beach years ago.

The thought instantly pulled me back to those early days, remembering how much time I spent sitting in the sand, contemplating my next move. Luck seemed to be on my side when the concierge of the largest hotel in town quit days after my arrival.

It turns out that luck had never been my strong suit.

The car behind me loudly honked, breaking me out of my memories. With the line finally cleared, I slammed on the gas, rushing toward the bridge that led to work. After parking my car in the staff lot, I dashed up the path toward the Isadora Resort, the bane of my existence for the past three years.

Looking at the expansive, elegant estate, you'd think it was paradise. Between the lush greenery and pristine architecture, it was the definition of luxury. The employees worked tirelessly to guarantee the guests wanted for nothing during their stay.

But for the people who worked behind the scenes?

It was a prison of our own making.

Don't get me wrong—when I first got the job of head concierge, I was flattered, especially given that I had minimal experience in the field. But with every passing year, I was growing resentful of its demands.

The hours were long, and the expectations were next to impossible. No matter how hard you worked, someone wasn't satisfied. I would have cut and run years ago if it weren't for the benefits and pay. There were a ton of smaller hotels and inns surrounding our lakeside town, but no one ever wanted to cross the owner. If you left the Isadora on bad terms, good luck ever getting another job in this town.

Hopefully something I wouldn't experience firsthand anytime soon.

I snuck a peek at the clock as I turned the corner, swearing to myself as the minute hand clicked past seven. Officially late. For any other job, one minute late wouldn't be the end of the world, but here, you might as well burn your timecard on the way out the door.

I bolted up the path toward the back of the resort. No one was around, so my tardiness was my little secret. My hips swayed a little more with each triumphant step.

Right before I could breathe a sigh of relief, though, I glanced up at the employee's entrance. Standing in the doorway in a crisp white business suit was my mortal enemy—Diane Winters.

My boss.

"You're late."

***

"I ASSUME you have an excuse for your tardiness."

Speak of the devil, and she shall appear. My body shuddered as Diane's cool, calm words sliced through me like a sharpened blade. *Dammit.* Did I really think I could sneak in before my boss, the Baroness of Bullshit, caught me?

Count this as strike three for today.

There was a time I'd admired Diane. When I interviewed for my position, she made the *best* first impression. She was kind, empathetic, and made me feel like I was joining a solid team.

However, that shiny, kind illusion quickly faded, leaving behind a micromanaging, controlling narcissist—the kind of boss whose sole mission in life was to torture her employees. Our salaries were basically hazard pay.

With a heavy sigh, I stepped forward, trying not to cower under her withering stare. If making people feel small was an Olympic event, Diane would win the gold medal every time. I tried not to buckle under the weight of her stare.

Her red hair was cut to her shoulders, her pale skin dusted with youthful freckles. There were even light wrinkles that lined her cheeks and mouth, proof that she used to smile at some point, but that was the only evidence of it now. As she stared at me, her immaculately buffed nails tapped into the skin of her crossed arms. She belonged in a workforce warning, ever the picture of corporate annoyance.

I gave her an apologetic frown. "I'm sorry. You know how congested it gets downtown. I got stuck behind some tourists—"

"I don't care."

One. Two. Three. Breathe in. Breathe out. Do not murder your boss. You do not have the patience nor filter to survive long in prison.

"Your shift started at seven," she said. My lower lip found itself tucked between my teeth as I nodded. "You recall our conversation regarding the VIP party joining us today? I expected you to be here on time and ready to greet them before they arrive."

"Yes," I forced out through gritted teeth. "I have all of their requests ready--"

"Alexandria," she said, her voice lowering to an even more threatening decibel. "This is your final warning. I give you leniency because of your connection to my daughter, but I will not stand for you embarrassing me or this resort. Do I make myself clear?"

"Of course." I smiled, hating myself for holding back my words Even if I could've afforded to quit, my friendship with Diane's daughter, Calla, made my feelings even more complicated. I thought Diane was the devil incarnate, but my best friend loved her mother, even with her hurtful brand of care.

Besides, nothing good ever came from arguing with Diane. She ruled the resort with an iron fist and did not hesitate to fire people who tried to "undermine" her. Last month, a cook got fired for merely suggesting some tweaks to the main restaurant. Funny how Diane managed to come up with a brilliant plan to revitalize the menu days after he left...

As she turned the corner toward the front lawn, I rushed inside, chucking the rest of my stuff into my locker before taking off into the lobby. As soon as my hand touched the door, my feet stopped. *You can do this. You will be fine.* I breathed out the lies, trying to make them ring true.

When I twisted the handle, my carefully curated smile was in place. After about ten minutes, it made my face hurt, but it was part of the job. Diane and the rest of the board expected the brightest and most gravity-defying expressions from all their employees. No other emotions were allowed.

Luckily for me, I had a lot of practice faking happiness when inside, I was screaming.

As I crossed into the lobby's main atrium, my smile became

a little more genuine. While I might hate the demands of this job, it would be a lie if I said the hotel itself wasn't immaculate. Nestled in the Adirondack mountains, the building had been here hundreds of years, long before the town grew around it. It had been updated several times since then, but it somehow managed to hold onto its original charm.

My feet slowed as I stared up at the glass dome above the lobby. The soft, subtle glow of the morning light made the interior of the resort feel ethereal. The aroma of the forest and the breeze from the lake filled the space, as did the dwindling embers from the large fireplace on the south wall. With these relaxing and natural vibes, the tightness in my chest started to ease.

With one last inhale, I resumed my steps, moving past the front desk. It was too early for check-ins, but there were a few couples checking out. They were still looking around the room, trying to commit every detail to memory.

Eventually, I made my way to my station—the concierge desk at the far side of the lobby. The dark wooden station was nothing special, but the backdrop never failed to take my breath away. When you arrived at the Isadora, it looked like typical colonial-style building. The other side, however, was a different story. Floor-to-ceiling windows lined the entire back wall, showcasing the most amazing view of Saint Stephen's Lake.

It was the main reason I took this job. When I left the interview, I thought it couldn't be that bad if I got to stare out at this view every day. As I said—past Alex was a naive fool.

All too soon, I broke my gaze away and moved behind the concierge desk I called home.

Or hell.

It depended on the day.

Javier, one of my closest friends and partner in crime,

smirked at me as I ducked under the counter. "Told you to set another alarm."

I tried to scowl, but it came out like a smirk instead. No matter how much Javier messed with me, I could never stay mad at him. He was one of the first people I met when I started working at the resort, and he had become my lifeline in this place. From the moment we met, I fell head over heels in love. Not only because he was ridiculously tall and built like a professional athlete, with smooth, dark skin and a smile that made most patrons' toes curl, but also because he was the kindest person I'd ever met. He took me in when I was at my lowest, declaring that I was now part of his family.

If only he weren't married to the most fantastic guy. Otherwise, he'd be my soulmate.

"You know..." I breathed out. "*Someone* was supposed to call me earlier in case my alarm decided not to go off again." I gave him a pointed stare. "But he called me too late. Last time I ask him for help."

"*Or*," he countered, "instead of blaming your friend, the same one who showed up fifteen minutes early to cover your ass, you could be an adult and get an alarm clock that works. I told you to stop buying things based on the cute factor."

I rolled my eyes. He might have had a point on that one. But the clock looked like a sloth, and it was way too cute to resist, even if it tended to shut down every time I hit snooze.

As I stepped closer, Javier held out his hand. "Watch out," he said, nodding toward the floor. "You've got a visitor hiding under your station."

It was half a second too late; my foot caught on a precarious pile of books stacked underneath my computer.

"Seriously?" I huffed, grabbing the edge of the desk before I fell. "You decided that was the best place to hide out?"

"I tried to tell her that twenty minutes ago," Javier said, his eyes never leaving his computer screen.

My other best friend, Calla, smirked from her spot on the floor, surrounded by countless romance books and stacks of Post-its. She'd twisted her auburn hair into a messy bun, with pens and highlighters sticking out of the middle. Her long limbs were curled underneath her, making her look much younger and innocent, but reality was a very different story. Exhibit A: none of those books were suitable for anyone under eighteen.

She shook her head. "I saw this video on annotating romance books so you can always find the best moments, and I...*might* have gotten carried away?"

"Might?"

"It's better than the alternative." Calla shrugged. "My mother already threatened to kick me out if she sees me."

As if on cue, Diane poked her head out of her office, scanning the lobby for her errant daughter. My spine stiffened at her presence. If I gave off the slightest hint of joy, she'd come storming over here. After several long seconds, Diane deflated, walking off into a different room in search of Calla.

Shaking my head, I leaned back down. "Don't you think you're a little old to be hiding from your mother?"

"You know her, Alex." Calla lifted her hand, letting me help her to her feet. "I'm not up for another round of the whole *'you're throwing your life away'* conversation."

"You still haven't told her that you deferred law school again?"

She wrinkled her nose in disgust. "Hard pass."

"What are you going to do in January? You promised you were going next semester. I think she's going to notice if you're still hanging around here in the spring."

"That's another day's problem," Calla grumbled. "Besides,

if I tell her I'm not going to school, she's going to push me to take a job in my step-dad's company."

As I watched her face fall, guilt sunk into my stomach. I should have known better than to bring up the law school thing. If there was one thing that could sour Calla's mood, it was her parents' involvement in her life. Her mother and stepfather developed "the plan," or so she dubbed it in the eighth grade, to ensure she continued to build their family's legacy. They gave the same speech to each of her sisters, and they followed it every step of the way. The eldest, Laurel, was a high ranking officer in their stepfather's company, while Devyn recently started as an associate at one of the premier law firms in the city.

Calla has been the only one to resist—the only one of the three who dared to question the role she'd been assigned.

With a shake of her head, Calla's easy smile returned, a sign she was changing the subject. "So...did you learn any more about the VIP?"

"Nope," Javier said, his words clipped. "Your mother is refusing to tell us who it is."

"Do you think it has anything to do with the movie they're filming in town?"

"What movie?" Javier and I asked in unison, turning to face Calla.

"I swear, it's like you don't even try to pay attention," she sighed, pulling her phone from her back pocket. With a stealthy glance around the lobby to make sure no one was approaching our station, she tapped the search engine, typing too fast for me to make out the words. "No...no...yes! I knew I saw something!" She pushed her phone toward me. "They're filming some kind of period romance movie downtown. It's supposed to start next month or so. It's starring..." Calla scrunched her nose. "Everly Watson? Oh! I think that's the girl from that show. You know the one. And umm...oh. *Oh*."

I quirked a brow. "That good?"

"Adam. Rice."

"What?" Javier exclaimed while I asked, "Who?"

"Adam Rice!" "*The* Adam Rice." Calla and Javier snapped the words simultaneously before proceeding to recite the guy's entire resume page, as if that was going to make me join in.

"Never heard of him."

"Seriously?" Calla shrieked. "Alex, I love you, but you have got to get a life."

No shit. As I turned back to my computer, logging in to check for any requests that popped up last night, the two of them continued their conversation around me.

"I can't believe he's coming here!"

"Yup!" Calla said, taking back her phone to scroll through the article. "He's had enough superhero movies for a while and wants to try something different."

Even I have to admit, it would be pretty surreal to see a movie star walking around our town. We've always had a steady list of VIPs, but they tended to be managers of Fortune 500 companies, trust fund babies, or other legacies. You know — people who have a lot of clout and money but not necessarily the level of stardom and fame actors and celebrities possess.

As I imagined Adam Rice walking around our town, I almost chuckled. The morning gossip train was going to have a field day with that one. Saint Stephen's Lake was a small place, like, *painfully* small. When I moved here, it took less than twenty-four hours for the entire village to know my name.

I'd give it an hour from the time his fancy-pants SUV crossed the border for everyone in town to know he was here. A strange knot twisted in my stomach as I took a peek at our reservation page. Trailing my finger down the screen, I stopped once I hit the private villas. *Just as I thought.* The biggest one was marked off as VIP for the next two months.

"Holy shit. *He's* the VIP," I whispered.

It must have been loud enough to cut through Javier and Calla's conversation because they both turned toward me, eyes wide and mouths hanging open.

"No…" Calla said. "He can't be." She shifted my computer monitor, studying the same reservation block as me. "It's not his name, but we all know actors *never* reserve rooms under their real names."

"We do?"

"Duh," Calla chuckled. "They can't have the public finding out where they are, so most of them use aliases." She shakes her head. "Have I mentioned you need to get out more?"

"Once or twice."

"They're checking in at ten, so I guess we'll find out then," Javier said.

My jaw tensed. *The VIP wasn't checking in until ten?* Diane gave me hell because I showed up at 7:01. My hands clenched at the thought. She had the nerve to say *I* was the one embarrassing the resort?

There really was a special place in hell reserved for that woman.

* * *

The next couple of hours passed by painfully slowly. Every single guest was determined to trump the last for an over-the-top request. From hunting down a vintage canoe (*"it's for the aesthetic"*) to orchestrating an elaborate proposal complete with a horse-drawn carriage, I was mentally drained.

Luckily, Javier volunteered to give the VIPs their tour of the villa because my sparkle vanished shortly after my arrival.

As the sun rose high above the lake outside, the line in front of my desk finally cleared enough for me to take a breath. Once upon a time, I was better at this—at happily accommodating every outlandish request. My smile came more effortlessly, and I made myself bend for every single guest who walked through our doors.

Somewhere along the way, though, that changed. My happiness turned into a veneer, and every day seemed to grate more and more on my patience.

This job was supposed to be temporary, something to tide me over until I figured out what I wanted to do with my life. But here I was, three years later, and I haven't moved from this spot.

This fresh start was *supposed* to be exciting, a new chapter where I could reshape my fate. However, instead of crafting a life of my own, I'd become stagnant, chained to a career I never wanted in the first place.

"So stupid," I groaned into my palms. "So very, *very* stupid."

"Excuse me?" a deep voice called out.

Shit. I sent out a silent prayer that Javier returned from his lunch break early, that he was the one witnessing me acting like a fool, not a guest. But, as I peeked through my fingers, my stomach dropped.

Standing in front of my desk was one of the most beautiful men I'd seen in my life. I wasn't exactly tall, but this guy towered over me—definitely over six feet tall. A black baseball hat obscured most of his face, and he was wearing a flannel and jeans combination that many of the men in town favored, but even with his casual outfit, it was easy to see this man was in *shape*.

Once my gaze finished appraising his figure, it slid up to his face, and I almost let out a little gasp. It was lit up in a genuine grin, one that made his startling blue eyes crinkle at the edges. Everything about him was chiseled and confident.

"I'm sorry, sir. How can I help you?" I asked, coughing to cover up the way I was blatantly staring. Now that my shock had worn off, he started to look familiar, but I still couldn't quite place him.

"We checked in today, and I was told you were the person to ask about the town."

His deep voice sent a shiver down my spine, each word caressing a long-ignored part of me. It was smooth, almost unnaturally so, and so familiar, my brows furrowed.

It wasn't until he removed his hat, though, that it finally clicked, and my stomach dropped to my toes.

No. No, no, no. *No.*

This couldn't be my life.

Because the man who watched me have a meltdown behind my desk?

That would be Adam Rice.

The goddamn movie star.

TWO

Alex

Adam Rice stood less than two feet from me.

Adam *freaking* Rice.

How the hell did I not recognize his name earlier? I'd seen his face on almost every tabloid, declaring him one of the biggest stars on the planet. It was impossible to forget his hooded, dark blue eyes.

As he stared down at me with a grin, all sense left me. There were zero words in my brain; all my tact and grace had flown promptly out the window the moment he opened his mouth.

I always imagined if I bumped into a movie star, I'd keep my cool. *Oh, that was you?* You know the type—the people who hold onto their dignity even though they're talking to a celebrity.

Nope. Not me. Instead, I was giving complete deer-in-head-lights vibes, with a dropped jaw and everything.

His smile faltered as he leaned closer. "Miss, are you all right?"

No, I was not all right. One of the most recognizable actors in the *world* stood less than two feet in front of me, and I'd forgotten how to speak.

Now that his hat was gone, Adam's dark blond hair was on

display. The top was longer and slicked back, but the sides were trimmed shorter. His face was shaved clean, and every single piece of clothing, although casual, seemed like it had been plucked right off a runway.

A snort came from his side. "Is there someone else we can talk to? I think you broke this one, Rice."

That broke the stalemate in my brain. I whipped my gaze over, only now noticing the other guy leaning on my desk. I sent up a private prayer that he wasn't another movie star I'd forgotten, but thankfully, unlike Adam, nothing about him seemed familiar.

While Adam radiated charisma, the kind that made people turn as soon as he entered a room—his buddy looked like he'd just rolled out of bed after an all-night fight with his wife. Dark circles lined his deep brown eyes, a couple of shades darker than his shaggy, unkept chestnut hair. His skin was naturally tanned, more evidence of time outdoors than anything else. Stubble covered the bottom half of his face, the lines uneven, as if he hadn't shaved in over a week.

A tight smile formed on my face, camouflaging my annoyance. "My apologies. You, uh, caught me at a weak moment." I turned back to Adam. "How can I help you, sir?"

"Please, call me Adam," he said, holding out his hand. "I'm looking for Alexandria?"

"That's me," I said, placing my palm in his almost too enthusiastically. Holy hell, his skin was soft. Despite wanting to hold on much longer, I forced my hand back. "But I prefer Alex."

"Alex..." My name sounded smoother on his tongue, like honey flowing slowly from a jar. "I like that."

When his cobalt eyes captured mine again, I completely forgot what I was doing. Unfortunately for me, the same couldn't be said about the man standing next to him. While I was too focused on Adam, he hadn't missed a beat, prepared to shoot an arrow through my awestruck bubble.

He shook his head, nudging Adam out of the way. "Listen, I know you've got that whole star-struck thing going on, but we were told you could help us out." He ran a hand over his face. "All I want is a good place to go fishing, and then you can get back to your drooling."

"Excuse me?"

"Trust me," he continued, not caring about the glare I leveled at him. "You're not the first girl to lose her shit over my buddy, and you sure as hell won't be the last. But I was promised that this trip wouldn't be a gigantic waste of time, so it'd be great if you could do your job and help us out."

"Cole..." Adam warned.

What the hell? Listen, I'd had my fair share of rude guests. I'd been called more names than I cared to mention, and really, nothing this guy said was *that* bad. However, on top of the day, I'd already had, this smug son of a bitch was the last thing I wanted to deal with.

My hands clasped the edge of the desk. "What did you say to me?"

"We want to go fishing," he said, enunciating each syllable. "Isn't that your job?"

My eyes narrowed at him, hating that my knuckles were blanched white under the strain of my grip. *Hold the fuck up. Who the hell did this guy think he was?* Maybe on an average day, I would smile, ignore his comments, and move on.

But today, I'd had enough.

Leaning forward, I nodded my head to the side. "Sir, if you would?"

He followed me to the other end of the desk. As soon as we were out of sight of the other guests, I lowered my voice but kept my sugary, sweet grin firmly in place. "Listen here, you condescending prick. If you want my help, you're going to stop with the juvenile digs and talk to me with a hint of respect, or I promise you'll get the itchiest bedsheets every single night of your stay. Understood?"

He stared at me, trying to make me squirm under its weight. *Not likely, asshole.*

However, instead of the annoyed scowl I expected, he broke into a smirk. "Do you talk to all your guests this way? If so, you might be in the wrong line of work."

"Just the few who manage to piss me off."

"Honored to be a part of that club, sweetheart."

I saw red. "Listen to me, you arrogant son of a b—"

"How is everything going?"

A high-pitched voice crashed through the tension, probably saving this asshole's life. But when I met Diane's stare, I knew I was in trouble. Her eyes darted between the two of us, her lips tightly pursed, unimpressed by my behavior. My eyes widened, realizing how I'd just spoken to a paying guest of the resort. *Shit.* I needed to get it together quickly. Scooting back behind my computer, I plastered on my phoniest smile, pulling a pamphlet from one of my drawers.

"Good afternoon, Mrs. Winters. I was assisting Mr. Rice and..." *This asshole?* Probably not going to help my case. My nose crinkled as I forced out the words. "*His friend* with some places to fish." I placed the map on my desk, showcasing the designated fishing spots nearby. "If you would like, I can set up transportation for you."

"That would be great." Adam smiled, elbowing Cole when he didn't bother to say anything.

"Yeah, thanks," he muttered, a sly grin playing at the corners of his mouth. "And it's Campbell. Cole Campbell. Not *his friend.*"

Dick.

Diane glared at me while Adam and Cole looked over the map, sending all her venom in my direction. But I kept up my false sunny persona, mentally calculating the minutes until I was free.

Unfortunately, when Diane stared Adam, my stomach soured. Freedom seemed like a forgotten dream now. I'd seen that look before, and it never meant anything good for me.

She touched his forearm. "Mr. Rice, I have a wonderful idea. Since you are one of our most important guests, you shouldn't have to wait for service." Diane's eyes met mine with a sinister smile I knew well. *Don't do it. Don't you dare say it.* "Alex will be your personal concierge for the remainder of your stay."

Bile rose in the back of my throat as my gaze widened. This couldn't be happening. My eyes jumped up to find Cole's lips pursed together, barely containing his laughter. The pretentious prick was probably getting off on this. When another guest snagged Diane's attention, I itched the side of my ear with my middle finger, hoping he saw it.

Great—I'd wholly devolved into middle school territory.

Diane continued as she returned her attention to us. "Anything you need, any time of day, give Alex a call, and she will make sure it happens." She turned toward me as the side of her mouth tips up in a challenge. "Isn't that right, Alex?"

Holy hell, this woman really would be the death of me. *Any time of day?* Apparently, having a personal life was a new concept for Diane because she didn't even blink an eye. I could picture it now: *oh, Alex, you should move into the room with Mr. Rice. We don't want him to have to wait even a second for his requests.* Quitting was looking better and better by the minute.

As always, I swallowed my rage instead, prioritizing my paycheck over my pride.

"Of course, Diane," I managed through gritted teeth. "I'd love to."

THREE

"Never again. You will *never* convince me to go fishing again."

Adam dropped his tackle box by the door, not even bothering to change before flopping down onto the leather couch. I stepped over it and picked it up, dropping it on the counter. The pristine plastic container looked the same as it did in the store earlier. The damn price tag was even attached to the lid.

Ridiculous. I told Adam that he'd only need a pole and some bait, but my best friend was determined to have everything he needed. He'd basically bought out everything in the fishing aisle. I swear, the man was incapable of doing anything half-assed.

Not that it helped. Even with all that high-end equipment, we still walked away without a single bite. I was starting to think the concierge sent as there as payback for my earlier attitude, knowing that we'd end up empty handed.

After I hung up my jacket on the hook by the door, I stepped into the room after Adam. My jaw tightened as I looked around. I still couldn't get over the size of this place. What the hell was the studio paying for it? Our rented "villa" sat on the edge of the resort's spatial property, a separate building for people who wanted more privacy. When Javier first showed us around, my jaw almost dropped. The damned thing was bigger than my parent's home.

The inside was as impressive as the outside, ripped straight from a page of Architectural Digest. The walls were painted in different shades of pale blue; each room accented with weathered or white-washed wooden furniture. Even the ceiling was covered with sheets of stained shiplap. With a full kitchen, dining room, four bedrooms, and as many bathrooms, it felt like a waste for only us.

But Adam liked having a buffer from the rest of the world, and I wasn't going to complain about nice lodging, especially with my back causing all kinds of hell after our long flight.

"That was brutal," Adam groaned, scrubbing his hands over his face. "Why the hell would anyone want to do that for fun?"

I bit my tongue, tempted to tell him that what we did barely qualified as fishing. You want brutal? Try sleeping in the middle of the desert, the heat making every part of your body want to combust, the sounds of bullets in the background causing every nerve to stand on end.

That was what I called brutal.

I dropped down next to him, kicking my feet up on the coffee table. Fumbling around for the remote, I tried not to laugh at Adam's exaggerated complaints—*tried*. Maybe it was mean to take him to the other side of the lake for the entire afternoon. After all, I knew Adam would instead do almost anything other than fish.

However, he was the one who dragged me across the country to a ridiculously small town in the middle of nowhere. While I usually thrived on quiet, there was something about this place that made my hackles rise. It was too picturesque, too unassuming. For fuck's sake, even the restaurants closed at nine o'clock at night.

Adam deserved a little payback.

Adam leaned forward, almost gagging after he sniffed his shirt. He reluctantly sat up, heading to the primary bedroom to change. "What do you feel like for dinner?"

While he was upstairs, I wandered into the kitchen, opening the fridge to look inside. There wasn't much lining the shelves besides a few prepackaged meals and bottles of water we brought with us. Well, those and the miniature bottles of liquor across the top shelf. I stared at them for a moment, both hating and loving that I couldn't remember the taste. My fingers ran along the small bronze coin in my pocket, tracing the lines and numbers I knew by heart. Walk away, Cole. But they were too tempting, sitting there, waiting for someone to drink them.

I walked over to the far cabinet, finding a small garbage liner. With a muttered curse, I wiped out the shelf, removing the temptation from view. If the resort tried to charge us, I'd happily pay. But with of the work I'd put in to get sober, the last thing I wanted was these bottles lingering only a few feet from my door.

Shaking my head, I tossed the bag in the garbage, then turned back toward the fridge, now focused on the food.

"I'm down for anything other than these bullshit macro-meals," I called out, glaring at the containers. "I don't know how you survive on this shit. Three almonds is not a goddamn meal."

Adam chuckled as he rejoined me. "You know Rebecca's got me on a strict regimen. You don't even want to know how many shirtless scenes are in this new movie. Speaking of...work out tomorrow?"

I nodded, stretching out my arms. It had been too long since I'd had a routine, and my body felt it. Running had been my outlet for most of my life, spending my early mornings racing through the woods back home.

That was before. Before the damaged nerves. Before the surgeries. Before I felt like a shell of my former self.

Now, not only could it be painful, but running didn't feel the same, especially in LA. It was too loud, too congested. It was near impossible to clear my head with so many people always around, and even though Adam's offered his state-of-the-art gym, I barely ever used it. I'd never get on board with running on a machine.

"You want to head out? Find something to eat in town?"

Adam sighed, placing his hands on his hips. "I don't know about that."

It didn't take a genius to understand why. For the past few years, Adam had barely been able to cross the street without being asked for an autograph. While it might be the cost of fame, it was also exhausting having to put on a smile and happy face all the damn time. If he showed even a hint of humanity or dared to feel frustrated about the lack of privacy, he risked his reputation—the career he spent so many years building.

"What about room service?" I answered, dropping back onto my same spot on the couch. Grabbing the remote, I started flipping through the channels. "They can probably bring something over."

Adam glanced at the guide on the counter, reading through the menu. "Shit," he sighed. "Closed. Looks like we're eating the salmon and kale salads. I really didn't want to see another fucking fish today."

Nothing about that option worked for me. Rebecca might have been a world-class private chef, but her meals were prepared based on Adam's demanding nutrition plan. No butter, no salt, no sugar, nothing that might make him look less than a camera-ready action star.

An evil idea popped into my head, and I nodded toward the phone. "What about the girl at the front desk?"

"Do you mean Alex?"

"The manager said she would be available at *all* hours."

"And Alex looked like she wanted to crawl under the desk," Adam said. "I don't want to inconvenience her."

That was why he was a better guy than me. Truth be told, riling Alex up was the most fun I'd had in a long time. My plan wasn't to be a dick at first; I'd never been called open and friendly, but I also didn't go out of my way to be an asshole to people. I blamed my shitty mood on the rocky flight and the press at the airport.

I'd already started my apology speech in my mind when Alex pulled me aside, but that plan died when she read me the riot act. The way her cheeks tinged pink and her eyes turned volcanic made a weird flicker happen in my chest.

For some reason, I wanted to do it again.

Usually, when I was with Adam, everyone tried to give their best impression to get into his good graces. Especially around people in his industry. When he was in the room, they'd slap me on the arm and pretend to ask my opinion about what we were filming, but the moment he left, they went right back to ignoring me, not bothering with someone who couldn't help them advance their careers or wallets.

I knew what they thought about me, that I was nothing more than a hanger-on, a professional best friend leaching off his successful buddy. It worked for me, though. They didn't know what I had been through, and I had no desire to explain it to anyone. I didn't give enough of a fuck to play their games.

But Alex didn't care about Adam standing there. She was willing to cut me down to my knees, consequences be damned. It was a far cry from the first impression I had of her, assuming she was going to be another name added to the long list of Adam's conquests. The dude had plenty of women willing to join him for a few nights of fun, but ever since his ex, a singer with a severe grudge, made their relationship the theme of her new album, his reputation had taken a bit of a hit.

My jaw tensed at the thought, remembering the conversation with his team after it was released. The tension radiated off the walls of the large conference room, the giant screen filled with headlines about Adam's perceived bad behavior. As they outlined all the ways he needed to improve his image, I watched my best friend deflate, taking their words to heart. It took weeks to get him out of his head.

I pulled myself back to the present, still wishing I had punched his manager, Theo, in the face.

As Adam walked inside, I shifted to one of the barstools, watching as he inspected his options. He looked as disappointed by the meals as I did. Shaking my head, I said, "Screw the meal plan. What do you want?"

"I'd kill for a cheeseburger right now."

Before he could argue, I grabbed my wallet and moved toward the door. "We'll make a deal: I'll go to the desk to see if Alex is there, and if she is, I'll ask if she can hook us up with some real food. If not, then we'll stick with Rebecca's plan."

He gave me a knowing glance as he took a step closer. "Cole...we're going to be here for at least two months."

"Your point?"

"Try not to piss Alex off on our first night."

Too late.

A FEW MINUTES LATER, I walked into the lobby, determined to get Alex to help us. As I crossed the room, my mind stalled, too distracted by the view of the lake. It took my breath away. The moonlight glowed through the large picture windows, highlighting the calm water and the lights of town. It was striking in the daylight, but there was something even more special about this place at night.

I missed sights like this the most when I was overseas. For months, all I saw was sand and then the sterile, white walls of the VA hospital. I missed nature, the quiet serenity of being surrounded by nothing but trees and sky.

The same feeling came over me when I spotted Alex at her station. She was one of the few employees left—the lobby was much emptier than earlier this afternoon. Besides the person handling the front desk, we were the only people in the room.

With her distracted, I took the opportunity to study her. Alex twirled her long brown hair into a bun on the top of her head, a couple of strands sneaking out to frame her face. Her ivory skin shined in the low lighting, making her appear softer. There was peace in her expression while she read whatever was on her monitor. As her pen tapped against her plush lower lip, she grinned to herself, pleased with whatever it was she was focused on.

But all I saw was her.

With no one else around, she stole all my attention.

As I stared at her a little longer, I started to think it'd be impossible to look away, even in a crowded room.

Shit. I ran my hand over my face. I should not be looking at anyone—especially not the woman who controlled our dinners like that. Based on how busy she seemed earlier, Alex already had enough on her plate. The last thing she needed was a guy like me leering at her across the room like a creep.

I pushed all thoughts of her out of my head as I stepped closer. Alex lifted her head, meeting my gaze. For a moment, I forgot why I'd come up here. One look from her had my head swimming with questions. *What made her smile like that? What color were her eyes?* From here, they looked light blue, paler than most I'd seen, almost like the water on a calm morning. They were striking, like they could see through to your very core.

However, as soon as she realized it was me, Alex's eyes narrowed in annoyance. That look worked just as well for me, though. There was something addicting about being the one who elicited that reaction. The corner of my lip quirked up as I resisted the urge to smirk.

When I kept moving, she muttered something under her breath, ducking her head behind her computer monitor.

This was going to be fun.

When I leaned over her desk, letting my arms rest against the wood, she didn't even bother to look up.

"Go away."

I chuckled. "What happened to that small-town hospitality I keep hearing about?"

She turned toward me, smiling tightly. "Go away, *please*, Mr. Campbell."

"That's better, sweetheart."

"Don't call me that," Alex snapped, turning back to glare at her computer screen. "In case you've forgotten my name, it's literally right here." Her finger tapped the small gold bar attached to the pocket of her navy blue blazer.

My eyes dropped down, trying not to let them linger on the curves hidden beneath the thick fabric. Instead, I did my damndest to focus on the name tag, smirking when I noticed it said something different. "Alexandria, huh? I think I like that more."

"What do you want, Cole?"

"Who says I want something?"

She groaned, squeezing the bridge of her nose with her fingers. "Listen, Cole, I have had a *very* long day and am in no mood for entertaining...*whatever* this is. So let's end this pathetic excuse for flirting and tell me what you want."

"Pathetic?"

"Solid 3 out of 10. If this were a bar, my drink would be in your face."

"Alright, you got me there," I chuckled. "But I do need your help. We're starving and can't find anything that's open."

She rolled her eyes. "And that's my problem because...."

"Besides it being your job?" I chuckled, leaning in a little closer. "Or did you forget that your boss said you were supposed to be available to us at any time?"

"I am supposed to be available for *Adam*," she said. "Not you. So if he needs something, *Adam* can call my desk. Otherwise, leave me alone."

She went back to her work with a winning smirk, probably thinking she had the last laugh. *Good luck with that.* I wasn't deterred that easily. Maybe Alex was used to people backing away when she bared her teeth, but she had no idea that she'd met her match. Stubborn was practically my middle name at this point, and verbally sparring with her had been the highlight of my day.

"Look," I said, tapping my fingers on her desk. "We could really use your help. Something tells me you know what's still open, and I'm borderline desperate here. A restaurant, any restaurant. That's all I need, and then I'll leave you alone for the rest of the night."

Alex stared at me, not saying a single word. With her arms crossed and lips pursed, I got a nasty flashback of visits to the principal's office. My palms started to sweat a little under the weight of her glare. After a long minute, she said, "Give me one good reason why I should help you."

"Seriously?"

"Yup," she answered, leaning back against the counter. "You've been unbelievably obnoxious since the moment we met, so I think some groveling is needed." She arched a brow. "Convince me."

I fan my hand over my face. "It's for Adam?"

"Err," she said, mimicking a buzzer. "Wrong answer. Have a great night."

"Okay, okay," I sighed, running my hand over my face. "Alex, look—I'm sorry for being a dick. I'd say it won't happen again, but I can't promise that. What I can promise is that I'll do my very best to treat you with respect."

She arched her brow. "And if you don't?"

"Then call me the fuck out. It's the least I'd deserve."

Alex stared at me as if trying to weigh the sincerity in my words. I meant every one of them, and I hoped she could see that. Eventually, she gave a resigned sigh. "Fine."

"Thank you. Thank you. Thank you."

"Don't push it." She scrunched her face, clearly trying to think of something. I knew we were testing our luck, but I wasn't kidding when I said I had faith in her. Alex clearly took her job seriously. She was the first one we saw when we walked in this morning, and she was still here long after her shift must have ended.

Besides, if she didn't figure something out, then I'd be stuck wandering around, trying to find food. From what I'd seen, the only thing open this late was a gas station on the very edge of town, and after a horrible bout of food poisoning from a Quick Mart sandwich years ago, I'd rather take my chances with the all-green option in our fridge.

Alex exhaled as she searched on her computer. "There's not much available right now. What are you in the mood for?"

"Anything greasy. Bonus points if it's a burger. Nothing vegan."

She nodded her head, her typing echoing in the quiet lobby. "I think I can figure something out. Give me about thirty minutes, and I'll have two meals sent down to your room."

"Thanks, sweetheart."

"For that, you're getting a veggie burger."

FOUR

Alex

"No, Mr. Walters," I muttered, rubbing my eyes with my fingers. *How was this man still complaining?* Twenty minutes of talking in circles should've been enough, but no. He needed to make sure I knew *exactly* how badly I messed up. "Yes, I understand you requested a private sauna in your room. However, as we discussed when you made your reservation, none of our rooms have that option."

I glanced over at Javier, rolling my eyes in exasperation. He chuckled, thankful Mr. Walters had taken a liking to me instead of him. "No, we cannot install one before tomorrow."

As Mr. Walters continued to prattle on in the background, I couldn't help but zone out. Would I get fired if I just hung up the phone? I glanced at the clock, watching as the minutes of my life tick by. *Might be worth it.* As Mr. Walters continued to bemoan my incompetence, I tried to type out a couple of emails for other requests, but even those seemed to make my eyes feel heavy.

"How am I supposed to plan a romantic evening without a sauna?" he screeched through the phone. "I *promised* my wife we would have one!"

Just as I was about to give Mr. Walters the same response for the fiftieth time, Adam strolled into the lobby, pulling all my attention away. He looked like the poster boy for coastal charm. His navy board shorts showcased his muscular calves—his white linen shirt unbuttoned enough to show a hint of the broad chest hidden beneath. It was almost unfair. How was I supposed to go about my everyday life when he waked around looking like that? As if able to read my thoughts, Adam caught my stare, giving me a little wave as he passed by. I tucked my chin, trying to hide the blush that covered my cheeks.

I wasn't the only one star-struck. A group of fans trailed behind Adam, people of all ages, watching his every movement. Their phones obscured most of their faces, trying to take photos and videos. Adam greeted them with a tight smile, taking their stalking with a grain of salt.

As I continued to watch his interactions, something seemed off. His smile wasn't the same blinding one from yesterday. No, it was almost...sad, strained. It took everything in me to stay at my desk, not to walk over there, and to shield Adam from people violating his privacy. It seemed cruel, like an animal trapped in the zoo.

"Are you even listening to me?"

Mr. Walter's shrill voice pulled me out of the daze. As the restaurant doors closed behind Adam, I tried to focus back on my phone conversation.

Luckily, it only took ten more minutes to talk Mr. Walters down, but by the time the call ended, my head throbbed, a tight knot forming around my temples. I rubbed in small circles to alleviate some of the pain, but it barely helped.

"How did it go?" Javier asked, as he handed me a fresh cup of coffee. I thank God for this man. He was one of the few people who understood my desperate need for caffeine and kept it in steady supply.

"Fine," I said after thanking him and inhaling one glorious sip. "All it took was a few free meals for him and his date. He was giggling by the time we ended the call."

"You have the magic touch."

"Don't go that far," I grumbled, staring at the computer screen. As I tried to focus on another request, the words went fuzzy. Leaning back, I rubbed my eyes, my dried contacts like sandpaper behind my lids. When I looked back at the screen, it was the same.

This day needed to end.

Last night, I tossed and turned, wondering if my phone would go off in the middle of the night. Although Cole and Adam seemed thankful when I dropped off their dinners, a part of me feared it was some sort of test, making me jump through hoops was some sick entertainment. While I might love my town, I wasn't under the illusion that it was as thrilling as cities like LA. They were probably crawling the walls in boredom.

I still wasn't sure why I agreed to help them. It would have been easy enough to pretend nothing had been open. They had no way of knowing that I had a connection to the best restaurant in town.

Maybe it was because Diane spent thirty minutes explaining how important it was that Adam Rice enjoyed his stay. With an influx of other people from the movie flying out soon, she could practically smell the dollar signs, which was why she had no problem sacrificing my mental health for her bankroll.

That had to be it—some sort of sick loyalty to the place that paid my bills.

It had *nothing* to do with Cole Campbell.

As if I conjured him by thoughts alone, Cole stepped into the lobby, stealing my breath differently. He looked better, more rested, than the last time I saw him. He wore a flannel shirt, buttons undone, with a white t-shirt underneath, and a pair of jeans. Nothing special, but his appearance still made my heart beat a little quicker.

While Adam drew your eyes to him with his charm and magnetism, Cole was a very different story. He didn't pull the room's attention like Adam; instead, it was like he tried to hide from the world.

Yet, for some unknown reason, I couldn't tear my eyes away.

It had to be because I couldn't read Cole and never knew what to expect when he opened his mouth. The man slung insults like compliments, and I didn't know how to respond to either. So far, my gut reaction had been annoyance. Even when I brought the food to the villa, all he did was nod in thanks.

No annoying dig, no sorry attempt at flirting.

A nod.

That was it, and it'd been messing with my head ever since. It wasn't because of him, per se—no, it was because he was a mystery, a puzzle I couldn't quite fit together.

It has nothing to do with his sexy little smirk or the way his forearms flexed when he leaned against my desk.

Why the hell was that so damn hot?

On the list of things I found attractive, forearms rarely cracked the top ten, but as Cole leaned forward, I pictured his arms around me, him lifting me on top of the wooden counter to satisfy all my needs. It was the most turned-on I'd been in months.

My eyes widened at the realization. *No, no, no.* Do not think about Cole that way. *Come on, Alex. Don't you remember how annoying he was with the flipping moods and surly attitude?* Those horrible qualities had to override his attractiveness.

This had to be from my self-imposed dry spell. When was the last time I even went out, much less took a man home? It had only been a couple of months, right?

I glanced at the calendar, trying to remember the guy's name. Brian? No, Bryce. *Shit*, it started with a B. Either way, it had been snowing when he drove me home, and he used it as an excuse to hang out a little longer.

Okay, that was more than a couple of months ago. No wonder that hint of muscle made me drool.

I debated checking cat adoptions when Adam strode toward me, his genuine grin back in place. I waited for that pitter-patter of my heart, the one that arrived last night when Cole visited me. But that fickle little bitch pumped a steady, slow rhythm. Don't get me wrong; I'd still relish in this gorgeous man's attention.

"Mr. Rice, it's nice to see you again," I said. "How may I help you?"

"It's lovely to see you too, Alex," he smiled. "And I told you, it's just Adam. Please."

"Okay, Adam," I said, earning a wide grin. Diane would have my head if she heard I called a guest by their first name, but his smile alone was worth it. "How can I assist you this afternoon?"

"I wanted to thank you for your help last night," he answered. "You saved me from one of Cole's hunger rants."

My eyes rolled all on their own. "That sounds like a long night."

"You have no idea," Adam laughed. "I hope he wasn't too harsh when he came up here."

"Nothing I can't handle."

"Good," he said. "That's...it's good to hear." He fidgeted with his hands, bringing them up to the counter, only to place them back in his pockets seconds later. "Listen, I would like to show my appreciation. Can I take you to dinner?"

I choked a little on the air. *This was a joke.* It *had* to be a joke. Some elaborate prank Javier dreamed up to test my reaction. There was no way that this man was asking me on a date, not when he had been with almost every model who walked Fashion Week.

But then, a sobering thought hit me: perhaps he wanted to be nice. He never said the word "date," after all. Just an ill-advised attempt to get back in my good graces after last night's late-night food run. Feeling silly for my presumptions, I smiled politely back at him. "That's very kind of you, but I promise, it's unnecessary. I was only doing my job."

"Then let me rephrase," Adam said, leaning further over the counter. "I would like to take you out, Alex. I'd love to get to know you better."

Holy fuck. What did I even say to that? My brain once again short-circuited, as it was apt to do in this man's presence. A large part of me wanted to say yes, to open myself up to the opportunity.

Before it could escape my lips, another face popped into my mind. *Cole.* I tried to shake him from my mind, to force myself to accept Adam's offer, but nothing came.

As I tried to formulate the words, Javier slid to my side, answering for me. "Alex would love to. Her shift ends at eight. Meet her in the employee parking lot?"

Adam winked back at me. "It's a date."

"THIS IS the worst idea in the entire world."

I stood in front of the mirror, plucking at the ridiculous dress Calla forced me to try on. It was better suited for her taller frame, so on Calla, it looked spectacular. Me? I looked like a toddler playing dress up in her mother's closet. The fabric fell past my knees, making me look much shorter than my five-foot-four stature.

Running my hands over my face, I mumbled, "I should call the whole thing off."

"Don't you dare!" Calla said as she came back into the room, arms filled with a dozen more dresses. "You are living my literal dream. If you cancel on Adam Rice, I will disinherit you as a friend."

I shot her a look. "You love me too much for that."

"Don't test that theory," she answered, shaking her head as she looked in the mirror at my reflection. "Take that off. It doesn't work at all."

I sighed and dropped on her bed. The plush mattress enveloped me, making me long for my bed. I grabbed one of her satin-covered pillows and pulled it over my face.

This whole night, I didn't feel like myself. Like someone else invaded my body and forced me out of my happy comfort bubble. Once upon a time, I'd put hours into my hair and makeup, coordinating picture-perfect outfits to match the occasion. My top priorities were my reputation and making connections, but that life came with unlimited strings, ties to places and people—ones I had no problem cutting once I moved up here.

Now, I was a creature of simple routines, enjoying my solitude too much to give up a quiet evening for a potentially awkward dinner date. I'd tried dating apps, but all they'd left me with was a headache. Honestly, it was easier to accept being alone than to put myself out there.

Besides, my last relationship left me with enough literal and figurative scars to last a lifetime. I wasn't in a rush to give my bruised and tattered heart away again.

Calla plopped down next to me, nudging me with her elbow. "What's really going on in that big brain of yours?"

I groaned, dropping the pillow down to my chest. When I sat up, I cradled the thing like a safety net. "I can't do this."

"Which part?"

"All of it," I whispered. "Every time I go on a date, I'm so uncomfortable that I end up spouting some useless knowledge or something ridiculous. Then, I end up counting the minutes until it's over, hating that I've wasted an evening when I could have been at home enjoying myself. I have to see this guy every day, Calla. Your mom made it clear that—his happiness is my number one priority. What am I going to do if this goes terribly wrong?" My eyes drop down to my trembling hands. "What if he realizes I'm a hermit who uses the word fuck like a comma? Adam Rice does *not* date women like me, Calla."

Calla laughed, standing up and pulling my hand. She brought me in front of the mirror, placing her chin on my shoulder. "Listen, I know it's hard, but for tonight, I want you to let go of all that. Enjoy the moment for once. Even if it goes badly, I know you. You'd never let it interfere with your job." She squeezes my shoulders. "But Alex, this is a once-in-a-lifetime kind of thing. You don't pass those opportunities up, and I'd be a shitty friend if I let you." She twisted me, leaving her hands on my shoulders as she stared into my eyes. "Promise me you'll have some fun tonight."

I rolled my eyes. "You're asking a lot here."

She smiled back at me. "Well, it's a good thing that you love me and will do whatever it takes to make me happy. For tonight, that means you're going out with one of the sexiest men alive." She snapped her fingers. "Now, try on that blue dress I laid out. We're going to make sure you take Adam's breath away."

FIVE

Alex

Twenty minutes later, I stood in the side parking lot, waiting for Adam to arrive. As I tried not to stare at the path to the guest villas, I fidgeted with the hem of my dress. By some sort of miracle, Calla found something in her closet that fit me properly.

The light blue sundress was *everything*. Delicate straps held up the sweetheart neckline, showing off the golden tan I'd gotten over the past few months. The flowing skirt stopped right above my knees. My favorite part, though, was the eyelet design. They were sewn into the linen fabric with such care that I wondered if it was handmade.

After much convincing, Calla let me wear my white slip-ons instead of the heels she picked out. She could dress me up and put as much product in my hair as she wanted, but I drew the line at those death traps. I had enough trouble staying on my own two feet without the additional three inches strapped to my ankle.

I touched my light curls, running my fingers through the loose ringlets. I hated to admit it, but Calla was a master with a curling iron. It was probably due to her experience with two older sisters, but I was happy to reap the benefits. My unruly waves had been tamed into slick tendrils cascading down my back. It made me feel beautiful, especially when they whipped up in the night breeze.

"Holy shit."

The whispered words came from over my shoulder, making me turn to meet Adam's stare. His gaze trailed down the length of my body before rising again to meet my eyes. He rubbed his hand over the stubble on his chin, barely hiding his wide grin. "Wow, Alex. I'm lost for words."

"It's going to be a long night then," I chuckled, trying to fight the unease brewing in my chest.

He laughed, ducking his head down. "What I meant to say is that you look beautiful, Alex. I'm so glad you agreed to go out with me."

"I doubt many people turn down an invitation from *the* Adam Rice."

He cringed at my words. As I was about to apologize, he took a step closer, lowering his voice. "For tonight, I want to leave all that behind us. I'm just Adam, a man who cannot believe he's lucky enough to take you out. Nothing else matters."

My cheeks blushed, unable to hold back my grin. Unsure what to say, I nodded toward the parking lot. "Did you have somewhere in mind for dinner?"

He shook his head. "So far, I've only been to that giant superstore at the edge of town and that fishing spot," he smirked. "I'm trusting your judgment."

I smiled, instantly knowing where we should go. There weren't many good places to eat in town, even fewer that weren't mobbed with tourists during the long summer nights, but if you've lived here long enough, you learned the hidden treasures, the ones we save for ourselves.

Which, for tonight, sounded perfect.

I led Adam toward my car, trying not to cringe when my busted blue Jeep Wrangler came into view. It was the first car I bought for myself, and I loved her, even with all her bumps and bruises. I was fiercely defensive of old Bertha, but Adam set all my nerves on fire. As he came to her side, I grimaced. "Sorry, I know this isn't what you're used to."

"Don't worry about me," Adam said. "My first car was a Honda Civic with a hole in the roof. This is a luxury compared to that junker."

"Please tell me you still have it."

"Not anymore," he sighed. "When I decided to move to LA, I drove that old rust bucket the whole way. It made it to the city limits and then died right on the side of the road."

I snorted a laugh. "Most people would take that as a sign."

"I did." He smirked. "If it hadn't made it there, I would have probably turned back around and headed back to Texas, tail tucked between my legs. That it waited until I was in LA made me think it was meant to be." He shrugged as I unlocked the car, climbing into the passenger seat. "Luckily, I was right."

"So, Texas?" I asked, putting the car in reverse and pulling out of the parking lot. "What was it like to grow up there?"

"Depends," he smiled back at me. "How much do you know about dairy farms?"

"YOU'VE GOTTA BE JOKING!"

My stomach ached from laughter, and I was captivated by the man across the table. Adam lit up as he spoke, animatedly telling his story. His eyes were watering from laughing almost as hard as me.

"I swear," he said, holding up his hand. "I thought a monster was attacking me! You should've seen Cole bust into my trailer.

I wish I recorded his scream for a ringtone." He lets out a high-pitched scream, waving his hands in the air. "Love the guy, but he's a shit bodyguard. That girl would have mauled me if it wasn't for the rest of my security team."

"Did they even figure out how long she'd been hiding out?"

"Three weeks!" Adam said. "She had been using some of the extra paint in the make-up trailer to try to blend into the movie backdrops. By the time she finally got the nerve to break into my trailer, she looked like a Picasso painting."

"That's terrifying," I said, taking another sip of my wine. "I hope you pressed charges or at least reinforced the locks on your trailer."

"Yeah, it was handled..." As his voice trailed off, his smile started to falter. He glanced down at the table, running a hand over the creased, plaid tablecloth before he cleared his throat. "Tell me more about the' hotel. How long have you worked there?"

Oh. Apparently, that was Adam's way of changing the subject. Gone was the laughter he couldn't contain moments earlier. Now, it was replaced by a visible tension stretching his jaw.

At the abrupt shift in his demeanor, empathy for his situation overwhelmed me. I'd known fear like that—the fear of not knowing what someone was truly capable of. But where I knew my threat, a stranger had targeted him. I couldn't imagine having someone break into my home, confusing me for a character I played. As much as Adam tried to play it off, it was clear the constant attention got to him. I reached out, placing my hand on top of his. "I'm sorry she did that to you."

He shook his head, his carefully curated smile returning. It was the same one from his interviews on the red carpet...not that I would know. I *definitely* did not spend hours googling him after he asked me out.

"It comes with the territory," he sighed, sitting a little straighter in his chair. "People see you on screen and think they know you. They think you *owe* them a piece of yourself."

As the haunted look lingered in his eyes, I made it my mission to give him more moments like this one. When we entered the restaurant, Adam was on edge, waiting for someone to recognize him. After a couple of minutes without anyone paying him any mind, he relaxed. You could see the weight lift off his shoulders, helping to melt away his public persona and reveal the real man underneath.

"So, you want to know about working at the hotel?" I asked, wanting to see his smile again. "How much do you want to know? The usual, or do you want the truth?"

He smirked, leaning forward like we were sharing some dark secret. "The truth. Always. Give me all the sordid details."

As I told him all about working at the Isadora, I realized that tonight had been one of the best dates of my life. We'd been here for hours, laughing and telling ridiculous stories about our lives. The restaurant closed almost an hour ago, but the owners were my neighbors, so they let us hang out a little longer if we promised to lock up.

Adam let out one last, long laugh before his breathing returned to normal as he looked behind me, taking in the rest of the restaurant. From the outside, The Lost Tavern didn't look like much. Hell, on the inside, it still didn't. The dark brown wooden siding was aged and worn, lined with pictures of patrons. The lighting and decor hadn't changed in the last thirty years, and I got the feeling that it never would. It was the kind of place most people would drive right on by, not realizing their mistake.

The magic of this place really was its owners, Marta and Curt Anders. They were two of the kindest people you'd ever meet, and they made a mean burger. On my first night in town, I accidentally stumbled on the Lost Tavern. They greeted me like an old friend, taking me under their wing.

Marta and Curt helped me find my house, conveniently forgetting to mention that they lived right next door. Curt visited most weekends, offering to fix up things that I would have never noticed. Last summer, Marta planted a bunch of sunflowers in my garden after hearing they were my favorite. She came over to water them often, which was the only reason they were still alive.

Adam glanced at me. "What are you thinking about right now?"

"Honestly? I'm thinking about Marta and Curt and the rest of the people in this town." I sighed, trying not to get emotional. "Moving here, I didn't know what to expect, but now...I'm starting to feel like I belong. I've never felt that way before."

"Oh," Adam said. "I assumed you grew up here. Where are you originally from?"

My smile dropped momentarily, but I recovered quickly, hoping he didn't notice the change. My past was one of the things I abandoned alongside the highway. I tried to forget everything about my former life when I crossed the border into Saint Stephen's Lake. Even if it were something I was willing to talk about, I'd never spoil our evening with that tale.

So instead, I shook my head. "I moved up here about three years ago, and now, I think it's starting to feel like home."

He nodded. "There is a certain charm about towns like this one. It's quiet, and everything seems to move a little slower."

My lips puckered at the word *"slower."* I was used to hearing it as a slight. Adam must have picked up on the shift in my demeanor because he chuckled.

"I meant that as a compliment. Back home, even away from the city, it's like the world is moving too fast. There's never a moment that's not scheduled or about my schedule. It's nice to take a couple of weeks to unwind."

I nodded, pretending to understand when I didn't. I thrived on my alone time, needing it to unwind from the social demands of my job. I couldn't imagine not having that. "I was surprised when you showed up. I was expecting a full entourage."

"Thought I'd be some high-maintenance guest?"

"Absolutely," I chuckled. "After Diane said I was supposed to be at your beck and call, I was prepared to be miserable."

"Not my style," he said, smirking as he leaned back in his chair. "But something tells me you're going to be seeing a lot more of me."

SIX

Alex

Adam and I left the restaurant sometime later, our stomachs filled and our throats sore from laughter. The hours had passed seamlessly, like talking to an old friend rather than someone I just met. We told stories, laughed about our families, and even traded some of our dreams for the future. By the time we got into the car to drive home, I felt lighter than I had in months.

But that all changed as my car traveled along Main Street, and Adam placed his hand on mine. "I'm not ready to call it a night yet."

My fingers instinctively tightened on the steering wheel. *That's not what he meant. Shit, is that what he meant?* Maybe I should have thought about the ending of this evening before I agreed to come out. It wasn't that I was opposed to taking things further with Adam in the future, but tonight, I wasn't ready. No matter how easy it was to spend time with him, I was still holding back. Whether it was nerves or wariness, I wasn't sure.

Luckily, before my thoughts spiraled too far out of control, Adam continued. "Show me more of your town?"

"Really?"

"Of course," he said. "You've spoken so highly of it tonight. I want to see it through your eyes. Show me what makes it so special."

The earnestness of his words made my heart grow, lifting away my panic. I pursed my lips as I thought of the perfect place to take him. Many came to mind, all the parts of Saint Stephen's Lake that made it home, but there was only one place I wanted to be tonight.

When the sign for Guardian's Beach appeared on the side of the road, I flicked the blinker and turned into one of the empty parking lots. As soon as I parked, the pristine strip of rocky beach came into view, and the full moon highlighted the lake.

At the sight, the same relief washed over me as it did three years ago. I could still remember that night clearly, the way the waves broke through my weathered walls, allowing me to let go of my fears and regrets finally. Ever since that night, I'd come here often. Whether it was a difficult choice or a bad day, this spot called to me. It wasn't a secret I shared with anyone, but something about Adam told me that it would be safe with him.

He softly exhaled as he climbed out of my car. "This is beautiful, Alex."

I nodded as I joined him. "It's one of my favorite places in the whole world." I lifted to my tiptoes, pointing across the lake. "You can see the hotel right down there."

Adam stood at my side, letting out a contented sigh. I almost wished I was experiencing this place for the first time like he was.

I'd learned the hard way that there are many wonders people take for granted, the magical marvels visitors gaped at, yet residents walked by every day like they were ordinary. New York was a prime example of that. After a lifetime in the city, I barely even noticed the sights and wonders others beheld. I'd wasted too much time ignoring the world around me. I refused to do that now.

Even if I spent the rest of my days in Saint Stephen's Lake, I would never let go of this feeling.

The light breeze ruffled my hair as we walked toward the shore, bringing in the clear coastal air. I kicked off my shoes as we walked along the rocky sand, dangling them from my fingers. Some laughter echoed from the public section of the beach, a frequent gathering place for high school kids.

But here?

It was only us and the moonlight.

Taking Adam's hand, I led him to a washed-up log, prompting him to take a seat. He did without hesitation, and I almost giggled. *Well, my first impression was dead wrong.* I honestly thought he'd go running the moment we walked into The Lost Tavern. Most celebrities would probably have had a heart attack if they saw the peanut shells on the floor and the grease-stained kitchen walls.

But every time I thought I had Adam figured out, he surprised me. He was nothing like the cocky playboy portrayed in the media. He'd been the perfect gentleman all night, with nothing more than a couple of light touches on my hand or wrist.

It was nice spending time with someone new, with no expectations or judgment of my past. While my friends were amazing and always there for me, they knew me, my faults and all. It felt freeing hide the bits of my wounded pride and relax with another person.

Adam nudged me with his shoulder. "You went quiet on me."

"Just thinking how much fun I've had tonight," I said. "It's been a long time since I've had a night like this."

"Same here."

"Thank you for asking me out."

"Don't thank me yet," Adam chuckled. "If this next part goes well, I'm hoping to have many more nights like this."

"Next part?"

My thoughts cut off as Adam turned his head toward me, brushing the lightest of kisses against my lips. It was barely even a touch, more delicate than the breeze passing through us. Before I could comprehend what was happening, he pulled back, searching my eyes for permission. When I nodded my head, he leaned forward again, and I met his kiss, both curious and hungry for more.

When our mouths met, I expected electricity, to feel that all-consuming urge to take over, that magical moment when my heart would scream out, telling me that this was precisely what I needed.

There was *nothing*.

Refusing to accept that, I lifted my chin, taking his lips more ferociously. He followed my lead, meeting me kiss for kiss, his hand moving to my jaw.

It was...*nice?*

Okay, it wasn't that nice. It felt wrong, like our bodies knew this was a line we shouldn't cross. I cursed my stupid head, heart, or whatever body part was ruining this moment because Adam was everything I should want. He was kind, friendly, and made me feel special.

But *nothing* about this kiss worked for me.

Adam stopped, pulling back to face me with a sheepish smile. "So, uh, that was..."

"Not great," I answered, dropping my face into my hands. As soon as I realized what I said, my head popped back up, shaking wildly at Adam. "Not that you're not great! You are, I mean, of course you are! It's me; there's something wrong with me."

Adam chuckled, placing his fingers on my chin. As he tilted my face up to meet his, he smiled softly. "There's nothing wrong with you, Alex. The chemistry's not there, and that's no one's fault."

I rolled my eyes. "You sure about that? I've seen some of your movies. You seem to have chemistry with everyone else on the planet."

Adam shook his head, "Did you see my last movie? The one with the girl from that dragon show?" I nodded. "She was the *worst* kisser I've ever worked with. Not only was there zero chemistry between us, but she smoked like a chimney. It was like playing tonsil hockey with an ashtray."

I couldn't help but laugh, happy that some of the tension had broken. I glanced back at Adam. "I did have a good time tonight."

"I did, too," Adam replied.

"Maybe we can still hang out," I said. "You know, as friends."

Adam nodded, mulling over my words before replying. "You know what? I think I would like that. Friends."

He put out his hand with a goofy smile, waiting until I placed my palm in his before pulling me into a tight hug. We sat like that for a few moments, enjoying the silence of the world around us.

At least until it came crashing down around us.

"Holy crap, I told you it was Adam Rice!"

A group of teenagers emerged from the other side of the trees, their cell phones clutched in their hands. Adam and I scrambled up, trying to ignore the flurry of photos and videos as we jogged back to the car. Even as he climbed into my Jeep, they followed, knocking on Adam's window. It made my blood boil how little they cared about privacy. *Idiots.*

"Ignore it," Adam said. "They don't mean any harm."

"To hell with that," I muttered, cranking down my window. "Mark Fischer, get your hands off my car before I call your mother! She still owes me for taking care of your dog last month. Hit my window again, and I'm posting *all* your baby pictures online!"

Mark jumped back almost a whole foot, placing his hands up in the air. The rest followed his lead, probably not wanting to be on the receiving end of my threats.

As the car finally pulled away, Adam chuckled. "That's one way to do it. Think it'll work with the paparazzi back home?"

I winked back at him. "Best part of living in a small town. Know where to hit 'em where it hurts."

THE FOLLOWING DAY, my phone trilled to life *way* too early. My head ached from lack of sleep, too busy replaying my date with Adam. Poking my head out from under my cocoon of covers, I glanced at the clock before smacking the screen.

Not even six a.m.

"Too early," I mumbled.

I got two days off a week. Well, at least I did in theory. Most of the time, I still ended up getting called in to fix someone else's mistake. However, today, I was determined to take the entire day for myself. I wished I could have said that it was to do something productive, but in truth, I planned to wallow in my self-hatred for letting my stupid brain ruin the end of my date, and that would take a pint of ice cream and a binge of my comfort show.

After I slept in for the first time in months.

Apparently, though, my phone didn't get that message. The damn thing continued to ring, determined to interrupt my sleep.

"What the fuck?" I hissed under my breath. I *hated* whoever was calling right now. With the exception of life-threatening injuries or death, there was no good reason to bother anyone at this hour. With my luck, it was Diane on the other end, prepared to berate me for some obnoxious reason.

After a few more seconds, the phone finally stopped ringing, and the silence was almost blissful. But as soon as my eyes drifted closed again, text messages started pouring in. I swore each incoming text sounded angrier than the last. Refusing to climb out of my covers, I stretched, feeling around my end table with my fingertips.

By the time I found my phone, the texts had stopped, and it was ringing again. Pulling it under the covers with me, I cracked open one eye, seeing Calla's name blowing up my screen. With an annoyed huff, I slid the bar over to answer her call.

"Are you dying?" I grumbled.

"No, but—"

Click.

Maybe it was rude, but no one has ever accused me of being a morning person. All my friends knew I had a no-talking before coffee policy, which they abided by because they valued their lives. *Especially* Calla.

The thought made me sit up, chewing my lip at the way I answered her call. Rummaging through my comforter, I grabbed my phone, dialing her back as I ambled down the stairs to the kitchen. As it rang, a familiar jingle came from the other side of my door.

Calla burst through the side entrance, barely more put together than me. Her hair was still wild from sleep, and she was wearing her old college shirt, the one Calla *never* left the house in. Hell, she still had her slippers on.

"Who died?" I asked, trying to brace myself for what was coming next.

"What?" Calla said, shaking her head. "Why would you even ask that?"

I glanced at the clock with a pointed stare. "Cal, it's barely even light out, and you don't have one of your signature bribe lattes. Not to mention..." I arched my brow at her choice of footwear. "So either someone is dead, or they are about to be."

"Hold that thought," Calla sighed, settling on one of my barstools at the counter. "Remind me again. How did your date go last night?" Starting the coffee pot, I furrowed my brow, knowing damn well I gave her a rundown of everything that happened last night. "I know, I know. Humor me, please."

"It was good. Well, it was great. At least it was until Adam kissed me, and there was not a single spark." I rubbed my hand over my face, still embarrassed at the turn the evening had taken. "Seriously, it was almost criminally bad."

"And you guys talked, right?" Calla asked, studying my face with an intensity that made my hackles raise. "You *both* agreed just to be friends?"

I stared at her, noting how her lower lip tucked between her teeth—classic Calla nervous tick. Placing my hands on the counter, I sighed. "I am going to need you to tell me what is going on. Right now."

Reluctantly, Calla stopped toying with the phone in her hand and slid it across the counter to me. "Remember, don't shoot the messenger."

I frowned as I grabbed it, trying to read the words, even though my eyes were still clouded from sleep. "What is this?"

Calla motioned to the device. "Keep reading."

As I scrolled, my eyes suddenly snagged on a picture of two people cuddled up together on a beach—two *very* familiar people.

Huh? That was weird. The woman's dress and hairstyle were so similar to my outfit last night, and next to her was a man who looked *a lot* like Adam. As I kept staring at the image, my pulse started to race. I scrolled through the photos, my heart rate spiking with each one.

Nope.

Not happening.

This entire morning was some messed up dream. This is what I got for daring to sleep in.

Even when I got to the last one, where the couple appeared to be kissing passionately on the beach, I still refused to believe what I saw, and I didn't let a single one of the images or words sink through my deep cloak of denial.

At least until I read the title of the article.

"Super Hero, or Super Player? Weeks after his latest break-up, Adam Rice caught in late night make-out session on location for his new movie."

SEVEN

"You had one rule, Adam. *One!*"

Adam sat on the couch, blankly staring at the phone on the coffee table. His agent, Theo's, voice rang out across the room, echoing through the whole villa. As he continued his rant, Adam's hands clenched, and his knee wouldn't stop bouncing. It was the same position I found him in almost an hour ago, woken up by Theo's yells. With another shake of his head, Adam muttered, "I know."

"All you had to do was avoid any publicity about your personal life until we got this Ivy thing under control."

"Shit, Theo! I know! This whole thing was supposed to have blown over by now."

From my seat in the armchair, I chuckled, knowing it was going to be a damn while before that happened. I told Adam not to mess around with a songwriter, but did he listen? *Nope.* Now, just like her last three boyfriends, he had an Ivy Abrams album dedicated to him, filled with details of their relationship. Not gonna lie, even though they made Adam sound like a dick, those are some damn catchy songs.

"I know, Theo," Adam snapped, running his hand through his hair again. If he kept it up, he'd be bald before thirty-five. "I told you—I didn't know anyone got pictures of us. The only people who saw us were some kids. How was I supposed to know their videos would go viral?"

Theo sighed, a sound I was pretty damn familiar with. I could picture his expression as if he was in the room with us, pinching the bridge of his nose. In the four years since becoming Adam's agent, I'd only seen the gesture a handful of times, saved for the moments when he thought Adam had really messed up. According to him, Adam paid him way too much money not to listen to his advice.

"Do you think the girl sold the photos?" Theo asked.

"No," Adam snapped. "Alex wouldn't do that."

"You barely know her. You have no idea what she's capable of. She probably set up the whole thing."

That got me to my feet. I was used to hearing Theo and Adam's talks. My best friend had thick skin and knew how to block Theo out, but for him to insinuate that Alex was behind the leak? For some reason, that shit made my blood boil.

"Drop it," I said, inserting myself into the conversation. The minute he heard my voice, Theo muttered something under his breath, too low for me to hear. I didn't have a great reputation among Adam's team. Adam tended to let them dictate every part of his life, not bothering to put up much of a fight. I tended to tell them to fuck all the way off. "If Adam says she wouldn't do that, then it's done."

Adam nodded gratefully before continuing. "Cole's right. I know Alex didn't have anything to do with the pictures, but we do need to figure out the next steps."

"That's what we're working on now," Theo said, shuffling around papers in the background. "I've got my assistant scouring social media to see if this story is gaining any traction. Until we get a handle on your image, please, for fuck's sake, lay low. I'm going to head out there in the morning once we know more."

"Theo, you don't have to—"

The line clicked off.

Adam sat back on the couch, tossing his phone to the side before scrubbing his face with his palms. After a long pause, he finally placed them in his lap, laughing humorlessly. "So... Theo's coming."

"Surprised it took him this long," I scoffed. "You know he hated the idea of you being out here by yourself."

"Maybe he was right."

Adam's face scrunched up with worry. I knew he hated every second of this. It was exhausting, having every date or conversation splashed all over the headlines. He always said it was a small price to pay for getting to live his dream, but I called bullshit. No one should have to be worried if the person across the table is using them.

I sat down next to my friend, clapping him on the back. "You didn't do anything wrong. You went on a date. You're allowed to do that, no matter what that asshole says."

Adam shook his head. "I know, man, but it's not even that part that bothers me. It's Alex. She doesn't deserve any of this." He paused, scrubbing his hand over his face. "Especially after the way we ended things last night."

A strange twist forms in my gut, one I've never had before. Shit, I knew that plant-based protein powder seemed off, but Rebecca told me I wouldn't even notice the difference. Last time I trusted her advice.

Adam continued. "Last night was the most fun I've had in a long time. Alex, she's...I don't even know how to describe her.

She's warm and so damn real. It's something I didn't even know I was missing until now."

I tried to focus on his words, but each one made the pain in my stomach amplify. Damn, I really was a mess. The more Adam talked about their date, the worse it got. *It wasn't because of her, right?* I barely knew Alex, and during our two conversations, I'd managed to come off as an ass, but I'd be lying if I said I didn't get the feeling Adam was describing. There was something about Alex that drew me in, even though I spent most of my time trying to hide from others.

I swallowed, trying to ignore the lump in my throat. "What happened?"

Adam chuckled, running his hand over his face. "We kissed."

Fuck. My stomach bottomed out. I tried to push thoughts of Alex out of my mind. She was off-limits now. Guy code—once your buddy hooked up with a girl, she was strictly off-limits unless he gave his blessing. But for me, once a girl had been with Adam, she was off limits forever—not that any of his exes ever showed any interest in me. Once you'd been with a movie star, his loser buddy was a significant drop.

I nodded, lifting myself off the couch, needing some space to clear my head. Maybe I should go for a run, something to get this itchy feeling off my skin.

"It wasn't good."

I turned to face Adam, stopping in my tracks. "What do you mean?"

"I mean..." He laughed. "It was like kissing your cousin. Everything about it felt wrong."

My jaw dropped. No, literally, that shit was almost on the floor. "Wait, wait, wait..." I said, crossing my hands in the air. "You're telling me you had a fantastic date, and when you kissed her, there wasn't anything?"

"Nope," Adam said. "Nothing. Even my little soldier wasn't feeling it."

I shuddered. "Dude, you gotta stop talking about your dick in the third person. You know that shit freaks me out."

"Don't talk like that. You'll hurt his feelings."

"I don't give a single fuck about his feelings," I sighed. "So that's it? You're done with Alex?"

Adam shrugged. "We decided to be friends. It'll be cool having someone to hang out with while we're here. Hell, maybe you can come with us and make sure no one thinks we're dating." He groaned. "You know, after Theo gets here and rips me a new one for trying to have a life."

ADAM DECIDED to spend the rest of the afternoon going over the movie's script, so I grabbed my running shoes. When I stepped outside, I started toward town, impulsively deciding to test out one of the trails I found yesterday. It didn't take long to run across the bridge, the road leading right to Main Street. Despite the chill in the air, there were still a fair number of people loitering around, but fewer seemed to be on the beach.

I continued down the street, heading away from the cluster of businesses and toward the thick woods. My legs were aching from the exertion, and my back called out for me to stop, but I kept pushing, needing to feel that rush I used to crave.

So many days, when life got too heavy, I'd head out into the world, letting my feet guide me where they wanted. But that was years ago, back when my problems were much more minor than I realized. Now, it took a lot longer to escape the things that chased me.

As I hit the trailhead, I paused, stretching out my spine and legs. Maybe today, I'd try to push myself to see if all that physical therapy had made an impact. While I looked around, my phone rang out from my armband, and I hesitated when I saw the picture on the screen.

Shit.

Taking it out of the pouch, I place the phone up to my ear.

"How's my favorite girl?" I said, trying to hide my guilt.

A loud chuckle filled the line. "You say that to all the girls."

"Yes, but you know I only mean it with you, Dani."

She sighed, trying to hide how much she loved my cheesy lines. "Checking in. It's been three days, and I haven't heard a peep outta you. Keeping yourself out of trouble, right?"

"Trying."

"Good," she said. A voice in the background called her, so I knew our all-too-brief time was up. "Gotta go, but you know you can call anytime you need. Miss you, Cole."

"Miss you too, Dani."

We ended the call with little fanfare. As I resumed my run, the phone call lingered in my mind. Should I have told Dani about what was going on with Adam? No, definitely not. Not that Dani wouldn't understand, but she had always drawn a firm line in the sand. Our relationship was about us, not him, but it wasn't that easy for me to turn it off. When a guy has had your back for over twenty-five years, you don't walk away from him. Ours was a bond no one else could ever understand.

The trail twisted and turned through the forest, going deeper until I could no longer hear the sounds of town. My only focus was my breathing and my feet hitting the ground, one after the other. That was my favorite part of working out and the reason I got back into it when I had lost my other outlets. It was a chance to clear my head, to focus on my body and none of the other shit tying me down.

It worked.

Usually.

Today, though, my thoughts kept going to Alex and what Adam said about their date. How the hell could he not have chemistry with a girl like that? Shit, I saw the pictures, so I knew something had happened between them, and based on the images, I started to think a lot more went down than an awkward kiss.

Not that it mattered to me—they were consenting adults, and they could do whatever they wanted. But Alex had been stuck in my head for the past few days. I couldn't shake the feeling that I wanted to know more about her.

As I turned past a thick brush, my mind still entirely focused on Alex, I slammed into someone, sending them flying back into the dirt.

"Fuck!" I hissed. "I'm so sorry. I wasn't paying attention."

"No shit," a familiar voice groaned.

My eyes widened when I realized the woman I slammed into was the same one I couldn't get out of my head. Alex was laid out on her back, glaring up at me from the ground. With her sprawled out on the ground, with her sports bra and tight shorts clinging to all the right places, it was hard not to picture all the other places I wouldn't mind seeing her on her back.

"Seriously," she huffed, turning to get up. "First, you knock me on my ass, and then you just stand there?"

Shit.

I jumped into action, bending down to help lift her from the ground. My back twinged with a sharp pain, but I pushed it back down to focus on Alex. As she brushed off her knees, I picked a few leaves and branches out of her hair and lowered my voice. "Sorry about that."

Alex looked up at me, and my breath caught in my throat. Her blue eyes were brighter than usual, but that was because they were red-rimmed and puffy. The sight of her upset made the knot in my chest only grow, conflicted between tracking down the person who hurt her or pulling her into my arms, whispering promises that it would all be okay.

But as soon as she was up, she took a little step back, wincing when she put weight on her ankle. I reached out, taking her arm in my hand. Shit, her skin was smooth. That was something I shouldn't have noticed, and I definitely shouldn't have been moving my thumb to feel it a little longer. Taking a step back, I cleared my throat. "You okay?"

"Yeah, great," she scoffed. "Never better."

"Liar," I teased.

I waited for that usual spark of hers, the one that loved to knock me on my ass, but it was nowhere to be found. "It's fine," she said quickly, her voice filled with defeat. "I'm having a crappy morning."

"Guess that means you saw the article?"

Alex's eyes snapped up to mine, her mouth forming a tight line. "Oh, you mean the one that said I'm just Adam's latest fling? Or the one that called me "Townie Trash"?

"Shit."

"Yeah, that was pretty much my reaction," she scoffed, shaking her head. "Along with a ton of other swears. I thought a run would help, get me out of the house, and escape my phone for a little bit." She motioned to her scraped knees. "But the universe thought I needed to be knocked down a few more pegs today."

"Look, Adam's going to fix this," I said, shifting closer to her. "And even if he can't, it'll brush over quickly."

She nodded, but it was clear she didn't believe me. Alex glanced over her shoulder. "I should get home. Running was a shit plan. I feel cookie dough calling my name." She half-heartedly waved as she turned away from me.

"Hey, Alex," I called out, waiting until she stopped before

continuing. "Remember—those articles are bullshit. You're none of those things."

She rolled her eyes, "You barely know me, *Mr.* Campbell."

As she headed back down the path, only one thought played in my head.

That was going to have to change.

EIGHT

Alex

I stared at the employee entrance of the Isadora, the simple white-painted door blending in the background. Only the black sign marking it as the employee entrance made it stand out from the rest of the walls. The seconds kept ticking by, but I stayed standing there. It was only ten feet, but it felt like a million miles.

No matter how hard I tried, I couldn't quite convince my feet to move any closer. It had been almost twenty minutes since I first stopped in this spot, and I hadn't made it any closer to the inside.

I already knew what awaited me on the other side.

Questions.

Too many questions.

I avoided these questions for the past five days, thanks to my ridiculous number of sick days.

But based on the number of calls and messages from Diane, my grace period was officially over. She'd been circling for days, waiting for my head to pop out of my burrow to strike. As tempted as I was to steer clear of the rest of the world, it was time to face the music.

According to my call-outs, I'd been battling strep throat. In reality, it was much more a case of I-avoid-awkward-things-at-all-costs. For the past five days, Javier and Calla alternated checking on me, fluctuating between sympathy and tough love. They tried to understand my situation, but neither really could. They both lived fearlessly, not worried about who was watching their every move. Me? I had to be much more selective about the information that got out into the world.

A cold chill ran up my spine, and I wondered who else had seen the photos. Plenty of old friends had come out of the woodwork when the story broke, wanting to know all about Adam and me. Luckily, that seemed to be it.

My phone chirped in my pocket, alerting me to another comment about the photos. I shut it off without another look, not wanting to hear another stranger's opinion of me. That was a lesson I learned in hour five of this situation, figuring out all too quickly how much vitriol people spewed when they hid behind a keyboard.

Not that it mattered. They were all words I'd heard before.

With a reluctant groan, I forced my way inside the resort, stopping to drop off my stuff before crossing into the lobby. Hopefully, it would be an easy day, one with minimal guest interaction.

That wish was quickly squashed when my name rang out before I even reached my desk.

"Thank God you're here," Adam said as he rushed to my side. "Calla said you were sick, but I had to see for myself. Please tell me you're okay. The pictures, I swear, I had no idea—"

I shook my head, not ready to talk about the article. Instead, I arched my brow at him. "How did you know I would be here?"

He smiled sheepishly. "I might have bribed your counterpart a little bit: a bunch of signed items in exchange for your work schedule."

Over his shoulder, Javier lets out a little wave. "Talk. To. Him," he mouthed, emphasizing his point with a stern look.

Traitor.

"Adam..." I sighed, glancing around the room. This was not the place for this conversation. Too many sets of eyes were watching us, trying to listen in inconspicuously.

I grabbed his arm, dragging him into one of the event rooms off the main lobby.

Once he crossed the threshold, I closed the doors and turned the lock, but as soon as it was the two of us, my emotions started to get the best of me. Everything hit me at once. My skin was usually thick, but reading and hearing people's comments over the past few days had unearthed past wounds, ones that had taken years to heal.

Adam came closer, placing his hands on my shoulders. "I'm so sorry, Alex. I had no idea...I didn't think..." He cut himself off, taking a step back to run his hand through his hair. "You shouldn't have gotten dragged into this."

"It's not your fault, Adam."

"Of course it is," he said. "How are you doing? Honestly."

"I've had better weeks," I chuckled, trying to push away the words eating away at me. Nothing had happened with Adam, but the assumptions hurt the most. *Whore. Slut.* Too many people had no problem slinging those words like weapons.

Adam stared at me, trying to read through my mask. *Don't break.* His forlorn expression was *almost* enough to shatter my walls, but I refused to place my insecurities on his shoulders. Instead, I quickly wiped the corner of my eye. "I want to get back to work and pretend like this whole mess never happened."

Adam dropped his gaze down to his feet. "Look, if this means you don't want to hang out again, I get it," he said, his voice cracking a little with each word. "If you don't sign up for this life...I know it can be a lot. Shit, it's a lot, even if you did. It can be frustrating. Invasive. I...I've had people walk away for less."

The shame and fear in his eyes almost made me stumble. It was as real as the paintings on the wall. The idea of Adam losing people because of things out of his control crushed me. Those bitter, self-conscious rumblings turned to anger, hating that he gave so much of himself for so little in return.

I smiled up at him, and this time, it was a little more genuine. "Not gonna happen. We said we're friends, so we're going to be friends. Maybe no more kissing on public beaches?"

Adam breathed a long sigh of relief. "You've got a deal."

He pulled me into a tight hug, his head nestling on top of mine. His strong arms enveloped me, holding me tight against his chest as I nuzzled into him, the smell of cedar and spice calming my spiraling feelings. It was soothing having someone hold me like this, something I didn't even realize I desperately needed at the moment. My heart thumped loudly in my chest—not in desire, but in comfort. Adam was a fantastic hugger. I pulled back, wiping a few errant tears from my eyes. "I should get back out there. Javier's already pissed I've left him alone for three days."

"Of course," Adam said, but his eyes darted around the room. *Uh oh.* "So, listen...I need to ask for one more favor."

My brow arched at his words and the sudden shift in his demeanor.

Adam continued, "My agent flew in to help with the media coverage and to get ahead of any stories about us. He wants to sit down with the two of us to discuss the next steps."

"Next steps? I figured this would be over as soon as another story broke."

"Me too," he said, "but I'm still dealing with some of the

fallout from my last relationship. We've been working on cleaning up my image, but this kind of threw a wrench in that." He took my hand in his. "I get it if you don't want to meet with him, and I would never ask you to do anything if it made you uncomfortable, but I had to ask."

"And this is important to you?"

He stared down at me with his picturesque blue eyes, and I was hit with the urge to soothe his pain again. Whoever his ex was, damn her for putting that sadness in his soul. Without thinking about the consequences, I nodded my head.

"Then I guess I'm in."

———

I ALWAYS BELIEVED Calla was the most energetic person I knew, but I was very wrong. She was practically comatose compared to the pacing man in front of me. Theo stood slightly shorter than Adam, his frame much slenderer, but he commanded every single inch of the villa. As he stood in the center of the room in his three-piece designer suit, he looked like the villain out of a Bond movie, and his not-so-sunny reaction to my arrival didn't do much to sway me in his favor.

When Adam picked me up after my shift, he spent the walk to his room trying to prepare me for Theo, but no amount of prep could have readied me for this meeting. Theo covered the entire dining table with printouts of articles and social media pages covering our impromptu photoshoot. Did I mention the spreadsheets and charts? Oh yeah, because he had those too. Overall, it felt more like an investor's pitch than a discussion about a man's personal life.

As Theo waxed on about the colossal mistake Adam made with me (*thanks, buddy*), he sat there silently, staring out into space. It struck me that Adam had heard this whole speech many times, and my heart cracked a little more. Without think-ing, I reached out, taking his hand under the table.

He jumped a little at the contact before squeezing my hand back. He needed my support, whether he'd asked or not. It was odd that Cole wasn't here, but it shouldn't have been. Adam said earlier that he tried to keep his friend away from these meetings because he hated them so much. Apparently, Cole tended to tell Theo to shut his mouth.

At that moment, I didn't see the problem.

Theo suddenly stopped moving, ending his tirade mid-sentence as he snapped his attention back to Adam. "Have you heard anything else from Ivy?"

He glanced over at me quickly before answering. "She called a couple of times, but I didn't answer."

Theo nodded. "Good, good. We don't need this being spun into her next single."

Wait.

"Holy shit, Ivy Abrams is your ex?" I said, connecting the dots in their conversation to my past ones with Adam. He nods. "That's crazy," I continued. "I love her new song—you know the one. Crap, how does it go?"

He grimaced, "Please don't."

My eyes practically bugged out of my head as I turned to him. "No! Please tell me that's not about you."

"Yup. Most of the songs on her new album are."

Yikes. I'd only heard a couple on the radio, but those songs cut deep. Calla and I had had car sing-a-longs to a few of them. I remembered wishing I was the one throwing the hurtful words into my ex's face. They embodied female rage in a way I could never dream.

But the man in her lyrics was so different from the Adam I was starting to know. He was gracious, kind, and even thoughtful—not the guy a song called "Narcissist" would be penned after.

He ran his hand over his face. "We didn't date for long, but Ivy thought it was a lot more serious than I did. When I tried to end things, she didn't take it well. I can't lie. I didn't do a great job with the whole break-up, but I also never set out to hurt her. Apparently, she disagrees."

"And now, she's making a goddamn fortune painting our golden boy as a jerk who uses women," Theo said, finally dropping into the chair across from us. "We've been working for months to try to repair his image with no luck, but I think we might have caught an unexpected break."

"What do you mean?" Adam asked.

"We've been watching the coverage around your photos. While we still have the usual trolls, most of the press has been positive, especially about Alex. They like the idea of Adam dating someone outside Hollywood."

"But we're not dating," I interrupted. "It was one date, and that was it."

"Are you sure?"

Adam and I glanced at each other, probably both thinking of the mangled kiss that got us into this mess. He nodded first. "Positive. Just friendship here."

"Too bad," Theo tutted, "but not a complete deal breaker."

Adam started shaking his head before Theo even finished his thought. "No way, man. I told you—*never* again."

"What happened with Everly isn't going to happen again. We won't make that mistake twice."

"Absolutely not."

I leaned forward, raising my hand in the air. "Hey, I'm still here. Do either of you want to fill me in on what you're talking about?"

"No," Adam said at the same time as Theo nodded his head.

Theo pointed a sharp glare at Adam. "Let's at least discuss it. You pay me way too much money for this exact reason: I get results. This set-up will help your image. You know it's true." He leaned back in his chair. "Let's at least run it by Alex and see if she would be game."

"Game for what?" I asked, my head swiveling between them. This whole talking around me thing was starting to get on my nerves. Whatever plan Theo had concocted needed me to work, which already made me feel unsteady—not to mention the massive frown on Adam's face.

He stared at Theo for a long minute, who still did not back down. Eventually, Adam groaned and then turned to me. "You don't have to do this."

"Do what?" I finally snapped. "What do you want us to do?"

Theo smirked across the table. "We need you to pretend to be Adam's girlfriend."

NINE

"Excuse me?"

My voice came out too squawky and too loud, unable to hide my shock. Theo wanted me to be Adam's *pretend girlfriend?* How was that even an option? Sure, I'd seen movies and read books with the whole fake-dating thing, but to hear it suggested out loud boggled my mind.

Theo and Adam were looking at me like this was a completely normal request, like this was a normal conversation. If I ever had any doubts that Adam and I were from two very different worlds, they'd be dead now.

"You two would pretend to date," Theo continued. "Some scheduled events and strategically planned candid photos." He slowed his speech as if the words were what I was failing to grasp. "It's a very common occurrence."

"Oh, well, then it makes complete sense," I snorted. "This is insane. You know that, right?"

"You sound like you have questions," Theo says.

"No shit."

He scowled at me but passed over a stack of papers. "If you both agree to this plan, we will draft a contract stating all the terms and conditions. This is what a standard one would look like."

"And you happened to have this on hand?" I asked, trying to read the words on the page. None of them made sense, and all the legal jargon went over my head. Maybe under normal conditions, I would understand, but right now, my brain was too foggy even to try.

"As I said, it's a prevalent practice in Hollywood."

Adam leaned forward in his chair, reading over my shoulder. Eventually, I gave up and passed the entire thing to him. He read through it, nodding as he turned through the pages. "How long?"

"At least until the end of filming," Theo said. "Once the movie has wrapped, you'll return to LA. We'll say that your relationship ran its course. We can even throw in that Alex wasn't willing to relocate." He shrugged. "Simple as that."

Simple? To this man, this insane, bullshit plan seemed *simple*. Instantly, I started laughing, unable to hold it back any longer. Theo stared at me like I lost my mind, and maybe I had. That was the only way this night made any sense. When I calmed down, I shook my head. "I thought the whole point was to get Adam's love life *out* of the news."

"Originally, it was," Theo answered. "But after our research, we found that audiences preferred seeing him in a committed relationship. It changes the narrative from playboy to relationship material. Much better for his image."

"Then it can wait until he finds a real girlfriend!" I shrieked. "Not some random girl off the street!"

"Would love to, darling, but you're the one in the photos," he said. "Plus, people like that you're the girl next door. It's a bit of a Cinderella story, and people eat that shit up."

I turned to Adam, throwing my hands in the air. "Are you really buying this?"

"I have no idea," he said. "But then again, it wouldn't be my first time in the fake dating arena."

"Seriously? How many times have you done this before?"

"Twice," he winced. "And no, I can't tell you who. We had to sign NDAs as well."

"NDA?" I asked, directing my question back to Theo.

"Non-disclosure agreement. You agree not to speak of the arrangement to anyone."

My eyes narrowed. "And if I do?"

"Then you would run the risk of a major lawsuit," Theo said. "That is non-negotiable. After Adam's latest dating disaster, we do not want any unauthorized stories about your relationship getting leaked."

That made sense. At least, it made sense that it would work in Theo's mind, but the idea of lying to everyone in my life gave me pause.

"I can't tell anyone the truth?" I asked. "Not even my best friends? I know them. They would never say anything."

"No one." Theo shakes his head. "That's the only way to make certain the plan works." He turned his attention back to Adam. "That brings us to Cole."

Adam instantly tensed. "What about him?"

"You can't tell him about this."

"Not gonna happen," Adam snapped. "I don't keep shit like this from him."

Theo ran his hands across his face. "Do I have to remind you about the Santa Monica incident?"

Adam's face instantly fell. "Point taken."

My head volleyed between Theo and Adam, trying to pick up on their conversation. As they debated what Cole could know, I sat back in my chair, staring out at the lake from the window.

How the hell did I even get here? A couple of days ago, I

was living a completely normal, albeit boring, life, and now, I was sitting with a movie star, contemplating playing his fake girlfriend.

The more we discussed the plan, the more absurd it seemed.

No one, and I did mean *no one,* would buy that Adam and I were a real couple. Hell, we didn't have enough chemistry to make it through one lackluster kiss. How in the hell was anyone supposed to believe we were in love?

Adam might have had dozens of films under his belt, but my acting experience was limited to the Spring Musical in the third grade. There was a reason I was assigned to the stage crew in the fourth.

Adam took my hand. "Alex, you do not have to do this. We will find a way to fix this mess. You don't need to get involved."

Great, that worked for me. Where was the door again?

But before I could stand up, I met Adam's eyes, recognizing hurt and hope lurking in them. Every time I thought my heart couldn't break anymore for the man, it did a little more. To the outside world, he had it all, but now, after getting to know the real man behind Adam Rice's brand, it was clear he was lonely. He was almost entirely alone except for the people he paid. Cole was the only one who seemed to have his back out of loyalty.

The whole situation still made me nervous, and I hated the idea of putting myself in the spotlight. As much as I wanted to help Adam, there were some risks I wasn't willing to take.

But even as I told myself all the reasons this was a terrible idea, I couldn't bring myself to say no. Instead, I sighed, shifting in my chair. "Can I think about it?"

"Of course," Theo said. "Just don't take too much time. We want to get this matter settled before filming begins in a couple of weeks."

I nodded, standing from my chair as Adam did the same. He walked me to the front door, barely waiting for Theo to call out goodnight before ushering me outside. As soon as the cold breeze hit my skin, breathing became a little easier. The last half an hour had felt like a fever dream.

"I'm sorry about that," Adam muttered as we walked back to my car. "I promise; I did not know this was the direction Theo was going to go."

Turning to face him, I asked, "What do you think about it?"

"It seems like a very strategic and thought-out idea."

I rolled my eyes. "Adam, this isn't a press junket. Between you and me, how do you feel?"

"Exhausted," he answered, letting his mask drop for a second. "I'm so tired of putting on an act and being the man everyone wants me to be, tired of having to ask for permission to live my life. That was why I had so much fun with you: I could be myself. But if we decide to do this…"

"Then it all goes back to being an act," I finish for him.

"Exactly," Adam said. "I hate the idea of lying to everyone, especially Cole, but at the same time, I selfishly like the idea of doing this with you."

"Well, I am pretty good company." I smiled at my quip. "If I agree, will you tell me who the other two girls were?"

"Nope," he said, crossing his finger over his chest. "I know better than to fuck with Theo and his NDAs. I swear, he's going to be buried with them." Adam stepped closer to me. "But seriously, Alex, there's no pressure to say yes. If you want to give this a go, I promise we'll make it worth your while. If it's too much, then everything will go back to how it was before. Either way, we're good."

"Promise?"

"On everything I am."

"YOU NEED to explain this to me again."

Calla stared at me from the opposite barstool, and her eyes narrowed in confusion. Her long, red waves flowed over her shoulder, having lost her hair tie after our first couple of drinks. For most of our evening, she'd been her usual self, laughing and singing along to whatever was playing on the jukebox.

That was one of the reasons I picked Paddy's Wake for our girl's night out. It was originally an Irish pub, but the owners moved to Florida to escape the cold long before I moved here. Even though the new management kept the name, the decor had drastically changed over the years. Most of the time, it was crawling with tourists, the locals preferring the quieter bars away from Main Street, but the owners banked on the summertime traffic and made every effort to live up to the beach bar vibe. The drinks were cheap and gimmicky, and the music was constantly blasting old tunes everyone knew by heart. Images of patrons and partiers over the years lined the walls. The glow of the neon beer signs was the only light in the central area. It was the kind of bar that didn't care if you came in sweatpants or your prom dress, just as long as you paid your tab at the end of the night and kept fighting to a minimum.

In short, the perfect place to forget all your troubles from the outside world.

Tonight, Calla and I were doing just that—her to forget what a witch her mother could be and me to ignore the offer looming over my head. It was working...until I let it slip that I was talking to Adam about going out again.

That was the moment Calla switched from carefree to curious, the drunken giggles disappearing immediately. It was a shame she had no desire to become a lawyer like the rest of her family. The girl had the iron will of a shark when she sensed something was up.

Case in point: Calla stared at me as she stirred the swivel stick in her drink. After spearing the cherry at the bottom, she pointed it at me. "So, based on what you said about your first date, you have zero interest in him romantically. How did you phrase it?" She paused, tapping her pointer finger against her lower lip. "Oh, yes. It was *criminally* bad. So why in the hell do you want to go out with him again?"

Fort Knox, I was not. Considering that I hadn't signed the NDA yet, I figured it wouldn't be the worst thing in the world to confide a little in my best friend. Granted, I skipped the whole fake part of our dating scheme.

I shrugged my shoulders, keeping my eyes trained on my drink. "Adam asked for another chance. I figured there was no harm in going out again."

Calla shook her head. "I don't buy it. You're the girl who makes up *any* excuse to get out of a social event. Who are you, and what have you done with my best friend?"

I chewed on my lower lip, unable to meet her knowing stare. God, lying to her was the *worst*. How was I supposed to keep this up for *months*? Another reason on the long list of reasons why I should say no to the arrangement. But instead of admitting that to Calla, I doubled down on the lie. "Well, maybe you've finally rubbed off on me."

"About damn time," she smiled, holding her empty glass in the air as the bartender swung by our table. "Okay, give me the pro-con list."

"I didn't make one."

"If you're going to keep trying to lie to me, we're switching over to shots."

I glanced behind the bar, seeing Aaron standing behind me. The burly man was a giant teddy bear, but I swore he could mess up a tequila shot. The last time we ordered lemon drops, we got a literal cup of vodka, and lemon slices chucked at us.

Wincing, I turned back to Calla. "I swear, this time, I didn't make one." *Mostly because I wasn't sure if the list would count as violating an NDA.* "I'm trying not to overthink things and do what feels right."

"And that's being with Adam?"

It wasn't that simple. How could I explain to Calla that being with Adam wasn't the right move for me but that helping him was? There was a connection between us, but it was almost like kindred spirits. We both knew how it felt to be alone in a room full of people, wishing someone would see the person hiding underneath. While our situations were very different, I couldn't help but wonder what my life would be like now if someone had helped when I truly needed it.

Feeling more resolute in my choice, I nodded. "Yeah, I think it does."

Calla smiled brightly back at me. "Then I wholeheartedly agree with this choice. It's about damn time you did something for the hell of it!"

I groaned, dropping my head down to my hands. "If you think this is the right choice, maybe I should reconsider."

"Nope," she smirked. "You said it. Now you have to follow through."

Fuck my life.

Shaking my head as she tried to flag down Aaron, I decided the best evasive maneuver was to steer the conversation to another topic.

"What about you, Cal?" She frowned at me. "Are you going to tell me what the blow-up with your mom was about?"

She groaned, sinking more into her chair. "You know, the usual stuff. She thinks I'm throwing my life away because I refuse to follow her 'advice.'" She rolled her eyes. "It's like she is incapable of understanding why I don't want to be her."

My hands clenched into tight fists under the table. Diane's favorite activity after berating her employees was pointing out her youngest daughter's flaws. Forget the fact that Calla graduated at the top of her undergraduate class; in Diane's eyes, because she didn't go directly to law school and snag a rich husband, her daughter was a failure. "Fuck that," I muttered. "Have you shown her your ideas yet?"

For the past year, Calla had shadowed the events department at The Isadora, helping plan most of their high-end banquets and weddings. While she didn't like to take credit, everyone at work knew she had all the best ideas. Lately, Calla had been toying with the idea of making it a full-time job, hoping to upgrade our dated ballroom and modernize the space.

Calla chewed on her lower lip. "Nope. I want to have the details worked out before I present the idea to my parents. It's one thing to say that I want to help out around the resort, but actually doing it is a completely different story. There are so many variables, especially if I want to start my own event planning company. I don't even know where to start. I've got Devyn looking into the legalities, but otherwise, I'm still trying to get my bearings."

"And Devyn's been supportive?"

I hated to voice the question, knowing Devyn was the only sister Calla regularly spoke to. Her older sister, Laurel, was a clone of their mom and made no secret of her disdain for Calla's life. From the few times I met Devyn, though, she seemed like a good blend of her two sisters. While she was guarded, she also had a soft spot for her younger sister. Devyn was there whenever Calla needed her.

Calla nodded. "She's been great about the whole thing.

She's busy at work, of course, but she's been trying to help in her limited free time."

"That's great," I said honestly. "I know I can't tell a peony from a dahlia, but I'll help you any way I can."

She reached across the table to take my hand. "You already are. Being here and listening to me bitch is the best thing right now." Her lips twitched in a devious way. "But there is one thing you can do for me..."

"If it has something to do with Adam, you're walking home."

"That wasn't what I was thinking, but now that you mention it..."

"Calla!"

"Okay, okay," she giggled, holding her glass in the air. "Aaron, it's time for lemon drops! We're celebrating!"

I shook my head, both excited and terrified for what the next few hours held. As Aaron dropped a large jug of vodka in front of us, I leaned over to ask Calla, "What are we celebrating?"

She shrugged. "You're taking a risk on Adam, and I'm trying to get my shit together. Seems like as good a reason as any other."

Now, that was logic I could agree with.

Emerging from the church's basement, I gave a quick wave over my shoulder, leaving the rest of the group to head further into town. While everyone else liked to gather at the local diner after our meetings, I was the outsider. Worked for me. Another reminder that this was all temporary.

I pulled out my phone, debating whether to take an Uber. *Fuck it.* It was a nice enough night. The stars were out and welcoming, and there was the slightest hint of a chill in the air—not enough to make me grab a coat, but enough to show that autumn was on its way.

There was something to be said about this town in the middle of the night. Once the lights went down, the main street of Saint Stephen's Lake felt like a different place. Gone were the tourist traps and the visitors who typically lined the streets. The mini-golf park and various novelty shops turned off their signs hours ago. Instead, under the antique street lamps, you could see the old-world charm this town still held.

There were no pretenses, nothing fake about it. Saint Stephen's Lake might have its flaws, but they didn't bother to hide them. It was a trait I rarely saw back in LA.

The thought of my so-called home made my steps stutter a little. What would it be like to go back? Would it be a relief? Or would I still be thinking of quiet evenings here, wishing I was staring out at the glossy black waters instead of the Hollywood hills?

I already knew the answer. Being in Saint Stephen's Lake, I felt lighter than I had in years. While LA was where I needed to be, it wasn't home. It never would be. It was like trying to swim upstream. Uncomfortable. Unnatural. Necessary all the same.

As I tried to ignore that thought, a loud bark of laughter pulled at my attention. It came from the top floor of a double-decker bar on the corner of Main and Woodcrest streets. It was a fucking dumb idea, but I moved closer, my curiosity getting the best of me.

A flickering neon sign showcased the name of the bar: Paddy's Wake. It stuck out among the rest of the town, designed to look like a tacky beach-side attraction. The obnoxious paint colors and surfboards littering the walls would have pissed me off in most circumstances, but here, it was even more irritating.

I stopped, turning to look at the building. While the lower floor was closed off, the top one had all open windows, wooden slats pushed open, held by chains covered in fake vines. Even from across the street, the drunken wails of Journey's "Don't Stop Believing" reached me. As much as I tried to fight it, I smirked, imagining what the bar was like on the inside.

A few years ago, I would have grabbed a beer before joining them for a round or two. But now, it was like that bar was covered in bright warning signs urging me to stay the fuck away. No matter how much fun it could be, it would never be worth the self-loathing in the morning.

I'd worked too hard, too fucking long, to throw it away for a single night.

I forced myself to keep walking, hoping that I'd killed

enough time for Theo and Adam to talk. My jaw tensed, thinking about their conversation. Good thing I wasn't there. Every time I sat in on one of Adam's meetings, I had to toe the line, which often ended with my foot in my mouth instead. While Adam took it all in stride, there had been plenty of times when I'd blown a fuse, sick to damn death of those people telling Adam how to live his life. His team managed everything, from his schedule to his diet. They knew everything about him, never allowing a moment when he could think for himself.

Another reason I'd never wanted Adam's life. I might have made a lot of mistakes, but they were mine to own, and no agents or reps were waiting to call me out for any missteps.

As I debated heading back to the hotel, two girls stumbled out the bar's front door. The first one captured my attention, her red hair glowing under the neon signs, but as soon as her friend came into view, she became a distant afterthought. The shorter brunette was the only person I could see, the broad smile on her face making the air zip right out of my lungs.

I'd only seen Alex with a scowl or a smirk, never this bold happiness. If she aimed that smile at me, I'd drop to my knees.

I didn't notice the two men following them until they called out their names.

"C'mon, baby, one more drink..." one of the men called out, grabbing Alex by the waist.

She glanced down at his hand with a sneer before pushing it off her. "And we said no. Go back inside, boys. You're gonna have much better luck in there than out here."

"Seriously, Mitch," the redhead next to her snorted. "When are you gonna learn that it's never gonna happen?"

The asshole didn't even flinch. Instead, he took Alex's hand, pressing his lips to her knuckles. "Can't blame me for trying."

My fist tightened at the sight. Who the fuck was this guy, and why did he think it was okay to touch her like that? If she were into it, I'd keep my fucking distance, but I knew that look on her face, having been on the receiving end more than once.

The guy was half a second from becoming a eunuch.

Ignoring my brain's warning, I stepped into the parking lot, beelining for Alex's side. Her friend stared at me as if trying to figure out if I was another threat. I wasn't, at least not to her or Alex, but if these assholes didn't get the hint, that would be another story.

"Hey, sweetheart," I said, stepping to Alex's side. My arm wrapped around her shoulders, pulling her closer to my side. At the contact, her blue eyes widened with shock. Not even half a second later, they narrowed, and her lips thinned. *Fuck.* Maybe I was the one facing castration tonight. But when I winked at her, some of her irritation faded, finally figuring out what I was doing. She even started to relax into my touch.

"Hey babe," Alex said, snuggling into my side as her hands slid around my chest. "I missed you."

"Not as much as I missed you," I answered, tucking her even closer to me. Damn, she fit so perfectly against me. I could smell her shampoo, floral, and warm scents filling the small space between us. I shook off the thought, directing my attention back to the guy gaping across from us. "Who are your friends?"

"This is Mitch and his buddy Pete. We were reminding them of the importance of consent." Alex smirked back at them. "We good, guys?"

They both nodded, muttering under their breath as they walked back through the bar's front doors.

As soon as they were gone, her friend doubled over, holding her stomach while loudly laughing. "Oh my God, I wish I had my phone out for that! Mitch's jaw hit the floor when you came over."

"Don't tell him that, Calla," Alex groaned, shoving me away

from her. She even wiped her hands on her jeans as if touching me repulsed her. "You'll only make his ego bigger."

I smirked down at her. "That's a strange way to thank me."

"For what?" She rolled her eyes. "I had that covered."

"I could tell," I said. "But you seemed about five seconds away from committing murder, so I thought I'd step in and save you some jail time."

"Our hero." Calla placed her hand on her heart, pretending to swoon, while Alex just continued to scowl at me.

"Then consider your job done," Alex said with a flick of her wrist. "We were about to walk home, so you're good to go."

I glanced around, not liking the idea of two girls walking through the darkness. There were too many things that could go wrong at night. Alex had car keys clenched in her hands. "Why aren't you driving?"

"This one," Alex pointed over her shoulder to Calla, who was watching our exchange intently, "made me do shots."

"We were celebrating," Calla added quickly, earning another glare from Alex.

Alex pressed her fingers to her forehead. "It's fine. Aaron would rather me leave my car here than risk driving. I'll come grab it in the morning."

"The fuck you will," I said, reaching my hand out. "Look, I'll drive you two home and then hitch a ride back to the hotel."

Calla jumped up, wrapping a hug around my neck. "That would be the best! These shoes are cute, but they suck for walking."

I pat her back, lowering her to the ground, but I didn't miss the way Alex's eyes tracked all my movements, her lips forming a cute scowl. Alex snapped the keys back when Calla tried to grab them.

"This isn't some excuse to get us alone to murder us, right?"

"Alex!"

"What?" she snarled, turning back to her friend. "You don't know this guy. He can't stand me. Who knows if this is some elaborate trap?"

I reached over, snatching the keys from her hands. "First of all, if I was going to murder you, announcing myself as your boyfriend would probably be a stupid idea. And second, I never said I didn't like you."

"Then why do you give me so much shit?"

I clicked the unlock button, smiling when an older model Jeep Wrangler's lights blinked on. This was going to be fun. As I walked past Alex to get to the driver's side, I lowered myself down to her ear, speaking low enough so only she could hear.

"Because, sweetheart, you make it so easy."

ELEVEN

Alex barely said two words to me after we dropped Calla off at the hotel. A thick tension had grown between us, a visceral wall erected across the console. It had been easier on the drive over with Calla. She was happy to fill the silence, telling her entire life story during the ten-minute drive. She grew up in the city, but her family moved here when her grandfather passed away, and her mother inherited the hotel. Her father still lived in Manhattan, a named partner in one of the best law firms in the country, with her two older sisters following in his footsteps. She was the only one who chose to stay here, living in one of the suites in the hotel with her mother.

I'd never met someone who spoke so much in such a short amount of time, but now that Calla was gone, I almost missed the constant stream of words. At least it broke up the tension between Alex and me.

"You know, you're going to have to talk to me eventually," I said as we crossed over the bridge into town.

"Not necessarily."

"Unless you want to spend the whole night driving around,

you're going to have to give some kind of directions," I smirked back at her. "Your choice, sweetheart."

She groaned loudly. "Turn right at the end of the bridge," she muttered before turning to glare at me. "What is with that stupid nickname?"

"What—sweetheart?"

"Yes," she said. "I don't get why you can't call me by my name like everyone else."

I slowed down to make the turn, taking a moment to turn and steal a look at her. She crossed her arms around her chest and scowled at me. It was adorable.

"I don't know," I answered honestly. "It's not something I usually do. It kind of slipped out the first time, and then you flipped out and were so damn funny, I wanted to do it again."

Her brow furrowed. "That seems like a dumb reason."

"Maybe." I shrugged. "But I don't have a lot of other things going on right now, so I'll take whatever entertainment I can get."

"Is that why you were wandering around town like a lost puppy?"

"Not exactly," I said, not wanting to share the entire reason I was in town. "Adam was meeting with his agent, so I got out of there for a bit." Alex turned to study me curiously, so I continued. "It's complicated. Adam and I have been friends for a long time, and I want the best for him. All these people..." I shook my head, cutting off my words. "Forget it."

"You can tell me. I...I'd like to know more," Alex whispered, her voice a little shaky. "How long have you and Adam been friends?"

"Since the third grade. I was the new kid, and he helped me out. It was weird—we just clicked. We've been best friends ever since."

"That's amazing." Alex pointed toward a side street, and I

hit the blinker. "To still be friends after all that time, especially with Adam's career."

As we turned, I said, "I can't lie and say things aren't different. When it's Adam and me, it's like nothing has changed. He's still the same guy I grew up with. But when he's around everyone else..." I shook my head, struggling to put my feelings into words. How did you say you loved your friend but hated the person he's becoming without sounding like a dick? "His team...They make him doubt everything, make him act like someone he's not. It's too much bullshit, and he barely ever says anything. I can't keep my mouth shut, though, so when they meet, I make myself scarce. I want as little to do with that part of his life as possible."

Alex shifted in her seat, turning to face me more. "So then, why do you stay?"

"What do you mean?"

"I mean, that's Adam's life. His choices, his career. What about you?" She stared at me, her blue eyes wide with curiosity. "Don't take this the wrong way, but it seems like you're more concerned with his life than yours."

"Ouch," I chuckled, trying to hide how close to home her comment struck.

She rolled her eyes. "That's not what I meant. I'm just wondering why you stick around If you hate what's happening so much?"

I sighed, weighing her question. I'd be lying if I said it wasn't something I thought about. Often. There were many reasons why I stayed with Adam, even when I didn't like the path he chose.

But too many of those reasons led to questions, ones I wasn't willing to discuss with anyone, much less with a girl I barely knew.

"I owe him a lot," I answered honestly. "The best way I can

repay him is by being there now. He needs someone who knows him, who's looking out for his best interests instead of the bottom line. So, as long as he needs me, I'm gonna be there."

"Sounds like he's lucky to have you," Alex said as she tucked herself into the seat a little more. "Maybe you're not as much of an ass as I thought."

"Thanks, sweetheart."

"I take it back."

A COUPLE more turns and Alex directed me to pull into a dirt driveway, the only thing marking the place a rickety old mailbox. The number twenty-eight was plastered on the side, the edges of the vinyl starting to pull away. At first, I thought she was messing with me, leading me into the woods to play a nasty trick. With all her questions about my intentions, maybe I should have been the one questioning her.

My self-preservation instincts must have been rusty because I kept driving until we reached the end. Luckily, when the trees broke, there was a little cabin surrounded by sunflowers and other wildflowers.

I shifted the car into park and took in Alex's home for the first time. It was nothing compared to the houses back in LA, but even from here, it felt cozy and comfortable: all the things a home should make you feel. Little lights lined the stone path to the front porch. The exterior walls were painted with washed white, dove gray shutters on each window. In fact, the only color besides the flowers was the bright teal door.

Alex tucked her bottom lip between her teeth as she climbed out of the passenger seat. "So, this is my place. I know it's small..."

"It looks amazing," I said, meaning every word.

Alex grinned back at me, the smile taking up almost her whole face. It made that knot in my stomach reappear. It was so genuine. She was terrible about hiding her emotions; her face gave her away every time. Knowing that I was the one who made her smile filled me with an irrational level of pride.

The thought made my feet stall. What I felt was unfamiliar, but at the same time, strangely not. An idea popped into my head, but I pushed it away. There was no chance I had feelings for Alex. I couldn't. It was off the table. Not only had she gone out with Adam, but any sort of relationship was the last thing I needed.

The last thing I deserved.

Clearing my throat, I dropped my gaze back to the keys in my hand before I handed them to Alex. "These are yours. You should head inside; I'll be good out here."

"Yeah, I can grab you the number for a cab–" Her eyes widened almost comically. "Oh fuck."

"What?"

"The only cab company in town closed ten minutes ago."

I dryly laughed, shaking my head. "Then I guess I better start walking."

Alex paused for a moment, glancing at her house and then back at me. "Or you could stay here."

Nope, definitely not. There was not a single scenario in which that was a good idea. If I wanted to get Alex out of my head, the last thing I should do was walk into her home.

"I really shouldn't."

"Cole..." Alex said slowly. "Do you even know how to get back to the hotel from here?"

Shit. Never once on the drive over did I think about where we were going. My brain was too focused on Alex. Rookie mistake. Considering that the town was barely a few miles wide, I was sure I could figure it out, but the last thing I wanted to be doing in the middle of the night was wandering around in circles.

As if she could read my mind, Alex opened her door, motioning for me to follow her inside. "Listen, I'll never hear the end of it if you get hurt walking back. I'd give you my car, but I don't let anyone borrow Bertha. You're lucky I even let you drive her." She nodded. "C'mon. I promise my couch is comfy."

"How comfy are we talking?" I asked. Without a proper mattress, my back would be in a lot of pain tomorrow. In the past, sleeping in random places had never phased me. Now, I needed to be selective about where I decided to lay my head. But as Alex stared at me with those wide blue eyes, I knew I couldn't say no to her. Despite my mind screaming out reasons not to enter her house, my feet were already heading up the path, eager to get closer to her.

"The best," she promised. "Not gonna lie, I crash on it a lot, on nights when I'm too burnt out to make it to my bed."

As I climbed up her front stairs, her face came into view, illuminated by the porch lights. Now that she mentioned it, there were dark circles under her eyes. My fingers ached to reach out and soothe them, but I held back. "Does that happen a lot?"

"Getting burnt out?" Alex laughed. "More than you know."

Without another word, she pushed open the door. As we both entered, she took her keys back from me and placed them in a bowl on a console table. She smiled sheepishly as she held out her arm. "So, this is my place..."

Her home was as cozy as the outside suggested. The inside was decorated with the same warm, natural elements as the outside, making you instantly relax. The walls were a subtle mint green, each one decorated with photographs and paintings. Wooden bookshelves lined many of them, filled with different colored spines and photos. Most of the pictures were of Alex,

Calla, and Javier, the other concierge at the hotel. It was a hint of her world, but it was enough to make me want to learn more.

This place felt like a home.

A sharp pang hit my chest, knowing nowhere I'd lived during the last few years felt like this. From the sterile walls of my first beat-up apartment, which was an over-priced shoe box, to the army barracks and, most recently, Adam's pool house, everything was temporary. None felt like a place I wanted to spend my life.

Settling down roots hadn't crossed my mind before. It was always something out of reach. But maybe when this movie wrapped, and Adam and I headed back to LA, it would be time to look for a place for myself, something that was mine.

"Are you okay?"

Alex's voice broke me out of my head. I turned to see her standing at the bottom of the stairs, her eyes too focused on me. Somehow, while I zoned out on the pathetic state of my life, she snuck into her room to change. Gone were the jeans practically painted onto her. I thought it'd be a nice reprieve, but instead, she wore a black satin cami and the tiniest pair of shorts I'd ever seen.

Look, there was no question that this girl was gorgeous. I'd been trying and failing to ignore that fact since the moment we met, but her standing in front of me now? With her long hair free of its usual bun and the make-up erased from her face? The sight made my dick harden, straining behind my jeans.

What was wrong with me? Alex had opened her home to me, and I was standing here, rocking a semi like a teenager. I needed to snap out of it.

"Cole?"

"Sorry," I said, rubbing my eyes to keep from gawking. "More tired than I thought."

She gave me a look but walked over to the couch to pull out

a spare blanket and pillow. "Remote is on the table. Feel free to grab anything from the kitchen." She glanced up at the clock on the wall. "I have to be at work by seven. Is that okay for you?"

"Yup." I nodded, trying to look at anything but her. "I'm an early riser anyway."

We stood there in awkward silence, not sure what to say to each other. After the clock quietly chimed on the wall, Alex cleared her throat, looking down at her toes. "Well, I'll let you get some sleep."

My brow arched at her words. "Aren't you heading to bed?"

She shook her head. "Not really. I feel tired, but my brain's having trouble turning it off. I'll watch a movie or something until I fall asleep."

As I glanced at the television on the wall, an idea popped into my head. It was probably a bad idea. No, strike that—it was definitely a bad idea, but the words came anyway. "Same here. You want to hang for a bit until you're tired?"

She stared at me as if trying to read the meaning behind my words. I shook my head. "Get your head out of the gutter, sweetheart. I literally mean hang out."

Alex pulled her lip between her teeth, glancing from me to the stairs and back again. Slowly, she grinned. "Yeah, sounds good."

I waited until she was settled on the couch before sitting on the opposite side, trying to keep as much space between us as possible. It was easy to do as Alex tucked her feet under herself, nestling against the armrest. She grabbed the remote from the side table and flicked on a streaming app. "What works for you?"

"Anything," I said, trying not to notice how the blue light made her seem softer. It was taking everything in me not to pull her to my side, not even looking for anything but to hold her close. I rubbed my hand over my face, forcing myself to think of anything but Alex. It was useless. My mind was focused on only one thing- the one person I should not be thinking about.

Alex scanned the titles until she found an older sitcom, glancing at me to see if I was cool with it. Nodding at the choice, I settled against the cushion, letting an episode I'd seen a million times before distract me.

But I couldn't take my eyes off Alex.

From the way she giggled to the way her hair fell in front of her face, there was too much about her that intrigued me. I wanted to tuck the hair behind her ear to see if it was as silky as it appeared. I wanted to feel the weight of her leaning against my chest, nestled into my side like it was a usual occurrence. There were so few moments where it was Alex and me, no other eyes, no distractions. It made my mind spin, imagining scenarios I had no right to picture.

"I can feel you staring at me."

"Sorry," I chuckled, my cheeks heating with embarrassment.

She shifted on the couch to face me. "What are you thinking right now, Cole?"

That I want to kiss you.

The thought almost knocked me on my ass. I didn't know how, but Alex had gotten under my skin tonight—maybe even before if I was being honest. It was confusing and frustrating, but it also made me feel more alive than I had in years.

Instead of saying that, I shrugged my shoulders. "Trying to figure you out."

"I'm not that interesting," Alex answered, shifting back to face the screen. "My life is pretty much work, and then my limited free time is spent with my friends."

I nodded to the pictures on the shelf. "Calla and Javier, right?"

She arched her brow back at me. "Yeah...."

"Don't look so shocked, Alex. I'm not the ass you seem to think I am."

"Debatable," she said. "But yes, those two are the closest I have to family. Well, them and my neighbors. They became my surrogate parents when I moved here."

I quirked my head. "You didn't grow up in town?"

The question seemed innocent enough, but the moment it left my mouth, Alex's whole body stiffened. She fidgeted with the hem of her tank, refusing to meet my eyes. "Um, no. I grew up in the city. New York, I mean."

Her reaction made me want to know everything, desperate to find out what caused her plump lips to pout, but her body language screamed that it wasn't a question for right now.

I nodded to the TV. "Watch this. It's the best part of the whole episode."

"You've seen it before?" she asked, a bright smile on her lips.

"A dozen times or so."

"Me too," she squealed, reaching forward to put her hands on my leg. "I ate a butterfly," she said, quoting the next scene by heart.

I could act out the whole damn thing, but right now, my only focus was her hands on my thigh, the spark of warmth that accompanied her touch. God, what would I give to feel her touch everywhere? As if she realized it at the same time I did, she jumped back, toying with her hair.

"You know what?" she said, leaping to her feet, "I should head to bed."

"You sure?"

"Yup!" she said, giving a little wave over her shoulder.

Disappointment filled my bones. That was how our night ended? As much as it had been weird and unnerving, I wasn't ready for it to be over—not that I wanted to try anything, but because I liked spending time with Alex. She made me laugh, and that was rare these days. There weren't many people I trusted, but Alex had worked her way through my walls without even trying. It scared the shit out of me. This was a losing game, anyway. I scrubbed my hands through my hair, reciting the reasons why I was fucked.

She went on a date with Adam. You live 3,000 miles away. You haven't had a real relationship in almost a decade. You're too screwed up for someone like her. She'd run for the hills the moment she saw the real you.

The reasons didn't feel as solid as they did earlier, more like questions than definitive statements. Could Alex ever see me as something other than Adam's friend? Would it be worth finding out if there was something real here?

It didn't matter. Given how quickly Alex rushed out of the room, she didn't feel the same. That was fine. In fact, it was for the best. The last thing I needed was to get my head all twisted over some girl. Still, no matter how hard I tried to believe that, the words felt like ash on my tongue.

I waited until I heard her bedroom door close before settling on the couch. Damn. Alex was right—this thing was more comfortable than some of the beds I'd crashed in. As soon as I started to pull my flannel off, light footsteps echoed from the stairs.

"Hey Cole?" Alex called out from the landing, her voice suddenly shy. She linked her fingers together, her eyes focused on them and not me. "Thanks for helping me out tonight. It meant a lot."

"You're welcome, sweetheart."

She lifted her gaze, tucking a strand of hair behind her ear and smiling softly before turning back upstairs, stealing one last look at me before disappearing into the hall.

I grinned to myself. Maybe I wasn't such a lost cause after all.

TWELVE

Alex

The following day came way too quickly. Not only did my alarm wake me up from a *very* exciting dream, but when my eyes reluctantly opened, my head felt like someone had dropped an anvil on it.

"Damn you, Calla," I muttered as I lumbered toward the shower. Hopefully, the water would wash some of my pain away. But even as it ran down my skin, scrubbing away the lingering smell of vodka and poor choices, I couldn't help but think about last night. I came so close to telling Calla about Adam and his offer. If I took him up on it, could I really keep all of it from her?

Shit, I wouldn't have a choice. Based on the look Theo gave me when I asked about violating the NDA, I had no doubt he would sue me for breach of contract. Not that he would get much from me—this house was the only thing in my name besides my fifteen-year-old Jeep, and while I loved Bertha, very few people felt the same.

Even with the lie hanging over my head, other things were holding me back from diving straight in, no matter what I told Calla last night. I had a lot of questions about what I would have to do and what would be written about me. Who would read about my "relationship" with Adam? Would it drag up old ghosts I'd rather keep buried?

I chewed my lip as I washed the shampoo from my hair, trying to ignore the name on the tip of my tongue, the new, unexpected complication: Cole.

Before last night, I only saw him as an ever-present thorn in my side—the broody ying to Adam's charismatic yang. While there might have been an undeniable spark between us, I attributed it more to annoyance than anything else.

Until last night.

When he offered to drive us home, I half expected it to be a prank. Even in my semi-drunken state, my brain knew it wasn't wise to be alone with him, but instead of fear and annoyance, there was a quiet sense of comfort, of safety.

Maybe it was the way he let Calla rattle on about her family, only interjecting a couple of times to ask clarifying questions. Perhaps it was how he talked with so much admiration about Adam that made me look at both of them differently. Whatever the reason, I was starting to realize that my first impression of Cole was flawed, and this version of him? That was someone I wanted to know better.

No! That was the worst place my brain could go. I was supposed to decide if I wanted to fake date Adam, not date his friend for real. Not that it was even on the table—Cole might have turned off his asshole-ness for one night, but that was a far cry from being someone I wanted to date. Besides that, there were plenty of other reasons why it would be the worst idea.

Feeling settled on the topic, I quickly rinsed my hair, jumping out of the shower before the hot water dried up. As I scrambled into my closet to get changed, an odd smell caught my attention.

Smoke.

"Fuck," I hissed, throwing on the first clothes I could find before running out of my bedroom. By the time I reached the kitchen, all the smoke detectors were blaring, earning a string of stronger curses from my lips. "Motherfucker. Fucking shit-balls alarm."

"Damn, sweetheart," Cole chuckled from the front of the oven, fanning it with one of my baking sheets. "Didn't know you had such a mouth on you."

"What did you do?" I screamed, shoving him to the side. "Are you trying to burn my goddamn house down?"

He turned to the window, cracking it open wider before he resumed fanning the smoke detector. "I was *trying* to make you some breakfast before work. How was I supposed to know that you hadn't cleaned your oven in a decade?"

As the alarm stopped blaring, I let out a sigh of relief, dropping my head down to the counter. "It's mostly ornamental," I said from under my arms. "I don't think I've ever turned it on."

"Seriously?" Cole laughs. "You've got this big kitchen, and you don't even use it?"

"I use the microwave," I objected. "And the coffee pot lives here, so it's one of my favorite rooms." I lifted my head to glare at him. "Which is why I'm really pissed you almost set it on fire."

He rolled his eyes, trying to hide his shit-eating grin. "Relax, Alex. There weren't any flames. I cut the gas before there was too much smoke."

I was about to argue more when my front door suddenly smashed open. Marta and Curt bolted inside without a single knock, barreling into the kitchen. Normally, I'd be pissed, but the sight was almost comical. Marta held an oversized watering can while Curt dragged a fire extinguisher that was as old as me.

"Where's the fire?" Marta yelled.

"Nowhere," I said, trying to hold back my laughter. "My friend got a little overenthusiastic and tried to use my oven."

"Big mistake, son," Curt chuckled. "This girl can't cook for shit. You're lucky the damned thing didn't explode."

"Hey!" I objected. It was true, but only I was allowed to mock my terrible culinary skills.

Curt playfully grinned at me. "No offense, darling, but we all know it."

"Remember when you tried to thank us for the flowers by making lemon bars?" Marta piled on.

My whole body grimaced. "In my defense, sugar and salt look very similar."

Cole barked a loud laugh behind me, turning all the attention in the room to him. The sound made my heart beat a little faster, not having seen him this relaxed before. It was intoxicating, much like his smile. Marta gave me an appreciative wink while Curt studied him as if Cole was picking up his daughter on prom night.

Curt straightened to his full height. "And who is this?"

To my surprise, Cole didn't miss a beat as he stepped up to my neighbors, offering them a hearty handshake. "Cole Campbell. I gave Alex a ride home last night, and she graciously offered up her couch so I wouldn't get lost driving back to the hotel."

"Is that what the kids are calling it these days?" Marta smirked.

"Okay, well, as you can see, nothing is on fire," I said, hastily guiding them toward the door. "So you two can get back to whatever it is you were doing,"

"That is one fine man," Curt whispered. Marta glared at him, and he shrugged. "What? You'd have to be blind not to notice."

"That might be true, but he's a giant pain in the ass," I quipped.

"The best ones always are," Marta said, earning a mock scowl from her husband. "Good luck with him, dear. I can tell he'll be trouble in the best way."

As soon as they left, I shut the door, making sure it was locked this time. But instead of returning to the kitchen, I slumped against it, not used to starting my day with such chaos. It was bullshit, especially before caffeine had hit my bloodstream.

"So..." Cole called out from the other room. "Those are your neighbors."

"Yup," I answered, skulking back to the kitchen to find him rooting through my cabinets. "They're basically the overbearing parents I never asked for, but I love them anyway."

"They clearly feel the same about you."

I shook my head, trying to wrap my head around what was happening in my kitchen. "Are you making pancakes?"

"Trying," Cole said. "I was going to make something else, but your fridge is a joke. Even your baking soda is expired. How the hell are you still alive?"

"Take-out menus."

Cole muttered something under his breath about the pathetic state of my diet as he poured the batter into the only pan I owned. I plopped onto the counter, carefully watching him work. He was more methodical than I expected; it was almost cute the way his brow furrowed while flipping each one, stacking them in a nice pile next to me.

After the third one, I couldn't hold it in anymore and grabbed the pancake on top, taking a large bite. My tongue burned a little, but the taste definitely made up for it—it was fluffy and pretty damn perfect.

"I can toss it in the freezer for a few months if that'd make it more your style."

Reaching out, I shoved his chest. "Shut up."

"Did you really try to push me?" He chuckled. "Real mature, sweetheart."

I did it again, trying to ignore the strength hiding underneath his t-shirt. Holy hell that was a lot of muscle tone. This time, though, he grabbed my hand before I could snatch it away, holding it tight against his chest. My fingers tensed, wanting to dig into his shirt and rip it away from him. Who the hell was I? I was never this bold. Ever. It was the muscles; it had to be. The veins on his forearms were making my brain dumb.

And horny, if I was being honest.

As if he could read the dark turn my thoughts took, Cole stepped forward, moving between my legs. His nearness took my breath away; I had a hard time remembering what I was doing, much less saying, with him this close. Stupidly, I glanced up, meeting the dark chestnut of his eyes, now narrowed in amusement. Underneath, a heat swirled that made my toes curl.

"What now?" He leaned forward to whisper, "Nothing to say?"

No words, brain empty. All I could do was gape at him, hating the way my heart thrummed wildly in my chest. I'd never been this close to him before. How had I missed the golden threads that weaved through his irises, breaking up the warm brown? I was desperate to memorize every inch of his face, from the small scar that intersected his brow to how his lips curved in amusement.

As Cole continued to stare at me, his hand shifted, his fingers linking around mine. His gaze dropped down to my lips, and all I could think was how much I wanted him to close the distance. I had no idea what was happening between us, but right now, I couldn't care less. All I wanted was his lips on mine.

Just as he leaned in, the smell of burned batter filled the air.

"Shit," Cole hissed, pushing away from me and returning to the stove. He pulled the pan off the stove, grabbing the burnt remnants of a pancake with the spatula.

As he shoved the smoldering pan into the sink, my brain finally caught up to my libido. What just happened? Was I really about to kiss Cole in my kitchen? There was something wrong with me. How the hell had I let this happen? Unwilling to talk about whatever transpired between us, I jumped down off the counter, using the distraction to slide out of the room without further incident.

"I've got to finish getting ready. Try not to burn my house down," I squeaked as I bolted away from the kitchen, unable to even look in his direction. Clearly, this was some sort of after-effect of all the alcohol I consumed last night. I thought the gift of poor decision-making was supposed to wear off when you sobered up. Apparently, that wasn't the case for me. One stare and Cole could have done whatever he wanted to me.

He tried to grab my wrist as I scurried toward the stairs. "Alex, I'm–"

"Nope. It's fine," I called out, hating that my voice was a million levels higher than usual. "Everything is good! Peachy, even!"

Ugh, did those words come out of my mouth? Without waiting for his reply, I leaped up the stairs, taking two at a time to reach the safety of my bedroom as fast as I could. As soon as I stepped inside, I shut the door, leaning against the cool surface of the wood.

What the hell was I thinking? Was I really about to kiss Cole, of all people?

Even worse, why was I so disappointed that it didn't happen?

THIRTEEN

Alex

The rest of the day did *not* go any smoother. From the moment I walked into the Isadora, it felt like the world was out to get me. That was why drinking on a work night was a terrible life choice. I wasn't great at tuning out the nonsense on a good day. Now, it seemed impossible.

I couldn't even blame anyone else for my bad day. All the guests were polite, and even Diane seemed to stay away. It was all me; my head was anywhere but in my work. I could barely focus on a single task, too tangled up in indecision and self-loathing. There were too many things weighing on my mind, too many unknowns I couldn't work out.

Almost twenty-four hours later, I was still no closer to an answer for Adam. Theo offered time to think things through, but who knew how long his grace period would last?

As much as I wanted to jump in headfirst, there was too much weighing on me—especially the lack of privacy. The idea of people watching me, judging me, had haunted me all night.

But now, in the daylight, my concerns had nothing to do with the cameras or the media.

Instead, it had *everything* to do with the man who made me

pancakes this morning. My mind kept spinning back to last night. I hadn't expected to feel so comfortable around Cole. Seeing his unguarded smile made my heart skip several beats. He was unlike most people I knew, who smiled freely and often. Instead, every single one was earned, and I liked being the one to earn it.

If that fact alone hadn't been enough to shake me to my core, then he had to go and almost kiss me.

When the hell had that even become an option? Every other time we'd spoken, we'd battled, trading barbs like oxygen, but after he picked me up last night, it was like something shifted. The animosity seemed to break down, leading the way to some common understanding.

However, as I started to think more about Cole, my mind inevitably drifted back to Adam. Guilt filled my core—should I tell Adam about what happened? Would it even matter? The contract wasn't signed. It wasn't like Adam was sitting around pining for me, but it still felt wrong. Cole said they were like brothers. The last thing I ever wanted was to get in the middle of them.

"You're being ridiculous," I grumbled under my breath. "Nothing even happened."

"Uh oh," Javier said from my side. "Talking to yourself again? That's never a good sign." He nudged me with his shoulder. "C'mon, spill."

I paused, unable to meet his eyes. With a huff, I quietly admitted, "I think I messed up."

"On second thought, maybe I don't want to know. Did you make poor drunken choices?" Javi chuckled, placing his arm around my shoulders. I leaned my head against his chest, savoring his comfort. "It couldn't have been too bad. You seem a million times better than Calla. She looks like death warmed over."

"Nothing like that," I said, chewing on my lower lip. "I...I think I might have feelings for someone."

"No shit, doll. The entire world saw that picture of you and Adam on the beach."

I took a deep breath. "No, I don't mean him."

Javi turned, his eyes wide as he took in my sullen expression. With a glance around the lobby, he beckoned over one of the girls from the front desk. "Hey Marisol, could you cover for us for a couple of minutes? We have to go check on one of our VIPs."

As she nodded, he took my hand, dragging me to the stairway. Luckily, no one used the back stairs unless there was an emergency, so we were in the clear. It was the place of many friendship-defining conversations, from my opening up about my past to debating whether Javier was going to accept his husband's proposal. At least that conversation ended on a happy note.

When the door clicked closed behind us, I slunk over to the wall, letting my legs twist underneath me. Javi stood across from me, folding his arms over his chest. "Tell me everything."

My mind raced, trying to figure out how to explain what was going on without spilling too many of Adam's secrets. In the end, the lie I fed to Calla won out. "I talked to Adam, and he wants to take me out on a second date. He thinks there could be something between us."

"And the problem is..."

"It feels complicated and incredibly messy," I said. "There are too many questions, too many things that could go wrong. You know me; I don't do well in situations like this. It feels like I'm setting myself up for failure. And then there's Cole...."

Javi shot me a look. "Wait...Cole, as in Adam's friend?"

I cringed. "That would be the one."

"Okay…" he sighed, pacing the space between us. "What happened with Cole?"

"That's the thing: *nothing* happened. Calla and I ran into Cole when we were leaving Paddy's, and he drove us home because we'd been drinking. When he got back to my place, it was late, and I offered up my couch. I didn't think anything of it, and then we stayed up watching a show. We were talking, laughing…" I pushed a breath between my teeth. "There was something there, Javi. I know there was. And then this morning, I thought he was going to kiss me—"

"Oh hell," Javi said, running his hand over his short, cropped hair. "This is messy, even for you."

"No shit," I muttered. "We didn't kiss. I promise. Which, logically, I know is a good thing. The last thing I need is another complication."

"But?"

"But I really, *really* wanted him to kiss me."

Javi sat down next to me, taking my hand in his lap. As he rubbed soothing circles against the back of it, even more words came tumbling out of my mouth.

"Now, I have no idea what I'm supposed to do. I promised Adam I'd think about his offer, and there's a big part of me that wants to take him up on it. He's such a good guy, and I like spending time with him. Then again, Cole makes me feel…" I sighed, dropping my gaze down to our joined hands. "Like he sees me."

I glanced up at Javi to find his eyes were a bit glassy as he gave me a knowing smile. For years, I'd been hiding, shrinking myself to fit everyone else's mold. Besides my close friends, it felt like so long since someone had actually seen the woman I was trying to hide; too scared to let someone in, but Cole had done it effortlessly, and that scared the shit out of me. I shook my head, pulling myself out of the moment. "Maybe it's all in my head. I don't know anymore." I looked up at him. "So tell me what to do."

"That's not up to me, Alex," Javi answered. "I can't tell you what to do next. However, before you make any decisions, I think you should talk to Cole."

I groaned, dropping my forehead on his shoulder. "What if he thinks I'm crazy and he was only being nice yesterday?"

"Then it's better to know now before you let your mind get away from you." He bumped his shoulder with mine. "I know you, Alex. You start seeing red flags before there's even a chance. If you like this guy, you need to talk to him. Be honest with how you're feeling. It's the only way you'll figure out what could be between you."

"Dammit," I sighed. "I hate when you use logic on me."

Javi pulled me closer to his side, dropping a kiss on the top of my head. "It's what I'm here for."

AS I APPROACHED THE VILLA, every part of my body buzzed with anticipation. If you had told me yesterday that I would go to talk to Cole, I would have died laughing. It was unbelievable how one night had changed so many things, making me question everything I knew about Cole. I prided myself on my intuition, being able to read people quickly and accurately.

Cole was the exception.

The man I saw last night was someone I wanted to get to know better.

When I reached the door, I sucked in a short breath, forcing myself to knock, but before I could, the door swung open, revealing Cole on the other side.

A *shirtless* Cole.

Fuck my life.

If I thought touching him this morning was brain-melting, then seeing him without his shirt on was another level. The man was cut, his body defined from years of hard work and exercise. Between his chiseled abs and the thick cords of muscle that worked down his forearms, I was a total goner.

"Alex?" His voice broke me out of my stupor. God, I hoped my drooling wasn't too noticeable. I dropped my eyes down to the ground. "You okay?"

"Yes!" I said, my voice way too high to be truthful. "I'm great. Perfect, even."

"Okay..." Cole said, scrubbing his hand through his hair. "If you need Adam, he's out for a bit."

"I'm here to talk to you."

"Oh..." he answered slowly, clearly taken aback by my statement. He shifted to the side. "Then I guess you should come on in."

Walking into the cabin, you'd think that I'd never been here before. Despite knowing every inch of the hotel property like the back of my hand, it felt foreign, like I didn't belong in this space. It was different than yesterday at the meeting with Adam and Theo when my nerves got the best of me. Now, it was all about the uneasiness of not knowing what Cole would say.

As I lurked in the main living area, Cole ran into one of the bedrooms, returning with a shirt. Thank God. I was pretty sure that if I had to keep staring at his chest, I'd never be able to get out what I needed to say.

"So..." Cole said, sitting down on the edge of the couch. "What's up?"

I took a deep breath, trying to collect my thoughts calmly. I replayed the speech I perfected on the way over here in my mind, the one where I told him what last night meant to me and how I wanted to explore this connection—the calm, rational conversation I knew we needed to have.

But instead, I blurted out, "Were you going to kiss me this morning?"

Well, there goes that plan.

Cole stared at me for a long moment before he dropped his gaze down to his hands. When he finally answered, his voice was low, hard to hear even in the empty room. "Yeah, Alex. I wanted to kiss you. Last night, too, if I'm being honest."

His words cut through me. I wasn't expecting him to admit that. His honesty was refreshing but also intimidating. Part of me wanted to take it back, pretending we'd never had this conversation. On the other hand, another part of me wanted to crawl into his lap and claim his lips for myself.

Just as my imagination started to get the best of me, Cole continued. "I'm glad we didn't cross that line."

"Oh..." I said, trying to bite back the hurt written on my face.

He shook his head and then ran his hand down his face. "Look, Alex. You seem great, but this..." he motioned between us, "can't happen. This morning...it was a mistake. I don't know what the hell I was thinking." He glanced up at me. "I'm sorry, Alex."

With his apology and pitying look, the hurt shifted into anger. I don't even know why I was surprised. It wasn't like we had some passionate affair or had fallen in love. It was a moment, and it was gone. For him to look at me like I'm some wronged woman—or worse, like he broke my heart—was too much for my fragile ego to take.

"It's fine," I said, letting the lie fall too easily from my tongue. "Like you said, it's for the best anyway. Adam asked me out again, and I think I'm going to take him up on it. I don't want there to be any weirdness between us."

Cole stared up at me, something hard flashing in his eyes as he stood from the couch, brushing past me to go into the kitchen. Grabbing a bottle of water from the fridge, he downed a good portion of it before speaking again. "Good for you two."

My brow furrowed, hating the chill in his voice. My head spun, unable to keep up with the consistent shifts of his moods. Not that I was any better; I hadn't said anything to contradict him. Instead, I played into his disinterest.

For a moment, Javi's words played in my mind, begging me to tell Cole the truth. But what even was the truth? That a brief moment between us felt like more? That he was the first person I'd felt something for in years?

No. All those words would be wasted, given that Cole already admitted whatever passed between us was nothing more than a mistake. Anything more would be giving him ammunition to hurt me, to make me feel more foolish than I already did.

So, instead, I chose to say nothing.

Turning toward the front door, I forwent a goodbye, wanting to be out of the room as quickly as possible. Just as freedom was within my reach, the door handle turned, and Adam stepped inside.

He glanced at Cole and me, hopefully, unable to read the mounting tension between us. "Hey guys..."

"Hey," Cole called out, his words still brisk. "Alex told me about your second date." He clapped Adam on the shoulder before heading to the door. "Have fun, man."

I winced at his words, his kindness from last night replaced by the cold indifference of his first few days here.

As Cole walked outside, he glanced over his shoulder, meeting my gaze, and I let out a quiet gasp, finding it anything but cold.

FOURTEEN

Alex

"You decided to sign the contract?"

I hated the excitement in Adam's voice. It felt like fraud, like I was capitalizing on his kindness to strike someone else down. In truth, the contract was the last thing on my mind when I told Cole about dating Adam. Instead, I was too busy trying to hurt him because I was hurt.

Immature? Definitely.

Pathetic? Oh, absolutely.

However, once I said it, I couldn't take it back—not when Adam looked at me like his salvation. No matter how badly I screwed up with Cole, I couldn't make the same mistake with Adam. I needed to be honest and think through my choices.

"I have some questions first," I said. "If we can work out all of the details, then I guess I'm in."

Adam nodded, shuffling me toward the dining room. "Of course, whatever you need to be comfortable with this arrangement. Let me call Theo. He'll be here as soon as he can."

As we waited for Theo, Adam was a gracious host. He offered me coffee and told me stories about some of his first acting jobs. Apparently, for his first credited job, he was paid with a Walmart gift card and lukewarm craft service meals, which was like gold to a struggling actor.

The conversation inevitably shifted to my background, but that was Pandora's box, and I wasn't willing to share that with him yet. Instead, I answered in the most basic ways possible, leaving out any details that might bring up more questions. *Yes, I grew up in New York City. No, I've only lived here for three years. No, I didn't always plan on working in hospitality.*

Adam listened carefully, hanging on each word. It was different from my conversation with Cole last night—that one flowed easily, with shared jokes and knowing smirks. This one felt more like an interview like I was on the couch of a late-night show, and he was the host.

I hated even to think that way. Adam had been nothing but kind and supportive. On our date, I thought our conversation had flowed so smoothly, almost like we were old friends reconnecting after their time apart. Now, there was a divide between us, and I was the one to blame. What was wrong with me? It had to be my head doing what it did best: overthinking and finding flaws where they didn't exist.

Almost thirty minutes later, Theo glided into the room, looking as dapper as ever in his three-piece suit. I nearly laughed; around here, people only broke out their suits for weddings and funerals. Anyone who needed to dress formally for work left them at the office, trading in their ties for comfort wear as soon as they got home.

"Sorry, it took me so long," Theo said, dropping his briefcase on the table. "I wanted to ensure we had everything covered."

Adam nodded, shifting forward in his seat. "Alex might want to sign. She has questions first, though."

Theo turned to me. "Ask away."

"How long are we talking? I know we said until the end of

filming, but that could take months. I would like a solid end date before we begin."

"That's fair," Adam acknowledged. "How about six months?"

Clearly, he'd been talking more with Theo since our last meeting. While he seemed as shocked as I was before, now they both appeared to be on the same page. It made me feel out of my league, like I was a child sitting at the adult table for the first time.

Instead of letting my insecurities get the best of me, I tried to keep my voice as steady as possible as I said, "That sounds reasonable. What would I have to do?"

Theo pushed a schedule and other documents over to me. "We've plotted some planned dates and other events we would need you to attend. Next to each one is the level of affection we would like to see."

"How romantic," I snorted.

"This is a job, Miss Green," Theo said firmly. "There is little room for romance in these arrangements. It would lead to...*complications*."

"Fair enough." I read through the page, tapping my finger at the bottom. "What about other people?" I turned to Adam. "What if you find someone you want to date for real?"

"Then we would come back to the table and renegotiate," he said. "It is important to note that there is a clause in our contract that states neither of us will be with anyone else for the duration of our relationship."

Oh shit. That made my palms sweat a little. I tried to ignore it, but a little thought nagged at the back of my mind, hating that this shut the door on whatever was happening between Cole and me. Then again, there was nothing to wonder about. What did he call it this morning? *A mistake?* Being Adam's fake girlfriend was one thing; Cole calling me a mistake was another.

Pushing aside my schedule and any thoughts of Cole, I looked over the NDA. It was tempting to call Calla to help me decode it, but there was no way Theo would let her in the room. Instead, I did the best I could to read through all the legal jargon, but some of the terms and language went over my head. Was this all a huge mistake? As I read it thoroughly, my palms started to sweat, especially when I got to the last section.

My eyes bulged out of my head. "I get *how much* if I complete our deal?"

"Half a million dollars," Theo said.

His tone was downright dismissive, as if he was offering me bare scraps. Maybe to him, five hundred thousand dollars felt like that. Considering that Adam made at least ten times that for each movie, they were used to dealing with ridiculous amounts of money.

I, however, felt nauseous.

Pushing the contract back across the table, I shook my head. "No. I can't accept that. It's too much money."

Adam placed his hand on top of mine. "Yes, you can. This will cover any missed salary or expenses along the way. Please let me compensate you for your time."

"It feels like I'm taking advantage," I said. "I'm not doing this for the money."

"I know," Adam chuckled. "Which is another reason why you're perfect. It's standard for this type of arrangement. If I'm asking you to be available for six months, the least I can do is make it worth your time."

When he put it that way—well, it still felt like way too much. This would not only cover my daily expenses, but I'd be able to pay off my house and maybe even take that vacation I'd been dreaming about forever. I reluctantly nodded, returning to the NDA. "And the only people who know about this deal are the three of us?"

"And my assistant," Theo added. "When it comes to contracts like this, discretion is of the utmost importance. The public doesn't like to imagine relationships as transactions. However, in this business, it's sometimes the best way to achieve your goals. We would hate for any of this to leak and mess with Adam's reputation even more."

Adam squeezed my hand again as I nodded, a quiet comfort to remind me we were in this together. It was nice having him at my side. I still hated that I couldn't tell my friends, but having him in my corner made it a little less lonely.

"And if I slip?" I nervously asked.

"Don't," Theo said sternly.

"I'm not going to do it intentionally. What if I mess up and say something to one of my friends or something like that?"

"Depends on the damage," Theo answered. "In an instance like that, we would need to know so we could get the other person to sign an NDA as well. However, if it was to make it to the press, we could pursue punitive damages."

"You'd sue me?"

Theo said, "Yes," as Adam frantically shook his head no, glaring at his agent. "That is the most extreme situation. We wouldn't do it unless we had no other choice, like if you booked yourself on the Late Show and tried to sell your story."

I almost snorted at the idea. However, as Adam passed me the pen, I hesitated. Signing this paper was literally signing my privacy away, a right I'd fought hard to keep over the past few years. What if a reporter dug into my past and brought all those dirty details to light? It would take some serious sleuthing, considering most of my closest friends didn't even know the full extent of what happened in the city. If watching procedural dramas had taught me anything, nothing stayed buried forever.

Chewing on my lower lip, I debated telling Adam and Theo about what drove me up to Saint Stephen's Lake, but acid burned in the back of my throat at the thought. Not only was it painful to relive, but that girl was a far cry from the person I wanted to be. Leaving her in the past was the best thing I'd ever done, and I wasn't sure I was ready to think about her again.

As I toyed with the pen, Adam spoke to Theo. "And there's nothing else we have to worry about, correct? Once the contract is signed, we're good to go?"

Theo nodded. "Yes. Everything else looks good. The story is still trending positively; Alex's background check came back clear, so we are all set."

My what? My eyes darted up, meeting Theo's dark ones. I tried to keep my face from slacking, not wanting him to see the confusion and relief in my gaze. "You ran a background check on me?" *And it came back with no red flags?*

"Of course," Theo said calmly. "We needed to make sure nothing would pop up that could hurt Adam's image." He leaned forward, staring at me more intensely. "Unless there's anything else you need to tell us?"

I thought about sharing my secrets with them, knowing that it might change everything. Maybe it was time to have it all out in the open, to finally try to let go of some of the fears that had been weighing me down.

But to give them a voice would mean giving them life, to dredge up a past I desperately wanted to forget.

So, I kept my mouth shut, forcing my hand to sign on the line.

"There it is," I sighed. "When do we start?"

Theo took the documents and packed them into his suitcase. "In due time. Right now, you need to prepare for what comes next."

I knew that was too easy.

FIFTEEN

Alex

Two weeks had passed since I signed the fake dating contract, and I still felt unprepared. The day after we worked out the details, Adam went back to Los Angeles for some last-minute rehearsals before filming started. Since he'd left, it had been a non-stop stream of producers and actors checking into the resort, taking up almost all of our private villas and luxury suites on the top floor. From what I'd heard, many of the crew members were staying closer to town, making the local businesses extremely happy.

The movie was all anyone could talk about. Even Marta and Curt were conspiring to get a walk-on role, trying to convince me to talk to Adam every chance they got.

I just was doing my best not to get in anyone's way.

While everyone else was prepping for the movie, Adam had been constantly checking in on me, making sure that I wasn't getting cold feet about our deal. Every day, he sent me questions designed to help us get to know each other better. At first, it was odd trying to answer his little icebreakers, but as they got more and more ridiculous, they became kind of fun.

For example, this morning's question:

ADAM

If a wizard turned you into a monkey, what's the first thing you'd do?

ME

Besides, throw my poop at annoying people?

ADAM

That's terrifying

ME

Like to keep you on your toes, Rice. What about you?

ADAM

Find the zookeeper and trick him into giving me all the bananas

ME

Okay, Curious George

ADAM

Technically, he was an ape

My mouth twitched into a smile, reading back all our past conversations. There was nothing remotely flirty, only nonsense and sharing stories from our lives. Adam told me all about his stay in California and even sent pictures of his unbelievable home. While not nearly as interesting, I'd been giving him updates on life around here. Each conversation went smoother than the last. I wasn't even hesitating anymore when he asked if I was ready for our first fake date.

The only thing I had to lie about?

Cole.

Almost every day, Adam asked me how he was doing, and truth be told, I had no idea. I'd only seen him once since the whole kitchen debacle when we bumped into each other in the lobby. He acted like he'd touched something poisonous, practically running to get away from me before I could even say hello.

I hated that it bothered me, that each day spent apart ate away at me a little more. We had only just started becoming friends, and Cole closed the door on even that. Being cut off hurt much more than I thought it would.

Honestly, it pissed me off. I was contracted to spend time at Adam's side. If Cole was going to bolt out of the room every time I showed up, it was going to be an awkward six months.

As my phone chimed on the counter again, Javi glanced at me and said, "Mr. Perfect is keeping you busy this morning."

"He's checking in," I said as I rolled my eyes. "Making sure the crew has settled in well."

"Right," he said sardonically. "He's checking on the crew. Whatever you tell yourself." He gave me a knowing smile, but it didn't quite reach his eyes. He was the only one who seemed to pick up on my foul mood.

I ignored Adam's question; if Cole wanted to pretend I didn't exist, I'd do the same. Two can play that game.

"Who's lying to themselves?" Calla asked as she turned the corner, hopping up to sit on the counter. "And who's blowing up your phone, Alex?"

"Adam Rice," Javi smirked. "He's been texting Alex every ten minutes for days."

"Lucky girl," she grinned. "When does he come back, anyway?"

"Tomorrow, hopefully," I said. "They're supposed to start principal photography on Monday, so he wants a couple of days here to relax before they begin."

"And are you going to be helping him relax?" Calla asked, wiggling her eyebrows. "You could find out what's underneath all that spandex. You would be the real hero!"

"I can't with you," I groaned, hiding my face behind my hands. "If you nosy brats must know, yes, we have plans for Sunday night." I swat at her, pushing off my desk, "Now, get your ass down here and help me figure out what we should do."

"My specialty," Calla said, joining me behind the counter. "What about kayaking? You could take him down to the lake, to that little seaside stand?"

"Don't do that," a deep voice grumbled from behind my computer. I glanced up, meeting Cole's cold stare. I hated that the deep timber of his voice made me stand a little straighter. My breath lodged in my throat for a moment, ensnared by his eyes. If it was possible, he looked more disheveled than before, like he hadn't been sleeping. What was keeping him up? Was he feeling as listless as I was? My stomach dropped. Had he met someone? Was that why he was exhausted?

Cole continued as I blankly stared at him, clearly not as affected. "Adam's not an outdoorsy kind of guy. He especially hates water sports besides swimming laps in his pool."

Calla popped a brow. "Then what would you suggest?"

Cole reached out, twisting the computer screen so he could see it. Frowning, he scanned the options until he tapped the screen with his pointer finger. "There."

"A farmer's market?"

"Yup." Cole nodded. "That's the kind of shit Adam loves but doesn't get to do often."

"As long as Alex doesn't have to cook for him," Calla laughed. "She almost burned down her dorm with microwavable mac n' cheese."

Cole turned his focus toward me, his lips tipping up in a hint of a smile. "How the hell did you manage that?"

All the words left my brain, too busy fixating on his lazy grin, the one that made my inside light up like the sky on the Fourth of July.

"I forgot the water," I eventually mumbled, kicking my past self for telling Calla about that.

"And you gave me shit for almost burning down your kitchen."

Calla's gaze volleyed between the two of us. "Wait...when were you at Alex's house?"

My blood ran cold as guilt filled my veins. Even though it had been an innocent situation, I never mentioned it to Calla. Well, mostly innocent. Glancing at Cole, I said a silent prayer that his brain was working better than mine.

He grinned at her. "It was the night I drove you guys home. I was stuck, so Alex let me sleep on her couch. I tried to cook her breakfast as a thank you, but her oven had other plans."

I nodded along, hating that even though it was the truth, he left out so much more—like the hour we spent in comfortable silence on my couch, the laughter we shared, and how his hand felt over mine, the heavy pounding of his heartbeat trapped underneath. My cheeks started to fill with color, so I ducked my head, pretending to focus on my computer screen, but Calla continued to stare at me as if she knew there was more to the story. She had the uncanny ability to read people's emotions. It was both one of her best and most annoying attributes.

However, before she could question me more, her mother stormed out of the office and made a beeline to our station. On instinct, both Javi and I looked away, pretending to be model employees. Even Cole busied himself, studying the brochures I'd lined up on the counter.

"Calla," Diane said when she reached her daughter. "Do you have any idea why Columbia Law School just returned my tuition check?"

Calla's face turned almost as red as her hair. "Maybe there was a clerical error."

"That's what I thought as well," her mother said. "So I called the bursar's office, and after I screamed at them for their incompetence for twenty minutes, they informed me that you were no longer enrolled."

Oh fuck.

Glancing up, I met Cole's eyes, which were almost as wide as mine. He mouthed, *"What is happening?"* to me, and I bit my tongue, trying to swallow my giggle.

"Get in my office," Diane seethed, staring down at her daughter. "Now. The rest of you, do your goddamn jobs and stop gawking at us."

As Calla followed her mother into the office, she smiled sadly over her shoulder at us. My heart broke for her. I hated that she wasn't free to be her own person, always stuck following her family's expectations. Growing up with successful parents came with many benefits, but she also lived in a gilded cage. In truth, it was a future I once imagined for myself, one I only escaped by blowing my life up spectacularly.

Not the route I'd recommend.

"Damn," Cole whispered to me. "Is she always that scary?"

"Not normally in front of guests. She usually tries to hide her nastiness so that only her children and employees get to experience it." The fact that she'd done it in front of him showed the depth of her rage.

Cole cleared his throat, running his hand through his hair. "So...I, uh...I came up here to ask you for your help."

I stared up at him, hating how viscerally I reacted to his presence. My palms started to warm, and my heart beat a little louder in my chest. Everything else around us faded away, leaving him as the center of my attention. It felt as if I'd been waiting for him to come back around to prove that the other night wasn't a fluke, that there was a connection here. It wasn't one that either of us expected or wanted, but it was developing between us anyway.

"I've been going stir-crazy these past few weeks," Cole said.

"Everyone's focused on getting ready to film." He sighed, running a calloused finger over the bridge of his nose. "I need some normalcy before I break a camera."

"And how can I help you with that?"

Cole smiled at me. "You know all the good places around here. At this point, I don't care if it's a walk through the woods; I just need to get out of here for a couple of hours."

I scanned my desk, thinking through the options. There were plenty of trails nearby, ones we usually recommended to visitors, especially if they didn't know the area well, but they were likely still packed with people. If I'd learned anything about Cole, he needed a break from the rest of the world, a feeling I understood all too well.

"You know what's gorgeous right now?" Javi said as he stepped to my side. "That trail by Beekman's Pass. You should check it out."

Cole nodded, his smile now tight. "Thanks, man. Do you have a map?"

"Oh no," Javi laughed. "It's a local secret, so it's not clearly marked. You need an experienced hiker to lead you through it. In fact..." He smiled down at me, and an icy dread jumped through my bones. "Alex knows it better than anyone. She'll be your guide."

"What?" I snapped, my gaze darting between the two men. "Oh no, I can't. You're supposed to be leaving soon, Javi. I can't leave you here by yourself. I can find another trail, or at the very least, someone else to help Mr. Campbell out."

"Don't be silly," Javi said, his eyes narrowing. "Go enjoy the hike. You and I both know you deserve a break."

I turned to Cole, hating that I couldn't read his expression. Was he as torn as I was? Was this the worst idea ever?

It didn't matter—the tension between us had to break eventually, and today was as good a day as any. Besides, I really didn't want to have to explain to Adam why Cole and I couldn't be in the same room.

I slowly slid around the counter, leading Cole toward the employee's lounge. I lifted my thumb over my shoulder, pointing to the employees-only entrance. "Give me five, and I'll meet you in the parking lot."

"You really don't have to," Cole said, his eyes shifting around the room. "I didn't mean... I was planning on going by myself."

"Oh. Yeah, of course," I say, shaking my head to brush off his stinging dismissal. I was going to murder Javi as soon as I got back to work. "You're right. I'll just..."

"Shit," Cole mumbled. He started to reach out to me but seemed to think better of it, dropping his hand back to his side and flexing his fingers. "That's not what I meant. You can come. You should come." He sighed. "I...I'd like it if you came along."

Maybe it was the slight hesitancy in his voice or the rare moment of vulnerability, but either way, I could feel myself soften to him again. "Are you sure?" I asked, nudging him in the ribs. "I could send you to one of the easier trails. There's one only a couple of miles away that I usually recommend for junior hikers."

For a moment, his lip curled up into an almost smile. "Damn, Alex. Know how to hurt a guy's ego, don't you?"

I smirked up at him. "It's a special talent for you alone." Then I stop myself, staring up at him. "But seriously, if you don't want me to come, I get it. Say the word, and I'll head back to work."

Cole stared at me for a long moment; there was no way he'd agree to this. To my surprise, he swallowed instead. "Yeah, you should come."

"Really?" As much as I tried to hide it, I couldn't help my

beaming smile. Cole continued to stare at me like it was the first time he saw someone react that way.

"Yeah. I'd like that," Cole said. "Besides, Javi's right. If anyone needs a day off, it's you."

"What's that supposed to mean?"

He motioned to the end of my ponytail, the curls a sad facsimile of what they were this morning. "You're looking a little rough there, Alex."

"Asshole," I chuckled, shoving at his chest. "And it's not like you're one to talk."

Cole stared down at me, and once again, I was back in my kitchen, imagining how his lips would feel like on mine. Would they be as sweet or demanding as I expected? I could already feel the scrape of his callouses against my skin, begging for more.

Cole cleared his throat, pressing open the door behind me. "Get your shit, Alex. You've got five minutes."

"And you'll wait for me?"

He stared at me, taking longer than I'd expected to answer. "It's not like I have much of a choice."

I inhaled a sharp breath, savoring the closeness between us. The same woodsy scent invaded my space, making me want to lean in. However, memories of a similar experience made my feet plant on the floor. It wasn't enough to stop my breath from catching when Cole leaned down, whispering in my ear.

"You're the one with the car."

This was a terrible idea.

Let the record show that I, Cole Campbell, made terrible decisions when left to my own devices. Not only did I break my promise to myself that I would stay as far away from Alex as possible, but now, I was back in her car, letting her lead me out of town.

The truth was, I had little willpower when it came to her. That became clear the moment in her kitchen when I almost kissed her. That was stupid, really fucking stupid, and I meant every word I said when I told her it was a mistake.

Alex was involved with my best friend. That meant she was completely off-limits. Guy code said that once your friend said he was interested in a girl, you were supposed to back off. If Alex weren't interested, that'd be a different story.

But she'd agreed to keep seeing Adam, and he was so damn happy about it that he spoke about her every time he called from LA.

Typically, when he mentioned girls he dated, it was all about their reputation and clout. This seemed to be a common thread in his actor circle: all friendships and relationships had a purpose, usually self-serving. Every interaction was a way to network—anything to ensure no one forgot their name.

I didn't know how the hell he did it.

However, his connection with Alex seemed to be the opposite. He seemed genuinely interested in her, and I almost messed it all up by thinking with my dick instead of my head. Logically, I knew she was taken, and I'd never do anything to mess with that.

But staring at her in the driver's seat, her long brown hair tangled from blowing in the wind, I couldn't help the images pouring into my head. They were the same ones that had been running wild since she exited the resort in a pair of cutoff jean shorts and a cropped shirt. It was such a far cry from her usual work attire it took me a minute to recognize her.

The further we drove from the hotel, the more Alex's guard lowered. Her smile became freer, her body looser. It was hypnotic to watch. Cursing under my breath, I rubbed my hand over my eyes. Not even a kiss and this girl had my head all fucked-up.

"You okay over there?" Alex asked.

"Getting a little car sick," I lied. "Who the hell taught you to drive?"

Alex rolled her eyes, giving me the middle finger while keeping her focus on the road. "Don't tell me you're one of those people who can't relax unless they're the one driving. You only got to drive that one night because I had too many drinks."

She didn't mean much with her words, but they still cut deep, striking a little too true for comfort. A familiar bolt of grief struck through my chest, trying to pull me down to the dark place in my head, but after years, I'd become used to it being there, waiting to knock me down. If this were last year, the comment alone would have been enough to trigger a spiral.

However, now, I smiled tightly and changed the subject. "Where are you taking me anyway?"

"You'll have to wait and see," she smiled back.

"HOLY SHIT."

"I told you it would be worth it," Alex said, coming up to my side with her hands on her hips. "The trek up here is a bitch, but you can't get views like this anywhere else."

She wasn't joking. From the peak of the mountain, you could see the entire town, all the way from her house down to the Isadora. The wind drowned out the sounds, but you could still feel the bustle of Saint Stephen's Lake below us.

It was the most peaceful place I'd ever been.

Inhaling slowly, I let the fresh mountain air fill my lungs. It was what I needed. While Adam thrived on staying busy, I needed this: moments where you could switch your brain off and just take in the world around you.

Surprisingly, while I usually enjoyed being by myself, it was nice having Alex at my side. She kicked my ass on the trail, teasing me until I almost had to run to keep up with her. It was clear she'd been here plenty of times, knowing the path by heart.

I was about to ask her about it when she spoke instead. "When I first moved up here, I felt so lost. It was like my old life suddenly stopped, and I was expected to know exactly what to do next." She smiled up at me, but it didn't reach her eyes. "Marta suggested I try hiking. I hated it at first, but once I reached the top, I knew she was right. It put everything in perspective." Her voice lowered as she continued. "All of my problems seemed smaller from way up here like I wasn't so alone."

Turning my head, I took in the blissful expression on her face as she tilted it toward the sun, soaking in the rays. Without thinking, I took out my phone and snapped a picture before she noticed. This close, I stared at the little freckles that dusted her nose and cheeks. Matched with her soft smile, they made her look more peaceful as if I could see the girl hidden behind her walls.

Maybe it was a kindred spirit thing, but I could tell something was haunting her. It was in the way she ducked any questions about her past, in how her life seemed to start when she got to this town. Even in her home, there were no pictures from her old life, none that featured anyone looking like family.

Curiosity got the best of me, so I asked, "Why did you move up here?"

Her face instantly lost its smile, her lips twisting into a tight line. "It's a long story."

"I have time."

Alex looked over at me, studying me with those wide, bright blue eyes. I needed to find the name for the color, wanting to memorize it for when she wasn't around.

Who the fuck had I become?

But as she hesitated, I continued, "If you don't want to talk about it, I'll drop it."

"It's not worth talking about," she quietly answered, scraping the toe of her shoe in the dirt. "Shit happened, and I had to make a choice." Alex shrugged, looking out over the horizon. "I've always been better at running from my actions than sticking around to deal with the consequences."

Join the club.

"I get it," I added. "Sometimes, it's easier to let the past stay there than try to deal with it."

She turned her head, shielding her eyes to stare at me for a moment. I kept my gaze trained ahead, not trusting myself if I looked at her. There was too much temptation to open up to her, to drop my baggage at her feet and see if it helped with the weight, to know if she'd look at me the same way if she knew who I really was.

So, instead, I said the one thing I knew would prevent me from doing something stupid.

"Adam told me about your date."

Alex instantly recoiled, taking a sizeable step away from me. Damn. Even though it was what needed to happen, the new distance between us cut me like a knife.

She slowly nodded, keeping her eyes trained on the lake below. "Yeah, we're supposed to go out on Saturday after he gets back."

"Gotta say, that surprised me."

"That he asked me out again?"

"Yup," I said, unable to keep the bitterness out of my voice. "Seemed like you two didn't have a great time on your last date."

Alex dropped her eyes, staring at her shoes. "It was a great date. I got in my head, and...." She shook her head. "Forget it. You don't need to know any more than that. All that matters is that Adam and I are excited for Saturday."

My hands tightened on instinct, feeling like there was something more Alex wanted to say. Still, pushing it wasn't my place, not when she was talking about my best friend.

Instead, I grunted out a half-hearted "Great."

Alex whipped her head toward me. "What's your problem?"

"I don't have one."

"Don't," she snaps. "Don't do that. If you have an issue with me, then tell me."

"I don't."

"Bullshit," she seethes. "You've been avoiding me for weeks, and now you want to give me a hard time because I'm hanging out with Adam? You were the one who said that our almost kiss, whatever that was, was a mistake, so stop taking it out on me." She chuckled to herself, but there was no humor in the sound. "You know, I thought we were becoming friends, but every time, you shut me out. I don't know what you want, Cole."

My jaw tightened so much I was afraid my teeth were going to crack. I wanted Alex, and that was the problem. She had invaded my bloodstream from our first conversation, and every new moment I spent with her only increased that feeling. But it didn't make what I said any less true. Yes, it was a mistake to think about kissing her, but I did, and in truth, I'd thought about it a million times since then—how it would feel to claim her lips with mine, to wrap her hair in my fist and expose the delicate skin of her throat, to make her scream my name so many times, her throat went hoarse.

The thought alone had my blood rushing to the worst possible place. Closing my eyes, I forced my thoughts to anything else: my grandmother, Theo's smug face, literally *anything* other than her.

When I opened them, Alex was still glaring at me, her hands propped on her hips. There was so much I wanted to say to her, but none of it would help. Instead, I went with the words I knew I should say.

"Look, Alex, I'm not taking anything out on you," I lied. "Yes, we had a moment, but that can't—no, it won't happen again. But we're also not friends. We don't even know each other. If you're looking for someone to spend time with because you're lonely, Adam's your guy. So just stop, Alex. Stop trying to get to know me. Stop trying to be my goddamn friend. Please." My voice broke a little, so I coughed to cover it up. "Leave it alone, Alex."

I hated myself the minute the words left my mouth, but I knew I had to be that harsh. Anything less, and I'd break. It wasn't only that Adam was interested in her—it was that he was the best guy I knew, the kind of man who deserved her. I was too broken, too fucked-up, to make something good last for more than a night. If she stuck around, she'd see through me. I couldn't take that risk, for either of our sakes.

Alex hastily wiped the corner of her eye, and it cut deep into my chest. This was the second time I'd made her upset, and I hated myself a little more for it. But even with my self-loathing, I was still desperate for her anger. I selfishly needed her to fight back, to show that spark I'd started to crave.

Instead, Alex shook her head, twisting to turn back down the trail. All I could hear as she started to descend was a muttered, "Go to hell, Cole."

SEVENTEEN

Alex

The drive back to the hotel was one of the longest of my life. It was barely over five miles, but it felt like an eternity, thanks to the man glowering in my passenger seat. I knew I should have locked my doors and ditched him on the side of the mountain.

But no, I had to be the bigger person—now, I was stuck driving back to the resort in awkward silence, and that was fine. I had nothing to say to him anyway. His words unearthed a pain deep inside my chest, one I'd tried to bury for a long time. This was why I didn't get close to many people. Not only did you have to show them your vulnerabilities, but it gave people the power to turn them against you.

As soon as we parked in the staff lot, I hopped out of the car, barely waiting for Cole to open the passenger side door. Fuck him, and fuck everything he said. Even as he faded out of sight, my emotions ricocheted between anger and sadness. I hated every second of it.

Once I reached the employee locker room, I quickly grabbed my uniform and changed before heading back to my station. Javi arched a brow when he saw me approaching.

"I'd ask how it went, but it's written all over your face."

"I don't want to talk about it," I snapped, hating that I was taking out my annoyance on my friend. Cole was the one who deserved all my vitriol. However, that would require me to speak to him, and I had zero intention of ever doing that again. "We are not going to talk about today or a certain asshole ever again."

"Shit..." Javi said, coming to my side. "I'm sorry, Alex. I thought it was going to help."

"It's not your fault," I said.

It was Cole's.

And mine.

I should have seen this coming. Cole spelled his intentions out to me; *I* was the one who ignored all the red flags. Shit, I even convinced myself he wanted to spend time with me, that he felt the same spark I did. *What an idiot.*

In usual fashion, my bad luck streak was far from over. The moment I got myself together, I spotted Diane storming over to me, rage set in her emerald-green eyes. She didn't acknowledge anyone else; she just beelined straight to my station.

"Alex," she snapped. "My office. *Now.*"

Without waiting for my response, she turned on her heel, marching into her lair, and I dropped my head into my hands. "Well, it was nice knowing you. When the cops find my body, tell them Diane is responsible."

"It might not be that bad," Javi said, nudging my elbow. "Remember, I'll still love you, even if you get fired."

"Promises, promises," I muttered as I lifted the counter, dragging myself across the lobby.

As I stepped into Diane's office, the temperature dropped ten degrees. I instantly shivered as I took a seat in the stiff, white leather chair across from her oversized desk. Calla told me that there used to be an antique mahogany desk at the center of the room. It had been gifted to her grandfather by local woodworkers when they were building the hotel. It stood in the center of the room from his first day as owner to the day he died, and it was one of the first things Diane removed, replacing it with a glass and chrome monstrosity. It fit Diane's aesthetic—cold and void of any personality. I was pretty sure if she could convince the board, she'd strip the entire resort of all its warmth.

As I settled into my seat, Diane stared at me, her hands steepled in front of her face. A clock ticked in the background, echoing the time slipping through my fingers as we sat in tense silence. After several minutes, she sighed, sitting up in her seat. "I assume you know why I asked you in here."

Not a clue. Maybe I had drawn the short straw, so it was my turn to be tortured. Still, I kept my mouth shut.

Diane reached across her desk, pulling a glossy magazine out from its hiding place. She slammed it down in front of me, and I flinched. The cover was one I knew too well, one of several tabloids that tried to figure out my identity and the nature of my relationship with Adam. If they had any idea...

"You have been cavorting with one of our guests," Diane said, leaving no room for rebuttal. "The board was very interested to hear about the extracurricular services you offered Mr. Rice."

Jesus Christ. She made it sound like I was pimping myself out for extra tips. Not that there was anything wrong with sex work, but it made my blood boil that they made such assumptions about our relationship.

I pushed the magazine back toward her. "Mr. Rice and I are spending time together," I answered. Despite the nerves radiating through my veins, I refused to let Diane see me flinch. "There is nothing in our employee handbook that says we are not allowed to fraternize with guests during our time off." That I knew was true. Theo read over every page of the thing with a fine-toothed comb to check that dating Adam wouldn't violate my contract.

"It is frowned upon," Diane said.

"I understand," I answered, sitting up a little straighter. "Has my relationship with Mr. Rice affected my work?"

"No, but–"

"I didn't think so," I snapped back. "I understand why you and the board are concerned, and if our relationship starts to affect my work, I will accept the consequences. But for now, our top guest is happy, and the hotel is getting positive publicity." I arched my brow, daring for her to argue my point, but her lips tightened instead. "Now, if you would excuse me, I have a couple more hours on my shift, and I want to relieve Javi."

I didn't wait for her to dismiss me. My legs felt like jelly as I stood, and my nerves were hopelessly frayed, but Diane didn't have the last word, and that was a victory in and of itself.

As soon as the office door closed behind me, I leaned against the wall, pressing my hand to my chest, trying to get my breathing under control. Never before had I stood up for myself with Diane and holy shit, it felt amazing.

When I stepped behind my desk again, waving Javi off for the night, a beautiful woman wandered over, smiling brightly at me. She was dressed like an old Hollywood film star, down to the patterned scarf wrapped around her hair and the oversized sunglasses. One glance at the expensive handbag she plopped on the counter was enough to make me sigh enviously.

Tipping down her glasses, she smiled brightly. "Hi. I was hoping you could help me."

"Of course," I answered. "Are you a guest of the resort?"

"Yes," she said, motioning behind her to the front desk. "I just checked in. I'll be staying in one of the lakeside villas."

"Wonderful," I said, injecting a false cheeriness into my

words. "Those are some of our best rooms. How can I help you today?"

"I heard that Adam Rice is staying here as well. We're old friends, and I wanted to drop off a gift for him."

My chest tightened at her words. Now that she'd shed her disguise, it was easy to declare that she was the most gorgeous woman I'd ever seen. Her dark umber skin glowed with a youthful radiance, her hair crafted into intricate braids that fell past her waist. Still, none of her features held a candle to her smile. It was the kind that lit up the whole room.

All my insecurities came crashing down around me, exacerbated by Cole's rejection. What was Adam thinking? Why would he pick me when he had a plethora of beautiful women surrounding him? No wonder those articles questioned him dating me.

"I'm sorry, Miss," I answered. "Unfortunately, we cannot give out that information. If you would like, you can leave it at the desk, and I will ensure he gets it."

She frowned and then looked down at my name tag. I braced myself for a verbal lashing. Instead, she grinned widely. "Alexandria? As in Adam's Alex?"

"I wouldn't go that far," I chuckled.

"I would! He spent all last week talking about you. You've made quite an impression on him. Oh, where are my manners?" She held out her hand for me to shake. "I'm Everly Watson. I'm going to be the other lead on this project."

"Oh!" I said, quickly meeting her handshake. "Of course. I'm sorry, I didn't recognize you."

"That's what I was going for," she winked. "Has Adam returned yet?"

"No." I shook my head. "He should be back tomorrow."

"Pity." She frowned. "You and I have to go out one night. Adam has talked all about this town, and I'd love to see it through your eyes. It would help me figure out what this place means to my character."

What it meant to her character? I didn't even understand what she was asking, much less how I could help her. I didn't think I'd ever be able to wrap my head around actor mentalities. First, it was fake dating, and now, it was trying to embody their characters. For the first time, I was grateful for my straightforward job. It might have had its negatives, but at least I didn't have to shift into another person entirely.

"That sounds great, Ms. Watson," I said, pulling myself from my thoughts. "I'll let Mr. Rice know you were asking for him."

As she walked away with a little wave, Javi bumped my hip with his. "I cannot believe that was the Everly Watson. She's literally in almost all my favorite movies."

"Why does that not surprise me?"

"Don't blame a guy for loving a good rom-com," he replied. "Those happy endings get me in the heart every time. And who knows?" He pointed to my now lit-up phone. "You might be living one."

"Right," I dryly laughed as I picked up my phone. However, the number wasn't one I recognized. As I tapped the messaging app open, my heart almost instantly skipped a beat.

UNKNOWN

Hey...It's Cole. I got your number from Adam.

I know I'm the last person you want to talk to, but I thought you might like this.

I gasped as I opened the attached image. It was the best picture of me I'd ever seen. The light highlighted my gentle, genuine smile. Surrounded by one of my favorite places in the world, I looked like someone I didn't recognize—someone full of hope who still dared to dream—the girl I desperately wanted to be.

For the second time today, tears made my vision blur. It was almost enough to take away the sting of Cole's words, hating how he crafted such a painful memory in a place I loved. But looking at the image, I knew it wouldn't matter in the long run.

I'd already proven that I was stronger than I realized.

Nothing, especially not Cole Campbell, was going to change that.

A LITTLE AFTER MIDNIGHT, I trudged into my house, letting the door slam closed behind me. I didn't even bother kicking off my shoes in the doorway, instead face-planting into my couch. Each day seemed longer than the last.

Have a movie film in your town, they said. It'll be fun, they promised. It'd be a story you can share for years. Funny how no one mentioned the constant demands from the actors and the endless equipment filling every spare space in the resort. No joke, one of the supporting roles sent back their room service four times because they insisted they could taste the gluten in their salad. Considering that none of the items in their order even contained gluten, it was hard not to flip out.

All of that was before I tried to drive home. Three different roads were blocked off to start some of the background shots and tests for next week. In a town with limited traffic patterns to begin with, it was a giant pain in the ass to get back to my house. My standard ten-minute drive took over an hour, and I was exhausted.

As my eyes started to drift closed, my phone chirped to life in my purse. Too tired to even move, I kicked it off the table with my foot. I stretched my fingers as far as possible, snagging the strap and lazily dragging it closer to me.

ADAM

Guess where I am?

A picture followed almost immediately after, and I instantly recognized the Albany airport behind him. I sat up on the couch, texting him back.

ME

Thank God you're back! I need someone normal to break through the hysteria. I don't know how you do it. I'm not even in the movie, and my stress levels are through the roof.

ADAM

I'd say you'll get used to it, but that's a lie. I'll be there soon to help in any way I can.

Speaking of– are we still on for Sunday?

My fingers paused on the screen, not quite sure what to say. It wasn't like this was an actual date. Theo had selected the time and place, and I'd already agreed to it, so there was no way to back out now. My signature on the contract promised that.

However, Everly's words played back in my mind, stopping me from replying. Was I leading Adam on? While he agreed that our relationship was for show, I couldn't help worrying he wanted more. With our daily conversations, he was quickly becoming one of my closest friends, and I didn't want to do anything to jeopardize that. I was willing to play pretend for a few months, but in the long run, I wanted the real thing, that all-consuming love I hoped existed...just not with Adam.

As I debated my answer, my phone suddenly rang in my hand.

"Hey, Adam," I answered, "I was about to write back to you."

"Maybe I wanted to hear your voice," Adam said on the other side of the line. My pulse spiked, and not in a good way. Fuck. Did we already need to have this conversation? All I wanted were my sweatpants and my bed, not to dive into awkward misunderstandings. Thankfully, his laughter interrupted my panic. "Just kidding. The driver was listening in, and I was trying to do my best impression of a man in love. I shut the divider so we can talk freely."

"You scared me for a minute," I chuckled.

"Don't worry, Alex. I meant what I said before: strictly friends. Remember, this isn't my first time acting this part."

"Your past fake relationships?"

"Yes," Adam sighed. "Although, I wouldn't classify those women as friends. They are more like business associates. Once the cameras were down, we barely even spoke."

"They didn't get your question of the day texts?"

"Those are special, just for you," Adam teased. "How was the rest of your day? You went silent for a while."

"Oh..." I fumbled. Should I tell him about the hike? Was spending time with Cole a violation of the terms of our contract? There were already too many lies floating around in my head, and I refused to keep anything else hidden. "I ended up going for a hike. Cole needed to get out of the resort for a while, so I offered to show him a couple of trails."

Simple and close enough to the truth. No need to mention the soul-crushing conversation afterward or how I spent most of my day plotting Cole's death.

"That's great," Adam answered. "I'm glad he went to you. I've been worried about him while I was gone."

"What do you mean?"

It was silent on the other end for so long that I checked to see if we'd been disconnected. Eventually, Adam continued. "It's not my place to say..." He let out a long sigh, seemingly debating what to say next. "Cole...he's had a tough road. He doesn't open up to, well, anyone. I was lucky enough to get in before he sealed himself off from the world. He's been better lately, but I still worry he's going back to that dark place."

Curiosity flooded my veins. What did he mean? Cole's had a tough road? It didn't take a genius to realize the man had thicker walls than Fort Knox. However, in my annoyance, I never stopped to wonder why. I searched my mind for the perfect thing to say, the right words to soothe Adam's worries, but nothing came to mind.

"I wish there were something I could do to help," I settled on.

"You already are," Adam said. "He's changed since we came into town. I think being out of California has been good for him."

"Good," I said. "I hope it keeps helping. If there's anything else I can do, let me know." *From a distance, far away from Cole and his stupid, intoxicating smile.*

"Actually, I think there is a way," Adam said slowly. His pause made my hackles rise, terrified of what he was thinking. When he finally spoke, the words were worse than I thought. "You know your friend Calla?"

"Of course."

"Well...I was thinking that Sunday might be awkward, considering that it's going to be our first staged date. It might help if we brought along another couple to break some of that tension." My brain disconnected, refusing to process what he was saying. "Like a double date."

Holy shit. What the hell did I say to that? No, I didn't want to set your best friend up with mine because I couldn't stay away from him? That if Cole started his shit with me again, I'd probably lose my mind and ruin our first fake date?

Adam continued, ignorant of my moral dilemma. "When he got home the other day, he talked about Calla a lot. I think they might hit it off."

I had to breathe slowly to control my temper. It wasn't logical or deserved, but I wanted to smash the phone and pretend the conversation never happened.

Instead, I gritted my teeth, forcing out my fakest voice. "Sounds like a great idea."

EIGHTEEN

Alex

"Does this look okay?" I glanced at myself in my floor-length mirror, checking all angles of my outfit.

The days had flown by since Adam returned from his trip. Even still, when it was time for our date, I felt utterly unprepared. I'd rehearsed with Theo until my eyes bled, primarily practicing how to handle the cameras— ways that showed I noticed the photographers but also wasn't trying to garner their attention. I learned how to exit the car without flashing my underwear, how to pose so no unflattering images showed up on the internet, and even how to stand next to Adam naturally without blocking the photographer's shot.

I was exhausted.

The only saving grace was that Calla agreed to come with us, all too willing to tag along on our date. She refused to call it a double date, and for some reason, that calmed the anxiety that had been wrecking me for days.

As I twirled in front of the mirror again, Calla peeked out of the bathroom, only one of her eyelids covered in shadow. "I guess it works..." Her face scrunched as she took in my preplanned outfit. "If you're going for the whole casual, *I-don't-care-how-I-look* kind of vibe."

Nope. Not the one I'm going for at all. Maybe I should have taken Theo up on his offer for a new wardrobe. He tried to ship over an entire stack of outfits with his stamp of approval, but I told him it wasn't necessary. So damn stupid.

I'd been standing in the middle of my bedroom for over an hour, hating every single piece of clothing in my closet. Everything felt like too much or not enough. Even worse—none of it felt like me.

But then again, I was playing a role tonight. I wasn't Alex Green, a self-imposed hermit and maker of terrible decisions. I was Adam's love-struck girlfriend, and I had to play that part to perfection.

Calla came to my side, making me feel like even more of a hot mess. Even without trying, she looked like she belonged on the runway. She bumped my hip with hers. "Still no luck?"

"Nothing," I answered, snapping my gaze away from the mirror. "Did Adam tell you anything about his plans?"

"Nope," she said, a little too peppy to be truthful. "Adam said he wanted a couple of suggestions and that he would take it from there. You know I hate you a little? You've got the perfect man, and all he wants to do is spoil you. I'd kill to be in your shoes."

I bit my lip, trying to keep the words on my tongue. In truth, Adam had nothing to do with the date. I tried to make plans to surprise him, but Theo dashed all of those. He was the one who arranged everything. He'd scoured the whole town, looking for the ideal backdrop for the photoshoot. All we had to do was show up and look like a couple in love.

As if it was that easy.

My palms started to sweat as I tried to remember all the tips he gave me. When he said he'd be hosting Adam Rice boot camp, Theo wasn't kidding. I spent all of my free time learning as much as I could about my new "boyfriend." If he were a topic on Jeopardy, I'd ace it.

Not all of it was painful, however. When Theo told me to watch all of Adam's movies, I thought it would be unbearable. I'd never enjoyed superhero movies before, especially the big ensemble ones. The constant threat of the world ending was not good for my overactive imagination.

Surprisingly, I ended up enjoying them, having a marathon all by myself. The action sequences kept my attention, and there was no shortage of people to ogle.

The definite highlights were when Adam came on screen.

He was charismatic in person, but on screen, he was even more enthralling. He made his character effortlessly charming, swaying even the most reluctant enemy. No wonder audiences fell in love with him.

A knock came on my front door, and I instantly jumped. Glancing down at my mismatched outfit, I cursed; I hated losing track of time. You would think that as someone who was perpetually late, I would be used to it by now. I always had the best intentions of being on time, but it never seemed to work out in my favor.

Calla must have noticed the panic on my face because she headed to the door. "I'll go get the guys. You pick something and stick to it. Maybe try one of your sundresses?"

As the door shut behind her, I headed back to my closet, rummaging through the back. Hidden by dozens of sweaters and faded tees were dresses Calla convinced me to splurge on a few months ago. Despite never having a place to wear them, I still bought a couple, loving the way they fit my frame.

Glancing at the three dresses, I instinctively pulled out the last one. I tugged it over my head, stopping to adjust the top to make it fit me properly. Turning around to face the mirror, I smiled as I took in the small details I'd forgotten about. Along the white linen fabric, embroidered flowers covered the bodice and skirt. It was short enough to hit right above my knees, making me look taller than usual. Even the thin straps seemed to suit me, showing off the deep golden tan I'd developed by some kind of miracle.

With one last glance, I stepped out of my bedroom, stopping at the top of the stairs. Calla and Adam were talking, laughing about something I couldn't hear, but that wasn't what stole my attention.

Cole stood by their sides, his attention focused on the top of the stairs. His eyes darkened as they met mine, and a chill coasted down my spine, but I was unable to look away. When his eyes finally trailed away from me, I took in his outfit. His usual flannel had been traded for a white Henley, with the top couple of buttons undone. His jeans were dark and fitted, sculpting his muscular thighs into a work of art. Even his messy stubble was gone, his face freshly shaved.

Fuck, he looked good.

The image was almost enough to erase our last conversation, the one where he told me to stop trying to be his friend. After three days, my temper had finally simmered down. Well, mostly —I'd replayed the conversation a million times in my mind, wishing that I'd handled it differently. With some distance, it was easy to tell why Cole kept throwing up walls between us. He had no idea about the contract, about the truth of my relationship with Adam. Cole thought he was betraying his friend, and I was all too willing to let him. No wonder he was so pissed.

However, as his chestnut eyes followed me down the stairs, the sting of his cutting words faded away, leaving behind only a sense of need—*of longing*.

My mind must have been playing tricks on me because I swore I saw the same look reflected on Cole's face. Typically, having any kind of attention on me made my skin itch. However, Cole's stare made me feel more confident and beautiful. His eyes never left mine as I descended the stairs.

As soon as I reached the last step, he came closer, reaching out his hand, almost as if he wanted to take mine, before pulling back suddenly. "Alex..." he whispered, his voice little more than a harsh whisper. "About what I said..."

"Don't worry about it," I said, trying not to get lost in the heavy look in his eyes.

"No," Cole said. "What I said was out of line. I– I don't know how to do this, how to be your friend." He ran his hand through his hair. "But I want to try if it's still on the table."

Now, he wanted to be friends? What was with this man giving me perpetual whiplash? I didn't know if it was still an option, not after our last conversation. He was right to pull away. No matter what connection I felt between us, real or imaginary, Cole had to believe I was with Adam.

Before I could respond, Adam stepped closer, blocking Cole from my view. That broke the spell between us. My cheeks flushed as I realized I'd been basically eye-fucking Cole as he stood right next to my date. *A fake date, but that's semantics.*

"You look stunning," Adam said as he wrapped his arms around me.

I grinned back up at him. "You do, too. You clean up very nicely, Rice."

"You should see me when I break out my tux." He winked. "Are you ready to go?"

As he backed away, Cole came back into view. His gaze was downright frigid. Gone was the warmth and appreciation I saw minutes earlier. Now, he almost looked lethal.

He nodded toward the door as I sighed. "Let's get this over with."

"I CAN'T BELIEVE you picked mini-golf," Calla said, her eyes darting between me and the course. "This used to be one of my favorite spots."

She gave me a warning look, a silent reminder that it was my fault she spoke in the past tense. I trailed a few feet behind her and Cole, standing next to Adam. My tension was already at an all-time high. Calla and Cole laughed together the entire drive over. What happened to the snarky asshole I had to deal with? Why did she get the nice guy when I had to deal with his bullshit?

My fists tightened as Calla pulled Cole into the shed to pick clubs, leaving Adam and me alone outside. Once they were inside, he leaned closer to me. "I hope you don't mind; this was one of the best options on Theo's list. I thought it could be fun."

I gulped, not sure how to tell him this was probably the worst option. Between mini golf and Robo-Cole, I was ready to go home and call the whole thing off. However, as Adam squeezed my arm, I knew it wasn't a choice. This wasn't for me. Adam needed this. I could keep myself together for one night.

So, instead, I nodded and led Adam to the main entrance. After paying, we each picked out our preferred colored golf ball and walked over to the first hole.

The Landlubber Golf Course was a town staple. Created in the eighties, it had barely been renovated since opening day. The course was littered with nautical decor, complete with the bow of a sailboat and mannequins dressed like sailors. The place had always given me the creeps, but everybody else loved it. It was only open for the summer stretch, and the first few weeks of fall, so both the locals and tourists made the most of it during those months.

When we lined up at the first hole, Adam motioned for me

to go ahead of him, and my heart instantly started to race. Lining up the ball with the hole, I tried to hit it at the right speed, but it ended up being too much. The ball rebounded off the brick border, bouncing into the bushes behind the hole.

"Crap," I muttered, jutting out my hip and glaring at the errant ball. That was not where it was supposed to go. Stupid wall.

Adam gave me a golf clap. "Nice effort. Don't worry, there's still a lot of game left to play."

"Hopefully, the next one will stay on the turf," Cole chuckled from his side.

"You think it's so easy?" I glared at him. I should have known our new-found truce would be short-lived. "Let's see you do it."

He raised his brow in a challenge, joining me at the starting point. He dropped his stance, bending at the knee to get a better view of the shrunken course.

"You've got to be kidding me," I muttered. "You're one of those people?"

"You might want to try it," Cole answered back, setting up his stance and tapping the ball down the course. For a moment, it looked like he overshot as well, but at the last second, the ball curved, dipping into the cup. As he straightened, he had the audacity to wink at me. "Watch and learn."

"Oh no," Calla whispered from behind us. "There's two of them."

NINETEEN

Alex

"You cheated!"

I shrugged nonchalantly, inspecting the end of my neon purple golf club. "Prove it."

Cole stepped closer to me, his hands on his hips. "You know you hit me with your club. Admit it."

"Over my dead body."

"Guys..." Adam called out, looking at the group forming around us. "Maybe we should call it a night."

"No way," Cole and I answered in unison.

Okay, remember when I said that mini-golf was a terrible idea? This would be why. It probably sounded ridiculous, but this game brought out my fierce, competitive streak. Well, that and every other game you could win.

Gracious winner?

Yeah, we don't know her.

As much as I hated losing, I had to admit that it was kind of fun to play with someone just as competitive as me, especially when we both resorted to dirty tactics to keep the other from winning.

I might have knocked Cole's ball into one of the blue-dyed

lakes, but he *definitely* put my ball in the lap of one of the creepy mannequins. It took almost five whole minutes for me to get up the nerve to grab it.

However, the biggest distraction of the night? That would be when Cole lifted his shirt to scratch his abs. I'd never seen that much definition on a man's torso before. It was unfair. Too busy staring, wishing I could trace my finger along his toned skin, my ball flew into a bush a good ten feet from the hole.

I tried to play it off like I had tripped in my shoe. I thought I'd gotten away with it, but then the damned bastard had to go and smirk at me like he knew exactly why I missed my shot.

Calla and Adam watched us like exasperated parents all night. Every time one of us pulled a move, they both smiled sheepishly at the employees, waiting for us to get kicked out.

I glanced over, seeing Mark Fischer watching us with a guilty look on his face. *That's right, jackass, you still owe me. You're the reason I'm in this whole mess.*

Well, that's not entirely true. Mark might have started the fire when he posted those pictures of Adam and me, but I was the one who let it burn out of control.

Shit. In my need to win, I'd almost forgotten the true purpose of this date. I looked at Adam, trying to convey a silent apology. Still, he just smiled at me, seemingly unworried about our lack of physical touches at least, until his eyes narrowed on something over the fence.

Before I could turn to see what caught his attention, Adam came to my side, draping his arm over my shoulder. As he dipped his lips down to my hair, he whispered so only I could hear, "The photographers are over by the parking lot." When my head whipped to the side, his fingers traced my jaw, keeping my eyes trained on him. "Don't look. Try to act natural."

"Easier said than done," I muttered.

Adam chuckled, continuing our quiet conversation as Calla

stepped up to the green. As she wiggled her hips like she was golfing on a PGA course, his lowered voice tickled my ear. "One of my old acting coaches told me the key to chemistry is imagination. Pretend you really are in love, and then it'll feel more natural."

"Does it work?"

He shrugged. "Sometimes. Try it and see if it does for you."

I closed my eyes, doubting that this would be the solution. It had been so long since I'd been with someone that I didn't even remember what it felt like. All my experiences with love were stained with pain, and that was the last thing I wanted to convey in pictures. But then Cole laughed, the sound profound and consuming as it invaded my thoughts. Instantly, everything changed. The person holding me, his fingertips brushing my bare shoulder? It was Cole.

I nestled closer to the hard body at my side, waiting for that familiar hint of leather and spice to invade my senses. Instead, there was only the clean aroma of fresh laundry and summer days. Pleasant, but not the one I wanted to cling to my skin.

Adam laughed, holding me a little closer. "Seems like it's working well for you. Picturing anyone in particular?"

"Jason Momoa," I lied.

"Damn," he smiled. "Hitting a guy where it hurts. That whole tall, dark, and handsome vibe works for you?"

My eyes instinctively met Cole's, and I shuddered under the intensity of his glare. It was like the world had melted away around us, leaving us alone in our tense stare-down. When Adam squeezed my shoulder, I broke away first, not wanting to acknowledge the moment that passed between us.

It felt like a betrayal to Adam. Despite our arrangement being fake, it still felt wrong to be in his arms while picturing someone else. The guilt snapped the tether between us, and I backed up. Clearing my throat, I gave him a sheepish smile. "Do you think that was enough?"

He nodded. "It'll be good for now. Keep close in case they want any more shots."

Sure. Can do.

The photographers hung out for a few more minutes before the owners ushered them away. I couldn't be more grateful; even though I expected it, experiencing it was very different.

The idea of being photographed didn't sound that bad. However, standing there, knowing they were waiting to capture a private moment between Adam and me, felt invasive. I felt like I was in a fishbowl with someone tapping the walls. I couldn't imagine this as my everyday life.

How did Adam manage the attention? No wonder he asked me for help. Even with my limited view of his life, I had started to see past the shiny veneer. From the outside, it looked like his life was perfect, but in truth, it seemed lonely. Isolated.

So when Adam reached his hand out toward me, I took it without hesitating. I promised him I'd help him; I was determined to get this right.

No matter what my head was trying to tell me.

AS WE REACHED the last hole, Cole and I were neck and neck, him two shots behind me. From the glint in his eyes, I could tell he was planning something gnarly for the end of the game, so I glanced around the putting course, trying to figure out his master plan.

"Don't even think about it," Cole chuckled from a couple of feet away. "You're never gonna see me coming."

My brow quirked in curiosity. "If you're so confident, then why don't we make this interesting?"

"Name the stakes."

"Loser buys a round of drinks at Paddy's."

I expected him to agree instantly, but instead, Cole's jaw tightened, and he glanced at Adam over my shoulder. A secret conversation passed between the two of them; Calla looked at me in question, and I lifted one shoulder in a shrug.

"Better plan," Cole finally said. "The loser has to do an activity of the winner's choice. Nothing dangerous or unethical, but they have to complete it."

My heart raced, thinking of all the ways this could go wrong. Or right, if I was being honest. My mind flashed with images of Cole pressing me against the wall, evidence of his desire taking my breath away, the way he'd grasp my wrists, and the filthy words he'd whisper in my ear.

"With Adam and Calla, of course," he quickly added.

Right. Our *actual* dates. While mine was pre-arranged, theirs was definitely not. A strange tug happened in my stomach, and I wondered if they were connecting. *Would they go home together? What if this turned into a serious relationship?* A swirl of nausea almost took me out.

I lifted my eyes to find Cole already looking at me, and his smile dipped. Did he know how my thoughts had turned? He started to step closer to me, but I held my hand up. "You're on."

His eyes bore a hole into mine, almost as if he could read the lie on my tongue, but my work persona had taken over, leaving little room for messy things like my emotions. This thing with Cole was a fantasy, nothing more. If he and Calla hit it off, I would be happy for them. In truth, she was a much better person than I could ever be, and if she brought out this softer, gentile side of Cole, maybe it would be in everyone's best interest.

Besides, I had other things that required my focus.

I had six months with Adam. That was it. Once all of this

was over, they would return to their real lives, and I would return to mine. It might not be the most exciting existence, but that could change. Maybe I'd find a new job and finally take those vacations I'd always dreamed of.

Cole Campbell was nothing more than a blip in my world, and I needed to remember that.

Fucking hell, I was in trouble.

I couldn't believe Adam insisted I come on this bullshit double date. Even after he called in every favor I owed, I still said no. He only got me to agree because Alex was nervous about the date. I pictured her the morning after the photos leaked: she looked so broken, as if she had memorized every vile word those assholes wrote and etched them onto her skin like scars.

So tonight, when a photographer popped out of the bushes behind the mini-golf course, I wanted to smash their damn camera into a million pieces. Back home, it wasn't as big of a deal when those leeches made their inevitable appearance, especially when Adam brushed them off, not bothering to let them rattle him.

Here, however, they were too out of place, too invasive to ignore.

Luckily, only a few had managed to find us, sticking out like a sore thumb among all the residents. They stayed off the course, but I could see the flashes go off every few minutes. Alex flinched every time they did, even though she tried to look like the photographers didn't bother her. However, I knew her genuine smile, having borne witness to it once or twice. The picture of her from our hike was burned into the back of my mind—the photo I sent to her and promptly deleted, feeling like a creep for taking it in the first place.

The one I wished I held onto.

There was no sign of that carefree girl here. Alex was too tense, too anxious, to act like herself. Instead, she'd morphed into a picture-perfect princess, grinning up at Adam and censoring her mouth every time her ball veered off course.

I hated it. Alex already acted like a damn robot at work, and it wasn't fair that she was playing one here, too. She was perfect just as she was. Alex was the only person who didn't realize that.

Adam's thumb traced comforting circles along her shoulder, keeping her tucked against his side. It wasn't the first time I envied him tonight, and it sure as fuck wouldn't be the last. When the hell had I become this guy? The one wishing I was the one following her freckles, drawing constellations on her skin? All I wanted in that moment was to be the one she sidled up to, my arm draped over her torso.

Shaking my head, I turned back to Calla, my actual date. She was lively and fun, everything that I should have wanted. I needed someone sweet and kind in my life, not a girl who constantly gave me shit, someone who could balance out my asshole tendencies. It also didn't hurt that Calla was gorgeous, no questions about it. She looked like a real-life mermaid, with her long red hair flowing down her back and her innocent smile. She was perfect.

When I tried to talk to her, though, there was nothing between us. I didn't feel a need to be close to her, to get to know every thought in her head. Not the way I did with Alex.

Alex was the girl who crawled under my skin, refusing to let go.

I wish I could've said I hated the feeling.

I didn't.

I hated the guilt that came with it.

We both waited as Alex stepped up to the tee, placing her teal ball on top of it. She squinted her eyes as she lined up her shot, biting the corner of her lip in concentration. It was cute how seriously she took this game. I couldn't give a fuck if I won or lost—getting a rise out of her was becoming my newest addiction.

She peeked over her shoulder before her swing, staring daggers back at me, waiting for me to make my move. In truth, I had nothing planned, but I enjoyed planting those seeds of doubt in her head.

With a deep breath, Alex tapped the ball, and we all watched with bated breath as it slid down the hill. It felt like the whole course was silent as it bounced off a stone at the base. It looked like it was going to stop, but as it rounded the hill, the ball grazed the outside wall, causing it to turn ever so slightly.

One slight tweak and it slid right into the cup. *Hole in fucking one.*

"Yes!" Alex screamed, holding her club up in victory and pointing it at me. "Suck on that, you motherfu—"

"Miss Green!" a voice called out from behind us. A woman glared at us, her hands covering a small boy's ears. He smiled cheekily up at his mother, probably crafting some questions for later in his mind.

Alex's cheeks turned various shades of red. "Sorry, Mrs. Patterson," she muttered while I smirked back at her. She pointed her finger in my direction. "Don't you dare say anything."

"Wouldn't dream of it."

The rest of us finished our games, not even coming close to beating Alex. The bright smile on her face lit up the entire course, making it almost impossible to look away.

As my mind started getting lost in thoughts of Alex again, Adam came to my side, nudging me with his elbow. "You good?"

Clearing my throat, I lowered my gaze, hating how easy it was to forget that Alex was here with my best friend, not me. "Fine."

"About the bet..."

"Don't," I cut him off. "There's no need. I appreciate you looking out for me."

"Always, Cole."

My stomach dropped at the simple exchange, a reminder of how much Adam had done for me. If it weren't for him, I would probably still be stuck in my hometown, drinking myself into an early grave, wishing I hadn't lost my purpose in an instant, hating the aimless loser I'd become. I owed him my life, which was a debt I could never repay

A good place to start would be to get my dick under control. No more thinking about Alex—at all. Looking away from the woman stuck in my head, I studied Calla. It was unfair that I'd never given her a chance.

So when it came time to leave, and Adam asked if we wanted to go to dinner together, I gave Calla a questioning look. "I was thinking we could grab some food just the two of us."

She smiled back at me. "That sounds great."

* * *

"Wait, are you serious? Friday Night Lights is a real thing?"

Calla stared at me, trying to understand my childhood. Growing up in rural Texas and New York City were vastly different experiences. While I was surrounded by livestock and miles of open land, she spent her days in a penthouse apartment with a doorman.

Despite our differences, we were having a good time. Calla took me to a small beachside shack that served some of the best burgers I'd ever eaten. It was barely even a restaurant, more a one-person operation behind the grill. Wooden picnic tables lined the concrete slab, and the red and white striped plastic roof gave the whole place a warm glow. As we sat on opposite sides of the table, I turned, staring out at the lake the town was named after.

As I watched the world go by, I started to imagine what it would be like to live here. Could I do it? The laid-back atmosphere suited me better than LA, that was for damn sure. Could I picture myself here five, even ten years down the line? I started to push the thought away, but that usual unease about the future was missing. For the first time in a long time, the idea of putting down roots didn't turn my stomach.

"Last call!" the guy behind the counter bellowed, tossing a couple of spare hotdogs onto the counter. After tossing out our trash, Calla grabbed one and took it with her as we walked toward her car. With her living at the resort, it was an easy call to head back together.

As we drove, we talked about anything and everything, from sports to her dream vacations. I kept waiting for that spark of interest to ignite, something that would make me want to do this again. I enjoyed talking to Calla; she was funny and smart as hell, much more serious than I initially gave her credit for. She was someone I should want to get to know better.

That was before a foul-mouthed brunette had taken over all my thoughts.

Once we got back to the hotel, I walked Calla to the front entrance, waiting awkwardly as she searched her purse for her keys. I tucked my hands in my pockets, unsure how we were supposed to wrap this up. *Hey, I hope you had a good time, but not too good because your best friend has my head all fucked up?*

When she pulled her keys out, she smiled up at me. "Well, that was certainly a date I'll never forget."

"Same," I laughed. In truth, it was one of the most memorable dates of my life. I had no idea mini-golf could get that heated. I cleared my throat, rubbing the back of my head. "Thanks for keeping me company. I had a good time."

"Yeah, I did, too." Calla smiled softly back at me. "Even though we both know I'm not who you wanted to be on that date with tonight."

My brows furrowed, hating that she saw so clearly what I was trying to hide. I decided to play dumb. "What do you mean?"

She rolled her eyes as she took a big step back. "Stubborn matches made in heaven. Or hell, if that game is to be believed." She glanced at the back lawn of the Isadora, across the pool toward the dark lake. Her expression seemed conflicted, and I didn't have the right words to say, so I stood there staring at her until, finally, she sighed. "Has Alex opened up to you at all about why she moved here?"

My jaw tightened, nerves already on edge at her apprehensive tone, one that told me that someone hurt Alex more than she let on. Afraid of what I would say, I shook my head, keeping my mouth shut.

"Didn't think so," she sighed. "Look, Alex is my favorite person in the world. I love her more than anyone, but she has got some serious issues letting people in. Whatever is going on with Adam, it doesn't seem like he's going to push her to open up."

"You think I can?"

"I think you have a shot." She shrugged her shoulders. "All I know is how she looks at you—like she wants you to see her, the real her. The only other people she's opened up to are Javi and me." Her eyes narrowed. "Just...whatever you decide to do next, please don't hurt her. She puts up a good front, but Alex is sensitive and takes people's words to heart. She tends to think the worst of herself. If you want any sort of chance with her, start with being her friend. She deserves to have more people looking out for her."

Without another word, Calla reached around my neck, giving me a chaste hug before scurrying inside, leaving me reeling. My head was spinning, trying to digest everything she told me.

Someone hurt Alex. Even if she didn't say it directly, that was what Calla meant, and no matter how long ago it happened, it still bothered her and caused her to keep people at arm's length.

And then, there was me: bringing her closer, only to shove her away when my feelings started to become too real, toying with her emotions, never telling her why I was so hot and cold. She asked for my friendship, and I couldn't even offer that, too wrapped up in my own shit to see the olive branch until it was almost too late.

Calla was right. I needed to show her that I could be her friend and that I would support her no matter what happened next.

Before I could start to make amends, there was something I had to do first.

I had to talk to Adam.

Alex

The week after our date felt like it moved at warp speed. With the movie starting to film in town, everyone was desperate for a glimpse behind the scenes. The media had been flooding our hotel lines, trying to get us to confirm our guest lists. There are only so many polite ways you could tell people it was none of their damn business.

Despite the new distractions, my days hadn't changed too much. I was swamped with requests, but most came from Adam's costars. I'd spent some time getting to know them and found that most were very down to Earth.

Well, except for Everly.

The girl was used to the city lifestyle and didn't understand why she couldn't order ahi tuna to her room at two in the morning. Usually, I hate all the over-the-top requests, but she was so sweet when I told her it wouldn't work that I didn't mind trying. She stopped by after shooting almost every day, dropping off a coffee to thank me for all my hard work. With that and the tips she always forced into my hands, she quickly became my favorite guest.

My other favorite guest barely had enough time to text,

much less spend some face-to-face time with me. Every time I saw Adam, he was rushing somewhere. He'd explained he was trying to be as hands-on as possible with the film. From what he told me, he was hoping this movie would break him from being type-cast as one of America's favorite superheroes.

As I tried to process another one of Everly's requests (not quite sure where to find goat yoga locally), Adam dashed through the lobby, barely looking up from the script pages as he pressed through the crowds of waiting fans. I climbed out from my station, blocking his path before he could walk right past me.

But I underestimated how invested he was in the pages. He barely slowed down when he ran into me. As I started to topple to the floor, Adam dropped the script to his side, looping his arm around my waist. "Oh shit, I'm so sorry, Alex. Are you okay?"

"Fine." I smiled up at him as he righted me. Adam took a moment, tucking a stray hair behind my ear before stepping back from me. I glanced around the lobby, then lowered my voice so only he could hear. "But you've been neglecting your fake girlfriend, buddy."

The pictures from our date last week had gone viral, and even I had to admit it: they were compelling. From the way Adam hugged me to the candle-lit dinner we shared afterward, we looked like a couple in love. Only we seemed to know the truth.

Well, we were *supposed* to be the only ones, but I was starting to get the sneaking suspicion that Calla was on to us. She questioned me non-stop all week, curious how I felt about Adam. I tried to sell it the best I could, but I was getting to my breaking point. NDA or not, I hated lying to my best friend. She was one of the few people who saw directly through me, and it was only a matter of time before she found out the truth. God forbid she found out from another source. Then, there would be hell to pay.

Adam chuckled, bringing me back to the present as he pressed a quick kiss to my forehead. "Sorry about that. I tend to get hyper-focused on projects and forget to come up for air."

"You have a break in filming tonight, right?" He nodded, so I continued. "I was thinking I could take you to dinner. You know, help you clear your mind a little bit."

His smile almost blinded me. "I'd love that. Lost Tavern?"

"You know it."

When we reviewed the contract, we decided some places needed to be off-limits to the cameras. The Lost Tavern was one of them. Not only had it become a little sanctuary for Adam, but Curt and Marta would also kill me if the tourists and fangirls invaded their space.

He glanced at the call sheet attached to the script. "Meet me here at...eight? Does that work for you?"

"It's perfect." I grin, excited to leave my desk for another night. I was getting used to being around other people, and my house had become too quiet for my liking. Being alone used to be my solace. Now, it made my bones ache with loneliness.

For the past week, I'd been spending almost all my nights at work, not wanting to feel that familiar ache in my empty house. A couple of times, I'd fallen asleep at my desk, and Javi had to drive me home.

Tonight, that wouldn't be a problem. A dinner with my fake boyfriend sounded perfect. Even though we were staying strictly in the friend zone, Adam was quickly becoming one of my favorite people. From the way he told me about his day to how he spoke so passionately about his craft, it made my heart clench.

It had been years since I'd felt that passionate about my career. Actually, I didn't know if I'd ever had that feeling. In the past, I'd picked my job because of stability. I was more concerned about being comfortable than happy.

Now, I wanted both.

Only I had no idea where to start.

With three years of experience in hospitality, it made logical sense to keep on this track. None of the other properties in town would hire me; they were too terrified of Diane's wrath to poach one of her people, but maybe I could find a way to utilize my experience while finding a job I preferred.

As I glanced outside the large picture windows, the tickle of a plan started to scratch the back of my mind. I did have things I loved, and most of them were about this town and the beautiful landscape surrounding it.

A slow smile pulled at my lips as I opened another search window on my computer. Perhaps it wasn't as hopeless as I thought.

"ALEX?" a voice called out, breaking me from my thoughts.

All afternoon, I had been researching what it would take to start my own business, like maybe even an inn or bed and breakfast, something much smaller and more personal than the Isadora. There were plenty of older properties deeper in town, ones that needed some love and care but had terrific bones.

I never pictured myself as a small business owner, but the more I thought about it, the more sense it made. I'd spent years studying finance and marketing, ready for a career in a Fortune 500 company when I graduated. Maybe this wasn't in my plans before, but plans were meant to change. I was living proof of that.

If I waited until I was ready, who knew when that would be? Maybe I was being impulsive. No, scratch that—this was definitely impulsive. But I was tired of weighing every choice, of acting like a passenger in my own life. Looking didn't mean that I had to purchase anything; it was just worth it to explore some options. Maybe this pipe dream could ever become a reality.

"Alex?"

My head snapped up, meeting Everly's surprised gaze. "Sorry, I didn't mean to disturb you."

"Don't be silly," I said. "You're not disturbing me at all." I glanced at the clock: 8:30. *Shit, had I zoned out that long?* My eyes roamed the lobby, searching for Adam, but he was nowhere to be found.

"Looking for someone?" Everly asked, arching one of her perfectly manicured brows.

"Adam was supposed to pick me up when he finished filming. I guess he's running late." I gave a half-hearted shrug. "Oh well, gives me more time to get some work done. What can I help you with tonight?"

"You can have a drink with me." She smiled brightly back at me. "I'm desperate for some girl time, and all my friends are on the other side of the country."

"Oh..." I glanced toward the door. "I don't know if I should; Adam's expecting me to have dinner with him."

"Last time I saw him, he was reviewing the day's reels with the directors," Everly answered. "I doubt he'll be back anytime soon."

Oh. I rechecked my phone, searching for any missed calls or texts. *Nothing.* I know it shouldn't hurt, but it still stung that Adam hadn't even bothered to message me.

"Well," I smiled tightly, "then I'm in."

"Perfect!" Everly leaned back, clapping her hands together. "I'll give you some time to get ready, and then we can go at what...ten?"

"Everly..."

"You're right—no one good shows their face until at least 11."

"Everly, the bar closes at 10:30."

She groaned, dropping her head back. "I don't understand why you chose to live here. It's like the entire world shuts down after the sun sets."

That's precisely what it was like around here, but I wasn't about to argue with her, not when she looked so defeated. "How about this," I said. "We'll grab a drink at Paddy's Wake, and then we can have a bottle of wine at my place." Everly beamed back at me. "Do you mind if I invite a couple of friends to join us?"

"The more the merrier," she cheered. "Just make sure they're up for a good time. I've spent the whole day playing a woman pining for a guy who doesn't want her, and that shit is depressing. I need to have some fun to shake it off."

I smirked to myself. I knew exactly how she felt.

TWENTY-TWO

"And then I told that disgusting perv if he tried to touch me with his teeny-weeny again, I'd cut it off and blend it into a smoothie."

Javi and Calla almost fell off my couch in laughter as I sat there in disbelief at Everly's story. I shook my head, unable to hold back a smile of my own. "I'm guessing you didn't get the part."

"Nope," she grinned. "But after that audition, I got a call for an even bigger movie, and we blew his out of the water."

"I think you're my hero," Calla called out, wiping tears from her eyes.

Though I was nervous about how tonight would go, Everly was an easy addition to our group. She gave great advice to Calla, commiserated with Javier about being the eldest child, and even took a moment to review some of the properties I'd found.

Overall, it was one of the best nights I'd had in a while.

Everly pointed at Calla. "Are you single?" She smirked at Javi. "I already know this one is married. He's got that happiness glow that only comes from true love." She plopped down on the couch next to Calla. "But you...I can't put my finger on."

"Oh, I am definitely single," Calla said.

"*Happily* single?"

"Most of the time," Calla answered honestly. "I'm satisfied by myself." All of us turned to look at her with smug smiles, and she buried her face in her hands. "Get your minds out of the gutter; I didn't mean like that! I meant that I have too much to deal with as it is. I can't even imagine adding someone else to the mix. Maybe when I'm more settled, I'll try dating, but for now, I'm putting myself first."

"Damn straight," Everly said, tipping her glass to Calla's. "My last girlfriend tried to force me to choose between her and an acting job. I didn't want to be with someone who put me in a position like that. As I always say, choose you."

Javi nodded in agreement as Calla stared back at her with wide-eyed wonder. I chewed on my lower lip, taking her words to heart. When was the last time I chose me? When I moved here? That was more an act of self-preservation than a proper choice.

Looking at the printouts of different vacant properties scattered all over my coffee table, I felt that same twinge of excitement. Opening an inn might not have been my forever dream, but it quickly became my newest one. If I could take everything I'd learned at the Isadora and turn it into a career I loved, maybe my time there would have been worth it.

Javi peered over my shoulder. "Which one are you leaning toward?"

"The cheapest one," I answered honestly. "If I scrape together all my savings, I should have enough to cover most of the down payment, but I'll need a lot more capital once I start the renovations."

Adam's payment for my fake-dating services would hopefully be enough to cover those expenses, but I kept that thought to myself.

"You should look for investors," Everly said, sitting across from me on the floor. "I've contributed to some low-income housing projects back home. You could get plenty of people interested if you market it right."

My brow tightened. It was sage advice, but the idea of handing off a piece of my dream, even a brand new one, created a knot in the back of my throat. I'd heard enough of the ramblings of the board at work to know that I didn't want that life. I didn't want to have to answer other people about my property.

"Oh! Oh!" She clapped her hands together. "You should ask Adam! I bet he'd love to help you out."

He already was.

But she couldn't know that, so instead, I offered her an uneasy smile. "I don't want to ask Adam. We just started dating. I don't want him to think I'm using him for his money."

I didn't have to turn to know Calla's eyes were drilling holes into the back of my head. She'd tried to get me alone multiple times tonight to figure out what was happening between Adam and me; luckily, I'd managed to evade her so far.

"I guess that's a good point." Everly pouted, deep in thought for several seconds before she snapped her fingers. "I know! Marry him, and then all his money will be your money, too. Problem solved."

Javi's wine came flying out of his nose.

"Relax," she laughed. "I'm kidding...*mostly.* My mother claimed she was the reincarnation of Elizabeth Taylor. Her advice was always to get married. Probably why I'm never going to." She stood, shaking the empty wine bottle on the table. "I'm going to run to the bathroom and then get us a refill. Does anybody need anything else?"

"We're good," I answered.

As soon as the bathroom door closed, Calla and Javi dropped their smiles, turning to face me as Calla spoke. "Okay, spill. I know you're hiding something, and Javi knows it too. You're not leaving this room until you tell us what's happening."

My eyes widened, flashing down the hall. Javi stepped into view. "If you don't want Everly to hear, then I suggest you hurry up."

"Guys, I can't tell you. I would if I could."

Calla's eyes widened to the size of quarters. "What? What do you mean? Are you in danger? Oh my God! Are you pregnant?"

"No, and fuck no! I haven't had sex in almost a year."

"A year?" Javi snapped at me. "Damn, girl. That's almost criminal."

"Table that for another day," Calla said, silencing him with her hands. "What do you mean you can't say anything?" Her eyes flashed with hurt. "Do you not trust us?"

"You know I do." I ran my hands over my face. "More than anyone in the world. But what you're asking about...it's not my secret to tell. Not really."

Calla shifted forward, taking my hands in hers. "Okay."

"What?" Javi said, leaning back as he glared at Calla, his eyes widening. "I thought we were having an intervention tonight."

"We promised to make sure our friend was okay." She turned back to me. "If you can't tell us, we won't push, but remember, we love you, and we will *never* break your confidence. If you decide you want to talk, we'll always be here for you."

My eyes darted between her and Javi, heart so full of love (and cheap Moscato) that it felt like I might cry. With that simple assurance, all my walls broke, unable to keep the words inside for a moment longer.

"Adam and I aren't really dating."

The words came out jumbled in my haste to spit them out, and Calla and Javi looked at me with twin confused faces. Javi turned toward Calla. "Did she say they're hibernating?"

Calla shook her head. "I think she said it's liberating?" She glanced down at her glass. "No, that can't be right."

"No," I snapped. "Adam and I aren't really dating. This whole thing, our relationship, it's an arrangement. It's all fake."

A COUPLE of hours and several bottles of wine later, Calla and Javier sat in my living room, processing everything I had told them. After I dropped the initial bomb, Everly fluttered back into the room, and the conversation ended just as quickly as it began.

But I knew my time was running out. When Everly yawned and declared she was crashing in my guest room, Calla and Javi wasted no time asking for all the details. Once everything was out in the open, they stared at me with twin looks of shock and confusion.

"Wow," Calla sighed, leaning against the couch and rubbing her temples. "I knew something was up after that awkward date, but I didn't think it was going to be this deep. What the hell are you going to do?"

"I'm going to keep up my end of the contract," I said as if it was the simplest thing in the world. "Enough people have let Adam down. I'm not going to be one of them."

Javi's eyes darted to Calla, and she tucked her lip between her teeth, the telltale sign that she was holding something back. My brow raised. "What?"

"Look, I didn't want to say anything because I wanted you to figure out by yourself that Adam wasn't the guy for you. But if you're saying it's not real between you guys..."

Wait, *what?* Calla thought Adam was wrong for me? Of all the people in my life, I thought she'd be the most crushed by the fakeness of our relationship. I was prepared for tears and possible anger, not this strange sense of relief.

"What's going on?" I said.

"Well..." She sighed, looking up at the ceiling. "I think there's another person you should consider before you go all in with Adam." My heart beat wildly in my chest. "You should consider...Cole."

There went all the air in my lungs.

I shook my head, standing up to wash my glass. No more wine tonight. It made me forget about silly little things like NDAs and how Theo could sue me for my life savings if he found out I spilled.

"Nothing is going on between Cole and me," I said.

Javi followed behind me, propping his hip against the counter as I turned on the faucet. "Liar, liar. Are you blanking on a little conversation we had under the stairs last month?"

No, I hadn't, but I hoped he did.

"That was me being stupid," I muttered, rolling my eyes. "I was seeing signs that weren't even there. Cole does not see me as anything other than Adam's girlfriend."

"Yeah, that's bullshit," Calla said, earning a confused glare from me. "I talked to him after our double date. That man is really into you, Alex. You'd have to be blind not to see it."

"Or deep in denial," Javi added.

I stared blankly back at them, unable to clearly process what they were saying. A small glimmer of hope rose in my chest, wondering if all those moments weren't as in my head as I had imagined.

After the last disaster with Cole, I'd shoved down every feeling, refusing to think about him as anything at all. Still, I'd be lying if my heart didn't do some weird somersault whenever Cole came around. It was different with him than any other people I had dated. Where I once sought comfort, Cole made me feel on edge, like I was teetering on a precipice, unsure of what awaited me on the other side. It should frighten me.

Instead, it made me feel alive.

My hand abruptly stopped rinsing the glass. *No. I wasn't going there. Not again.* Cole had slammed the door to anything more between us multiple times, taking my insecurities and wielding them like a weapon.

Even if Cole had feelings for me, which I was having a hard time believing, he'd gone out of his way to make it appear the opposite. No matter what he said to Calla, there was no taking his words back.

"No," I said firmly. "Even if he does, it's a non-starter. I've tried to open up to him twice, and he's left me feeling like a fool. I'm not giving him the chance for a third."

Calla sighed into her wine glass. "Fine. But if the sparks I saw between the two of you are anything close to real, I think you're making a mistake."

"Maybe," I said, effectively ending the conversation. "But it's my mistake to make."

TWENTY-THREE

Adam was avoiding me.

It had been over a week since we'd spent more than five minutes in a room together. It didn't matter if we were in our villa or on set—the moment I walked into a room, Adam immediately walked out of it.

I tried to tell myself this was normal. This was how Adam always was when filming. He'd get so invested in his role he'd forget about his real life. Adam tended to take on a lot of his character's burdens and channeled them into every scene. He spent all his free time scouring the dailies, checking his performance.

Even after the movie wrapped, it took time for him to get back to his usual self.

Usually, I'd push for him to talk to me, to get his head out of the role for at least a few hours a day, but my head was so fucked up lately that the distance was a relief.

Ever since that double date, I hadn't been able to get Alex out of my mind. She invaded my goddamn brain, chasing me down even when I purposely tried to forget her.

Calla exposed a raw nerve, which I thought no one else

had noticed. When she confronted me about my feelings for Alex, they became too real, and I felt like the world's worst friend.

Usually, Adam was the one I went to when I needed to sort my shit out. This time, though, I couldn't. My head was all wrapped up about the girl *he* was dating.

Suddenly, the room started to feel too small, robbing the air from my lungs. My hands began to shake, and my vision blurred. I needed air.

I stumbled out of the villa, my hands landing on my knees when I got outside. Even the open air offered no relief. Being at the hotel only reminded me of Alex. She'd tainted every piece of the property, making me constantly on edge.

I needed to get out, even if it was just for a few hours.

There had to be something in this damn town that could take my mind off of Alex.

Hopefully.

THE WALK in the woods did little to clear my clouded mind. Usually, being away from people allowed me to breathe and let down my guard for a short time.

Now, all I felt was alone.

Coming to Saint Stephen's Lake was supposed to be a break from reality, a chance to support Adam as he pursued his new dream.

All this time away had shown me one thing, though: I was stuck. I hid behind him because I didn't want to face my past. For the past two years, I'd avoided all my triggers, including my family and hometown. How long had it been since I even talked to my sister? Our last phone call was quick but tense. I didn't know if she'd ever fully forgive me for how hard I hit rock bottom, for my words and actions when I was in a bad head space.

Without realizing it, I'd cut off all meaningful relationships from my life. Well, besides Adam, but let's be honest—he was only still around because he fought like hell to stay friends. No one else would go through that level of effort.

Not that I tried to let people in—that was clear with my dating track record. Ever since moving to LA, all I had were meaningless one-night stands, nothing more than a single moment shared. Letting someone in meant exposing your secrets, and mine were guarded better than Fort Knox. Even if I did open up, very few people could move past what I'd done.

Hell knows I hadn't.

Realizing the familiar turn my thoughts were taking, I pulled my phone out, scrolling until I found the right contact.

My favorite girl.

She answered on the third ring. "Hey, kid."

"Hey, Dani."

"How's the least coast?"

I rub my hand over my face. "You gonna call it that forever?"

Dani grew up in New York, fleeing to the land of milk and honey as soon as she was old enough. From how she told it, you would think this side of the country was consistently shrouded in a cloud. It'd been decades, and Dani refused to return to this side of the country. I never asked what caused her to cut out this part of her history, as she never pried too heavily into things I wasn't willing to share. Perhaps that was what brought us together: the mutual desire to start completely new lives, the desire to escape our demons.

"Don't worry about that," she said. "What's going on with you?"

I sighed, then explained everything that had happened since

we arrived—how Adam had taken on a more active role in this project, the boredom, the loneliness.

Alex.

"Sounds like you've met someone pretty special," Dani quietly said once I finished.

"She seems to be," I sighed. "The thing is, she's dating Adam, so I need to get my shit together and get her out of my head."

Dani took a long breath, probably inhaling one of the menthol cigarettes she refused to quit no matter how often I asked. "Is that what you want?"

No. The answer rang out before I could even give it a thought. Everything about Alex called to me, got under my skin, and refused to let go. She was beautiful, but there was so much more to her than that. There was a life inside of her that made me want to wake up, stop hiding, and rejoin the world again, to finally release myself from the chains that had been holding me back for years.

However, none of that mattered, not when my best friend's heart was also on the line.

"It doesn't matter what I want," I said.

"It does if she feels the same way about you. Kid, you're making your mind up for both of you."

"She's with Adam—"

"Are they married?" Dani asked. "Engaged? Are they even exclusive?"

"Not that I know of."

Dani muttered a curse before speaking again. "Then pull your head out of your ass and *talk* to her. Even if she's gone on a couple of dates with your friend, she doesn't belong to anyone. She's not a pet, Cole. Adam can't claim her unless she wants to be claimed."

The words made sense in my mind, but the swirling of guilt

in my gut told me it wasn't that simple. Dani was one of the few people in the world who knew how Adam saved me; she understood our bond better than most. He wasn't some passing friend. He was my brother, closer to me than my actual family. I'd rather live with regrets than hurt him.

Besides, he was everything Alex deserved. If they kept dating, he could give her the world. I had nothing to my name—no real job, not even a place to call my own. What could I possibly offer her?

As if sensing my internal battle, Dani spoke again. "None of this matters if you can't forgive yourself, kid. You won't be any good to anyone if you can't love yourself first."

I rolled my eyes, used to this speech. She gave it every time we met up, always advocating that you needed to love yourself before you could even think about letting someone else into your life. I wanted to mention that she'd been single the whole time I'd known her, but even I wasn't stupid enough to step on that grenade.

"Love you, Dani."

"Love you more, Cole. Tell that girl how you feel, or I'm going to kick your ass until kingdom comes."

We hung up, and I kept moving up the trail, stopping to look at some of the sights along the way. Eventually, I found my way to one of the main roads, trying to get my bearings. Though it wasn't a far distance from the resort, the air back here was completely different. While the resort was perfectly curated to scream relaxation, these properties looked more like they were carved from the forest itself.

I walked along the road, taking in the different homes and motels until, eventually, I stumbled upon one for sale. In the front, there sat a large wooden cabin—a sign hung from the porch that read "Fox Creek Lodge." Behind the main building was a field with ten smaller cabins. Evergreen and Balsam trees lined the background, making it picturesque, precisely the kind of image you'd want to see in a brochure for Saint Stephen's Lake.

Even from a distance, though, I could tell it needed some help. It'd probably been vacant for years. But even with age and wear, there was something about the lodge that called to me.

"Do you think the owner would budge on price?" A voice called out in the distance. "Factoring in the repairs, I don't know if it'll be in my price range."

"It never hurts to ask," another person answered. "That's the reason it's still on the market. We got flooded with above-ask offers from developers, but the owner refused to sell. He wants someone who will keep the original feel of the property."

The conversation faded as they walked around one of the cabins, and my curiosity had me moving closer to them. As Alex emerged, she spotted me instantly, jumping a little at the unexpected sight.

"What are you doing here?" she hissed.

Okay, so she might still be pissed at me from all the shit I'd pulled over the past week. Trusting Calla's advice, I tried to offer some words of support. "This place seems great."

"Seriously?" She rolled her eyes. "Which part? The crumbling roofs or the rotting floors?"

"Those things can be fixed," I said. "But the bones are great. It could be something amazing if someone knew what they were doing."

That seemed to soften her glare. Alex sighed, resting her hand along the wooden porch. "I think so too. It's been vacant for years. I'd love to bring it back to life."

The woman, who I assumed was a real estate agent, followed behind Alex, checking something on her phone. "Do you mind if I take this?"

Alex shook her head, still looking up at the ancient cabin

with stars in her eyes. As the woman started down the hill, I stepped closer to her. "You're thinking of buying this place?"

"I don't know," she sighed. "Maybe? I was trying to get a feel for the available properties in town and to get a budget scope before I drafted my business plan. That was before we came here, and I fell in love."

"How long have you been thinking about this?"

"Oh, about twenty-four hours," Alex laughed. "You probably think I've lost my mind, and maybe I have. I'm not normally this impulsive. It's just...once this idea came into my head, everything started to make sense." Her bright blue eyes met mine. "Have you ever had one of those realizations?"

I swallowed, dodging her question. "I thought you hated your job?"

"I hate the politics of it," she sighed. "The drama and bullshit I have to put up with daily, people who are too busy taking selfies to enjoy the world they're using as a backdrop. The idea of carving out a piece of this town for myself? Helping people see why this place is so special? That means everything to me." She blushed as she stared up at me. "Or I've lost the last of my brain cells, and this is the biggest mistake of my life."

Unsure exactly what to say, I reached out, placing my hand on hers. It was soft, almost softer than I imagined, and it fit perfectly with mine. Almost as quickly as I realized what I'd done, I pulled my hand back, pictures of Adam flashing in my mind. I brushed the back of my hair with the same hand, trying to forget the feel of her as I nodded to the cabins. "Show me what you see."

Her gaze dipped from her hand on the railing back up to my eyes, and for a moment, I thought she was going to say no, tell me to fuck off. Instead, she smiled brightly back at me.

"Come on."

HOURS LATER, Alex dropped me back at the resort with a renewed sense of purpose in her eyes. I don't know how anyone could doubt that this was what she was meant to do. The way she talked about the property and her vision blew me away.

Maybe that's why I offered my limited skills: to help her bring her vision to life.

There was also a selfish part of me that wanted to take her dream and make it a project for me. A purpose. It had been years since I felt like I had one, not to mention the added benefit of spending more time with Alex. Every minute we spent together today confirmed what I already suspected: I had feelings for her, feelings that I had no right to have but were there anyway.

For the first time in a long time, I wanted the chance to try, to fight for someone I could care about—to prove I wasn't the asshole I'd shown her.

After spending the evening at Alex's house, Calla told me I had some serious groveling to do. It was clear that my plan to get Alex to hate me worked a little too well—there was a wall between us that wasn't there before like she was keeping me at arm's length.

That was fine. I'd atoned for bigger sins in my life. I'd spend the rest of our time here convincing her I wouldn't hurt her again.

Despite Dani's advice, I needed to talk to Adam first. I owed him that. His reaction wouldn't stop me from spending time with Alex, not if she wanted me as much as I wanted her, but the least I could do was be open about my intentions.

When I returned to the room, I pushed the front door open, revealing an exhausted Adam on the other side. He laid on the couch, his arm draped over his eyes. When he heard me enter, he muttered, "Whoever decided we needed to be on set before the sun came up is the world's biggest douche."

"Sorry, man," I said, anxiously shifting to the seat across from him. "Did you at least get the shots you needed?"

"Think so," he said, resting his head on the back of the couch. "Had to shoot it fifteen times because Everly was asleep on her feet. She couldn't get her lines straight. They had to bring out cue cards, man. Thank God this day is done."

My hands flexed, trying to do something to dispel the anxiousness inside me. I knew Adam better than most people in this world—this was the wrong moment to push him. Everything in me screamed to run out and let this whole Alex thing go.

Actually, that sounded like the best plan I'd had in a long time.

As I lifted out of the chair, a flash of Alex's bright smile came into my mind, forcing me to sit back down. No. I'd avoided this conversation for too long already. My feelings for Alex weren't going away, and it was time to tell Adam the truth. As soon as he knew, I could see if she'd give me a chance. We weren't going to be in Saint Stephen's Lake forever, and my window with Alex was closing too quickly for my liking.

"Look, Adam," I said, running my hand through my hair. "I need to talk to you about something."

"Shit," Adam said, sitting straighter on the couch. "I was going to say that to you."

My palms started to sweat, thinking of anyone who could have told him first. The only people I talked to about this were Calla and Dani. Dani would never betray my trust, so I doubted she'd sell me out—Calla was more of a wildcard. From what I'd learned, she didn't seem like the type to share anyone else's secrets. I'd been wrong before, though.

Shifting back in my seat, I tried to play it cool, but my leg wouldn't stop shaking. "What's up?"

Adam sighed, running his hand over his face. "Before you say anything, I know this was probably a mistake. I promise, I thought this through this time."

My eyes narrowed, already hating the turn this conversation had taken. This had nothing to do with Alex. His tone had somebody else written all over it.

Theo. My fists instinctively tightened, "What did he rope you into this time?"

Adam winced, and that's how I knew he'd messed up. "Look, I wanted to tell you before the date. Theo convinced me it wasn't a good idea, but I'm not lying to your face."

"Adam, tell me what's going on."

"Alex and me...it's not real."

"What do you mean?"

"We're only pretending to date for the cameras," he sighed. "Everything between us, our entire relationship—it's all fake."

TWENTY-FOUR

Alex

Dozens of print-outs and pictures were piled all over my counter. It was impossible even to see the butcher block lurking underneath all of them. Despite the towering pile of photos, they still didn't feel like enough. I could have taken a thousand more.

Every single day, I drove by the Fox Creek Lodge, and yet, I'd never once given it a second thought. Not until Paula, the real estate agent, pulled into the gravel drive. The grass was overgrown, its only inhabitants raccoons and squirrels, but it was special, the kind of vacation that would take up a permanent place in your memories. It reminded me of summer camp as a kid, of the power of escaping your life for a few days, just enjoying the world around you.

Every step I took further onto the property cemented the fact that it was meant to be *mine.*

I could feel it in my bones.

Granted, a million things had to happen first, and the owner had to be willing to lower his price drastically, but I wasn't going to think negatively. Sure, so much could go wrong, but I was determined to make this new dream a reality.

I could picture it: spending each day guiding tourists through our town, crafting nature trails and other activities. I'd rebuild each of the cabins to give them more personality, blending nature and comfort to match my style, and plan excursions for my guests, letting them experience all the beauty Saint Stephens' Lake had to offer. The idea made me smile; maybe everything I learned at the Isadora wouldn't be worthless after all.

I'd repay the town that brought me back to life—make them proud.

I let out a little squeal and danced in the middle of my kitchen, not giving a single fuck about being ridiculous. There was a light at the end of the tunnel, a future where I might not dread heading to work each morning. Maybe I wouldn't get to travel the world as much as I originally planned, but there was something to be said about living a life you loved at home.

I reviewed Paula's paperwork one last time, and the number in bold made my stomach lurch a little. It was a significant dip in the asking price, but considering how long the property had been sitting vacant, it seemed like a reasonable ask. I'd already started the process of obtaining a loan to cover the mortgage, and my savings would be enough for the down payment, but the renovations were another story. I would need the money from the contract with Adam to get everything back up to code, much less in the style I wanted them.

My stomach dropped a little at the thought, still apprehensive about the money part of our agreement. I would have helped Adam without it, but it would be enough to make this new dream come true. Even if I scrimped every one of my pennies for the next ten years, I'd never be able to match it.

Pushing the thought from my head, I gathered the paperwork and tucked it into a folder. Just as I placed it in the drawer, three subsequent bangs sounded from my front door, and I stopped instantly, glancing up at the clock on the wall. It was almost midnight. No one bothered to call me at this hour, much less tried to break down my door. Calla and Javi would have come through the kitchen door, considering they both have a key. Marta and Curt were asleep by now, and they would have called or texted if something was seriously wrong.

Grabbing the baseball bat from the coat closet, I summoned all my strength as I stepped behind the door. "Whoever you are, get out of here before I bash your head in!"

"It's me, Alex."

Cole? My heart beat erratically as I pulled the door open, revealing him waiting on the other side. With his fist resting on the door frame, I took him in. His breathing was ragged, almost like he ran the entire way here, but other than that, he wasn't bleeding or showing any other signs of distress.

"Are you okay?" I asked, shoving his coat to the side to check for injuries.

"Fine. I just needed to see you."

"What the hell?" I hissed, pulling him inside. "You scared the shit out of me pounding on the door like that! Have you lost your mind?"

"Yeah..." he said, staring at me with an intensity I'd never seen before. "You're damn right I have."

Without another word, he crashed his lips to mine, making me gasp. It took a moment for my brain to catch up with his actions, and I was suddenly very aware that Cole was kissing me.

Cole was *kissing* me.

And holy hell, it felt amazing.

My brain screamed out questions, but my body had other plans, cataloging how incredible his lips felt on mine. His strong hands gripped my hips tightly, dragging me closer to him, and was that...yep, that was his erection, poking me in the stomach with a mind of its own. The sensations were all too much and not enough at the same time—I wanted him everywhere. When his hand started to stray further north, his thumb brushed a bare patch of my skin.

The slight action broke the spell between us, and I placed my hand on his chest, shoving him out of my space. "What do you think you're doing? Adam—"

"Told me everything," he answered quietly, his eyes still trained on my lips. "I know your relationship isn't real. When he told me that..." Cole lifted his gaze to meet my eyes, and I swore my knees went weak. No one had ever looked at me like he did, like I alone had the power to save him or damn him. "Alex, I've been such a fucking idiot. I kept pushing you away because I thought we were going to hurt my friend, but now that I know the truth...."

"Nothing changes," I forced out, dropping my gaze down to my feet. If Cole kept staring at me like I was his salvation, I'd break. His kiss felt too good; his hands belonged on my body, but none of that changed the facts. Cole had already pushed me away. Twice. Was it worth the risk to see if he would do it again? Maybe other people would jump right in, but with my history, I was cautious to a fault. I'd pick the safe route almost every time, and as much as I hated to admit it, Cole would never be the safe choice.

"You're right. This thing between Adam and I, it's all business," I said. "We're friends, nothing more, but that doesn't mean you and I are anything either."

"But we could be," Cole quietly said as he took my hand, lacing his fingers with mine. "You feel this, sweetheart. I know you do."

I shook my head. "That's not it."

He waited, watching as my chest rose and fell with the war raging inside me. My heart screeched for me to let go, to throw caution to the wind, but my heart had always dictated my actions, and that had only led to heartache and pain. Perhaps it was time to let my brain take the lead, and it was telling me that this was a mistake.

"Cole..." I said, dropping his hand. "I do feel something for you. I'm not denying that."

"But?"

"I don't trust you." The words drowned out everything around us, a silent tension replacing the lust that was there moments earlier. "I know you're a good man, but I've opened up to you a couple of times, and every time, you've knocked me down. I can't risk," I motioned between the two of us, "us becoming more and letting you hurt me. Not when I'm just starting to stand on my own two feet again."

Cole stepped back, running his hand through his hair. He stayed quiet for so long that I was worried he hadn't heard me. After several minutes, he turned back toward me, placing his hand on my jaw, his thumb tracing a delicate line along my cheek.

My heart, that traitorous bastard, almost purred at the move.

"I know I hurt you, Alex, and I'd promise it won't happen again, but words will never be enough to prove it to you."

"What do you mean?"

"I'm in this, sweetheart. You want to be friends, and we're friends. Hell, I'll be the first one running when you call. If it makes you smile, I don't care what it takes: jokes at my expense, beating me at mini-golf—fuck, I'll make you pancakes every goddamn morning if that's what you want." He stepped closer, tipping back my head until my eyes met his, his pupils darkened with desire. "In exchange, I'm asking for one thing."

I swallow, nodding because I didn't trust myself at the moment.

"You let me into that head of yours." His fingers shifted so he could brush a few strands of hair away from my face. "I'd never push you into anything you don't want. You say this won't work, and I'll stop trying. If you change your mind? You can be damn sure I'll be there waiting."

My heart almost cracked at his words. I should have told him no, but instead, all I could manage was a quiet "Why?"

He stared down at me, raw vulnerability bursting from his gaze. Cole swallowed, dropping his voice lower. "I've made a lot of mistakes in my life, Alex—more than you can even imagine. I know I don't deserve someone as good as you, that you deserve better than me, but I don't care. I've known there was something special about you since we met." His lips curved. "I had to tell you what I felt. I had to try. You're worth putting it on all on the line." He reached up, stroking my cheek with his calloused thumb. "Can we try?"

Yes. The word screamed in my mind, wanting nothing more than to be let free. But a steady fear held me back, unable to get past the lingering feelings of rejection. "I need to think about it."

Cole nodded, heading to the door without another word.

Before he could reach for the handle of my front door, my hand jutted out, grabbing him before he could leave. "I'm not saying no."

With that, Cole gifted me a bright smile, one so full of hope that it made my chest ache with uncertainty. I wanted to pull him back to me, to continue what had started in my doorway, to hear more of Cole's beautiful words that had already latched onto my heart. Instead, he pressed his lips to my forehead, lingering momentarily, giving my hand one last squeeze before heading out the door.

Even as I heard the car door close, I remained standing in the entryway, trying to figure out what the hell I got myself into.

TWENTY-FIVE

Alex

The next day, my brain refused to stop replaying Cole's words like an anthem. They echoed during my drive to work, following me as I tried to knock out the various guest requests that had piled up overnight. They even drowned out my fears about the business loan application in front of me. As much as I wanted to focus on it, I couldn't, not when Cole had said everything I wanted to hear from him over the past month.

Now that he had, I didn't know what to do with myself. All morning, I jumped when someone with dark brown hair entered the room. Not that I thought Cole would come looking for answers already, but I also didn't think he'd come to my house in the middle of the night and kiss me like his life depended on it, so what did I know?

Then, there was his promise to earn back my trust. What exactly did that entail? How long would it take him to get through my rapidly crumbling walls? While I knew I wanted him, I wasn't sure if I'd be willing to go there with Cole. Trust wasn't something you could hand over because you were dying to climb a man like a tree.

Holy hell, I couldn't believe I just thought that. Yes, I spent a ridiculous amount of time thinking about his kiss last night, using some of my battery-powered friends to help soothe the ache his touch left behind, but no matter how many times I saw stars, nothing seemed to satiate the lust in my bones. Cole awakened a feeling inside me that had been dormant for years. When was the last time I'd craved someone's touch? Not since—

No. Think of *anything* else.

As I tried to distract myself with images of the Fox Creek property, Adam came up to my desk, offering a short knock on the wooden surface. "Hey there, I was hoping you had a few minutes to talk. Somewhere private."

My eyes widened as I tried to smile at him. What did he know? Had Cole already told him? My heart leaped in my chest, unsure if I would be relieved or annoyed that everything was coming to the surface.

"Of course," I said, waving over one of the girls from reception. "Let me get someone to cover my desk, and I'll meet you in the conference room."

After a couple of minutes, I headed to the empty room, unease and anxiety swirling in my gut. I wished Cole was there to take some of the heat off me. Was Adam mad? Upset?

Oh shit, did him kissing me violate the terms of our contract?

I know it precluded dating other people, but Cole and I weren't dating. I didn't even invite him over. Although, I'd be lying if I said I didn't love him showing up at my house like that. It was the closest I've ever come to a scene from a rom-com, and I loved every second of it.

Adam closed the door behind me, the click of the latch echoing in the large, empty room. The resort primarily used this room for conferences; however, the film crew rented it out to store extra equipment for the movie. Luckily, very few people ventured in here, mostly only coming by at the beginning and the end of the day.

I was debating how to start the conversation when Adam dropped down into one of the chairs lining the wall, put his head in his hands, and spoke barely above a whisper.

"I messed up, Alex."

My brows lifted. "What do you mean?"

He ran his hand over his face, barely able to look at me. "I told Cole everything." My heart slowed in relief; I wanted to appease his guilt, but he continued before I could get a word out. "After all the shit Theo gave you about the NDA, I can't believe I messed up like this. I know he won't say anything. Fuck..." he muttered as he pulled on the ends of his hair. "Alex, I'm so sorry."

"Woah," I said, placing my hands on Adam's shoulder. "You don't need to apologize to me. Cole's your best friend; I always expected him to know. I'm not upset."

"You're not?"

I shook my head, wondering if now was the right time to mention that I also told my friends. It was on the tip of my tongue before Theo's disapproving glare popped into my mind. I had faith in Adam. I knew he would understand my need to tell them, but I didn't trust Theo, especially when my future was the one really at stake.

Twirling my fingers together, I asked the question on my mind. "How did Cole take it?"

"He was relieved," Adam laughed. "I thought he'd be pissed, threaten to hit me for hiding this from him." He glanced up at me. "No offense. It's not that he doesn't care for you, but after the Ivy debacle, he's been much more guarded than ever. Cole wouldn't approve of anyone."

Nausea ripped through my insides. While a large part of me understood why Cole hadn't told Adam, it left me in a precarious situation. Should I tell Adam what happened last night? Probably. Perhaps it was cowardly, but I knew I couldn't do it as I stared at him.

Adam said my name, and from his tone, I knew it wasn't the first time. "Yes?"

He smiled softly back at me. "I was making sure that you wanted to continue our arrangement. If you wanted to back out, I'd completely understand."

For a moment, I thought about it. It would be so much easier to decide what path I wanted to take with Cole without this fake relationship hanging over my head. Adam and I had said we'd tell each other if we met someone, but until I knew what I wanted with Cole, it seemed pointless to throw away our arrangement, not when Adam still needed and wanted my support.

"No," I said. "I'm in this, Adam. You're stuck with one devoted fake girlfriend until filming ends."

He smiles back widely at me. "Glad to hear it."

"THERE WE GO."

I sighed as my phone screen finally came back to life. It had died while I was at work, and my usual charger was missing from my locker.

I was still reeling from the kiss last night and my conversation with Adam earlier. The more I thought about it, the more I was sure I should have said something to Adam- even just casually mentioning that I was interested in someone else.

But then again, telling Adam would mean I'd decided what to do about Cole. My mind was still all screwed up, unsure how to handle my warring emotions about him. On one hand, I wanted to kiss him again—do a lot more than kiss. One brief moment together, and my body already craved him, desperate for his touch.

On the other hand, he scared me, and yes, part of that was because I didn't trust him, but it was more that I didn't trust myself. I'd been fooled before by a handsome face and all the right words before. It'd taken me a long time to recover from that heartbreak, and I wasn't sure I'd be able to recover from anything like that again.

As soon as my phone got service, a series of messages came in, blinking one after the other. My heart skipped a beat when I saw Marta's name, asking me to come to the house to look at something. She never asked for help, especially if Curt was home. He was handy, able to fix pretty much anything on his own. He was also a prideful man, so much so that she'd have to sneak maintenance workers in when he was at work. So, if she was reaching out to me, they must be in dire straits.

Leaving my phone behind, I rushed out the door and jogged over to their adjoining lot. It took me a moment to survey their property, and I sighed in relief when I heard laughter echoing from their garage.

Turning the corner, Curt stood next to the hood of his old pick-up, watching someone else rattle around with the engine. His face was obscured, buried deep in the belly of the truck, but I'd recognize that frame anywhere.

Marta emerged from the side door, holding a tray filled with coffee and her signature maple pecan bars. As I approached, she gasped. "Oh, Alex, I'm so sorry. Did you rush over here?"

"I got your messages," I huffed out. "I thought something happened."

"Oh no," she sighed, placing down the tray to poke her husband firmly in the shoulder. "See what happens when you never ask for help? Alex thought she'd find us dead because I texted!"

He smiled sheepishly back at me. "Sorry to scare you, kiddo. The truck's battery gave me a run for my money, and I needed help jumping it."

"Good thing you didn't," a gruff voice called out from below. My heart stuttered as Cole stood up, wiping his hands on a cloth folded over the front fender. His pushed-back sleeves showcased his forearms deliciously, each of the veins protruding in the very best way.

"Why?" Marta said, backing away from the car. "Is it going to blow?"

"No," Cole chuckled. "The problem's with the starter, not the battery. If you jumped it a couple of times, the starter would still be dead, and you'd need a new battery on top of it."

"Can you fix it, son?" Curt asked. Neither Marta nor I missed the term of endearment, shooting each other twin looks of surprise. Marta was the friendly one of the pair. As far as I knew, I was one of the few people Curt had a soft spot for. Apparently, Cole had weaseled his way into Curt's good graces, too.

Brow furrowing, I glanced up at him. "What are you even doing here?"

"Alex..." Marta warned.

"What?" I asked her. "How did he know you needed help?"

Cole stared at me, grinning at my annoyance. "I was going to see you, and Marta was walking toward your house. When I stopped, she told me what happened, and I offered to check out the truck." He stepped closer, lowering his voice so only I could hear. "That okay with you, sweetheart?"

I was so tempted to tell him no, but watching him with my surrogate parents softened my hardened heart. I loved that he went out of his way to help them.

My misplaced annoyance waned. "You were coming here to see me?"

"I was dropping off dinner." He nodded to the car in the Anders' driveway. "I saw Javi on his way out, and he said you were working late. Considering the state of your fridge, I thought you might be hungry."

My mouth dropped open, not used to someone taking care of me. It meant to the world that Cole dropped everything to help the Anders. But it meant just as much that he'd gone out of his way for me. Too many nights, my dinners consisted of pop-tarts or frozen pizzas stuffed in my face before collapsing into my bed.

I couldn't help the shy smile that graced my face. Cole stared at me in wonder, like he saw something special for the first time. When he glanced up at the clock on the garage wall, he grimaced. "It might not be warm anymore. I've been here for a while." He nodded to his car, which I now realized belonged to Calla. "Go ahead and take it in. I'm going to see if I can get this old girl running."

Marta smiled, taking his hand in hers. "Tell me how we can repay you. Anything you want."

"It's nothing, ma'am." He waved off her concern. "I'm happy to help."

"How about this? I'll cook you dinner tomorrow, both of you."

"No," I said quickly, brushing off her offer. "Marta, you don't have to do that."

"Don't be silly, darling. You know I live for this stuff."

Before I could say another word, Cole answered for the both of us.

"We'd love to." Then, his grin turned toward me. "It's a date."

"What the fuck am I doing?"

Staring in the goddamn mirror, I tried to figure out what all this shit in my hair was supposed to do. Was it supposed to look like I'd poured a vat of oil all over my head? If so, mission accomplished.

Glancing down at my phone, I wondered if I'd have time to shower before meeting Alex. If I'd known that helping her neighbors was the key to getting her to agree to dinner, I would have set up shop in their garage a week ago.

Even though she never called it a date, and joining her elderly neighbors for dinner was not what I had in mind for our first time out together, my nerves felt differently. My palms wouldn't stop sweating, and I had a severe amount of buyer's remorse over my clothes.

I'd never acted like this before. Something about Alex had taken all the rational thoughts from my brain and turned me back into a teenager, preparing for my first actual date.

"Fuck it," I muttered, shoving myself away from the counter. Alex had seen me at my worst more than once, and she hadn't gone running for the hills. Yet. Pulling on my favorite flannel, I headed to the cabin's front door, grabbing Calla's spare set of keys from the table by the door.

Thank God for that girl—she'd saved my ass more than once this week. Luckily, she only used her car on the rare occasions she left town, mostly preferring to walk or take an Uber. I'd tried to give her money several times, but she refused. All she asked was that I fill the tank before bringing it back. Before I left Saint Stephen's Lake, I was going to tear apart the car, make sure the damn thing ran like it was brand new.

When I left.

The familiar pang hit my chest. I hated how quickly time seemed to be ticking down. Adam was a week into filming, which meant we'd have seven more at the most. Even with reshoots and everything else, there was no guarantee we'd be back here anytime soon. Something about leaving this town made my chest throb; I hated the idea of heading back to California.

Even after five years in LA, it never felt like I belonged.

Saint Stephen's Lake felt like home.

At least, it could.

As soon as I pulled into Alex's driveway, she exited the house, holding a dish in her hands. I took in her appearance, loving how her dark jeans molded to her shapely thighs. She kept it simple with a red hoodie, which was still enough to make my mouth water. Goddamn, I wanted to kiss her again. I was pretty sure that her lips would be etched in my brain forever. She made a little mewl when I dragged her closer, needing her to know how much I wanted her.

I did want Alex. Badly.

Enough that I was willing to ignore all the red flags in our way. I still hadn't talked to Adam, wanting to wait until Alex made her decision. Well, mostly. I was also scared shitless. There was a reason that Adam and I had managed to be friends for so long. We both stuck to our lane, never encroaching on each other. Even if their relationship wasn't real, Adam might be pissed that I was pursuing her. I'd hate for something like this to come between us, but I'd already tried to stay away from Alex. It didn't work then, and it sure as hell wouldn't happen now that I'd gotten a taste of her.

I shook my head, pushing that thought out of my mind. Tonight was all about Alex and me. She had started to relax when we spent time with Marta and Curt; they held a significant place in her heart, and I could see why. They loved her dearly, and they were also the warmest people I'd ever met. Sure, they had grilled me about my intentions with Alex before she arrived, but once I was honest about my feelings, they welcomed me into their home with open arms.

I climbed out of Calla's car, meeting Alex at the end of her walkway. I reached out and took the pie dish from her hands, eyeing the container curiously. "What'd you make?"

Alex blushed. "I tried to make an apple pie. Calla walked me through all the steps, so it should be edible."

"Should?"

"60-40."

We stared at each other for a moment, unsure what to do with each other now that we were face to face. I bent down, dropping a soft kiss on her cheek. The same red color filled her cheeks. Damn, that could get addicting fast. I liked being the one to make her blush.

I reached out, lacing our fingers together with my free hand. "So, anything I need to know when we get in there?"

Alex scrunched her nose. "Not really. Curt and Marta are open books, so they'll expect you to be the same. Oh, and if you're a Cowboys fan, don't mention it. Curt is a die-hard Giants fanatic. That'll be the fastest way to get on his bad side."

She continued to talk about them as we walked toward their

property, following the convenient path that linked the two houses. When we reached the door, she forwent knocking and instead walked into the main living room. The house reminded me a lot of Alex's but with a more antiquated feel. The walls were a warm honey, accented with reds and oranges. The furniture looked hand-carved from hearty oak.

"Hello?" a voice echoed from the kitchen. "We're in here!"

Alex dragged me across the living room, where we found Marta and Curt in the large, open kitchen. The kitchen had the same vibe as the rest of the house, which instantly put me at ease. It reminded me a lot of my parents' home in Texas.

The thought made my face fall, and I suddenly missed my family with an unbearable ache. Alex must have noticed because she moved closer, squeezing my hand a little tighter.

Oblivious to the shift in my mood, Marta came over, taking the pie dish from my hand as she smiled tightly at Alex. "Darling, you didn't have to bring anything."

"I swear, it's edible."

Marta just good-heartedly chuckled, offering us both glasses of wine before ushering us into the dining room. I declined, going for a soda instead as Alex grabbed a glass of red, finding the spot at my side.

Once we were in our chairs, I looked around the room. Family photos covered the walls, evidence of a well-lived life. Almost all of them had a boy between Curt and Marta, who looked at him like he hung the whole moon.

I nodded toward the picture. "Their son?"

Alex followed my line of sight. "Oh! That's Grayson, or Gray, to most people. He's a couple of years older than me. I've only met him a handful of times. He's Calla's ex. They dated all through high school."

"What happened?"

"I don't know all the details." She shrugged. "I think it

fizzled out naturally. Gray went to Seattle to play college base-ball and got drafted into the MLB right after. He barely has time to come home because he's so busy. I don't think he has time for anything other than baseball."

I squinted at the picture, studying the man a little closer. "Holy shit, that's Gray Anders!"

"Shh," Alex said, putting her hand over my mouth. "Do not make a big deal out of it."

"Are you serious?" I said, shifting her hand away. "I am sitting in the dining room of a living legend. The man's stats–"

"Are not what this dinner is about." Alex gave me a stern look. "Marta and Curt are unbelievably proud of Gray, but they also have a rule about baseball talk in their house. They want this to be a place where Gray can escape, not having to worry about people asking him about his season. So please, do not mention it."

Our conversation stopped when Marta and Curt entered the dining room, and I stood, taking the plate from Marta so she could take a seat. She gave me a grateful smile as she took her place across from Alex.

"I hope you like chicken, son," Curt said as he passed the tray to me.

The rest of the night flowed in comfortable conversation; it was great to get to hang out with Alex without any expectations or hidden agendas. She was more at ease with Curt and Marta than anyone else I had seen so far, and I enjoyed getting to know them better, opening up more than I expected.

"So you've been in California for the past few years," Curt said. "Where were you before then?"

I swallowed slowly, debating if I should deflect the question. These people shared parts of their lives tonight, and I wanted to do the same—not because I was obligated, but because I wanted to share a piece of myself with them.

Especially Alex.

"I grew up in East Texas. My father was a career military man, but he retired right after my sister and I were born."

"Commendable," Marta murmured.

"It is," I continued. "I wanted to be just like him growing up. Seeing his medals and knowing what he had done for our country, I admired it. Signed up for the military the moment I turned eighteen."

Alex's head whipped toward me. I didn't share this story with many people, and maybe it was the coward's way out, telling her when she couldn't give her honest reactions, but I couldn't hold back a moment longer.

"I went to basic right after high school, and then I was deployed for a nine-month stint. I planned on making the army into my career, but I, uh." My voice shook a little, and I swallowed to try to cover it. "I was injured three months in. Honorably discharged." I sucked in a sharp breath, hating where this story led. "I had a rough time when I got home. I was angry for a long time and didn't handle it well. It took a lot to get me back on the right track. Now that I'm on the other side, I'm determined to keep going and find a new path." I turned slightly, taking in Alex's wonder-filled stare. "I like to think I'm starting to find my way."

THE REST of the night went by quickly; our stomachs filled to the brim by the time dessert came around. All four of us poked at Alex's apple pie, silently daring each other to take the first bite. Curt took one for the team, but the grimace on his face didn't inspire much confidence. Even Alex pushed hers away, not wanting to risk possible food poisoning.

As I walked her home, she was still shaking her head. "I

followed the damn thing word for word. It should not be this difficult."

"You know, my mom used to make pies every Sunday. I might be able to help you out and teach you some of the tricks I know."

She smiled at me. "I'd love that."

Tonight, something seemed to have shifted between us. The walls didn't seem as insurmountable. Alex's smiles were more effortless, much like when we hung out alone. As much as I wanted to pull her into my arms and show all the ways I wanted her, tonight was already a win in my book.

When she reached her porch, she turned back around, chewing on her lower lip. "I'd invite you in..."

"It's not a good idea," I finished for her. "I'm not in a rush, sweetheart. I'm just happy to spend some time with you tonight."

"And my hovering neighbors?" She nodded to the house behind me, where Curt and Marta were spying from the window. When I turned around, they dashed away, knowing we'd busted them spying.

I laughed, running my hand through my hair. "Yeah, even with them. I enjoyed getting to know them more."

"Me too," Alex sighed. "I liked getting to know you better, I mean. I was thinking...I don't know...if you'd like–"

"Alex..." I smirked. "Are you asking me out?"

She rolled her eyes. "Nope, forget it."

I reached out, taking her hand before she could turn around. I moved up the front steps, waiting until I stood directly in front of her to speak. "I'd love to go out with you."

Her cheeks flooded with color again, and she nodded. "When?"

"Tomorrow?"

She laughed. "A little eager there, Mr. Campbell?"

"For you? Always."

She tucked that damn lower lip between her lips again, hiding her full smile. That wasn't going to work for me. I reached out, loosening it with my thumb as she stared up at me, her eyes now lust-blown and heavy. Alex shook her head suddenly as if trying to focus on something other than my touch. "I can't tomorrow. I have to go with Adam to a crew dinner."

Shit, I was supposed to go to that too. I had forgotten entirely. Maybe I could find an excuse to bow out of it. There was no way I'd be able to sit there all night, watching Adam and Alex fawn over each other.

An idea popped into my head. "What about after?"

"After dinner?" She arched her brow. "Seems a little presumptuous."

"Nah, not like that. I know how these dinners always go: lots of egos and too little food. Trust me, you're going to want a real meal after."

"And where are we going?"

I lifted my hand, brushing the back of my fingers against her cheek. "Let me worry about that. You go have fun." I stared at her a little more intensely. "Not too much fun, though. I'll be here when you're done."

Alex lifted onto her toes, brushing a soft kiss on my cheek. "I like the sound of that."

TWENTY-SEVEN

Alex

The moment my house came into view, my body sagged in relief. It had been the longest evening ever. Nothing made you feel more like an outsider than sitting at a table surrounded by a film crew as they talked all about their project. Very few looked in my direction, much less spoke to me. I played my part, smiling when the cameras pointed toward Adam and me and staring at him adoringly when people asked about his process.

I felt like an accessory, something to be admired on Adam's arm, rather than a person of interest.

Which was fine. It was what I signed up for.

However, the pang in my chest told me it was not okay. I would never settle for a life like that. Every day, I learned more and more that Adam and I weren't compatible beyond friendship. His world revolved around his craft, which was an admirable quality. However, considering the amount of schmoozing and networking it required, acting felt like the most minimal part of his career. I would never have the disposition to stand by his side, smiling and nodding politely.

I shook the thought from my brain, hating that tonight made me look at Adam in a different light. He was still my friend, the guy who texted me constantly to ensure I was handling the media scrutiny—not that there had been much. After the initial shock wore off, people seemed to accept our relationship. Some trolls came out of the woodwork, but I was learning to tune them out.

There were still days when I wondered if my past would come back to haunt me. Every time a new post or article mentioned me, I anxiously watched my phone, wondering if it would finally be the day I feared.

So far, nothing had come out. No one from my past had shown up, and I knew I had Theo to thank for that. He was hyper-vigilant about Adam's publicity and worked hard to kill any story that might paint him negatively. I knew if he found something out, he would have told me.

Shaking my head, I killed the engine of my jeep, dragging my body through the front door, my stomach grumbling as soon as I walked inside. Cole was right. Apparently, when you're feeding a bunch of actors, meals are carefully crafted based on their dietary restrictions: no butter, no salt, no joy. It took three bites to turn my stomach.

I glanced at my phone, hoping Cole would be over soon. I texted him when I left the hotel, but there was no response yet.

However, when I shuffled into my living room, instead of the darkened quiet, I was greeted with the delicious smell of a home-cooked meal.

"Cole?"

"In here," a gruff, deep voice called out from my kitchen.

I couldn't help but smile when I entered the room. Cole was standing in the middle of my kitchen, wearing an apron I knew belonged to Curt as he smiled at me, making me forget about the "your opinion wasn't on the ingredient list" transcribed on the front of it.

"What are you doing here?" I finally asked, forcing my brain to stop sputtering. "I thought we were going to meet up later."

"Well..." Cole said, brushing the back of his head with his free hand. "I didn't want to wait, and I knew you'd be starving. Figured this would be better than scarfing down pop-tarts when you walked in the door."

Holy shit, this man was trying to kill me. It was a cruel joke —I hated Cole during our first meeting. I thought he was nothing more than a smug jerk destined to make me miserable. But in reality, he was one of the most thoughtful people I had ever met.

Unable to say anything else without making a fool of myself, I walked up to the stove, smelling the delectable aroma in a pan —a pan that was not mine. "Where did this come from?"

"I had to borrow a couple of things from next door. This kitchen needs some help, sweetheart."

"Not for me," I said, hopping up onto the kitchen island. I almost pulled out the box of pop-tarts to taunt him, but I stopped myself. "How did you get into my kitchen, anyway?"

"Calla," he chuckled. "I'm not the only one concerned about your eating habits. She said you have the palate of a five-year-old."

"Bullshit," I laughed. "My palate is not the problem. It's the cooking edible food part that gets me every time. There's only so much charr I can eat."

"No one ever taught you?"

"Nope."

As if able to sense that I wanted to drop the topic, Cole held out his hand. "Then c'mere." I arched my brow. "I'm not going to poison you, Alex. You wanna learn? I've heard I'm a hell of a teacher."

With a resigned sigh, I let him help me down and lead me to the stove. I stood in front of the bubbling...sauce? Yes, it smelled like some kind of sauce. I didn't dare to move, too scarred from too many failed kitchen experiments.

"Relax," Cole whispered, sidling in behind me to rest his hand on my hip. "It's just a simple chili. I didn't know what you liked, so I went with a family recipe." He took his other hand and placed the wooden spoon in mine. "All you have to do is stir." When my head whipped back to him, he lifted his hand, guiding my eyes back down to the pan. "You can't possibly screw it up."

"Easy for you to say," I muttered under my breath. However, as I let the spoon drift through the chili, I felt an odd sense of ease. At least, until I thought about Cole's earlier words. "So, is this your move?"

"What do you mean?"

I lifted my hand to him on the other side of my kitchen, slicing up a loaf of Italian bread. "This whole master chef thing. Is this your move to get into girl's pants?"

He laughed, and I couldn't help but smile. Cole didn't truly laugh often, but he should. The sound was much like his voice— rough and deep while also incredibly soothing. "No moves, sweetheart. I've never cooked with anyone else before."

Something about his tone made me take his words as fact. "Then who said you were a good teacher?"

As soon as the words escaped, a quiet tension crept between the two of us. For a moment, I thought Cole was going to change the subject, but after a long pause, he muttered, "My sister."

"You have a sister?"

"Yeah. Victoria."

The resigned tone made me turn around. Cole had a haunted look in his eyes as if talking about his sister physically pained him. Leaving the spoon in the pan, I took an apprehensive step toward him. Without overthinking, I brought my arms around his chest, placing my face against his back. He took a shuddered breath and put his hands on top of mine. "When I told you I went through a dark time, I wasn't kidding. It impacted my relationship with my parents, but I hurt Victoria the most."

"Have you talked to her?"

"Not as much as I should," he sighed.

"Do you ever think about visiting her?"

"Maybe..." he said; however, from his defeated tone, I could tell he wasn't really considering it. I was sure there was more to this story, but I wasn't going to push him, not when I was hiding parts of my past from him as well.

So, instead, I turned back to the stove, resuming stirring. "This smells amazing."

Cole came up behind me, and I let out a contented little sigh when his large hand retook my hip. "It's my grandmother's recipe. She spent years trying to get the spices right. When she moved to Texas from Mexico, she complained that nothing had enough flavor, especially with my grandfather. I swear, the man thought black pepper was too spicy. When she'd make him this, though, his whole damn face would light up. It's always been my favorite meal to make. When my sister and I were younger, we used to get whatever we could from my grandmother's garden, and she'd show us how to make it a meal." He laughed. "This time, I stuck with stuff from the market, so it still should be good."

As I continued stirring, his warmth crawled into my back. For a moment, I imagine what it would be like to sink into it, to let his hands linger on more than my hip.

Like he could sense the turn my thoughts had taken, Cole's hand tightened on my hip, making my lips part in excitement. "What's going through that head of yours, sweetheart?"

"Nothing," I lied, hoping he'd let it go.

Cole lowered his nose to the curve of my neck, dragging it

along the column before reaching my ear. "Are you imagining what would happen if I moved a little lower?"

I gulped, not trusting my words.

With a slow chuckle, he lightly kissed the sensitive spot behind my ear. "C'mon. We should eat."

What the ever-loving fuck?

I was about three point five seconds from stripping this man naked in my kitchen with one fleeting touch, and he wasn't affected at all? Looking down at my attire, I picked apart every single item of clothing. I knew Cole was attracted to me, but I couldn't help the negative thoughts taking over my mind. Maybe he wasn't as interested as I thought. Now that he had my attention, perhaps he'd figured out I wasn't worth the effort.

The thought stung more than I'd like.

When he realized I wasn't following him to the dining room, Cole stopped, taking in my sullen expression. "What's wrong?"

I pasted on my fakest smile, pretending I was back behind the desk at work, "Nothing. All good. We should eat before this amazing food goes cold."

When I tried to push past Cole, he stopped me, placing the plates on the counter. "Tell me the truth, Alex."

I shook my head, unable to meet his eyes. "Are you...are you attracted to me? It seemed like you were, and then—"

My words died as Cole lifted me onto the counter, pressing himself between my legs. Suddenly, I could feel all of him, every long, hard inch aching with the desire for more.

"Don't ever question how much I want you, Alex. I'm half a second away from ripping these pants off your gorgeous legs and eating you for dinner instead." He paused, forcing a breath past his lips. "But if I'm going to earn your trust, I gotta take things slower than that."

"Slow," I repeated as if it was the first time I'd heard the word.

"Yes, sweetheart, slow. Because if I ever get the chance to fuck you, I want to know it's because you choose me. That you trust me." He stepped back, adjusting the front of his pants. "Until then, it's a PG rating for us."

"Can we make it PG-13 at least?"

"No can do," Cole chuckled. "Because if I get a taste of that mouth again, I'm not sure I'll be able to stop."

TWENTY-EIGHT

The night flew by much quicker than I would have liked. The entire time, Alex transfixed me, and I was like a damn fool, hanging on her every word.

She opened up more than ever, telling me about her first few years here, about how she had found the town by accident and knew almost instantly that it was her new home. She even talked a little bit about her time in the city, but I could tell she was still holding back. She'd only give broad details, talking about her experiences in college and some of her work experience. There was a large piece of the puzzle that I was missing, but I wasn't about to push. She'd tell me in her own time—hopefully, once she started to trust me more,

The food went cold again, but neither of us tried to leave the table. I was pleasantly surprised; there'd barely been a beat of silence between us as the conversation flowed easily.

The way it only did with Alex.

When a clock chimed twelve times in the background, Alex hopped out of her chair, grabbing our plates before heading toward the kitchen, bumping me with her hip when I tried to take them back from her. "Not a chance, slick. You cooked.

There's no way I'm gonna let you clean. You're already spoiling me with all this food."

Gladly. The word echoes in my brain, making me grin with pride. I'd spoil her every day if she'd let me. Besides cooking, Alex was fiercely independent, and I knew she'd cut my balls off if I interfered too much.

And I was pretty attached to those.

As she placed the now-clean dishes on the rack, she turned and leaned against the sink. She stared at me, her eyes drifting down to my lips briefly before she inhaled slowly and shook her head. "We should probably call it a night."

I nodded, not because I wanted to, but because I wasn't about to push my luck. Calla put money down that Alex would attack me when she found me in the kitchen. Luckily, Marta and Curt had my back and thought she'd find it romantic.

Thank fuck they were right.

Alex glanced up at me, her wide, ocean-blue eyes filled with a weird apprehension. "Unless..." She turned, looking at the clock once again. "I know it's late. If you're not too tired, though, there's something I'd like to show you."

"Lead the way."

Alex stepped forward, lacing my fingers with hers as she pulled me outside. In the darkness beyond her porch, there are barely any other lights, no other sounds. It was peaceful, one that lulled my aching bones. Instead of heading toward the car, she turned right. I'd never noticed the winding pebble path beyond the driveway, and I followed her as we walked, getting a clear view of the lake beyond the trees.

Before we got too close, we reached a small clearing. There was a freshly mowed patch of grass, and in the middle, there was a stone fire pit with four wooden Adirondack chairs surrounding it. Alex shifted so she could meet my eyes. "What do you think?"

I lifted our linked hands, bringing her to my side as I softly kissed the side of her head. "It's perfect."

Alex moved away from me, and instantly, it was like the air dropped several degrees. She went over to a pile of wood, adding a few logs to the top of the fire pit before lighting a match. Small crackles of embers lit up instantly, clinging to the dried pieces of wood and other kindling she'd thrown in the pit.

When Alex was satisfied the fire would last, she motioned to one of the chairs. "Get comfortable."

I sat down in the closest chair, linking my fingers through one of her belt buckles. With a quick tug, I brought her into my lap, and she squirmed a little, her sweet, tight ass connecting with my groin. Holy hell. That shouldn't feel that good. As I tried to keep myself together, Alex rolled her eyes, smacking me in the chest. "This wasn't what I meant."

"You said to get comfortable. That's what I'm doing."

She snorted a curse under her breath but didn't get up, instead nuzzling further into my chest. We sat silently for a while, watching the fire crackle and burn. If it were under any other circumstances, I'd look for an exit after ten minutes. However, I'd never felt more content with Alex's soft sighs and her weight against my chest.

At least until my phone rang, breaking apart our peaceful bubble. When I pulled out my phone, Alex's eyes instinctively flashed to the screen. The moment she read the words "My Favorite Girl," Alex stiffened, leaping out of my lap and heading toward the house.

"Shit," I muttered, following quickly behind her. "Alex, it's not what you think."

"It's fine," she said, refusing to turn around. "I shouldn't have looked. It's none of my business."

I caught up to her the moment she reached the door. My hand encased hers on the doorknob, not letting it turn. I grabbed her hip, twisting her so she was facing me. From this closeness, it was impossible not to get swept away into her gaze. I hated the hurt in her eyes. I could practically see her frantically reassembling her walls, trying to place as much distance between us as possible.

As one tear fell from the corner of her eye, I lifted my thumb, brushing it away. "I promise, Alex, it's not what you think. That's what I call Dani. She's...."

"Your girlfriend back home," Alex answered for me.

"Fuck, no," I stammered. "Do you think I'd be here if I had someone back home?" I closed the distance between us, brushing my lips lightly over hers. "Alex, I want you. That's it."

Alex sighed, keeping her eyes closed as she nodded. When she looked back up, I could still see a question in her gaze. "You don't have to tell me."

My chest thundered, unsure if it was the right time to discuss that part of my past. I'd spent so many years hiding my faults, hoping that if I buried them deep enough, they couldn't affect me anymore. However, some demons didn't like to lay dormant; instead, they used your ignorance as a playground.

I exhaled slowly, taking a moment to savor this moment in case it was the last time I'd get to hold her. No matter how scared I was of her reaction, this was the right path.

If I wanted her trust, I also needed to give her mine.

"Dani's my sponsor."

Alex's brows shot up to the top of her forehead, but she didn't say anything, allowing me to continue. With one last, steadying breath, I released my truth.

"I'm an alcoholic." I exhale slowly. "It started after I got discharged from the VA hospital. I got home, and I, fuck, Alex, I was so damn lost. Everything I'd worked for had been ripped away in an instant. I was in pain, and they wouldn't give me any more pills. They could see how much I was struggling, trying to get me in to talk to someone instead. But I was too damn stubborn, a fucking fool." I sighed, stepping back to lean against the railing. "At first, the drinking was just to get some sleep at night, to escape the nightmares that kept me up. Then, that wasn't enough, and I'd start a little earlier. Almost a year after I got home, it was all day. I'd wake up and have a drink and not stop until I passed out for the night."

Saying the words out loud felt like dragging a knife through my chest. Even almost seven years later, I felt guilty for how I handled myself. I was weak and pathetic. I hated that Alex knew what a broken man I'd been.

Despite the shame, I forced myself to continue. "I've been sober for 19 months, and I'm doing well. Dani checks in daily to ensure I'm keeping on the right track, staying away from any stressors." When Alex said nothing, I stepped back, wishing I could see into her head more than ever. "Look, I get if this is a deal-breaker for you. My sobriety is the most important thing to me, so if you can't handle that, I'd rather know now."

It took everything in me to stay standing, to stay silent, as Alex studied me for several minutes. Part of me loved that she wasn't pacifying me with pretty words she didn't mean, but the other half desperately needed to know her thoughts.

After the longest silence of my goddamn life, she took a small step toward me, lifting herself on her toes to press her lips to mine. It started apprehensive, so I didn't dare move or ask for more. However, when she linked her arms around my neck, I lost the limited control I had left.

Lifting her into my arms, I pushed her against the door, pressing against her firmly, needing her to feel how much I wanted her. She let out a little moan when I shifted, my needy cock brushing against her core. I waited to see if it was too much, but instead, Alex surprised me, linking her legs around my waist and bringing me closer.

"Thank you," she whispered against my lips.

I pulled back enough to meet her eyes. "For what?"

"For trusting me."

"I do," I said quietly, taking in the desire swirling in her gaze. "More than you know."

"Then we should go inside."

TWENTY-NINE

Alex

Cole's lips were on mine before I even had a chance to think about my words. Not that I would have taken them back—I knew I wanted him, needed him even.

Hearing about his past made the last of my walls crumble. I was lost for this man, and for the first time in a long time, I didn't want to worry about the consequences or what the next day would bring. Despite what I claimed, I trusted Cole.

When I pushed the door open, he lifted me into his arms, holding me tightly against his chest. My legs wrapped around his waist, letting him bring me up the stairs before he stopped at the top of the landing. "You sure about this?"

I pressed a softer kiss on his lips. "Bedroom is on the left."

He set me back on the floor, waiting for me to let him into my room. As he walked inside after me, he slowly closed the door, taking in my space.

"Looking for a tour?" I asked, arching my brow.

All my humor died when he looked at me. Gone was the smirk I'd grown to love, replaced by a raw hunger in his eyes. I'd never felt so terrified and exhilarated at the same time. He came closer, brushing the hair away from my face, his hand resting on my neck as he brought his forehead to mine. "Are you sure you want this, Alex?"

I looked up at him, matching his intensity with my own. "I want you, Cole. Just you." I reached up on my toes, kissing the apple of his cheeks. He exhaled slowly, twisting his mouth so it could graze across my neck. The heat made my toes curl in my sneakers. "Only if you're sure you want this, too."

He pulled back, his grip on my neck tightening. "Don't ever question how much I want you, sweetheart. It's all I think about." He trailed his finger along my collarbone. "About the patch of freckles across your chest." His lips started to follow the same path. "Your curves." His hand grasped my ass. "What you're hiding underneath those fucking little dresses."

"Does that mean you like them?"

"Fuck yes," he growled, bunching the fabric of my shirt. "I've gotten off so many times imagining lifting the hem and finding you soaking wet for me."

"Nothing's stopping you now," I answered, my voice breathless, heavy with desire. I needed more. While these light caresses were driving me insane, my body ached for him to touch me for real, to release the tension that'd been brewing between us all night.

Without another word, he spun me around to face the bed, but he didn't move toward it. Instead, his hands drifted down, slowly and torturously unbuttoning my jeans. He slid them down a little, brushing the front of my underwear, just enough for a shock to rock my core.

"You want me to touch you, Alex?" Cole whispered into my ear.

"Yes. Now."

"So demanding," he chuckled, brushing his teeth against my lobe. "Sweetheart, I've spent weeks dreaming about having you at my mercy. I'm going to take my time and learn all the ways to drive you insane. And when you can't take it anymore, I'm going to make you scream my name so loud you'll never forget it."

Before I begged him to follow through, his fingers drifted down the front of my underwear while his other hand bracketed my throat—not enough to hurt, but enough to hold me steady against his chest. He dragged the lace of my panties to the side, letting out an appreciative moan when he found me already drenched for him. It started apprehensive, learning my body just as he promised, but when I let out a little gasp, he increased the pressure, turning my mind to mush.

It was too much and not enough at the same time. "Cole..." I whispered.

"You need more?"

I nodded, and his hand crept further down to press one of his long, thick fingers into my core. With his rough palm on my clit and his finger curling inside me, my knees buckled, but Cole wouldn't let me fall. Instead, he continued to work my body, eliciting all sorts of moans and gasps.

As I started to see stars, he suddenly extricated his fingers, leaving me confused and frustrated; I already missed having a part of him inside me.

When I turned to protest, he gripped my hips, tossing me back onto the mattress. I sunk into the pillows, watching as he reached for my jeans, pulling them the rest of the way down my legs. As he sat back on his haunches, I lifted my shirt over my head, tossing it and my bra off to the side.

I waited for Cole to make a move, but instead, he continued to sit there as his eyes traced every inch of my body, taking it in under the subtle moonlight. Typically, I would have tried to cover myself up, hating for anyone to see my flaws. Under his watchful gaze, though, I felt none of that shame or apprehension. I felt like a goddess, ready for him to worship me the rest of the night.

Cole leaned forward, brushing his lips over my stomach. "You're fucking perfect."

My heart somersaulted at his words, wishing I could see him too. "You have too many clothes on."

"And it's going to stay that way."

I sat up quickly, but Cole's large palm pushed me back against the pillows. His fingers started to tease my clit again, and then he shifted so his thumb was there, one of his fingers fucking me with steady, long strokes.

"Not because I don't want to, because fuck, I would give anything to be inside this tight pussy." He shifted down, his lips grazing the inside of my thighs. "But not tonight. Tonight is all about you."

"And if I want to fuck you?" I said, my words tight and hurried, every stroke of his fingers bringing me closer to bliss.

"Patience, sweetheart," Cole whispered against my core, pressing a kiss where his thumb brushed moments earlier. "We've got all the time in the world."

I wanted to argue more, but when his mouth descended onto my clit, I was done for. I lifted my hips, meeting every touch with a thrust of my own. Every press of his tongue and fingers made my mind go blank, wanting so desperately to come but not wanting this moment to end. If I could stay here with Cole forever, it still wouldn't be long enough.

As a second finger entered me, my hips bucked off the bed, unable to hold back for a second longer. "Cole, please..." I whined, not even recognizing my needy voice.

"You want to come, baby?"

I nodded frantically, staring down at the beautiful man grinning between my thighs. "Then let go, sweetheart."

With that, I fell over the edge, losing myself in the rush of pleasure as Cole continued working me through the waves of ecstasy, not letting go until I relaxed. As I collapsed back against the pillows, he continued to caress me with slow, feather-like touches of his fingers along my side. As I draped my arm over my eyes, trying to catch my breath, he lay next to me, his eyes never leaving my face.

Like a satiated kitten, I curled against him, leaning against his chest. Inhaling the scent of warm leather and cedar, I felt more relaxed than I had in years. Nothing could pull me from this bliss except for the need to make Cole feel as incredible as I did.

With a smirk, I popped up, sliding down to the zipper of his jeans.

Before I could pull it down, though, Cole placed his hand on top of mine. "You don't have to do that."

I slapped his hand away. "Don't you dare, Cole Campbell. I want to do this."

He smirked at me. "Only if you want to. I'm pretty fucking happy just to hold you all night."

"Oh, you're going to do that too," I chuckled. "Post-sex cuddles are a non-negotiable for me."

I pulled down his zipper, tugging down his jeans until they joined my discarded clothes on the floor. Holy crap. As he stripped off his boxers, my mouth started to water, needing to taste him. Usually, I didn't see the appeal of the male anatomy, but Cole's dick was long and thick, corded with deep-cut veins. He was beautiful.

He chuckled as he reached down to stroke himself. "Didn't take you for the cuddly kind, sweetheart."

"Hell, yes." I licked my lips. "I require hours of it. Now lie back and let me make you feel good."

"You already do."

His whispered words were almost too low for me to hear, but they made me smile as I reached down to taste the pre-cum pooling on the tip of his dick. He groaned at the light touch, and

I let my tongue explore first, tracing his shaft and the thick veins that made my knees weak. I couldn't wait to feel him inside me. I had the feeling he was right—I'd never forget being with Cole.

When he let out a frustrated growl, I chuckled, done teasing him. I brought my lips around his head, gliding up and down his length to get a feel for him. There was no way everything would fit inside my mouth, so I placed my hand at the base, twisting to mimic my mouth's movement.

"Fuck, yes," Cole moaned. "God, baby, you feel so damn good."

My thighs tightened at his words, loving how encouraging he was. After weeks of questioning where I stood with Cole, now, I had no doubts. His quiet words made me want to please him, want him to come as hard as I did. His hands reached down, playing with my hair, light enough to let me set the pace but enough to know he was there, barely able to hold back. I reached up with my free hand, pressing his hand into my hair harder, silently commanding him to take control.

That was all the invitation he needed. Cole started to lift his hips, now dictating the pace. It was all I could do to keep up with his movements, loving that I got to see him lose control. After a few more thrusts, I could feel him start to tighten, hissing my name. "Fuck, baby, I'm gonna come."

I released him, letting him paint my chest with his release. Looking down at where he marked me, something primal came over me—it was a badge of honor being claimed by this man. I almost wished I had a more permanent mark to show how lost I was to him.

"Shit," Cole chuckled. "I don't think I've ever come that hard."

"Same here," I sighed, resting on my heels. Cole sat up slowly, going into the hallway only to return a moment later, holding a warm washcloth. He reached out his hand, pulling me up. As he washed away the evidence of our tryst, his lips came to the top of my head.

"Are you okay?" he asked quietly. "I didn't hurt you, right?"

"No." I shook my head. "I wanted that. I liked seeing you lose control."

"Only for you, Alex." Cole leaned in and kissed me softly. "You made me forget my damn name."

"Was it enough to make you forget your no-sex rule?"

"Nope," Cole chuckled, pulling me back toward the bed. "Not tonight. Now, get your ass on that bed. I'm going to hold you for the rest of the night."

Sounded perfect to me.

THIRTY

Alex

"And then what did you do?"

Calla arched her brow. She'd been trying to get to the bottom of my night with Cole for almost an hour, but I'd refused to tell her much, preferring to keep the details to myself.

We'd barely slept at all, too wrapped up in each other even to consider closing our eyes. Still, I wasn't as exhausted as I expected. A weight had been lifted off my shoulders. Waking up with Cole in my bed felt right, like it was something I'd want to see every morning. I couldn't stop the smile on my face when I thought of him stretched out across my pillows, his black t-shirt clinging to his body.

"I call bullshit," Calla giggled. "You *totally* banged him. It's written all over your face."

"I did not!" I said, flopping onto her bed and hiding beneath one of the pillows. "And not because I didn't want to, because that man is very talented. Cole wanted to wait, give us something to look forward to later."

"Okay, yes," Calla said. "I can get on board with that logic. At least you know it'll be worth the wait. He looks like he knows what he's doing. Did he do that possessive thing where he grabbed you and pulled you into his arms?"

Yes, but I wasn't about to share that with Calla, even if she was my best friend. If it were a random guy, sure, I would have told her everything that happened last night, but talking about Cole in that much detail felt wrong, like an invasion of our shared intimacy. So, instead, I just smiled.

"Fine, don't tell me." She rolled her eyes. "So, is this official? Are you two an item? What does this mean with Adam?"

"Umm..." I trailed off, not sure how to answer her questions. They were similar to the ones Cole voiced last night, ones I also had no answers for. While I didn't regret taking that step, I hesitated when Cole asked me for more, and I had no idea what to do with the Adam situation. I felt guilty leaving him hanging, knowing I still had time left on my contract. Cole wanted to tell him, hating that he'd already hidden his feelings for me for so long.

I wasn't opposed to telling Adam—I wanted him to know almost as badly. However, the last few times we spoke, Adam was so fixated on the movie that he'd barely been sleeping. I didn't want to add to his stress, not if we could keep this between us a little bit longer.

I told Cole my reasons and ultimately left the decision in his hands. He was the one with decades of friendship; I was a temporary stop along the way.

Calla stared at me as if she kept up with the silent conversation in my head. She leaned against her dresser, crossing her arms around her chest. Instantly, my defenses rose; I was all too familiar with her interrogation stance.

"Okay, so riddle me this," Calla said. "You had an amazing night..."

"The best."

"So why are you still holding back?"

"What?" I snapped. "I'm not! I hooked up with him. You know that's rare for me."

"True," Calla said. "But you're also not pushing for more. I know you, Alex. You start looking for an out before there's even a reason. You're holding back. Why else would you commit to a fake relationship when the real thing is standing right in front of you?"

"Adam needs—"

"Adam Rice is a grown man, one who has lived in Hollywood for years without your help. You're using this arrangement as a way to keep Cole at arm's length. So tell me what's really holding you back."

I sighed, hating that she knew me that well. As much as I didn't want to admit it, I was using my "relationship" with Adam as an additional wall between Cole and me.

When I was with Cole, everything seemed so simple, like being together was the most obvious thing in the world. I couldn't help remembering his face when he told me about his drinking problem, his entire body poised for rejection. If anything, it made me fall for him a little bit more. His raw honesty made me want to open up about my past and tell him about the life I kept hidden away.

Despite my heart telling me it was time, a part of me couldn't release the words into the world. My shame was inked too deeply in my bones, and it was never going away. There were still too many unknowns and too many questions left lingering in my mind. There was no telling if Cole would accept my past. I accepted his past, but it wasn't a reciprocal thing. I couldn't ask him to forgive my sins just because I wanted him to move past his own. That wouldn't be fair. Still, a small part of me hoped that he would.

Calla laid down next to me, taking my hand in hers. "I can

see your thoughts spinning already. Is this really about Cole, or is it about—"

"Don't," I snapped, sitting up suddenly. "I know this isn't the same thing."

"There's a strong chance he's why you refuse to let Cole in." She lowered her voice to a whisper. "You should tell him."

I pondered her words momentarily before shaking my head. "No. He doesn't need to know. I don't want to let all that shit taint the good thing we have going. Besides, everything is already too complicated; it feels like this would set us up for failure even quicker."

"Who says it's going to fail?"

"What are the alternatives?" I sighed, hating that this was where my thoughts had gone. "He doesn't even live here, Calla. He literally lives on the other side of the country. Even if this goes well, there's an end date."

"People move all the time."

"It's not that simple," I answered quietly, brushing a tear from the corner of my eye. "He's got a whole life out there. Adam is out there. I can't ask him to give that up for me. Once the movie wraps, he'll be on a plane, and I'll be here, picking up the pieces. I don't know if I'm strong enough to do that again." I dryly chuckled. "Then again, I'm also not strong enough to stop seeing him. That sounds even worse than the pain of losing him."

Calla turned, shifting to stare at me. "First of all, don't you dare question my best friend's strength. She's the toughest person I know."

"C'mon, Calla, be serious."

"I am," she chuckled, whacking me with a pillow. "You came here with the clothes on your back. You started over from nothing, and now, you're a huge part of this community. You're about to buy a fucking lodge, for fuck's sake. Don't sit there and tell me a man has the power to break you. If he leaves, it will hurt, but at least you're opening yourself up again. After everything that happened, you let someone into your heart, even if it might end badly. That alone shows you have a strength that no one will ever be able to break."

Touched by her words, I pulled her into a tight hug. No matter what drove me here, I couldn't regret any of it because it led me to this moment with friends who are more like family and a home I truly loved.

"Just promise me one thing," Calla said.

"Why do I feel like I don't have a choice?"

"Because you don't," she grinned. "Cole did something really hard and told you the truth. All I'm asking is that you think about doing the same. Promise me that you'll consider telling him what happened in New York."

I sat up, chewing on my lower lip. "And what if it changes everything?"

"Then you know he isn't the one," she said. "For what it's worth, I have a good feeling that he's not going anywhere."

I mulled over her words, not able to say anything back. The optimist in me wanted nothing more than for Cole to accept all of me, but that girl had been burned too many times before. She'd begged too many people to believe her, only to have their doors shut in her face.

Just as I was about to admit as much to Calla, my phone rang in my pocket, and when I saw my bank's number on the screen, my heart instantly kicked up a thousand notches. They said they'd call once they had made their final decision. They couldn't be done yet, right? It hadn't even been a week. Shit, that probably meant they were saying no, rejecting me for some archaic reason.

Calla glanced at the screen and then back at me. "What the hell are you doing? Answer it!"

With one last breath, I hit the screen, trying to keep my voice calm and even. "Hello, Mr. Abbott. How are you today?"

My heart thumped so loudly in my chest that I almost couldn't make out his words. All I could do was nod along, trying to keep myself from screaming.

At the end of the call, I said, "Yes, thank you, Mr. Abbott. Yes, we will speak soon."

"And?" Calla asked slowly, closing her eyes as if to brace for disappointment.

"I...I got it," I said, still not believing the words. "The bank... they, uh...they approved my loan. I can make an offer for the Fox Creek property."

***

WHEN I WALKED into the resort, the air didn't feel as oppressive as it used to. Instead, there was a lightness surrounding me, as if my days behind this desk were numbered. I was replaying the conversation with the bank in my head, waiting for someone to pop out and say it was all an elaborate prank.

As soon as I finished freaking out with Calla, I hopped on the phone with Paula, hoping she could get the ball rolling on my offer. Once I had the finalized loan documents, we could send everything over to the owner's agent. Hopefully, we'll know if the seller accepted my offer in the next month or so.

I was still in complete disbelief that things were unfolding so quickly. Perhaps jumping into my own business was impulsive. Usually, I would have taken months, even years, to evaluate all my choices before deciding to move forward. Maybe it was because I had been stagnant for so long that I wasn't willing to wait on this. I knew the risks, knew the business. All I had to do was jump. Even if I failed, at least I could say I tried.

When I settled behind my desk, I started to tick off my checklist, but it was almost impossible to focus. Even more so when the smell of cedar and leather filled my senses. Without even looking up, I knew it was Cole, used to the weight his gaze left on my skin.

When I finally glanced up at him, I smiled wide, and he arched a brow. "Do I even want to know why you're looking at me like that?"

"Can't I just be happy to see you?"

"As much as I'd love for that to be true, especially after last night, you look like you're about to combust. What's going on?"

I bit my lower lip, trying to keep my voice low but failing. "I got the loan."

Cole's eyes widened, his bright, bold smile almost matching mine. "Holy shit, Alex. You did it." He reached out, taking my hand in his. "I'm so fucking proud of you."

The simple sentiment brought fresh tears to my eyes. How long had it been since someone said that to me and truly meant it? And hearing it from Cole meant even more. I dropped my head, trying to stealthily wipe away the tears collecting in the corner of my eyes. "I know there's still a lot that could go wrong, so I'm trying not to get too ahead of myself."

"Hey," Cole squeezed my hand a little tighter, "you've worked your ass off for this. It's going to work out. I know it is." With one last lingering squeeze, he let go of my hand. "I'm taking you away to celebrate as soon as your shift is done."

Now, my excitement was all due to him. As I was about to cross all my lines and pour my heart out to him, one of the few people with the power to sour my mood came into the lobby.

He scanned the room, narrowing his eyes when he spotted me, and I dropped Cole's hand, moving a few steps away with an apologetic smile. He furrowed his brow, not spotting Theo until he approached the desk.

True to his obnoxious from, Theo even rang the ornamental bell sitting next to my name, ignoring Cole at my side. "Hello, Alex."

"Theo," I said through a false smile. "How can I help you today?"

After our time together during Adam Rice boot camp, I'd be happy never to see this man again. Our core beliefs seemed to clash on every level. He looked at people like transactions and gauged every relationship on its ability to create positive publicity. For example, when I questioned what Adam wanted, Theo snapped at me, telling me that our goal was to promote his brand, not his desires.

"Did you get our itinerary?" Theo asked.

My brow lifted in question. "What are you talking about?"

"For New York," he said slowly, groaning when I still showed no signs of recognition. "I swear, it's like you want me to get more gray hair." He pushed a few things on his phone's screen, and then my phone chirped in my pocket. "Adam has two events coming up this weekend. You will be accompanying him. We're heading into the city for three nights. Be ready to leave by seven."

THIRTY-ONE

"Adam Rice! Adam! Over here!"

The chorus of photographers played out like a symphony, voices shouting over each other until they became one. The sound alone would have been overwhelming. Add in the constant flashes of the camera, and my skin was on fire. Even after a day of preparations, I felt the urgent need to run and hide.

Adam's arm settled on my hips, turning me to face the crowds. I gulped, trying to paste on the fake smile. I'd practiced for hours in the mirror, between Theo unleashing a team of stylists and make-up artists on me. Not to say they didn't do a fantastic job—on the outside, I felt more beautiful than ever.

Internally, though, I was a mess.

I resisted the urge to rub my palms along the green silk of my gown. Even with the gorgeous outfit, I felt like a fraud. It was as if, at any moment, someone was going to realize I didn't belong among this glitz and glamor and ask me to leave. The city was different than I remembered—louder, harsher. My brain was on the brink of spiraling out of control. The fact that this city was once my home seemed like a far-off memory, almost as if it was someone else's life.

I knew I'd changed when I moved away from Manhattan. Without the intense need to succeed pushing me forward, I had to find a new normal. This new version of me didn't belong here.

For the millionth time today, thoughts of Cole flooded my mind. We'd exchanged a few texts since I arrived in the city, but we hadn't gotten the chance to talk about what happened. I tried to hold onto how he made me feel two nights ago, the calm confidence he always exuded. I wished he was here with me right now, even though it would be awkward and ridiculous.

Too wrapped up in my head, I didn't notice when Theo ushered us inside. When we entered the lobby, my jaw fell open. Even when I lived in Manhattan, I could never afford to stay here.

Three years later, I was walking in on the arm of one of Hollywood's biggest stars.

Adam squeezed my hand as we walked across the room, following the other patrons into the main ballroom. I gasped when we stepped inside: the room was elegant, from the crystal-clad chandeliers to the exquisitely designed centerpieces on each table. The tables are decked in a thick, satin fabric, all in the same pale gold to match the accessories on the walls.

Adam leaned down, whispering to my ear. "Overwhelming, isn't it?"

I shifted to face him. "For you?"

"Of course," he nodded. "The first time I came to one of these things, I almost threw up. I'm completely out of my element right now."

"Then why do it?" I asked, taking a glass of champagne when the waiter passed us.

"It's a part of the job," Adam sighed. "If I want to give back to the community, then I need money at my disposal. While I'm willing to give as much as it takes, I can't do it alone. I need people like this to trust me, to respect me, so I have to play the part."

I held his hand a little tighter. "I think that's admirable, and clearly, a lot of money is being raised tonight for..." Shit. I was so distracted on the plane that I'd zoned out when Adam told me about the charity.

"New York Metro Hospital's Pediatric Cardio ward," Adam answered. "Most of the funds raised tonight will be used to upgrade their essential equipment." He ushered me toward a mock-up at the edge of the ballroom. "With these improvements, the hospital will have the cutting-edge technology they need to treat patients more effectively." He pointed to the center of the wing. "We're also adding in some adaptive play equipment to give the patients a chance to feel like children."

"That's amazing," I said. "But couldn't the foundation take the money from this party and put it toward the wing?" I shrugged. "Seems kind of frivolous to me."

"Oh, it is," Adam chuckled. "This is just how the game is played."

My face furrowed, still trying to understand when someone called Adam away. He kissed me softly on the side of my head before joining another group. Left alone, I wandered toward the bar, lifting my empty glass to the bartender at the other side. I might need to break my two-drink rule to get through this evening.

As the bartender poured me another glass, my phone chirped in my clutch, and I smiled when I saw a message from Cole waiting.

COLE

Ready to run for the hills yet?

ME

You have no idea. How'd you get out of these things?

COLE

Told a couple of execs what I thought about their movies. You should have seen Theo's face.

ME

Oh, you rebel…

COLE

If you don't want criticism, don't make a movie about biomec crocodiles battling the Loch Ness monster

I smiled as I tucked my phone away. Turning away from the bar, I slowly strolled through the crowd, taking in the photographs of past patients. I paused at each one, taking the time to read all their stories. As much as I hated the ostentatiousness of these events, I couldn't deny how much good they brought into the world. Dealing with the upper echelons of Manhattan seemed like a small price to pay if it meant more children got the medical care they needed.

When I reached the end of the display, I walked back toward the center of the room, searching for Adam. I found him on the other side of the dance floor, locked in a conversation with the other hosts for the evening. He turned slightly, giving me a wave to join them.

Before I could move, my skin started to prickle as the weight of someone's heavy stare trailed along my bare back, tracking every inch of my spine. A warning tone filled my mind, urging me not to turn around, but my curiosity won out.

I barely felt the champagne glass slip out of my hand. The liquid spilled along the front of my gown, and a waiter rushed over to my side. But I barely noticed. All I could see were the pair of steely blue eyes locked onto mine, making every fiber of my body tremble with nerves.

The space between us was silent, the packed ballroom empty to me now. There was nothing I wanted to do more than turn and run, go back home, and never come back to the city again.

However, as I locked eyes with the one person I never wanted to see again, I knew it wouldn't matter.

Nate Gibson, the man I once thought I would marry, was here, in the room with me. I escaped him once, and based on the look on his face, I wasn't about to again.

"NO, NO, NO," I hissed, scrubbing my dress with a paper towel. After my stare-down with Nate, someone pulled him into a conversation, giving me a chance to dash into the bathroom. I'd be hiding out in here for almost twenty minutes, fixated on the spot on the edge of the gown. These stains were never going to come out.

God, do designers take payment plans?

I was probably just making it worse. A couple of other women entered the bathroom, so I tucked into a stall, not ready to face another human being.

Especially not Nate Gibson.

What was he even doing here?

It was an easy question to answer. Nate hated charity, but he loved attention. His family name got him an invite to almost every event in the city—the Gibsons owned half the buildings on the Upper East Side, for fuck's sake.

I should have seen this coming. This was precisely the type of event he'd attend, getting to look like the good guy without getting his hands dirty.

After the other women left, I forced myself out of the stall, staring at myself in the mirror, running my finger along my ruined make-up. Gone was the elegant woman on the red carpet earlier. All I could see was an echo of the past, staring at an entirely different mirror, trying to cover up the bruises that marred my body, trying to force a smile without opening the cut on my lip. I showed no flaws or weaknesses in public, while in private, my entire world was falling to ashes around me.

My hands clenched the marble surface, trying to push the memories away, to move past the hurt, the fear, the anger, all the things he branded on my skin, not caring what scars he left behind. In Nate's mind, I'd belonged to him, so he had the right to do with me what he pleased. I could still feel his hands all over me, demanding pieces I wasn't willing to share. I remembered the fear and nausea that consumed me when I woke in his bed, naked and alone, with zero memories of the previous hours.

My stomach lurched, and I ran to the toilet, emptying its limited contents into the porcelain bowl. My hands shook as I pulled away, unsure how to face Nate—if I could face him again. I'd deluded myself into believing I would never see him again.

Maybe I'd get lucky, and Nate wouldn't even talk to me.

I chuckled to myself. Of course, he would; Nate got off on exerting power over others. If he knew I was in here, shaking at the thought of him, he'd probably smile.

As I washed my mouth out, my phone chimed on the counter. The latest message joined dozens of unanswered ones from Cole, Adam, and even Theo. I unlocked the screen, knowing I had to face them eventually and tell them what happened.

I read the newest one from Cole first.

COLE

Adam said you're upset. Do you need me?

My heart sang out for Cole, in disbelief that a few simple words could make me feel instantly lighter. He didn't even ask what was wrong; I doubted it would matter to him. If I was upset, no matter how big or small the issue, I knew he'd be there the moment I asked.

Despite wanting his calm confidence at my back, I had to face Nate alone. He'd been the demon haunting my memories for far too long, and I was done giving him the power to break me. It wasn't like before. I wasn't alone with him. I wasn't trapped under his spell. Besides, he only unleashed his monster behind closed doors, where the rest of the world couldn't see.

ME

I'm okay. Thanks for checking on me.

I turned off my phone and fixed my make-up as much as possible. With one last, steadying breath, I exited the bathroom and tried to stealthily make it back into the ballroom without running into Nate. Luckily, no one noticed me, which was a good sign. If I'd made a scene, the whispers and comments would have started when I reappeared.

Adam was at my side almost instantly. "What happened? Are you all right?" he asked quietly. "You looked like you were about to pass out."

"I'm fine," I said, smiling back at him tightly. Luckily for me, he couldn't tell my placating smile from my real one. "I forgot to eat before coming here and felt light-headed."

He stared at me for a long moment as if he didn't quite believe my words. Instead of pressing the question, he leaned down, kissing the side of my temple. "C'mon, let's have a seat. I think dinner is about to be served."

Adam led me across the room, but as I started to take my seat, I glanced across the table, freezing when I saw who was smirking on the other side.

"Alexandria," Nate called out, standing to greet us. "It's a pleasure to see you again."

THIRTY-TWO

Alex

The air instantly left the room as Nate stepped toward me. With Adam's hand on my back and hundreds of witnesses, rationally, I knew I was safe—however, nothing about being in the same room as Nate felt safe.

When he took my hand in his, I tried to resist trembling as he lifted it to his lips. "You look wonderful tonight."

Nate's words made my skin crawl. My memories were tainted with moments just like this one, especially when we first met. He'd whisper compliments in my ear, making me preen with his attention. Being around him, being with him, was intoxicating. After a lifetime of never feeling like enough, one of the most powerful men in the world wanted me. Chose me.

I'd love to say that I saw more in him than his status, but at twenty-one years old, his name and wealth impressed me. And I was proud that someone so special saw something in me.

Looking at the devilish gleam in his eyes, I felt only nausea.

"I wasn't aware you two knew each other," Adam chuckled, holding me a little tighter. If he sensed any tension, he didn't show it. "This works out better than I thought." Adam looked down at me. "While you were occupied, Mr. Gibson and I started talking. He wanted to know if there were more ways he could support the hospital. I thought it would be great for him to join us for the evening."

Fan-fucking-tastic. Forget two drinks—I needed an entire bottle of champagne.

Instead of returning to the other side of the table, Nate took the empty seat on my other side. Barely a few inches separated us; I could stab him with my fork if he got any ideas. Not that it would have worked; Nate was watching me too closely to try anything discreetly.

I tried to resist shivering under his stare. Adam ushered me into my seat before taking his own on my other side; I hoped Adam's presence would be enough to dissuade Nate, but I should have known better. I could feel his gaze sliding down, skimming my curves before looking back up to my face. "This new look suits you, Alexandria. I almost didn't recognize you at first."

Adam's hand found mine under the table, gripping it a little tighter. The silent show of support made breathing a little easier. With another sip of his champagne, Adam leaned forward on his free elbow, leveling Nate with a stern expression. "You never said how you knew my girlfriend."

"Girlfriend?" Nate asked, his jaw ticking in annoyance. "I thought I saw an article online about you two dating. I didn't realize it was serious. Good for you, Adam."

My blood ran cold at his words. At least I had my answer: that was why he was here. I couldn't believe how foolish I'd been. I thought three years was enough time for him to forget about me. He'd moved on pretty quickly, after all.

One reason Nate was so successful in business was that he never let things go. If he tried to absorb a company and they turned him down, he'd go out of their way to make their lives harder. Slowed shipments and canceled contracts;

anything he could do, legal or otherwise, to get them to reconsider.

So what made me think he'd be so quick to let me move on with my life?

Once upon a time, he'd set online alerts for business competitors and past lovers. He always said it was in case he needed to issue a public statement or avoid a scandal. Now, I knew the truth: the controlling bastard liked to keep people under his thumb, even when they tried to escape.

Nate took a sip of his bourbon and then tipped his glass in our direction. "As for us, Alexandria and I used to work together."

My teeth mashed at the simplistic version of our history. Not that I would want to share our dirty laundry with the rest of the world, but it still stung a little. We were together for over a year, and now, it's as if we passed each other in the hall on the way to our offices.

I smiled up at Adam, hoping to soothe some annoyance radiating off him. "I interned at his company's headquarters during my last year of college. When I graduated, Mr. Gibson graciously offered me a full-time position. I worked there for almost a year before I decided to move on."

A thud on the opposite side of the table pulled my attention from Adam. The ice in Nate's glass continued to clink from how hard he had hit it on the table as he gave the other guest a placating smile before turning back to me. "Alexandria made quite an impression during her tenure." He sighed as if speaking to a petulant child. "And you know better, Alexandria. I'll always be Nate to you."

This asshole. He was goading me. I knew he was. He was trying to poke and prod me until I made a scene and ruined the event. I'd seen it unfold too often to let it happen to me.

Yes, his presence had jarred me, but I would not let him

break me. Not ever again. I wasn't the same girl who bowed down to his every word, desperate to please him, the girl who would do anything to hold onto his love for a little bit longer.

The new version of me had teeth, and I wasn't afraid to use them.

"So Nate...how's your wife?"

Adam arched a brow at me, a slow, proud smile on his face. "Oh, you're married, Nate? I didn't realize. Will she be joining us for dinner?"

"No." His jaw tightened imperceptibly. "Sandra's well, Alexandria. Thank you for asking. She's currently vacationing in Aspen. I'll be joining her at the end of the week."

"How lovely for you," I said, giving him my most saccharine smile.

"How long have you been married?" Adam asked.

"Almost two years."

"Closer to three now, right, Nate?" I asked, cocking my brow. "I thought I heard you got married four months after I left the company."

Nate took another long sip and then slowly nodded his head. "Yes, that's right. Good memory, Alexandria."

I slowly sipped my drink, feeling better by the moment. I didn't know if it was having Adam at my side or the way Nate tensed at my questions, but I felt invincible.

Adam's head volleyed between the two of us, trying to decipher the subtext in our conversation. I squeezed his hand, a silent promise to fill him in later. Well, the Cliff Notes version. There was no reason to expose him to Nate's darker side.

After the first course was served, the conversation shifted to safer territory. The rest of the group excitedly discussed the hospital's improvements, including everything the children had requested. By the time the servers cleared our plates, I had started to relax, even laughing along with the conversation.

When an attendant came up behind us, whispering that it was time for Adam to give his speech, my blood ran cold. He stood, pressing a chaste kiss to my cheek before he walked up to the podium.

The lights dimmed, save for a spotlight pointing to the stage, illuminating one of the board members from the charity. She highlighted Adam's contributions to the hospital, emphasizing how much time he put in at the ward itself. The accompanying pictures of him in his superhero costume made the entire crowd melt with adoration.

The entire introduction made me beam with pride. Adam was such a good man, and not everyone got to see this side of him. I might not love the situation we found ourselves in, but I would never regret it. I was lucky to call Adam my friend.

"I see you've moved on," Nate whispered in my ear as the crowd began to clap for Adam.

I didn't give him the satisfaction of answering. Instead, I kept my eyes focused on Adam. Watching his speech, I was captivated by the emotion and sentiment in his words. He spoke eloquently about the hospital's hard work but reminded the crowd about how much was left to do. He ended his speech by calling out the names of some of the children he'd gotten to know during his visits and spoke about their experiences during their stays. By the time he wrapped up his speech, almost everyone in the room had tears in their eyes.

Save for the fuming man at my side.

"Don't ignore me, Alex," Nate hissed, his words shaky with rage and alcohol. When I continued to focus on Adam, he reached down and grabbed my thigh. "What the hell are you doing here? With him, of all people."

I tried shoving his hand off my leg, but that spurned him even further. He reached under the split I had loved so much earlier and gripped my bare skin. "I already told you," I whispered. "He's my boyfriend. Now, get your hands off me before I scream."

"Go ahead, princess," he said. "Let everyone here know that you're another classless gold-digger. I should have known you'd pull some stunt like this."

My head snapped to his, eyes narrowing in a dangerous glare. "What stunt?"

"Showing up here with another man," Nate hissed, his nails now leaving marks on my skin. "If you wanted my attention so badly, all you had to do was ask."

The room broke out in applause, and I hated Nate a little bit more for distracting me during Adam's moment. When he looked away, I took his thumb and wrenched it as far back as possible.

"Don't flatter yourself, asshole," I said through gritted teeth. "You are the last person I ever wanted to see again." I leaned a little closer, ensuring he could feel the venom lacing each of my words. "And if you ever touch me again, I will ruin you."

I expected to see anger radiating off him. Instead, Nate just smirked.

"Not if I ruin you first."

THIRTY-THREE

This drive was taking too fucking long.

I stared out the cab window, willing my leg to stop shaking. The closer I got to the hotel, the more my nerves were shot. The driver glanced at me through the rearview mirror, a look of concern crossing his face. I probably looked insane, but I didn't care.

I woke up this morning with a bad feeling. I thought it was residual guilt because I hadn't told Adam about what happened between Alex and me, but it lasted all day. No matter what I tried, I couldn't shake the lingering dread.

All it took was one text from Adam, and I was on the next train out of Saint Stephen's Lake. Alex had hidden herself in the bathroom at his event, and he wasn't getting an answer from her. That alone was enough to set off alarm bells in my mind. Once Alex turned off her phone and ignored calls from Calla and me, I knew it was more than nerves.

It took seven hours to get to New York—seven hours of imagining every worst-case scenario, wondering what the hell had made her go silent. Adam sent updates throughout the night, trying to calm me down. He was rattled, too. The moment his speech was over, Alex asked to leave the event. When she returned to the hotel, she locked herself in her room, barely sparing two words to say goodnight.

When Adam first called, I considered staying behind, knowing that between him and the security staff, they'd have any issues handled. I'd be overstepping by interfering with her weekend with Adam, but if Alex was hurting, I didn't give a single fuck what lines I had to cross.

I needed to know for myself that she was okay.

When the cab driver reached the hotel, I tapped my card and hopped out as quickly as possible. Luckily, I only had my old pack, which had random clothes shoved inside. Pacing in front of the elevator bay, I texted Adam to let him know I was there.

He texted back their room number almost immediately, and for a moment, my jealous side reared its ugly head, hating that they shared the same space. It was my fault; I should have had the guts to say something to Adam when I first caught feelings for Alex. Well, the goddamn cat was out of the bag now, and I didn't care who knew. I wanted to tell the world that Alex was mine, and I was hers. One night together, and my mind was fucked, already addicted to every inch of her. We needed to talk to figure out precisely what was happening between us but now was not the time.

Right now, I needed to see my girl with my own two eyes.

When the doors opened, I trudged down the hall, grateful Adam was waiting by the suite. I gave him a stiff nod, waiting for him to question me, but all he did was nod his head. "She's in the room on the left."

I dropped my pack on the side of the entryway and walked over to her room, tapping my knuckles on the doors, and waited to hear her voice on the other side. Nothing came. "Alex?" I called, hoping that maybe she'd fallen asleep.

Dread filled my stomach when her quiet voice came from the room. "Cole?"

She opened the door, and it took everything in me not to explode. Her blue eyes were puffy and red-rimmed, fresh tears spilling down her cheeks. She looked so small, so broken. Without another thought, I pulled her into my arms, lifting her so I could cradle her against my chest. Not wanting to embarrass her before Adam, I shut the door, bringing Alex over to the bed.

When I sat down, I pulled back a little, brushing back some of the hair from her face. Alex stared back at me, confused. "What...what are you doing here?"

I pressed a kiss to her forehead. "You were hurting, sweetheart. Where else would I be?"

"But Adam–"

"I'll talk to him," I quietly said, stroking my fingers through her ponytail. We sat there for a few minutes, Alex crying against my chest while I caught my breath, grateful to have her safe and in my arms.

My hands tightened around her, desperate to know what caused her to fall apart, but I refused to say anything until she did. All I knew was that Calla almost passed out when I said something had happened in the city. Her reaction alone was enough to get my head spiraling, hating that I didn't know enough about Alex's past to protect her.

"I'm sorry I turned off my phone." Alex sniffled. "I was already overwhelmed and just wanted to clear my mind. I didn't mean to make you worry."

"Hey," I said, brushing my fingers along her jaw so she'd look up at me. "You have nothing to apologize for. I don't care that you turned your phone off. I care that you're upset. Adam texted, and I..." I cleared my throat. "Fuck, Alex, my head went to the worst places. I know I shouldn't have come, but I needed to see you for myself."

"I'm glad you did," Alex said. "I wanted you here."

"You need me, I'm there."

Alex nudged out of my grip, leaning down to nestle under the covers. She took a shaky breath, her gaze focused on toying with a loose thread. "I saw my ex tonight."

I had to force myself to stay still. I already hated where this story was going. "What happened?"

Alex pushed another long breath through her lips. "I was stupid. I thought he'd moved on, that I could get away with fighting back." She laughed dryly. "That never ends well, not with him."

"Did he hurt you?"

Alex didn't answer for several minutes, and then her tears started again, flowing heavier than they had before. Eventually, she nodded.

I was going to kill this man. I didn't even have his name yet, and he was a dead man. Prison would be heaven compared to what was going to happen when I got my hands on him.

She looked up at me, her watery gaze breaking me even more. I had no question that I would do anything to ensure she never had to face this again. "Is it okay if we talk more tomorrow?" Her voice was hoarse from her sobs. "I'll tell you everything, just not tonight. I can't do it tonight."

"Whatever you need," I said, kissing her forehead. "I'm going to go make you some tea and then crash on the couch."

"No," Alex said, reaching out to take my hand. "Stay with me. Please?"

I couldn't say no to this girl on a good day. How did she think I'd say no to her now? I nodded, pressing another kiss to her cheek. "Get some rest. I'll be right back."

I waited until her eyes drifted closed to stand, creeping into the kitchen. I said the tea was for her, but in reality, I needed to get out of the room before I exploded. Anger made my sight turn red—anger at the man who hurt Alex, anger at the event staff for letting that asshole into the hotel, and even anger at Adam for leaving her alone.

I paced in the kitchen, unsure how to get rid of the ache in my chest. In the past, I would have buried it with booze, not wanting to deal with messy emotions, but no part of me wanted to go back down that path. The temptation was always there, but at times like this, it was almost overwhelming. I needed to be strong for Alex, for myself. I worked too hard to blow my sobriety when she needed me.

I stopped pacing when the door on the other side of the living room opened, Adam emerging from the other side. He crossed his arms around his chest and leaned against the opened door.

"I think we need to talk."

I stared at my best friend, unsure if this was the right time to have this conversation. I was too keyed up, too on edge. One wrong word and I had no clue how I'd react.

But this was Adam—the man who knew all sides of me. If I were going to trust anyone in the world, Alex would be it, and he'd be a very close second.

He motioned to one of the couches, and I sat in the armchair in the corner. Before joining him, I peeked in on Alex, who was softly sleeping in her bed. Seeing her more relaxed eased some of the stress from my shoulders, and I finally felt like I could breathe again.

I sat on the edge of the couch, resting my elbows on my knees. The minutes ticked by as Adam and I sat silently, unsure how to start the conversation I'd been dreading.

"I don't know how to tell you this..." I chuckled dryly, running my hand over my face. "And before I start, I need you to know that I'm aware I messed up. We should have had this conversation weeks ago. Be pissed, man. Yell at me, scream.

Hell, hit me if that's gonna make you feel better. Just don't take it out on Alex."

"You care about her," Adam said. The way he stared at me put me on edge.

"Yeah, I do," I said. "No, it's more than that: I'm falling for Alex, Adam. It took me a long time to get here, and now that I am, I'm not backing down. I'm pretty sure Alex is it for me."

I braced myself, waiting for a punch, a slew of curses, something. Just because their relationship wasn't real didn't mean I didn't break some friendship code by pursuing Alex behind Adam's back.

What happened next, I wasn't prepared for.

Adam laughed.

He fucking laughed.

"Shit..." he said. "I never thought you'd admit it. I thought you'd own up to it when you found out we weren't really dating. What took you so long?"

"You knew?" I snapped.

"Dude," Adam said. "Anyone with eyes can see that you two are crazy about each other. Why do you think I called you tonight?"

I hadn't given it a thought. I was so focused on Alex that asking why Adam was calling me about her never occurred to me. I ran my hand over my mouth. "I can't believe you knew."

"Well, I can't believe you didn't tell me," Adam said. "Sounds like things are serious."

"Feels that way," I answered honestly. "I don't know what the hell she sees in me, but she's everything to me, man."

Adam shifted in his chair, leaning in a little closer. "What does that mean when the movie wraps? Have you decided what you're going to do next?"

I had no fucking idea. I wasn't joking: I had no intention of letting Alex go. But Adam also needed me, and I didn't know how to exist in both of their worlds. It didn't help that Alex and I hadn't gotten a chance to talk about our future yet. I was fumbling in the dark, trying to read her mind.

"I need to talk to Alex," I sighed, rubbing my tired eyes. "Then we'll see what happens." I sat up straighter. "Now tell me everything. Don't spare a single detail."

Alex

The next morning, both my head and leg ached—side effects of dealing with my bastard ex.

My eyes fluttered open, warm sunlight streaming into the sleek, white hotel room. My arm snaked out across the comforter, seeking Cole's warmth. The sun had started to rise when he finally came to bed. I'd been up, a nightmare making it hard to fall back to sleep. As soon as his strong arm tugged me close, I was out.

I turned toward the door, straining to hear voices on the other side. Cole's voice was there...and so was Adam's. I cringed, hiding my head under the covers. How in the hell were we going to explain this one? Cole, barging into our room in the middle of the night, had to make Adam question our situation. Realistically, I knew this could mean a lot of trouble for me, but I couldn't bring myself to care. I needed Cole, and he was there. It was that simple, and it made me fall a little bit in love with him.

Standing from the bed, I stretched out my tense muscles. If only yesterday had been a dream, something I could have forgotten when I woke. After years of deleting Nate from my mind, he'd taken forty minutes to break me down again.

The smells from the kitchen were calling my name, but I wasn't ready to face the guys just yet. My head was too lost, too confused to try to converse normally. Even though I promised Cole I'd tell him what happened, I wasn't ready to talk about it.

I wasn't ready for him to see me differently.

There was no way I could pretend nothing happened. Adam bore witness to everything, and he was slowly connecting the pieces. He tried asking me about it on the ride home, but I insisted that I wasn't feeling well and that the champagne was getting to my head. He could see through my lies, no doubt. I was hanging on to my sanity by a thin thread. Even now, I was one memory away from crumbling into a pile of frayed nerves and past heartbreak.

Eventually, I forced myself up, trotting over to the bathroom to take in my reflection. Too worn to do anything other than pass out, I slept in my make-up, and now, I looked as haggard as I felt on the inside. Dark circles surrounded my eyes, and streaks of concealer caked in random spots on my cheeks.

None of that compared to the bruise marring my thigh, though. Lifting my sleep shorts, I let out a little gasp, taking in the dark purple blotches. Nate had grabbed me harder than I realized. It wasn't the first time he'd left marks on my skin, but it was the first time he'd acted so rashly in public.

Looking at the mark made my body tense, and I remembered all the bruises and scars I'd covered up when we were together. On one of our first actual dates, Nate took me to get my makeup professionally done, buying me all the high-end products I could never have afforded on my own. Who knew that a couple of months later, I'd be using them to cover a black eye? My crime? I spent too long talking to a male co-worker.

The next day, a hundred pink roses appeared at my door,

with a note begging me to forgive him. Foolishly, I thought it was a one-time thing. I convinced myself that his jealousy was a sign of his love, of how much he truly wanted to be with me. It was an endless cycle—his outbursts, then the subsequent groveling for forgiveness. Of walking on eggshells, waiting for the moment his anger lashed out, and then hating myself for loving his undivided attention afterward.

His fits became more frequent, and the loving periods got shorter and shorter. There were plenty of nights he'd wander into the apartment, reeking of alcohol and other women. I kept my mouth shut, hating that so much of my self-worth was tied to his opinion of me. Maybe, if I acted perfectly, he'd stop taking his anger out on me and stop seeing other women.

Maybe he'd realize I was enough.

The sad thing was, I wasn't even surprised that he got married so quickly after I left. His now-wife was a friend of his family, a woman who was always conveniently around when he needed a plus one and couldn't risk taking me. "What would the media think if I showed up with my former intern on my arm?" He'd chuckle, dismissing me like a petulant child.

I shuddered, thinking back on the night I finally had enough. After Nate left the apartment for a "work meeting," I forced myself to wait twenty minutes before grabbing my stashed suitcases. Taking only what I could carry, I threw everything in the back of my Jeep, praying that his date would keep him occupied.

I don't think I breathed for the first three months I was in Saint Stephen's Lake. I constantly looked over my shoulder, waiting for his face to pop out of the darkness. It wasn't until his wedding announcement that I finally believed I was free.

Slowly, I started to make friends and find a new family, people who I knew would look out for me no matter what—

friends like Calla and Javi, Marta and Curt. I found a home, one I wouldn't give up for anything.

A short knock on the door pulled me from my thoughts. "Be right there," I called out, pulling a longer pair of pants from my suitcase. I wasn't ready for anyone to accidentally see what Nate had done to my leg. As I tied them tighter, I opened the door.

I wasn't surprised to see Adam on the other side, knowing Cole would've come in to check on me without knocking.

"Come on in," I said to Adam as he stepped in from behind the door.

As he did, he ran his hands through his slightly matted hair. He looked like hell, almost as bad as me. I wondered if he'd gotten any sleep last night, either. A heavy guilt filled me, hating that I'd pulled him into my mess. Last night was all about him being honored for his charitable endeavors, and I'd made it about me and my past.

"How are you?" Adam asked, studying my face.

I let out a short scoff. "I'm fine. Did Cole send you in here to check on me?"

"Nope," he said. "I made him go down to the gym. The guy was about to pace a hole in the floor." Adam smiled sadly at me. "He's worried about you. We both are."

"Don't be," I answered quickly, shifting so he couldn't see the shame on my face. "I told you, I'm fine. I just had a minor freak-out last night. I'm–"

"Don't you dare say fine again," Adam said, arching his brow. I narrowed my eyes at him but didn't finish my sentence. "Changing the subject. So, Cole and I talked last night..."

My cheeks instantly flooded with color; I wasn't sure I was up for this conversation. "Look, before you say anything else, I know I screwed everything up–"

"Alex..." Adam sighed. "You didn't mess up anything." He

took my hand, leading me to the end of the bed. While I sat at the foot, he shifted the vanity seat so we could face each other. "You have no idea how grateful I am for you. Not only did you help me out when I needed it, you reminded me that there is so much more to life than my career and showed me that I want something real in my life." He tugged my hand, so I looked up at him. "If you've found that with Cole, then I'm happy for both of you."

"It feels real," I whispered, gazing down at our linked hands. Terrifying. Monumental. All the things I never thought I'd open myself up to feeling again. "I care about Cole."

"I'm glad to hear that," Adam answered. "Cole...he's been in a dark place for a long time. Don't get me wrong, he's come a long way, but for a while, he stopped living. Not until you came along. You've brought him back to life, Alex. I can't thank you enough—for helping me with our fake relationship and giving me my best friend back."

Tears started to prick my eyes again. Damn him. By the time we left the city, I'd have cried enough to fill the entire lake back home.

I nodded. "Thank you for trusting me."

"Of course," Adam said. "Now, I do have one more favor to ask."

"Anything."

"The industry party tonight. I'd understand if you weren't up for it, but I think we should still go. Get out of this hotel room and have some fun. Everly's been blowing up my phone, asking if you were coming tonight." He held out his hand. "What do you say, Alex? One last fake date?"

I thought about it for a minute, the word no on the tip of my tongue, but Adam was right. I'd already wasted so much worrying about Nate. He wasn't going to take any more time from me.

I smiled as I placed my hand in his. "One last fake date it is."

THIRTY-FIVE

Alex

After my talk with Adam, the rest of the day passed without incident. Before I knew it, it was evening, and once again, I barely recognized myself. The same hair and make-up team came to style me, working some kind of magic to hide all the blemishes and redness from last night. Looking in the mirror, I saw the face of someone entirely different from the girl who woke up in this room.

I leaned forward in the mirror, dabbing my pinkie nail on the false eyelash to ensure it was secure. As I inspected the rest of my reflection, I sighed, not sure how much of a happy act I could put on tonight. Yesterday, it was easy. The excitement and grandeur of the event made my cheeks hurt from joy. I felt like a queen, whereas tonight, I feel like the court jester.

The dress for tonight was much more form-fitting. It was like someone poured a vat of black ink over my skin. Luckily, the slit wasn't as high, so I didn't have to worry about anyone noticing the bruise on my leg.

It had taken extreme coordination and subterfuge to hide it from Cole. When he returned from the gym, he was in my room, silently pressing for answers about last night. He was smart enough not to push me, but his eyes never left me. He studied every movement of my body for signs of distress.

It was odd to have someone care about whether I was okay or not. My friends were amazing at checking in during difficult times, but having a partner at your side was different. Even if I didn't talk to him about what happened with Nate, his presence alone calmed me.

That, and finally clearing the air with Adam. Knowing that he took my relationship with Cole in stride lifted a boulder from my shoulders. Once this event was over, we'd head back to Saint Stephen's Lake. Away from the city, away from the constant threat of Nate lurking around every corner, maybe Cole and I could sit down and figure out what was happening between us.

Because as much as I tried to keep my heart from getting carried away, there was no use. The last threads of self-preservation snapped when he showed up at the hotel last night.

My heart was Cole's if he wanted it.

I sat back in the chair, wishing he was here now. He'd made himself scarce when Theo showed up, unsure he could keep his distance from me. He was getting himself a different room so no one would question our sleeping arrangements in the two-bedroom suite. The three of us agreed that Theo could not know about us until I dissolved the contract with Adam. Adam might trust that Theo would do the right thing, but I wasn't so sure.

As I stood to rummage through my jewelry options, a knock sounded on the door. "Come in," I called, expecting Adam on the other side.

"God damn."

The words made me stop, and I turned around slowly to face Cole. I smiled brightly at him before walking over and kissing him softly. "What are you doing here? I thought you were avoiding Theo."

"Fuck that," Cole chuckled. "No way he was keeping me away from my girl."

I laughed, pushing back to meet his eyes. "Oh, I'm your girl now?"

"Damn straight, sweetheart." His eyes darted down the length of my dress, rising slowly as if he wanted to take in every inch of me. "And I'll never stop thanking the stars for that."

When our eyes met again, there was no mistaking the hunger in his gaze. While that sort of attention usually made my skin itch, under his gaze, I felt empowered, like I could ruin him with a single brush of my lips. It was a heady, overwhelming sensation that almost took me out at the knees.

I managed to stay standing, barely moving until he did. Swallowing a knot in his throat, Cole stepped forward. "You're stunning, Alex."

My cheeks flooded with color, forcing my gaze back down to my feet. "Thanks. It's all the dress. I don't know who made it—"

He silenced my words when his fingers ghosted the line of my jaw, tilting my eyes back up until they met his steely ones. "Not the dress. You. You are the most beautiful woman I've ever seen."

We continued to take each other in, unable to move after that soft confession. Words I had no right to say, not this early, screamed in my head. However, it was becoming apparent how much I cared about this man. I couldn't imagine my life without him. I wanted him at my side for every milestone, the good and the terrible. I wanted to be his anchor in the storm, the peaceful calm he'd find solace in.

Instead, all I muttered was a quiet "Thank you."

Cole rubbed the back of his neck, suddenly filling the room with an anxious energy. "I got you something," he muttered, pulling a small blue box out of his pocket. "I was going to wait to give this to you when we got back home, but I'm an impatient bastard. Last week, a couple of us were walking downtown and saw this cool antique shop."

"Georgia's Treasures?"

Cole laughed. "That's the one. In the window, they had this necklace, and it made me think of you." He hesitated for a moment before he placed the box in my hand.

I cracked the lid open, absorbing the delicate gold chain. A pendant settled in the middle, and I ran my fingers along the design: a simple gold circle with intersecting lines.

"It's beautiful," I whispered, taking in the small diamonds in each of the crossings before closing the lid. "Cole, I can't accept it. It's too much."

He pushed the box back, taking my other hand and placing it on top of his. "It's not. Please, Alex. I want you to have it."

"Thank you." I smiled softly at him. "I love it. Will you put in on me?"

"Oh," He sighed. "You don't have to. You're already dressed, and I don't want to piss off the team."

Without another word, I turned around, gathering my hair to the side so Cole could put the chain around my neck. He paused, looking down at the jewels on the dressing table. It made me want to laugh—none of those held a candle to his gift, not when he picked it out for me.

"Please," I whispered, and he pulled the necklace from the box. As it laid against my skin, I pressed my fingers against the pendant, finally making sense of the shape. "A compass?"

Cole nodded, his fingers grazing the curve of my neck, sending shocks skittering across my skin. "It's how I see you, Alex. You led me back into the world and gave me a second shot at life." His eyes met mine in the mirror. "And I'll never be able to thank you enough for that. You saved me, Alex."

His words broke the last shred of doubt in my mind.

I loved him.

There was no question, no fear. I loved this man down to my very soul.

Despite our rocky beginning, Cole had become so much more than I could have imagined. Over the past months, he'd become my friend, my confidant, and it wasn't enough. I wanted him in a way I'd never wanted anyone before.

"Cole, I—"

A succession of swift knocks cut me off, and Adam popped his head into the room. "Are you ready to go?"

I smiled tightly, taking Cole's hand in mine for a moment. He had to know how much he meant to me. My words would have to wait.

My red-stained lips curved into an artificial smile. "Let's head out."

WHEN I USED to see pictures of industry parties filled with A-list actors and mega-producers, I was always jealous, dying to be a fly on the wall.

However, now that I was the one in the room, I only felt...*bored*. Between the never-ending photographs and ass-kissing conversations, this night was nothing like I'd imagined. Sure, it'd been amazing to see some of my favorite actors, but I'd trade this for a night on the lake in a heartbeat.

The silver lining was that I didn't need to worry about Nate. Adam had ensured his name was not on any of the lists, with explicit instructions to call the police if he tried to enter. Knowing that Nate would never risk his reputation with a public scene was enough for me to let my guard down.

I leaned against the metal rail separating the club's two floors, watching the party unfold around me. Adam was the center of attention, many of the power players trying to get him to commit to his next project. I'd have to ask him about that as well. The last time we spoke, he was mulling over five different scripts. Nothing was calling to him, though.

Not far behind him were Theo and Cole, locked in a tense conversation. I still couldn't believe Cole had agreed to come tonight. He looked up, almost immediately finding me in the crowd, and when Theo turned to talk to someone, he stealthily winked, making every part of me clench in anticipation.

God, I needed him inside me. All the build-up had been driving me insane.

"Alex!" a high-pitched voice came from behind me. Before I could even turn around, someone wrapped me in a tight hug. It took me a moment to realize it was Everly, her words slightly slurred. "I am so happy to see you!" she yelled over the pulsating music. "That hotel has been the most boring place since you left."

"I've only been gone a couple of days," I chuckled, holding her arms as she swayed.

From below, Cole frowned, arching his brow in question. I rolled my eyes teasingly before I gave him a soft smile to let him know I was okay. Even without any Nate sightings, he'd been watching me like a hawk. I had to draw the line at walking me to the bathroom—and not to fool around inside. Buzzkill.

Everly let out a loud laugh. "I know, but still. We only have a couple of weeks left to film, and I wanted to hang out more. Please tell me we can have another wine night before I go."

"You got it," I chuckled, leading her toward the leather chaises tucked in the far corner. "Do you want some water?"

She shook her head. "I'm okay. I didn't even drink that much, but my head feels like it's a balloon." She fumbled her phone from her purse, pulling up her messages. "I'm just going to text my driver and have him pick me up. I need my bed and a burrito the size of my face."

I held out my hand, helping her to her feet. She stumbled, probably due to both the alcohol and the five-inch heels. Weaving through the crowd, I started to lead her to the front door when she stopped in her tracks. "Nooo, can't go out there. Those damn paparazzi will get a picture of me like this. I cannot afford to have another negative article about my drinking. Theo's already threatening to send me to rehab if I don't get my shit together."

"Theo works for you, too?" I asked, not sure if I knew that information.

"Yup," she hiccuped. "He's been my agent for almost as long as Adam. He's a total asshole, but he gets stuff done. He's the whole reason I'm even in this movie."

"Then that's a point for him," I said. "Because otherwise, I never would have gotten to know you."

"That's true!" she squealed, pulling me into another tight hug. "Gah, you're the sweetest little nugget. Adam better not hurt you, or I'll kick his ass."

I shook my head as she pointed toward the back of the venue. It was much darker back there, and I had to squint to make out the hallway in front of us. Glancing over my shoulder, I searched for Cole in the crowd. He was nowhere to be found.

This was fine. I was fine. They'd banned Nate from every inch of this club, so I'd be fine.

As Everly pushed the back door open, letting the crisp breeze bust through the humidity inside, my stomach turned slightly. There was no one else out here. The only lights were the ones flickering above the door.

"Where's your car, Everly?" I asked, my blood running colder with each passing second.

She pulled her lip through her teeth, lifting herself onto her toes to get a better look. Just as my heart felt like it was going to implode in my chest, she broke out into a wide grin. "There he is!"

The town car pulled up in front of us, and the driver came around to open Everly's door. After he shut it, she rolled the window down, pouting. "You wanna come with? We can have a girls' night and binge eat terrible food in my hotel room."

"I'd love to," I laughed. "But I can't leave Adam to fend for himself. I should get back in there."

She smiled. "He's lucky to have you."

"I'm the lucky one."

With that, she closed the window, and I watched as the car took off down the alley, turning onto the city streets. Letting out one last breath of relief, I turned back to the door, pulling on the handle.

Nothing.

I tried it again and again, but nothing budged. I tried to ram my fist against the metal—still nothing. After a few minutes with no answer, I gave up. Muttering a slew of curses under my breath, I started to turn toward the alley, hoping I'd be able to get in the front entrance without Adam at my side.

When I took the first step, my eyes met someone else's: the same dark silver eyes that haunted my dreams, waking me in a pool of cold sweat. My head screamed out to run, to do something, but my body didn't obey.

When I finally started to scream, it was too late. Nate's hand was clasped around my mouth, blocking my airway.

"Nice to see you again, Alexandria. I think it's time we had a little chat, just the two of us."

"Shit."

The word slipped from my lips as I scanned the club, trying to find Alex in the crowd. Every moment I didn't have eyes on her, the more panicked I got. So many things could happen in a moment. I'd learned that lesson too many times to count.

I'd been gone for less than a minute, needing to hit the head after sipping on seltzer all night. Before I left, Alex was wrapped up in a conversation with Everly. It should have been fine.

Where the hell could she have gone? As Theo passed me by, I grabbed him by the arm. "Have you seen Alex?"

He shook his head. "Maybe ten minutes ago? Everly was heading out for the night, and she was helping her to the car."

Alex should have been back by now.

I knew there were too many variables to count. Everly's driver could be late, they could be talking outside, and Alex might have decided to return to the hotel with her.

No way. She would have texted me if she was leaving.

No matter how many excuses I gave myself, I knew something was wrong. Call it intuition, call it my gut, call it whatever the fuck you want—whatever it was, it had me bolting toward the door without a second thought.

I made it there without rushing, not wanting to draw any unnecessary attention to the situation. If Alex was fine, she was going to rip me a new one for overreacting, especially when she'd been giving me shit all night for hovering. My blood ran cold as I passed through the front doors. No one was waiting outside the club. There were no cars, only photographers scampering for pictures of celebrities leaving the party, hopefully in a state of inebriation.

To be sure, I headed out further, scanning the rest of the block. Cabs and other cars lined the street, and the only sound I heard was the blaring horns.

There was no sign of Alex.

Trying to keep my pulse steady, I grabbed my phone from my pocket, sending off quick messages to her, Adam, and Theo.

ME

Have you guys seen Alex? I lost track of her in the crowd

THEO

No sign of her up here. I'll keep looking

ADAM

Did you try the back? There's another private exit in case you want to avoid paps

ME

Trying It now

My patience finally snapped as I tried to shove through the throngs of people. One perk of being a big guy? I could quickly force people apart. I didn't care who I pissed off—I needed to see with my own two eyes that Alex was okay.

As soon as I got to the other side of the club, I found a darkened hallway leading toward the exit Adam mentioned. My hand hadn't even reached the door when I heard raised voices, loud enough to carry over the music inside. Shoving the door open, I searched for Alex, rushing into the alley to find the source of the noise.

That was when my heart stopped cold.

A towering figure had her pressed against the wall. He hovered over her, with his hand over her mouth. Her eyes were firmly closed, her head wildly shaking, trying to get him to release her.

I couldn't hear the words spewing out of his mouth—only the pounding of my heartbeat. Rage raced through my bones, unlike anything I'd ever felt before.

It only took two steps for me to reach them, ripping the man off her. Alex collapsed to the floor, and I instantly went to grab her, but he was fast and grabbed me around my neck. Unfortunately for him, I wasn't a stranger to dirty fighting tactics. With a swift jab of my elbow to his gut, he dropped back, panting for breath.

"You motherfucker!" I screamed, pulling my leg back so I could slam my boot into his side. The loud thud and subsequent cries weren't enough to soothe the beast inside me.

For hurting the woman I loved.

There was nothing but red.

I didn't know how many times I hit him or when he stopped fighting back, but after another heavy thud to his face, a slight, gentle touch on my back broke my haze.

"Cole?" Alex's quiet voice called, and without another thought, I stood, taking in her trembling body and tear-stained cheeks. "It's okay, I'm okay."

I looked down at the sad sack on the ground, and I couldn't bring myself to feel an ounce of remorse, not when he put his hands on my girl. He was lucky to be breathing at all. I brought my hands up to Alex's face, brushing the tears from her cheeks. As soon as our skin made contact, her knees gave out, and she practically collapsed into my arms.

I scooped her up, pulling her tightly into my chest. There were no words to describe the feeling overtaking me, the twin pangs of anger and relief battling for dominance. With a look over my shoulder to make sure the bastard hadn't moved, I carried Alex out of there.

He'd never lay a hand on her again.

ON THE RIDE back to the hotel, Alex stayed seated in my lap, no matter how many dirty looks the cab driver gave us. I doubted this was the oddest thing he'd ever witnessed back here, but even if it was, I didn't care. Alex was still trembling and not saying a word. There was no way I was letting her go.

I wanted to check every inch of her for marks, to erase any painful touch on her skin, but I didn't move, holding her against the crook of my neck. If it weren't for the light brushes of her eyelashes against my skin, I'd think she was asleep.

My phone buzzed in my pocket, but I ignored it, sure it was only Adam on the other end. Before leaving, I sent him a message telling him what happened. He immediately put Theo on the situation, and for once, I was glad he was in our corner. I was already starting to dread the consequences of my actions, but there wasn't an ounce of regret. That asshole hurt Alex; he was lucky to breathe at all still, and I'd do it all again if it meant she was here, safe with me.

When we arrived at the hotel, I shifted and got out first, helping her to her feet since she refused to let me carry her. "I need to walk in there on my own," Alex whispered– her first words since the alley. "I don't want someone to snap a picture and turn it into something against Adam."

Fuck that. I hated that was what Alex was concerned about. Adam's reputation should be the last thing on her mind. Apparently, whatever bullshit Theo had shoved down her throat sank in. I'd gotten the same speech more times than I cared to count, and most of the time, I tried to toe the line, to not let my actions reflect poorly on the man who saved my life.

Right now, though, I couldn't bring myself to care. I settled for my hand on her back, leading her to the elevator bay. As soon as the door shut, locking us in our little world, I pulled her back to me, still trying to convince myself that she was there.

If I was a couple of minutes late, if I hadn't gone looking for her—

No, I wasn't going to let my imagination go there. I'd never thought of myself as a violent man, but the moment I walked out into that alley, one thing became clear.

I would kill anyone who harmed Alex Green.

If that asshole ever put his hands on her again, he'd lose them.

After the doors opened, I released her, leading her into the hotel room she shared with Adam. Mine was a few floors below, but I couldn't leave, not yet. Once she was settled and asleep, I'd head back. The last thing she needed was for Theo to find out about us, opening another can of inconvenient worms.

Once she was asleep, once I knew Adam was back in case Alex needed something, I'd force myself to my room.

At least, that was what I told myself.

I opened the door, leading Alex over to the bed and helping her sit on the edge, trying not to growl when she grimaced in pain. She didn't even seem to notice; instead, she just stared off into space. She fidgeted with the pendant around her neck, trapped in her head, so I knelt in front of her, taking her hands in mine. "What do you need, sweetheart?"

She blinked a couple of times before her eyes finally focused on me. As soon as they did, they filled with tears, and she broke, lifting her arms around my neck to hold me close. Her body shook with the force of her cries, and I felt entirely helpless as I held her, rocking her slowly in my lap.

When her sobs started to fade, I leaned back on my haunches, lifting her chin so she was looking at me. My thumbs brushed away the trail of her tears as I smiled softly at her. "Let's get you ready for bed. Sleep away the rest of tonight."

She stood and turned in front of me, silently asking me to help her with her dress. My throat bobbed as I touched the slick metal clasp, unhooking it before pulling the zipper down her back. It took everything in me not to reach out and touch her, knowing that would be the last thing she needed right now.

Once the dress pooled on the floor at her feet, I turned, facing the opposite wall, while she grabbed an old shirt and leggings and climbed into the bed. Glancing over my shoulder, I made sure she was covered before turning to face her. I found Alex snuggled up on her side, curling the blanket around herself. Coming to her side of the bed, I leaned down, pressing a feather-light kiss on her forehead.

Without another word, she pulled back the blanket, silently willing me to join her. Shit. I should say no. The past two days had been emotionally draining. She was in a vulnerable state, and I needed to give her space.

I was also a man on the edge, and the need to be next to her outweighed everything else.

Kicking off my shoes and my suit jacket, I climbed into the bed next to Alex. Only a few minutes. Once she was asleep, I'd head into the living room and let her rest—an hour max.

As I listened to her breathing start to slow, my eyes closed for a moment. That was all I could allow myself. Yet, as soon as they fully closed, I drifted off, plagued with dreams of what could have been.

THIRTY-SEVEN

Alex

It was still dark when I woke. It took me a minute to realize that I was back in my hotel room, my brain still too worked up to make out many of the details. My entire body ached as if I'd run ten miles over the sand.

It took me a moment to gather my senses and realize that I wasn't alone. Someone's heavy arm draped over my stomach, and someone's very prominent erection pressed into my backside.

What the hell? I instantly stiffened, thrown back to when it was Nate holding me like this, overwhelmingly possessive, even in his sleep. The clawing smell of his sterilized apartment made my stomach turn, and I shut my eyes tight to keep out the fears. As my mind started to panic, my fight or flight instinct pushing me to look for the closest exit, the sleeping man next to me whispered in my ear.

"It's just me, sweetheart."

Cole. The tension instantly left, replaced by an overwhelming sense of comfort. As my heartbeat slowed, the nightmares faded away. The sterile smell that made me gag was replaced by the familiar aroma of leather and citrus as I shifted in the bed to face him. He was still in his suit from earlier, now rumpled from sleep. His messy hair covered part of his face, and I leaned down, brushing it back. His eyes reluctantly opened, giving me a soft smile when I buried myself in his chest.

This was precisely what I needed.

"How are you doing?" he said, reaching out to tuck my hair behind my ear. The gesture alone made me want to cry. After years of feeling lost, he was the first person I felt entirely safe with. Cared for. Loved.

Flashes of last night popped into my mind, from Nate's furious scowl to Cole's heavy-handed punches and kicks. My body must have tensed because he pulled me closer. "Hey, you're okay. I've got you, I promise."

I knew. Even when I was terrified last night, there were no doubts Cole would come. He had proven time and time again that he'd keep me safe, that he'd find me if I needed him. It made me want to hold him forever, to keep him from harm for the rest of his days, to love him for as long as he'd let me.

The words didn't come. Instead, I gingerly kissed Cole and whispered, "Thank you."

"For what?"

"For saving me."

He ticked his tongue, "Don't thank me for that." He abruptly sat up, running his hand through his hair. "You never should have been out there by yourself at all. It was my fault for losing track of you." He sighed, whispering to himself, "I fucked up."

I popped up to my knees, taking his face in my hands. Forcing him to look at me, I made my voice as stern as possible. "Don't you dare, Cole Campbell. You are not responsible for what happened. None of this is on your shoulders. It's all on Nate. Besides, I'm an adult; I chose to go out into the alley, and

I'll probably hate myself for it for a long time." I stared into his dark chestnut eyes, praying he heard me. "It was not your fault."

"You could have been hurt."

"I wasn't," I said. "Nate tried to grab me, and I fought back, Cole. I knew you'd be there, that you'd realize what was going on."

"You never should have been in that position, Alex! Now, that's all I can see—that bastard's hands on you."

Hearing his defeated tone almost shattered me. I was barely holding it together, but I needed to be strong, not only to prove to Cole that I was okay but also to prove it to myself. Three years ago, I would have cowered under Nate's rage, letting him drag me away from the party without so much as a word. This time, he was unprepared for me; he didn't think that I would fight back so viciously.

I pulled Cole's arm, trying to get him back into the bed, but he shook his head. "I shouldn't be here, Alex. You need rest. And space from me." He motioned down to his crotch, his dick at full attention. "And I can't control myself when you're pressed up against me."

"I like that you can't control yourself."

"No one should treat you like that, Alex. You need someone–"

"Stop, Cole." My voice came out harsher than I intended, but I was not about to let him spiral into treating me like a porcelain doll. "Please don't treat me differently now. I like that you want me so badly. It makes me feel treasured." I shook my head, looking up at the ceiling. "After I left Nate, it took me a long time to look in the mirror. Every time I did, all I would see was some weak girl who fell for an abusive narcissist. It's taken years to shake away that image. It would kill me if that were how you saw me, too."

Cole turned so quickly I tumbled over, landing on my back

against the mattress. He pressed on top of me, and for the briefest second, I panicked. But then, looking up into his intense stare, all my fear faded away. Even with his body hovering over mine, I knew Cole would rather die than hurt me.

"You are not weak," he said insistently. "You survived him. You ran and started a brand-new life for yourself without help from anyone. When I look at you, that's who I see: the same woman who makes me want to pull my hair out, who also makes me want to kiss her until I can't breathe. You're demanding, stubborn, and so beautiful; it hurts to look at you sometimes. I see you, Alex. Don't ever question that, not for a minute."

I quietly nodded, not able to do anything against the conviction of his words. It was intoxicating, having someone believe in me so much. He saw the strength I doubted, and it made me want to be that woman, the one he saw, the one he believed I was.

So, I did the hardest thing in the world.

"I want to tell you about it. Why I left."

Cole stared at me for a long moment as if appraising my words for any hesitation. When I showed no sign of flinching, he leaned away, shifting his back against the headboard. He reached out and pulled me to his side, laying me against his chest so his fingers could run through my tangled hair. It was entirely too comfortable, almost enough to lull me to sleep.

I'd been battling with these memories for too long, and I needed to let them go.

"I met Nate when I was an intern at his company," I started. "My college arranged for groups of seniors to go every year to make connections so we would have a leg-up after graduation. I was there for almost a month when I got called to the conference room, and Nate was standing there. I was in awe when he asked me to help him look over some documents. After all, who the hell was I? I was an undergrad business major, and he oversaw a multi-billion-dollar corporation.

"That was the first time we met, and I was...shit, I was infatuated. He kept asking for my help on different projects, and I felt so special. This guy wanted my feedback. Mine. It was one of those late nights when he finally kissed me for the first time."

I could feel Cole clench underneath me, so I spared the details of that evening, skipping ahead to when things started to change. "I knew we had to keep our relationship a secret at work. He told me some stories about not being able to be seen with me outside the office either. When it was the two of us, he'd promise me the world. After I graduated, he got me a job in his office, saying he wanted me as part of his team. In reality, he wanted to keep an eye on me."

"Was that when..." Cole started to say, then cut himself off.

"No," I answered quickly. "That didn't start until I moved in. We had only been dating for a couple of months, but he was insistent and said he wanted to wake up with me every morning. He told me his father owned his apartment and had rules about having other people officially live there, so he purchased a smaller one for me on a lower floor in the same building. At first, I was so excited. I was convinced we would live happily ever after."

"But that's not what happened."

"Not by a long shot," I sighed. "About a month after I moved in, I stayed late to help another team member with a new marketing campaign. When I got home, Nate was furious. He kept asking me what had happened. He thought I was sleeping around behind his back. When I said some snarky comment about being his little secret, he, um." I paused, trying to keep my voice from cracking. "He backhanded me across the face." I closed my eyes, unable to shake away the memory of the sting of his hand against my skin, the way my knees bruised when I fell to the floor, and him standing over me, screaming to show him every inch of my body to prove that no other man had touched what was his.

"That was the first time. The next morning, it was like a switch flipped, and Nate was so apologetic, telling me he was afraid he was going to lose me," I whispered, reaching up to brush a few stray tears from my eyes. "And stupidly, I believed him. I bought all his promises that it would never happen again. After that, we were happier than ever. He was back to the doting, caring guy I first met. Then, something else happened at work, and..." I closed my eyes, trying to remind myself that I was safe. Cole's arms tightened around me, silently letting me know I wasn't alone. Not anymore. "It kept happening. The same pattern of him losing his temper and then apologizing profusely for it afterward. I was too ashamed to leave, to tell people that I was letting this happen to me. Not only did I allow myself to become lost in his world, I let him hurt me, and I convinced myself that I deserved it, that I was the one upsetting him. I started doing everything he asked, hoping that if I made him happy, we would be back to what we once were."

Cole's fingers glided onto my chin, tilting it so I was looking up at him. "You got out." I nodded, dropping my gaze. "You don't have to tell me if you don't want to—"

"I thought I was pregnant." I winced when the words came out. "Nate was very strict about my birth control, but there were a few days when I was too hurt to take my pills. He must not have noticed. So, when my period was late, my mind went to dark places." I swallowed, forcing myself to continue. "Luckily, I wasn't. Instead, it was the wake-up call I needed. I needed to get out because that could have been my future if he didn't kill me first. I refused to bring a child into the world with that monster.

"The following day, when he went to work, I packed up two bags and got the hell out of there. The only thing left in my name was my Jeep, so I drove, no destination in mind, far enough away that he wouldn't look for me.

"It wasn't until I got to Saint Stephen's Lake that I finally took a breath. I pulled the Jeep up along the beach, parked, and just cried. I didn't even know how long—probably for hours. I was planning on moving on, but I stopped into the Lost Tavern for a quick bite. The minute I sat down, Marta spotted me. I think she could tell I needed a friend because she and Curt instantly took me in as one of their own. They even let me sleep in their guest room for the first couple of weeks. Without her, without Javi and Calla, I don't know where I'd be now. Because of them, I found a home."

I shifted shyly, meeting Cole's eyes for the first time since starting my story. I was worried that I'd see something in his gaze: worry, concern, or even worse—pity. There was none, though, only the same admiration he'd always shown when he looked at me. Without another word, he leaned down, lightly brushing my lips with his own. "I'm so proud of you, Alex."

"Don't be," I laughed sardonically. "I should have left after the first time Nate hit me."

"You left," Cole said, his fingers trailing along the line of my jaw. "That's all that matters. You got out."

The simple affirmation made my cracked and bruised heart beat stronger in my chest. I needed to release those words, needed to share my story so I could let go of it once and for all. I hated the idea of being defined by my past, but that was precisely what I'd been doing: holding back from forming new connections to keep from getting into that situation again.

Looking at Cole in the moonlight, a wave of adoration washed over me. I loved him. It wasn't a conscious choice, not a moment I could put my finger on. No, it was in all the small moments, the seemingly meaningless conversations. It was all the things people forget about, not the grand gestures: cooking dinner together, curling up at the fire pit, hell, even helping Curt and Marta fix their older-than-dirt truck.

All the things that make Cole, Cole.

"I love you."

The words rushed out all at once, unable to stay on my tongue for a second longer. I thought I'd feel nervous, even embarrassed, but instead, all I felt was relief. Cole deserved to know how much I cared about him.

He paused, staring at me in the darkness. Just as I started to panic, a wide, blinding smile broke out across his face. "Thank fuck." He grabbed my chin, kissing me with as much passion as he could muster. "Because I'm hopelessly in love with you, Alex Green. I want to spend the rest of my life showing you what you deserve."

Without another word, I crawled onto his lap, placing his hands on my hips. He gave me an unsure look, like he didn't know if he should touch me, so instead, I leaned down, kissing him with enough fervor that there was no way he didn't understand my intentions.

"Show me," I whispered against his lips.

That was all the encouragement he needed. Cole's hands gripped my ass as his tongue tangled with mine. Before we could get carried away, he pulled away, framing my face with his hands. "We shouldn't do this."

"Why?" I asked, leaning forward to steal another kiss. "Do you not want to?"

He arched a brow, thrusting his hips so his rock-hard cock slid against my core. Goddamn.

"That's the last time you question if I want you," Cole said. "I'm going out of my fucking mind right now, but you've had the night from hell, and I'm not about to let you do something you'll regret."

I smiled softly back at him, using my finger to brush back a few errant hairs on his forehead. "This has nothing to do with what happened tonight. This is about us. I want to be with you, Cole. I need to be with you."

"You mean that?"

"You're not the only one who has been losing their mind," I laughed, taking his hand in mine. Our gazes locked together, and I led him toward my leggings, bringing his fingers to my slick center. "This is how much I want you."

One quick brush at my clit, and I was in the air, thrown over Cole's shoulder as he burst toward the door. I let out a short giggle, clasping my hand over my mouth before asking, "Where are we going?"

"To my room," Cole answered. "I've had a while to think about everything I want to do to you, and I don't want to wake everyone up with you screaming my name."

"That sounds like a challenge."

"No, sweetheart," he said, swatting my ass as he opened my bedroom door. "It's a promise."

THIRTY-EIGHT

Alex

We barely waited until the elevator doors closed before kissing again. Maybe it was the months of built-up tension, but all I wanted was to rip his clothes off here and now. Even being practically on top of Cole, there was too much room between us.

When the doors opened, Cole took my hand and yanked me toward his room. His lack of patience was the biggest turn-on; I couldn't remember ever feeling this needed or wanted.

Then again, I'd never felt anything like what I felt for Cole.

When he opened the door, I took in the room, admiring its quiet coziness. It was different from the suite upstairs; it felt much more intimate as if there was barely enough air for the two of us.

Turning back to look over my shoulder, I expected to see Cole stalking toward me. Instead, he leaned against the door-frame, watching me.

"Why are you over there?" I arched my brow.

He smiled, rubbing his hand over his mouth. "Admiring the view. Deciding which way I want you first."

My body trembled at the thought; this side of him was everything I wanted, shaking me of all my insecurities. He took a couple of steps toward me, kissing me lightly on the lips before dropping down to the couch.

His hands gripped my arms, staring at me with an intensity that made my knees quake. "Strip."

"What?"

He leaned forward, propping his elbows on his knees. "Take your clothes off. Slowly."

I rolled my eyes. "Then you should get over here and show me how."

"Nope," he chuckled, leaning back on the couch and stretching his arms out over the cushions. "I've been dreaming of having you for months, Alex. I'm going to savor every single moment of tonight."

My thighs clenched together, unable to stop the rush of excitement at his tone. It had been a long time since I was intimate with anyone else, but I couldn't remember ever being this turned on. Cole's darkened gaze made me realize how mild my past sexual encounters had been. Just a few words and Cole had already ruined me.

I toyed with the hem of my t-shirt, dragging it up slowly. Cole's eyes blazed with desire as I pulled the shirt over my head, dropping the cotton fabric to the floor. Standing there in my leggings and my pale pink lace bra, I'd never felt sexier. After unclipping the hooks, I let my bra fall slowly down my arms, landing next to my discarded shirt.

"Fuck," Cole hissed, shifting in his seat. Seeing him struggling to keep his hands to himself spurred me on, loving that I could get such a reaction from five feet away.

My hands slid down my stomach, teasing the edge of my pants. My thumbs hooked the fabric, pushing it down my legs before I carefully stepped out of them. Cole's eyes tracked every one of my movements, his breath hitching as I stood there, bare and vulnerable.

Then, his gaze fixed on something, and his face fell. I realized my mistake too late. "Cole, I…"

He was already off the couch when I pulled my pants and underwear back up, covering the nasty bruise. I did not want him to see the evidence Nate had left behind.

Cole placed his hands on top of mine, stopping my movements. I glanced up at him, and I could see everything in his gaze: his rage, his worry, his love. It was so palpable I could almost taste it. Without a word, I removed my hands, letting him lower my leggings back to my ankles. He sank to his knees, running his thumb over the deep purple flesh.

I expected his rage and a slew of curses, but he shocked me by pressing a tender kiss to my leg, continuing until he had covered every bruised inch.

"Never again," he promised as his lips lightly grazed my skin. "That bastard will never hurt you again."

He lifted his hands, teasing the band of my underwear, looking up at me for permission. When I nodded, he continued, pulling them down until they joined the rest of my clothes in a pile on the floor.

Cole stood and placed his palm on my stomach, pressing me back until the cold window collided softly with my skin. I chewed on my lower lip. "Someone will see us."

"No, they won't," Cole said, lowering to his knees and lifting my leg to his shoulder. "The windows are tinted. I would never risk anyone else seeing you like this."

My fingers brushed through his chestnut waves as he kissed a path down my stomach. "And why is that?"

"Because I don't share well," he admitted, his fingers drifting higher to tease my slit lightly. "And I want you, Alex. All of you. For myself."

"You have me," I whispered, my voice losing more of its strength as he got closer to where I wanted him. "All of me."

"Not yet," Cole answered. "After tonight, this—this thing between us is real. We are real. No more hiding."

He paused, and I could tell he was waiting for my answer. If this was anyone else, the fear and dread would be overwhelming. I'd be running out of the room, terrified that giving my heart to someone else would lead to me losing myself again.

However, with Cole, there was nothing to fear. We'd fought and argued, but we still managed to find our way to each other. There were no more doubts, no more questions about what I wanted.

All I wanted was Cole.

"This is real. I don't want to hide this- hide you anymore."

With those simple words, he jerked my hips forward, letting his tongue lick through my folds. Holy shit. One touch and my head was already swimming. Cole continued his ministrations, alternating between slow brushes and suction of his lips. Based on his groans, this experience was as pleasurable for him as it was for me.

I couldn't even feel my body anymore. My hands alternated between slamming the glass behind me and holding onto his hair for dear life. His tongue made me feral, resorting to only my baser instincts. I needed him, needed all of this, the rest of the world be damned.

I almost hoped the people below could see me being ravished by this strong, caring, incredible man. I wanted the world to know we belonged to each other.

"Shit, Cole," I cried out, almost unable to stand with the power of the orgasm building inside me. My legs shook wildly, enough so that Cole propped me up on his shoulders before continuing his task. Now, in addition to his tongue, his fingers found my slick entrance, one entering me before he quickly added another. The sensation was too much.

With one last thrust and flick of his tongue against my clit, I crashed over the edge, clutching his hair to the point of pain. I couldn't stop. I didn't know what I was saying, much less what was happening to me. All I could think about was Cole and his magical tongue.

As the last of the aftershocks faded away, Cole lowered my trembling legs to the ground as he kissed along my thighs and stomach, staying in the moment with me until my eyes finally opened.

I giggled. "God, I think I'm addicted to your mouth."

Cole stood, pulling me into his arms. "Good to know, sweetheart." He lifted me into the air, and my legs wrapped around his waist, able to still feel his desire through his suit fabric. "But I'm just getting started with you tonight."

The sight of Alex naked on my bed was enough to make me fall to my knees. Her long, wavy brown hair lay across the pillows, her lips and cheeks still red from her last orgasm. If she were a siren, I'd happily follow her to my death, all too happy to worship at her feet.

I loved her more than I ever thought possible. Even when she was holding back, Alex ensnared me. Now that I'd earned her trust, there was no way in hell I'd ever lose it again. Not when she was looking at me like that, her eyes as clouded with lust as my own. I wanted nothing more than to make this good for her, to tease her until the sun came up. My dick had other plans, though, needing to be deep inside her and mark her as mine.

I'd never thought of myself as a possessive man, but Alex brought out that side of me. Without meaning to, my eyes drifted down to the gnarly bruise on her upper thigh. That fucking asshole; I should've hit him harder.

"Are you going to stand there all day?" Alex teased, lifting herself onto her elbows.

Chuckling, I finally stepped forward, taking her calf in my

unworthy hands. Her skin was like silk, such a difference from my own that I almost felt bad. From the way she was staring at me now, though, Alex didn't seem to mind. She popped up, moving until she knelt in front of me on the bed as I stood at its edge. She took my shirt in her hands, fumbling with the buttons until it was lying on the floor at my feet.

When the cool air hit my bare skin, I flinched instinctively, and Alex's brow furrowed. "Are you okay?"

Inhaling slowly, I forced myself to nod. "My back...." I turned so she could see my scarred skin, a souvenir from my brief tenure overseas. "I told you I was medically discharged from the army—this is why."

Alex inhaled sharply when my scars came into view. Almost a third of my back was ruined, twisted, and torn from the heat of the fire that nearly killed me. "What happened?" she whispered.

"IED." I'd told the story so many times that the words no longer carried the same weight. I wasn't ashamed of what happened anymore. I just hated the remainder of how derailed my life became because of one moment. "Our squad was doing a supply run when we hit a roadside bomb." I ran my hand through my hair. "The best part? Five Humvees passed it by and didn't trigger a thing. Ours hit it just right." I sucked in a sharp breath, turning to face Alex. "Five good men lost their lives that day, and I know I'm so damn lucky I wasn't one of them. It doesn't make a difference, though—I'll never be able to escape that moment, to erase those memories from my mind. Those scars? Every time I see them, I'm right back there."

Alex reached out, placing her hands on my heavy shoulders as her thumbs stroked my back. She leaned forward, pressing her lips to my chest. "I can't imagine what that was like. There's no timeline for healing, Cole. Give yourself more credit. Yes, you fell–" I started to interrupt, but she gave me a stern look.

"But you're not looking at how far you've come. I've only known you for a couple of months, and I can see how much you've grown. If you ever think you're going to that dark place again..." She placed my hand on her heart. "I'm here to help guide you home."

I reached up, gripping the back of her neck and bringing my lips to hers. "I love you so damn much."

"I love you too," Alex smiled. "Now, if we're done with the emotional part of this evening, I'd really like you to take your pants off."

"A little eager?"

"God, yes," she growled, smacking my hands away so she could unzip my pants. "I've wanted to see you naked since the first time you walked into the hotel."

"The first time?" I smirked, remembering all too well her threats of violence.

"Yup," she said. "Granted, it was to do painful things to you, but now, knowing what was lurking under those clothes..." She sighed. "What a waste that would have been."

My smirk returned at her words. All those excruciating hours of PT and grueling sessions with Adam were worth it for how she stared at me now.

With a few more tugs, we both stood nude in front of each other for the first time. We just stared at each other; I felt like I was a teenager again, so damn eager yet terrified at the same time. A silent conversation passed between us—there was no going back after this.

The wait almost killed me, but I let Alex take the lead. If she decided to call this whole thing off, I'd respect her choice, even if my balls would be aching for weeks.

Luckily, Alex put me out of my misery, wrapping her arms around my neck and dragging me on top of her on the bed. There was barely any light in the room, save for the city around us. The dim white light made Alex almost glow as if she had been plucked from my wildest fantasies.

"You're so beautiful," I whispered, pressing my lips along the column of her throat as I dug through the bedside drawer for a condom.

"You're one to talk," Alex said, nuzzling into my chest. I ripped the packet open and rolled it onto my shaft. As I did, Alex raked her nails across my lower back, and a shiver broke out across my skin.

My hand slipped between her thighs, letting out a hungry groan when I found her drenched and ready for me. Shifting to be fully on top of her, I lifted her leg around my hip, using the movement as leverage to slide my dick along her clit. Her head fell back to the pillow as she moaned my name and God, the sound got me harder than I thought possible.

"You ready?" I asked, continuing to glide along her folds, brushing her clit with the lightest pressure.

Alex nodded, her eyes darting between mine and the place our bodies were about to merge. Slowly, I pushed inside, letting her adjust. Fuck, she was so damn tight; I had to pause to get a handle on myself.

Alex looked up at me, her eyes wide and her cheeks flushed. "Are you okay?" she asked hurriedly.

"You need to relax for me, baby," I groaned, kissing her cheeks and forehead. "You feel too good, and if I come before you, I'll never forgive myself."

She chuckled, rubbing my arms. "We have all night, Cole. I'm not going anywhere."

As she laughed, her body relaxed, allowing me to seat myself inside her fully. This...this was indescribable. There was something about being joined with Alex that felt right. It was exactly where I was meant to be.

When I started to move, she pulled me down for a deep kiss,

her tongue tangling with mine as her nails left marks on my arms and lower back. I fucking loved it. Mark me, bruise me, Alex could do whatever she wanted. I'd wear her scratches like a badge of honor.

"Holy shit, Cole," she whispered against my lips.

"You okay?" I asked, brushing kisses along the bridge of her nose and cheeks.

"You feel so good," she said, a little breathless. "Fuck me harder, Cole. Fuck me like you never want to stop."

That was all the permission I needed. Moving back onto my haunches, I lifted her hips, pulling out as far as possible before slamming back home. She met me thrust for thrust, her need almost as strong as my own. Almost. I needed this woman like I needed to breathe. Tonight had only just begun, and I knew it would never be enough, not when we fit together like this.

With a few more thrusts, Alex started to fall apart, her walls constricting hard around my cock. As she screamed my name into the night, my body cramped, my spine tingling with the need to release. There was no damn way I'd last much longer, not with the way she was gripping me. Without warning, my orgasm ripped to the surface like a tsunami crashing against the beach. I swear, I almost blacked out. I couldn't feel any part of my body; legs, head, heart, all of them were happily numb, unable to focus on anything other than the woman underneath me.

I lowered myself, bringing my slick forehead against Alex's as her eyes started to close, a satisfied smile playing on her lips. "That was amazing," she said quietly. "I—"

"What?" I asked, pulling back to brush the hair away from her eyes.

She opened her eyes, and her smile turned shy. "I didn't know it could be like that. Sex has always felt like a chore before but with you...."

"It was fun?" I called over my shoulder as I rushed to the bathroom to clean up.

"It felt like a religious experience," she chuckled, turning on her side to watch me in the mirror. "Can we do it again?"

I laughed as I brought over a washcloth to clean her up. She watched as I brought the cotton towel between her legs, trying to be as gentle as possible in case she was sore. "Give me a little bit, sweetheart. Then, I'm all yours."

"Promises, promises," she teased, resting her head against the pillow.

By the time I climbed back in bed, she was breathing heavier, sleeping peacefully against the pillow. With a light kiss against her shoulder, I curled my arm around her stomach, shifting her closer to me. I told myself I'd stay up, content to watch her sleep for a little while. Maybe I'd wake her up again later with my head buried between those perfect thighs.

With the familiar rose and other florals invading my senses, I drifted off to a heavy sleep, more content than I'd been in years.

"OH MY GOD!"

The sound of Alex's sharp yelp pulled me from a fantastic dream. She was on her knees, begging for my cock. Oh wait—that might have been last night. After a brief nap, I woke up to that exact sight. We took turns waking each other up, our need for each other overriding the need for sleep.

This was a different kind of alarm.

As I sat up, rubbing the sleep from my eyes, Alex ran around the room, desperately trying to collect her clothing. My heart instantly plummeted to the ground: She regretted last night. The cold, callous voice in my head reminded me that this could happen, that she would get all of me and realize she deserved so much more. After all, this woman showed all her cards, exposing her darkest secrets and incredible strength.

No, I refused to accept that, not after we shared yesterday. Whatever was scaring her, we'd face it together. One night with her wasn't enough. Hell, the rest of my life might not be enough.

The thoughts were ripped from my head as my shirt smacked me in the face. "Get dressed," Alex yelled, pulling on her leggings.

Fuck this.

"Wait. Wait!" I said, hopping out of bed, not caring that I was completely naked. "What the hell is going on, Alex? Do you..." I swallowed, unable to meet her eyes. "Are you having second thoughts? Was last night too much?"

"What?" She whipped her head up to meet my eyes. "Why would you ever think that?"

"I woke up and you're freaking out!" I said, my words more panicked than I intended. "What am I supposed to think?"

"That we overslept, and Adam and Theo are currently waiting in the other room to talk to us," she said, her eyes widening in urgency. "So unless you have some kind of time machine or a hidden entrance, I think we're going to have to come clean."

"And you're not sure if you want to?" I asked, hating how needy and insecure my voice sounded. Fuck it—I didn't give a shit if this girl knew how gone I was for her, how it would kill me if she left now, keeping me as nothing more than a secret.

Alex lifted onto her toes, pressing a kiss to my lips. "I love you, Cole. I want everyone to know we're together, assuming that's what you want, too. I'm just nervous about what Theo is going to do. You weren't there when he went over that contract. He threatened me with a lawsuit, Cole. I can't deal with that, especially right now, when all the stuff with Fox Creek is still up in the air."

"He'll have to get through me first," I said, pulling her into my chest. "No one's going to destroy your dreams. Not while I'm around."

Alex smiled against my bare skin. "I know you will, and I love you even more for it, but until Adam and I officially nullify our contract, there can't be any surprises. Not with Theo involved."

"I'll think of something—maybe a distraction to get him out of the room so you can sneak back in. Maybe Adam can come up with something."

"You'd do that for me?"

"Don't you get it, Alex?" I said, pressing my lips to hers. "I'd do anything for you."

FORTY

Alex

The ride back upstairs was a stark difference from yesterday. While I could still feel the overwhelming pull to Cole, it was overridden by a different feeling entirely.

Guilt.

My talk with Adam had alleviated a lot of it, knowing he supported Cole and me. However, I promised to be by his side, promising to help him out of his bind with the press. Now, I was ending our contract months early because I fell for the one person I never expected. Adam might not own my heart, but he was still my friend, and I hated that I let him down when he needed me the most.

Cole's reflection caught my eye. His hands gripped the gold railing behind him, his gaze transfixed directly ahead of him. What was going through his head? If I was feeling guilty about us, was he feeling even worse?

My bond with Adam could never come close to the one he had with Cole. That kind of friendship couldn't be replicated, not with the history between them. It was something I'd never experienced for myself—most of my childhood friends were still back in my hometown, and we lost touch the minute I moved to

New York. What was that like, having someone to walk with during every phase of your life?

Would my relationship with Cole alter their friendship? Cole assured me Adam was happy for us, but Adam was an actor by nature. I knew he hid his more complex emotions behind his cheerful persona; was this bothering him more than he let on?

When the elevator doors opened, Cole stepped out immediately, but my feet refused to move, unable to face what was waiting for me on the other side of the room. I was a grown woman, and I owned my choices, but I was tired, so tired of feeling like I had to justify my actions, of feeling like I was under a microscope.

For the first time in years, I was truly happy, and I refused to let anyone take that away from me, not when I had just gotten a taste of what life could be like with Cole.

As he realized that I wasn't following him, Cole turned. "Alex..." he called out softly. "Are you okay?"

Was I? I felt like my emotions had run the gambit during that brief elevator ride. The only thing I knew for sure was that no matter what happened, Cole and I would face it. Together.

So, instead of giving my insecurities a voice, I took Cole's hand, giving it a soft squeeze before we got to the threshold of the suite. I barely had time to let go when Theo's face appeared in the doorway, his ever-present scowl more pronounced than ever before.

"Get in here. Now."

"Theo," Cole warned his hand going to my lower back and leading me inside.

"Don't," Theo said, following us into the sitting area where Adam was already waiting. "Do you have any idea of the shitstorm I've had to manage since last night?"

I looked over at Adam, hoping he could give more insight,

but he just rubbed the bridge of his nose. He looked exhausted like he'd been here with Theo for hours, trying to save us from his agent's wrath.

Theo continued, staring at Cole. "Did you think you could beat the living shit of one of the richest men in America, and he wouldn't try to press charges? The man is out for blood, Cole."

"I don't give a fuck," he snarled. "He was going to hurt Alex. He's lucky he's still breathing."

My entire body tensed at his tone, hating that he could face repercussions for my mistakes. I was the one who put Nate into his orbit. My thoughts started to spiral, and I was terrified about what would happen to Cole if Nate got his way.

Theo was practically radiating anger, but Adam spoke instead. "Alex, are you okay?"

My first instinct was to put on a happy face, to hide the depths of fear and rage that Nate had elicited inside me. That was my past, hiding his indiscretions for fear of other's judgments. I refused to let him break me or those I care about.

"No, I'm not," I said, turning toward Theo. "Nate Gibson and I used to be in a romantic relationship. He's an asshole who gets off on putting his hands on women. My leaving him has been a sore spot for a while, and last night, he tried to make me pay." I swallowed, trying not to think too deeply about the way Nate's eyes glared with unprecedented rage as he whispered that he would kill me.

Theo sighed, running his hand over his face. "Shit, I'm sorry, Alex. I'd love to say I'm surprised, but that guy's always come off like a controlling asshole." He leaned forward, tapping his fingers on his thigh. "However, without any proof, it's your word against his. He has the bruises Cole left behind, the hospital records, and the police report. Right now—well, honestly, we're pretty fucked."

"We?" Cole said, taking the word from my mouth.

Theo rolled his eyes. "Goddamnit, of course, we. Did you think I'd let some asshole ruin your name, Cole?"

Cole stared at him as if that was what he thought Theo would do. We'd both been under the impression that Theo only cared about Adam's reputation, willing to let everyone else take the downfall over his client. We'd underestimated him.

Adam shook his head, standing to walk to the window. "What does he want? Money?"

"I tried that," Theo answered. "He spewed some shit about wanting justice, tried to make it out like Cole's unstable and at risk of hurting other people for no reason."

"That's bullshit," I hissed, jumping to my feet.

"Hey," Cole said quietly, taking my hand and bringing me back down to the couch beside him. "It's okay. I knew this was a risk yesterday."

"It's not fair." My voice cracked, hating that Nate was getting the upper hand. Again. If he wanted to come for me, okay. I survived him once, and I could probably do it again, but to punish those I love for defending me? That was a new low, even for Nate.

Cole reached up, brushing away my falling tears with his thumbs. "He is not going to hurt you, Alex. I don't give a shit what I have to do. He's never going to hurt you again."

"And that's not all," Theo sighed, continuing to rub the bridge of his nose. He motioned between the two of us. "There's something else we have to deal with." He grabbed his tablet, found something, and then turned it toward us.

The grainy footage seemed like nothing at first, some kind of surveillance footage. It took me a minute to realize that it was from the hotel elevator. Oh shit. I knew where this was going before we even entered the frame. As my stomach started to twist, Cole and I entered the elevator, immediately locking lips in a passionate embrace. Fuck. Such a stupid move. I knew there were cameras; Theo had warned me to watch my actions, especially outside of the room. The moment Cole's lips touched mine, I didn't give Theo's words a single thought, too focused on him to even think about the consequences.

Cole leaned forward, slamming the tablet down. "Delete that. Now."

"Already done," Theo answered, taking the tablet and deleting the reel. "Don't worry, I paid off the security office, so this wouldn't make any headlines. We've got enough of a shit storm to deal with already." He stared at me. "You know that this voids your contract, right? I told you that you could not be caught with anyone else while you were with Adam, and now this?" He turned to Cole. "What were you thinking? Out of all the goddamn girls in the world."

"Enough."

Adam's quiet command broke the tension in the room, all of us turning to face him. "Theo, enough. I already knew about Alex and Cole. They told me a week ago. We were waiting until after the event last night to break things off."

I smiled at Adam, grateful that he smudged the timeline to make us look better. When Theo sat back on the couch, Adam winked at me, and all my nerves about him harboring resentment toward us faded away.

Theo nodded. "Fine. I'll draft a new agreement saying that we're terminating the contract, and none of the parties are to blame." He leaned forward, fixing me with his favorite stern stare. "However, this does not affect the NDA, Ms. Green. If you speak about Adam and the nature of your relationship to the press, I will not hesitate to file suit against you."

Cole tensed at my side, and I placed my hand on his knee, a quiet gesture to show I was okay with his terms. "Of course, Theo," I smirked at him. "I'd expect nothing less."

"I swear, dealing with the three of you is making me go

prematurely gray." He shifted, gathering his belongings from the coffee table. "Oh, and this will also affect your payment, Ms. Green. Since you did not fulfill the terms of the contract, your payment will be prorated for your time."

"That's fair," I said. My stomach churned, hating that I would have to borrow my funds if I wanted to get the hotel up to my standards. Even with Cole offering to help out, it was going to be a substantial investment.

"Actually," Adam said, clearing his throat. "I'd like to help with that. Cole's told me all about your project, and I would love to help finance it."

"You did?" I turned to Cole.

"Of course I did," he smiled. "I'm so proud of you, baby. I want everyone to know what a badass you are."

"Thank you," I said, leaning forward to kiss his shoulder. "But I can't accept your money, Adam. We're friends. I don't want you to think I'm taking advantage of you."

"You're not," Adam said, taking the seat across from me. "I'm asking to invest. If it makes you more comfortable, we can arrange a repayment plan." He holds up a finger to stop me from refusing again. "Only after you turn a profit."

"That could be years."

"Then it'll be years." Adam shrugged. "In case you haven't noticed, Alex, I'm doing pretty damn well for myself. I'm not going to miss the money, and you need it. What's stopping you from saying yes?"

I had no idea—some naive notion that if people helped me, it wouldn't really be mine? This was different than the board or the investor back at the Isadora. These were my people, ones who were willing to invest in me and my dreams. With their support, there was no way I could fail.

"Okay."

Adam beamed back at me. "Yeah? You mean it?"

"Yes, Adam," I said, standing to offer him my hand. "You can be an investor in the Fox Creek Property."

He took my hand and pulled me around the coffee table, engulfing me in a tight hug. "Thank you," I whispered.

"Thank you," Adam said. "For everything you've done for me, for Cole."

I grinned to myself as I pulled away, my tears turning from those of frustration to pure happiness. Unfortunately, they soured again when I thought of the elephant in the room. "As happy as I am about this development, what am I going to do about Nate?"

"What are we going to do," Cole insisted. "This is my problem, Alex. You're not going anywhere near it."

"No," I said, my voice firm and strong. "I have spent too long hiding from Nate and his games. This ends today."

Adam smiled at me. "I was hoping you'd say that."

Alex

The room dropped about thirty degrees when Nate and his lawyers walked inside. Theo had set up the meeting quickly, wanting to get everything under control before the story leaked. He'd commandeered one of the hotel conference rooms, which seemed like as good a place as any to meet.

The room was bathed in swatches of reds and oranges, giving it a warm and welcoming vibe. Cole, Adam, Theo, and I sat on one side of the table, leaving the other empty for Nate and his team. When they stepped inside, Theo greeted them and led them to the empty chairs.

I tried to keep my breathing steady, hopeful this would be the last time I'd ever have to be in a room with Nate, but my relaxed demeanor almost shattered when his smug smile met mine.

Granted, Cole did a real number on his face, making his sneer less menacing. Black and blue bruises covered his cheeks, and one of his eyes almost entirely shut. Nate limped as he joined us, wincing as he lowered himself into the chair.

You would think the ass-kicking would be an essential life lesson, but not for Nate. He still acted like the king of the castle, probably getting off on the fact that he held our fate in his hands.

"Well, well, well," Nate said. "Looks like the gang's all here. Alexandria…" He turned to me, his eyes lazily skimming down my front. "I wasn't aware you'd be joining us. What a pleasant surprise."

"Don't talk to her," Cole growled, his voice low and lethal.

"Oh," Nate chuckled. "Now I get it. She's got you wrapped around her finger. Alex has always had a talent for that. Enjoy it while you can, buddy. She'll be fucking around on you, just like she did me."

I bit my tongue so hard it almost bled. I wanted nothing more than to rage at him, to spew insults about his manhood until my voice was hoarse. That was what he wanted, though, so I forced myself to keep quiet until it was time.

Theo shook his head, pushing a folder across the table. "Why don't we get down to business? This is a generous compensation package to make up for any injuries or issues that might stem from the altercation last night."

"Altercation?" Nate snapped, ignoring his lawyer's warning. "This criminal attacked me for no reason!"

Cole started to speak, but I found his hand under the table, giving it a quick squeeze. He was half a minute away from launching across the table and finishing what he started.

I inhaled slowly, trying to steel my nerves. "Nate, can we talk for a minute? Alone?"

"Absolutely not," Cole snapped as Nate's lawyers insisted on the same thing in more professional terms.

They'd forgotten how well I knew this man, how much he hated that he had lost control of the situation. Nate's biggest downfall always was his ego, and I knew exactly how to use it against him.

"Please, Nate." I forced my voice to break a little. "I just want to talk, to apologize for what I did."

"You have nothing to apologize to this asshole for," Cole snapped, dropping my hand and standing abruptly. "I can't believe you'd do this shit, Alex. Fuck this." Without another word, he stormed out of the room, Theo and Adam rushing behind him.

Once I was alone on my side of the table, Nate's face contorted into a sly smile. "Leave us."

"Mr. Gibson..."

"Out. Now."

The moment the door closed behind his lawyers, a familiar dread clawed into my stomach. Being alone with Nate always put me on edge. I was too familiar with how his mind worked—he was already dreaming of ways to punish me, I was sure.

I clenched my fists, trying to keep my hands from shaking. This man didn't get to see his effect on me, not anymore. Images of Cole flashed through my mind; he gave me strength, even though he couldn't be with me right now. As soon as this was over, I could get back to him.

Nate smirked at me across the table, arching his brow. "You were saying?"

"That I'm sorry. Last night—things got out of hand."

He leaned back in his chair, steepling his hands. "Ah, that's a good start, Alex, but I need more."

"More?"

"You left me," Nate snarled. "I gave you everything, Alexandria. I loved you, and that was the thanks I got? You took off to some bum-fuck town in the middle of the night!" His veins protruded from his neck, his usual calm persona long gone. "I was kinder than you deserved. I let you go, and this is how you repay me?"

Every inch of me wanted to scream. How could Nate

water down our history to such basic terms? How could he have left out of the broken bones, the bruises, the manipulation? Looking back, that was how it had always been: everything was my fault, his actions only reactions to my failings. Of course, he'd twist the end of our relationship to suit his narrative.

"Now you come back here with that Neanderthal in tow and try to ruin my life?" Nate scoffed. "Newsflash, princess: you have nothing. No power, no cards left to play." He jammed his pointer finger into the table. "I own this town, and don't you dare forget that."

"I know," I whispered, tears flooding my eyes. "But if I'm going to apologize, you need to as well."

"For what?"

"You hurt me," I said, my voice gaining confidence. "You hit me. Beat me. Broke my arm because I was assigned to work on a team with another man. Made me feel like I wasn't worthy of anything but your toxic bullshit love. For making me doubt myself and who I am. For taking out all your sick, pathetic insecurities on me."

Nate dared to laugh at me. "Prove it, Alex." He observed my expression, "And that's the thing, isn't it? You can't because you weren't smart enough to document anything. Good thing you're pretty because you don't have a lot of other skills to lean back on."

"See, that's the thing," I said, mimicking his words. I finally dropped my contrite act, letting my true smile bloom. "I might not have physical proof on me, but there are hospital records, noise complaints from neighbors, and testimony from those who knew me—enough to tarnish your reputation if you decide to go forward with these bullshit charges. Because you can bet your ass that if you try to hurt Cole or Adam, I will come for you with everything I have."

"Bullshit," he hissed, leaning forward. "Try it, and I'll kill you. Put you in the ground like I should have last night."

I ticked my tongue. "Oh, Nate..." I pulled my phone out, showing him I'd recorded our entire conversation. "You really should think before you speak."

"What is that?" he snaps, pushing back in his chair. "You can't record me! You need my permission!"

"Maybe for a trial," I said, sending the recording to Theo and the others. "I could always anonymously give it to a reporter. Think about the coverage if it came out. How many other women would come forward? Would your wife stand by you?" I paused, pretending to tap my lip in thought. "Somehow, I doubt she would."

Nate's practically vibrating with anger. "What do you want?"

"When I walk out that door, you forget you ever met me," I said, leaning forward to ensure he heard me. "You forget about Adam, Cole, and everyone else I love. You live your life, but from now on, you think twice about putting your hands on another woman. Remember that old saying, Nate." I winked over my shoulder as I started toward the door. "Never fuck with a woman scorned."

With that, I pushed the doors open, not sparing even a glance over my shoulder. The moment they closed behind me, it felt like an anchor had been released from my chest. For years, I dreaded meeting Nate face to face, terrified he was lurking in the shadows. Now, I no longer had to fear that he was waiting for me.

I was free.

As soon as I got to the lobby, Cole, Adam, and Theo rushed over to me. "Did you get it?" Theo asked as Cole stood at my side, placing his hand on my back and rubbing soothing circles.

"Hook, line, and sinker." I smiled. "You know who to give this to?"

Theo nodded. "I have a couple of contacts in the New York press circuits. I'll give them the heads up and see what they can dig up on their own. I'll make sure they keep all our names out of it."

As Theo walked away to make the call, Cole scooped me up, pulling me into a tight embrace. "Shit, I hated every second of that, sweetheart."

"I did, too," I whispered into his neck. "It's done. We don't have to worry about him anymore."

"Thank fuck," he said, placing me down before he turned to Adam. "Now what?"

"Now, we head back to Saint Stephen's Lake and finish the movie."

"That sounds good to me," Cole said, holding his hand out to me. "Ready to go home?"

More than he even knew.

FORTY-TWO

Alex

It had been three weeks since we returned home from New York, and while everything in Saint Stephens Lake was the same as when we left, everything in my life had changed. Without Nate hanging over my head, it felt like I could finally breathe for the first time in years.

While that was a significant victory, it was not the best part. With the contract between Adam and me dissolved, Cole and I no longer had to hide. It was weird at first, and people questioned the timeline of our coupling, but neither of us cared.

When we got home, Cole practically moved into my house, only returning to the hotel to check on Adam or help with the movie. We'd created a routine, one of simple domesticity. Meals were cooked together, movies were watched on the couch, nights were spent tangled in each other's arms, and all of it was filled with more love than I'd ever known.

Despite the solace in our home, there was still an elephant in the room. In three days, the movie would be finished filming. Three days, and Adam would be returning to LA to decide his next project.

And I still had no idea what Cole was planning to do.

We'd spoken a little about him staying, but nothing was concrete. I didn't want to push, needing him to make this choice for himself. I wanted him here, with me. However, after years of desperately trying to prove that I was enough, I needed to pivot my actions. For the first time, I wanted someone to pick me, to choose me, and not because it was convenient, not because there weren't any other options.

Because my love was enough.

I stared out the window, taking in the early morning rays across the lake. There was a brisk chill in the air, a sure sign that winter was on its way. I took a sip of my coffee, letting the warmth settle my aching heart. All this indecision was driving me crazy. Did Cole not hear the ticking clock over our heads, signaling the end of the quiet bubble we'd built together?

What if he didn't care? What if this was all temporary to him?

No. I refused to let that part of my brain have the power. I'd always struggle with intrusive thoughts, but I didn't have to give in to my doubts. I knew Cole loved me—he proved it every single day.

As if I'd summoned him with my thoughts, Cole came up behind me, wrapping his arms around my waist as he pressed his lips to my neck. "What's on your mind, sweetheart?"

The truth sat on the edge of my tongue, begging for me to come clean. Instead, I gave him a tight smile. "Wondering when we'll get snow. The first time is always the most beautiful."

"Hmm..." he said, reaching down to take a sip of my coffee. "Gotta say, I'm looking forward to that. I've never really seen snow."

"What?" I turned so abruptly that my coffee almost spilled down the front of my shirt.

"Yeah," Cole shrugged. "Not a lot of snow in Texas or California. I'm kind of excited to see it. Not the shoveling part, though. We're going to have to get a plow or some shit to take care of your driveway. That's gotta be a bitch—"

"Hold on!" I snapped, stepping out of his hold. "You're skipping over some important information here, Campbell." I looked up at him, my eyes already starting to water. "You're staying?"

Cole's face furrowed as he stepped closer. "Of course I am, Alex." He shook his head. "I told you that I'm all in." He reached up, cupping my cheek with his hand. "I want to stay here, Alex, with you. I want us to live in this house and build a chaotic life together. I want to spend every day showing you how much I love you and how much your love means to me. So if you're good with it, sweetheart, I'm here for as long as you'll let me."

Now, the tears were freely flowing, and my emotions were unable to hold back. It was like a weight I didn't even know I'd been clutching was lifted from my arms, allowing me peace for the first time in weeks.

"What about Adam?" I asked. "What about Dani? Your life is in LA. I can't ask you to drop everything and move out here just for me."

"I already talked to Adam," Cole said. "He knew this was coming. Honestly, he knew before I even told him. We're always going to be best friends; distance isn't going to change that. Besides, he's thinking about making some changes as well."

"Changes?"

"Later," Cole promised. "As for Dani, she told me I'd be an idiot if I left. She'd drag my ass back here if I tried. We're still going to talk, and she'll always be a part of my life, but I've been going to meetings in town for the past couple of weeks, and I'm going to find a sponsor a little closer to home."

"Are you sure about this? I don't want you to regret—"

"Woman, stop asking questions, and let me kiss you."

I smiled happily up at him, wrapping my arms around his

neck to bring his lips to mine. "Yes," I mumbled against him. "I want you here—every day. I want to fall asleep with you and wake up in your arms. I can't wait to build a crazy, beautiful life with you, Cole Campbell."

"ALEXANDRIA," Diane called from the other side of my desk. "I need to see you in my office."

"Is it urgent?" I asked, frowning at my computer screen. "Mr. and Mrs. Martinez wanted me to book–"

"Yes. Get in there. Now."

I sighed, tempted to smack my head on the computer screen. So much for my fantastic morning. After Cole told me his plans, we spent a couple of hours celebrating in my bed and then in the shower immediately after. I was almost twenty minutes late to work, but it was worth it. Besides, my days here were numbered. Even if Diane decided to unleash her wrath, it was only a matter of time until I didn't have to deal with her anymore.

Every day, I waited with bated breath, hoping to hear back about the Fox Creek Lodge. As far as I knew, everything was in order. The loan had been approved, and the owner was willing to accept my low-ball offer. Everything seemed to be going my way, which made me anxious for the other shoe to drop.

With everything else going on in my life, I had almost forgotten about Diane. Between my fake relationship, my real relationship, and trying to navigate owning my own business, my mind was completely preoccupied.

I let out a weary sigh before moving from behind my desk, following my boss to her office on the other side of the lobby. As soon as the door opened, my brow furrowed, finding Calla already waiting inside. I glanced at her, arching my brow to see if she knew what was going on. She shrugged her shoulders, as in the dark as I was, apparently. Diane didn't even acknowledge her daughter as she walked inside and made her way over to her desk.

"Please, take a seat," Diane said as she steepled her hands on the surface of her desk. "I wanted to speak to both of you at the same time, so there was no confusion."

"About what?" Calla said, her voice already on edge.

Diane gave her a tight smile and then pulled out a file from her drawer, dropping it in front of me. It looked like nothing special, just a regular file folder stuffed with papers. She pushed it closer toward me, and I cautiously took it, lifting the cover to see a picture of the Fox Creek lodge. My heart dropped down to my toes. I scanned through the rest of my papers and found a copy of my offer and details on my bank loan. I shook my head, trying to wake up from this nightmare.

My hands shook as I put the file back on her desk. "What..." I cleared my throat, trying to get rid of the bubble already forming there. "How the hell did you get this?"

Diane narrowed her eyes at my question. "I am one of the prominent business owners in this town," she said, clearly bored. "Our company does more business than the rest of this town combined. Did you think I wouldn't find out?"

"This has nothing to do with you," I scoffed.

"That's where our opinions differ, Alexandria." Diane's voice was cold, almost lethal.

"Oh, please." I rolled my eyes, too angry to even give a shit that she was my boss. "Our businesses would operate in completely different circles. You wouldn't even notice we exist."

"Maybe," Diane said, a little too smug for my liking. "However, it doesn't matter anymore. The bank has decided to terminate your loan application. Turns out they didn't have a reference from your employer. I was more than happy to provide one."

"You can't do that!" I snapped. "It was already approved! You had no right to interfere. When everyone finds out what you've done—"

"How will they find out?" Diane tilted her head. "Besides, it's done. Even if you tarnish my name, it won't bring your sad little project back to life." She smiled, and my blood ran cold. "However, I can help you—if you are willing to agree to my terms."

My vision went red. I wanted to scream, to rage at this woman. All my dreams, my freedom, and my future were being washed down the drain as part of some sick game. Tears threatened to spill, but I forced them back, refusing to reveal any more weaknesses to Diane.

"What do you want?" I asked.

Diane leaned back in her chair. "I am willing to provide the start-up capital for your property. The board has been looking at different ways to expand The Isadora, and I think this would be a great place to start—a more...rustic experience for our guests. It would still be under our name, of course. You would be in charge of the day-to-day."

This was a joke, right? This had to be a joke. There was no way this woman was stealing my dream and then asking if I would run it for her. The level of audacity was ridiculous, even for Diane. She couldn't possibly think I'd ever trust a word she said.

"I'm not done," Diane said, her attention shifting over to her daughter. "This offer is conditional on Calla agreeing to work for her father's company."

"Are you serious?" Calla snapped, her mouth hanging open. "You're willing to screw over Alex to get me to go along with your plan? What is wrong with you?"

"Wrong with me?" Diane said, her voice dripping with anger. "I have given you everything, Calla. Everything. All I ask is that you do something with your life, not bum around this town with zero purpose. You're too damn smart to ruin your life with your lack of ambition." She scoffed. "You're an embarrassment to this family."

"Stop," I snapped, hating the look on Calla's face. My friend, the one who was always smiling, always finding joy in the world, looked utterly broken under the weight of her mother's words.

"Is that what you think of me?" she said quietly. "That I'm an embarrassment to this family?" She hastily wiped the tears from her eyes. "If that's how you feel, fine. I won't be a part of it anymore. I'm done, Mother."

Diane's eyes widened for a moment before her stoic mask slipped back into place. She shook her head. "You don't mean that."

Calla stood, placing her hands on her mother's desk and leaning forward. "Oh, I do. I'm done with your demands, done with you trying to push me to lead your life. If your love is that conditional, then I don't need it anymore."

"You'll change your mind," Diane sighed. "You'll see I only want the best for you."

"Are you sure?" I asked, taking Calla's hand and pulling her over to the corner of the office. "I'm behind you, no matter what. I don't want you to give up everything because of her. We'll find another way to fight back."

"Thanks, Alex," she smiled at me. "But this is something I've been thinking about for a while." She glared at her mother. "I'm tired of her guilting me, forcing me to follow her lead. I'm going to make my own choices, whether she likes it or not."

Diane rolled her eyes, ignoring her daughter in favor of

staring at me. "Are you going to talk some sense into her? Or are you willing to throw away your future along with my daughter?"

I looked at Calla, feeling empowered by her words and desire to get out from under her mother's thumb. The whole point of this project was to find something that was mine so I could put my mark on this town the way I wanted. If I accepted her offer, it would be the same bullshit I'd dealt with for the past three years.

As much as I loved the Fox Creek Lodge, there would be others.

"No," I said firmly, taking my place at Calla's side. "In fact, I quit."

"What?" Diane snapped.

"I quit. I'm done with you and this place. Maybe my plan didn't work out, but I'm not about to sign my life away to you." I took Calla's hand and led her out of the office. "My life will be as far from you and your bullshit as possible."

Alex

Holy shit. Holy shit. *Holy shit.* I quit my fucking job. After years of dreaming about leaving the Isadora, I'd finally done it.

And I felt...*okay?*

Alright, okay wasn't the right word. When I dreamed of this scenario, it was one where I held all the power, and I was walking away on my terms. In my dream, I had found success, and I could smugly tell Diane to kiss my ass.

Not because the horrible woman tried to blackmail me into staying on and working for her.

My heart sank again, thinking about Calla and her mother's words, how deep they seemed to cut, worse than anything Diane had ever hurled at her before. I knew that look on her face all too well, the one when you realized the person you'd been fighting for wasn't worthy of your loyalty.

As soon as we left the office, we went to Calla's suite, packing everything she needed. With Javi's help, we were able to box everything up and load the cars within two hours. The entire time, I thought Diane would apologize, but instead, she sent a security officer to ask Calla for her room key. That was a new low.

As soon as we got back to my house, Cole was waiting on the front porch. I'd texted him as soon as we left the resort, asking if he minded if Calla stayed with us for a while. The delay in his reply was just enough for me to start freaking out, wondering if he'd planned on getting his own apartment now. It seemed silly; we were already living together without the label. For the first time, I was happily willing to give up some of my space.

When he texted back, more than willing to let her crash in the guest room for as long as she needed, I couldn't help grinning. I wanted to pinch myself, not sure how I was lucky enough to have such a good man at my side. Maybe it was the universe rewarding me for surviving Nate.

I tried to tamp down my good mood for Calla's sake, but she noticed me tucking my lip between my teeth and rolled her eyes. "You don't have to pretend to be sad on my account, Alex."

"What?" I said, feigning ignorance. "I'm not–"

"Yes, you are," she laughed. "And I swear, I'm okay. I'm weirdly excited about this. I've always had my parents looking over my shoulder, so this is the first time I get to do what I want without their commentary." She pursed her lips. "I'm very tempted to get a giant tattoo."

"Hold off on that one," I chuckled.

She paused, tapping her fingers on her thighs. "Thank you again. I promise I won't bother you guys for too long."

"You're not bothering us."

"You guys just started dating," Calla said. "And now, there's a third wheel crashing with you. I promise I'm going to figure out what I'm doing sooner rather than later. I have a little bit of savings from my side gigs—maybe I'll try to get a place in town. Devyn owes me a lifetime of sister favors, so maybe I'll crash with her."

"New York would be a good adventure." I nudged her with

my elbow. "Take your time, Calla. There's no deadline here. Figure out your next steps, and we'll be here to help in any way we can."

Cole came to the driver's side of the car and knocked on the window. When I rolled it down, he stuck his head inside, giving me a brief kiss before looking over at Calla. "You good?"

"Sure," she chuckled. "I'm homeless and penniless, but otherwise, the world is looking up. At least I'm free from my demonic mother." Calla stretched out her arms. "That feels pretty damn good."

"Why don't you head up to the guest room and get settled?" I offered, climbing out of the car. While Calla walked inside, I took Cole's hand, keeping him outside with me a few minutes longer.

As soon as he turned to face me, he wrapped me in a tight hug, the smell of cedar and spice instantly soothing me. Having someone to help carry the burden when it got too heavy was a comfort I'd never really known before. Cole leaned back, brushing his hair behind my ear. "Are you okay?"

"Not really," I shrugged. "I've been telling myself there are plenty of other places I could buy, but I was so excited about that one. Fox Creek seemed perfect, and now..." I shuddered, thinking of what might happen to it.

"Me too, Alex." Cole kissed my forehead. "Like you said, this isn't the end of the world. We're going to make this dream come true, no matter what." He scratched the back of his head. "And, good news—you can take your time because Curt hooked me up with a job. You know Steve Kaplan?"

"The contractor?" I asked. "Yeah, he did some of the work in my bathroom."

"Well, he needed another guy for his crew, and Curt gave him my name. He's got a lot of projects coming up, and he thinks I'll be a good addition. I'm going to learn a lot, and I figured, when it's time, I can use what I've learned to help fix things up around your inn."

"Really?" I beamed up at him. "I can't believe you did that."

Cole just smiled, tipping my chin up to press his lips to mine. "One day, sweetheart, you're going to realize that I'd do anything to make you happy."

"You," I said. "You're all I need to be happy."

THE FOLLOWING WEEK, Cole insisted we go for a drive to check out other properties, but I wasn't quite ready. At this point, the couch had developed an Alex-sized hole in it.

I didn't see the point in going to look at anything else. Even with Adam's investment, there was no way I'd have enough without a sizable bank loan. After Diane pulled her move, I scheduled an appointment with the bank, trying to explain my situation. Not only was he petrified of Diane's wrath, but he also informed me that because I was no longer employed, I wasn't qualified for another loan. Lucky me.

Cole had been incredibly patient, waiting out my erratic mood swings as I tried to figure out my next moves. He insisted I take all the time I needed to figure it out, not wanting me to rush into another job I hated. Cole was thriving at his new job. His boss, Steve, said he was a natural, and working on his family farm had prepared him for the manual labor. His back still twinged, but with daily exercise, it wasn't as much of a nuisance.

I hopped into Cole's truck, not bothering to ask where we were going. I'd already tried that tactic earlier—naked. If he didn't tell me then, there was no way he'd cave now.

We drove to the other side of town, not stopping at any of the places I expected. When we approached the road for the

Fox Creek lodge, I instantly tensed, not ready to face my failure just yet. Instead of buzzing past it, Cole hit the turn signal, pulling into the lot.

I opened my eyes to see the sold sign swaying in the wind, and my lip instantly started to tremble, hating that someone else was going to give life to my dream. Or worse—that they'd be tearing it down to make some slick and modern motel.

Cole pulled the truck up to the main cabin, not waiting for me as he hopped outside. He came over to my door, meeting my scowl as he pulled it open. "What the hell are we going here?" I said, crossing my arms like a toddler.

"I've got something to show you."

Cole reached out his hand, but I refused to take it. I didn't want to be here. It was too soon.

He leaned in closer, pressing a kiss to my forehead. "C'mon, sweetheart." He presented his hand again. "You trust me?"

"With my life," I answered honestly. If there was anyone who could get me out of the truck, it was Cole.

I placed my hand in his, letting him guide me down to the ground. Even when I found my footing, he didn't let go of my hand as he nodded toward the main cabin. "So obviously, this would be the main entrance, with check-in and the dining room. Did you know that there's an apartment above the lobby? You could hire an onsite manager, and the housing would be a great perk. You'd have someone here 24/7 in case of any emergencies."

I shook my head, not processing his words. "Yeah, but–"

"And the dining room—it's got a lot of potential." He pulled me up the front stairs. "If you blew out that back wall, you could put in floor-to-ceiling windows, give your guests a view of the lake."

"My guests? What are you–"

He stopped at the top of the landing. "This would be a great spot for a porch swing. I could see us coming out here, admiring all your hard work, you reading one of those romance books Calla's always leaving around, me watching you."

"Cole, stop!" I snapped. "What are you doing?" I dropped his hand and started walking back to the car. "You know what? No, I don't care. I can't believe you'd bring me here, especially after someone else bought it."

"You bought it."

His calm demeanor made me even angrier. "Did you hit your head? You know I didn't buy it! You were there when I came home crying from the bank."

"Yeah, I was," he said, walking toward me and taking back my hand. "And the moment you fell asleep, Calla and I started talking about a plan."

A plan? My heart tripped over itself, trying not to get ahead of myself while also bracing for heartbreak. I kept my mouth shut, needing to know why we were there.

"Adam already committed to investing, so he was more than willing to lend more for the initial cost. Curt and Marta also wanted to help, so they contributed as well. Shit, even Theo was willing to invest." He shook his head. "Calla and I don't have much, but we're more than willing to put some sweat equity into this place. I'm going to try to tackle a lot of the repairs, and Steve offered to help with anything over my head. Calla was way too excited at the idea of using a sledgehammer, so I suggested she could help design the cabins instead."

He continued to talk about everyone in town who had stepped up, all wanting to see me achieve this goal. I couldn't hear him, too transfixed on the wonderful man in front of me, the one I never expected would be my person, and now, I knew I'd never want to live without him. If it were possible for a heart to burst from happiness truly, mine would have, all because of Cole.

Cole glanced down at me, and his brow furrowed. "Are you pissed?" He ran his hand over his face. "Look, I know this is supposed to be your thing, but dammit, Alex, you have to let people help you sometimes. You've got too many people who love you, who want to make sure you succeed." He started pacing, taking my stunned silence as annoyance rather than wonder. "If you're mad, be mad at me. This whole thing was my idea. Please, Alex, talk to me–"

I reached up on my tiptoes, fusing my lips with Cole's. He flinched for a moment at the sudden movement and then met me with the same intensity. He stepped back, pressing me against the passenger side door.

"I love you," I said as his lips trailed down my neck. "I can't believe you did all this for me."

Cole chuckled, pulling back to meet my eyes. His hand went to my cheek, his thumb brushing away my tears of joy. "I'd do anything for you, Alex."

With one last lingering kiss, he put me down and headed over to the other side of the truck. He opened the driver's side door, pulling out a stack of papers that were tucked under the seat.

"All you have to do is sign, sweetheart," he said, passing me a pen. "Then, the Fox Creek is yours."

"*Ours*," I said, glancing up at him. "I want you to do this with me."

He shook his head. "This was your dream, Alex. I just wanted to make sure you achieved it."

I tucked myself against his chest, letting my hands rest on his shoulders. "That's the thing, Cole—none of this matters without you. I want to run this place with you. Fill it with more love and happiness than I ever thought possible." I reached up, softly kissing him. "So let's make this place the start of our beautiful, crazy life together."

He stared down at me, a look so intense that if it were anyone else, I would have flinched. "Yeah," he finally said. "If you're sure."

"More than you'll ever know."

"Then I'm in." He reached down, hooking his hands under my thighs. As soon as he lifted me, my legs wrapped around his waist. Cole kissed me with reckless abandon, making every inch of my body sigh with contentment. "I love you."

"Not as much as I love you."

Alex

EPILOGUE

Six Months Later...

"And you're sure the plumbing is functional?" I sighed, checking out the shower for the fifth time. "I don't want them to stop working on our first night."

Cole shook his head, laughing at my incessant line of questions. "Yes, sweetheart. Steve checked over everything. Again. He said we're good to go."

"What about the stove?" I said, toying with the end of my braid. "One of the maintenance guys swore he smelled gas."

"Crossed that off the list, too. There's no problem. If the pilot light gives us any trouble, I know a guy who can come check it out." He fixed me with a knowing smirk. "Breathe, Alex. We've got everything covered. Tonight's going to be amazing. Please try to enjoy all your hard work."

Six months ago, I would have never thought we'd be here. Within the next couple of hours, all our friends and family would be joining us for the soft opening of the Fox Creek Lodge.

Cole and I had debated changing the name, but it felt

wrong. This place was a part of the landscape of Saint Stephen's Lake, and we wanted to honor that tradition.

We'd poured our blood, sweat, and tears into getting the lodge ready for guests. Cole had brought an entire crew to help gut the cabins, all of whom were willing to donate their time in exchange for a stay when we opened. We were more than happy to oblige. It seemed like the whole town had a hand in us getting to this moment.

I couldn't lie and say it was easy. We'd hit a ton of road-blocks along the way, especially once we realized how much damage the lodge had incurred when it sat vacant for years. There were nights I wanted to give up and take a nice, safe job downtown, but Cole kept me going, showing me how much progress we were making. That wasn't to say we didn't fight—sharing a home and a business would be stressful for any couple. Somehow, though, we managed to work through the problems together.

Every day, I fell a little more in love with Cole. Seeing all sides of him, watching him become a part of this community—it was more than I ever expected. Finally, having a partner who loved me so fiercely gave me an incredible amount of strength.

I scanned through the checklist one more time, much to Cole's annoyance, as he crossed his arms around his chest. "There's nothing left, Alex. We're ready."

"What about—"

He pulled me into his chest, his familiar scent calming my rapidly fraying nerves. "It's a soft opening. This is to work out any of the kinks before we have paying guests. Say it with me: it's going to be great."

"It's going to be great," I mumbled against him, not really feeling the words. I pulled out of his embrace, heading toward the door before he could catch me again. "I'm going to call Marta to check on the food."

"Woman, get your ass into the office and get ready." He slapped my ass as I hustled past him. "And if I catch you checking on one more thing, I'm locking you in the office until everyone shows up."

I stuck my tongue out at him as I walked out of the cabin, heading straight for the office as he instructed. As much as I loathed to admit it, Cole was right. We'd been planning this night for weeks, months, even. Everything was as ready as it could be. The only thing we needed now was for our friends to show up.

Walking into the office, I didn't even look up from my notes, too focused to notice the person sitting on top of my desk. When I finally looked up, I shrieked, not expecting someone in my office.

"Surprise!" Calla called out, throwing her hands in the air.

"What are you doing here?" I cried out, wrapping her in a tight hug. "I thought you were in California."

It had been almost four months since I'd seen Calla. Four long months. When she moved to Manhattan in the spring, I knew she'd be busy with her new job, but I had no idea how much I would miss her. Even though we talked daily, it wasn't the same as having her with me.

"Please," she teased. "There was no way I was going to miss this. I even convinced Mr. Sunshine to come tonight."

"How's that going?" I asked, laughing at the nickname Calla had christened Theo on her first day as his new assistant. Things had started rocky between them, with Theo threatening to fire her on a daily basis, but they seemed to be getting along better. At least I wasn't getting daily texts with the ways Calla was imagining murdering him.

"Eh," Calla shrugged. "It's been...different than I expected. Theo is..." Her voice trailed off, and she glanced down at her shoes. "He's different than I expected."

"In a good way?"

"Time will tell." Calla laughed, hopping off my desk and moving to the attached bathroom. "Now, I have five outfits for you to choose from." She held her hand up to stop my protests. "Yes, you have to wear one of them. This is a big night, Alex, and you deserve to be spoiled after all your hard work."

I shook my head and walked into the room without further protest. That was a battle I'd never win. The first dress on the pile drew my eye. Made from a navy blue, breezy material, it reminded me of the sky above the lake on fall nights, the kind I loved the most with Cole. These were nights when it was just the two of us sitting by the fire, talking about everything and nothing at the same time.

I pulled it over my head, knowing it was the one, without having to look at the others. Glancing in the mirror, I straightened my compass necklace, which Cole had given me when we first started. It never left my neck, a constant reminder of our ties to each other and that we would always help the other find their way home.

Calla's hand flew in front of her face when she saw me, and she nodded vigorously. "Yes, that's it. It's perfect!"

"This is probably ridiculous," I said, letting my hands run over the soft fabric. "It's going to be ruined in an hour."

"Trust me," Calla said, moving to my side. "You're going to want to be dressed up tonight." She pulled her lip between her teeth and then turned quickly, hiding a grin.

"What's going on?" I arched my brow. "Are you keeping something from me?"

"Nope," she answered quickly—a little too quickly. Sensing I was onto her, she shook her head. "You're not going to break me, Alex, so get your ass in that bathroom and finish getting ready. I have a feeling you're never going to forget tonight."

HOLY HELL, I'd never been this exhausted before. The past five hours had been beyond chaotic, and while my bones ached, I loved every minute of it. It was so surreal, having people staying in the lodge and the cabins. It made all the struggles over the past few months worth it.

There were still quite a few things we had to fix, issues we didn't catch until guests were staying with us, but Cole assured me we'd get to them after everyone left. Tonight was about celebrating how far we'd come with everyone we loved in one space.

The dining room was arranged with long tables facing the center so people could chat across the space. Everyone loved it. We decided to keep many of the rustic elements, from the wooden beams to the original hardwood floors. Cole was right about the windows. Opening the back wall not only brought more natural light into the room, but you could see the lake from every corner. It quickly became one of my favorite places in the world.

Cole draped his arm around me, pulling me into his side. "Can you believe this?"

"No," I laughed. "I'm pretty sure this is a dream. Don't pinch me, though—I never want to wake up."

Looking around the room, I was greeted by so many friendly faces. Dani sat with Javi, fussing over the view of the lake. Marta, Curt, and their son Gray were talking with Adam in the corner, Gray filling him in on his preseason games. Apparently, they were both huge fans of each other's. I didn't think I'd ever seen Adam as excited as when he shook hands with his favorite MLB player.

On the opposite side of the space, Calla was talking with Theo, who looked at her with something like amusement in his eyes. She'd made him participate in all the activities we'd planned today, even the nature hike, and I was shocked he agreed so readily. Even Cole thought Calla must have put a spell on him because Theo never wanted to do anything that wasn't work.

Others from town filled the rest of the chairs– all people who had helped us achieve this dream. Tonight was the first way we'd pay them back. It made me smile, seeing how much this town had accepted Cole, just as they had me. He fit in seamlessly, like he'd always belonged here.

There was one other person I knew Cole wanted here: Victoria, his sister. They'd been talking more than ever, and Cole was thinking about taking a trip to Texas once things were a little more manageable. He offered to fly her up, but she declined, always saying she was stuck at work. In fact, she seemed to have a lot of convenient excuses not to visit—not that I ever mentioned that to Cole. Hopefully, in time, she'd be with us at the table, laughing with the rest of our little family.

Cole cleared his throat, squeezing my shoulder before standing at the head of the table, holding up his glass of sparkling cider. "So I know Alex said a few words earlier, but I wanted to thank all of you for coming tonight. It means more to Alex and me than you'll ever know." He rubbed his hand over his face. "Shit, we wouldn't be here if it wasn't for most of you." He turned toward me, reaching out to take my hand in his.

"Nine months ago, my best friend took a role in this little art house movie no one had ever heard of. None of us wanted him to take it, but he was so damn determined. He even convinced me it'd be fun to go with him, to get an escape from everything in California." He chuckled. "Had I known what was waiting here for me, I'd have been on a plane then and there." Cole turned toward me, a soft sincerity filling his gaze. "Alex, I love you more than I can ever put into words. You're incredibly smart, kind, and so beautiful that it hurts to look at you some-times. I still have no idea how the hell you fell for a fool like me, but I thank the stars every single day that you did. You brought me back to life, sweetheart, and made me happier than I thought possible."

I frantically wiped the happy tears freely flowing down my cheeks as he lowered down to one knee, one hand holding mine while the other fished something out of his pocket. "I know we're in this together, Alex. Now, I want to make it official."

I gasped as he opened the green velvet box, revealing a gorgeous diamond ring. The bright center stone was an emerald cut with a baguette on each side—I recognized it instantly from family photos and stories. "This..." I said with a shaky breath. "That's your grandmother's ring."

"Yeah," he nodded, smiling brightly at me. "I've had it for years. I never thought there'd be a day I'd use it. Now, I know it was always meant to be yours." He pulled it out, holding it next to my hand. "So what do you say, sweetheart? Will you marry me?"

I stood up so fast that the chair flopped over behind me. "Of course I will!"

The room erupted in cheers, but I could barely hear it. I was too busy staring at the man in front of me—how, only a few years ago, I sat on the beach, wondering if my life was over or if I'd ever truly be happy.

After Cole slipped the ring on my finger, he stood and pulled me into him. He kissed me deeply, as if we were the only ones in the room before he rested his forehead on mine. "You ready to do this? Me and you forever?"

I smirked back at him. "Forever sounds perfect to me."

EXTENDED EPILOGUE

Want a glimpse of Alex and Cole's lives together, ten years after the events in (Un)Expected?

Join my newsletter to get your copy of this exclusive bonus epilogue!

Click here for your extended epilogue

ACKNOWLEDGMENTS

There are so many people that made this book possible, and without all of you, I would not be here.

To my family, that listened to me talk out various scenes and obsess over fictional characters, thank you for being my sounding board. And for insisting that we take a drive last Mother's Day, which literally inspired this entire series. You guys are world, my reason for everything.

Emmy- thank you so much for the years of support, encouragement, and seals of approval. You were the first person in my corner when I started to talk about this series, and I am so grateful to always have you there. You're my write or die forever.

To Alexa at Fiction Fix, thank you so much for everything you've done. I shudder to think what this story would look like without your edits. You helped me so much, and made me feel so much more confident about putting this out into the world.

Ainna- What would I do without your beautiful art? You took a teeny scrap of an idea, and brought my characters to life. You're so incredibly talented, and I am so lucky to work with you.

Books and Moods- I can't believe that I get to work with you. From the moment I saw your designs for the first time, I wanted to work with you. Your team is so incredibly talented and I am so blown away by what you created for this story.

And last- to the readers. The ones who inspire me,

encourage me, and are the most wonderful community. If you got an advanced copy, or are reading this, know that I appreciate you from the bottom of my heart. Readers make this world a better place.

SAINT STEPHEN'S LAKE SERIES:

(Un)Expected

A Dislike to Lovers, Small Town Romance

(Cole & Alex's Story)

(Un)Planned

A Grumpy x Sunshine, Workplace Romance

(Calla & Theo's Story)

(Un)Spoken

A Brother's Best Friend, Single Parent Romance

(Adam & Victoria's Story)

(Un)Rivaled

A Second Chance, Accidental Marriage Romance

(Devyn & Gray's Story)

ERIE CITY HAWKS SERIES:

Single Glance

A Single Dad, Baseball Romance

(*Cam and Hadley's Story*)

Double Down

A Friends with Benefits, Baseball Romance

Coming Fall 2025

ABOUT THE AUTHOR

K.C. Brooks is an avid romance reader who has always dreamed about turning her ideas into a book of her own. She lives for sunny days, iced cold coffees, and stories that make your heart ache for more. When not living in the fantasy worlds of her books, she resides in upstate New York with her husband, two children, and two fur babies.